An Apple From Eden

EMMA BLAIR

WARNER BOOKS

A *Warner* Book

First published in Great Britain in 1998
by Little, Brown and Company
This edition published by Warner Books in 1999

A CIP catalogue record for this book
is available from the British Library.

ISBN 0 7515 1859 X

Typeset in Adobe Garamond by
Palimpsest Book Production Limited,
Polmont, Stirlingshire
Printed and bound in Great Britain by
Clays Ltd, St Ives plc

Warner Books
A Division of
Little, Brown and Company (UK)
Brettenham House
Lancaster Place
London WC2E 7EN

An Apple From Eden

Chapter 1

'*L'amour.*'

Bridie Flynn sighed, then repeated the word. '*L'amour.*'

'You what?' queried Teresa Kelly in astonishment.

'It's French for love,' Bridie informed her. 'I go prickly all over every time I say it.'

Teresa shook her head. 'I suppose you learned that from one of those daft books you're always reading.'

'They're not daft at all!' Bridie retorted. 'Amongst other things they're very informative. Why, I'd be lost without my books. Thank Heavens for the library. The best thing I ever did was joining.'

Bridie glanced about her. The rest of the family were out – a rare enough event as there was usually someone else around in the evenings. Her mother, father and sister Alison had gone to visit Granny Flynn who was suffering from lumbago. As for her brother Sean, who knew where he was? He could be anywhere. Probably with one or some of his many pals.

'You know what I'd really like to have been in life,' Bridie suddenly stated.

'What?'

'A schoolteacher.'

Teresa gave a derisory laugh. 'You, a schoolteacher! My my, we have got ideas above our station, haven't we? Our kind don't become schoolteachers. That's for posh folk.'

Bridie pulled a face. 'I know. But a lassie can have dreams, can't she? If things had been different, if I hadn't been born into an ordinary working-class family, then that's what I'd like to have been. A spell at university, then training college followed by teaching.' Her eyes took on a faraway look. 'Oh but that would have been grand. The bee's knees.'

'Well, it's the lemonade factory for you, my girl, and thankful you should be that you have a job at all. There's many don't, as you well know.'

Bridie thought with distaste of the lemonade factory, her place of employment, as it was Teresa's, since leaving school.

'I don't know about *l'amour*, but if it's boys you're talking about, well, I'm certainly not against them. Quite the contrary.' Teresa giggled. 'I wonder what it's like?'

'What's what like?'

Teresa gave her friend a conspiratorial wink. '*That. L'amour.*'

Bridie reddened slightly. 'I'm not just talking about *that*, though of course it is part and parcel of love. No, I mean the act of being in love, of existing for someone else and they for you. On counting the hours, minutes and seconds till you see them again. The sheer elation of being in their company. The thrill when they touch you, the bliss of their lips on yours. The time spent together when the rest of the world ceases to exist.'

Teresa snorted. 'Well, there sure isn't much of that around here. Could you imagine my ma and da gazing adoringly into each other's eyes? The only thing my da stares adoringly at is food when it's put in front of him. Especially after a hard day's graft. Then he gazes adoringly enough. Particularly if it's his favourite mince, and potatoes. I swear he'd murder for a heaped plate of that.'

Bridie lean't further back into the rather ancient fireside chair which had belonged to Pat and Kathleen Flynn since early on in their marriage, one of the first items of furniture they'd acquired, and even then it had been second hand from Crown Showrooms in the town.

'You can mock all you like, Teresa Kelly, there's a Prince Charming out there for each and every one of us. Or if there isn't there should be. And one fine day I'm going to meet mine. I just know it.'

'You're away with the fairies, you are. Always have been in my recollection, and God knows I've known you long enough.' Teresa stared hard at her friend. 'Those silly books you've forever got your nose stuck in have a lot to answer for, and that's a fact. They've made you expect too much out of life. You'll settle for some nice lad just like all the rest of us, someone plain and ordinary and a far cry from a blinking Prince Charming. There'll be the wedding followed by weans and years of toil as is the case with all the women round here. There'll be precious little time for gazing adoringly into eyes when you'll be spending most of your time down the steamie boiling dirty nappies or else at home slaving over a hot stove and trying to make ends meet.'

Despair filled Bridie. What Teresa said was true enough, though she was reluctant in the extreme to accept it.

'Life's real, and hard,' Teresa went on. 'What you read in those books of yours are only stories. Sort of . . . well, things to get you out of yourself. A pretence if you wish.'

Bridie closed her eyes and pictured a handsome, dashing young man with flaxen hair and piercing blue eyes. '*L'amour*,' she breathed again. 'A meeting of souls.'

Teresa barked out a laugh. 'Your arse in parsley, hen. A meeting of souls indeed. Utter tosh.'

'It is not!' Bridie retorted fiercely.

'It is sought. Och, I admit when you find the right chap there should be a lot of lovey-dovey stuff during your courting. But that, from what I understand, is soon over once the wedding ring is on your finger. Then it's down to reality and getting on with it.'

Bridie came to her feet and leant against the mantelpiece. She suddenly wished her friend would leave so she could get back to her current book. There was still a while before bedtime, time enough for a couple of chapters at least.

Bridie started when she heard the front door open.

'Cooeee, we're home!' Kathleen Flynn called out. 'Get the kettle on.'

And so ended the conversation about *l'amour* and Prince Charming.

'Come in,' Willie Seaton responded to the knock on his study door. As he'd expected it was Ian, his only son.

'You wanted a word with me, Pa.'

Willie indicated an adjacent chair. 'Sit yourself down. And aye, I do wish a chat.'

Willie rubbed his eyes which were painful from long hours poring over ledgers. He was going to have to give in and see an optician, he told himself, something he'd been fighting against these past few years. But although he still considered himself a relatively young man at forty-four, time was beginning to take its toll.

'Would you care for a dram, son? I know I'm ready for one.'

Ian immediately rose although he'd only just sat. 'Yes, I will join you, Pa. I'll do it.'

Willie produced cigarettes and lit up, not offering the packet to Ian who didn't smoke.

'Hard day, Pa?'

Willie nodded. 'What about yourself? What have you been up to?'

'Did a bit of rabbit shooting earlier. Knocked over half a dozen of the buggers. Mrs Kilbride was pleased to get them.' Mrs Kilbride was their cook.

'So it'll be rabbit stew or pie tomorrow,' Willie mused, which pleased him. He enjoyed rabbit, hare even more.

'There you are,' declared Ian, placing Willie's drink in front of him, before returning to his chair.

'*Slainte!*' Willie toasted.

'*Slainte*, Pa.'

Willie tasted his drink, smiled in appreciation, then steadily regarded his son. 'It's a fortnight now since you returned home from your studies. I wanted to give you time to settle back in before speaking to you.'

Ian nodded, knowing what was coming next. 'What do you have in mind?'

'You've always been aware you'll be taking over from me some day. Though not for a while I hope. I have no wish to depart this world just yet.'

Ian laughed softly. He and his father got on extremely well, and always had done. With one exception that is, but that subject had long been accepted by Ian, the animosity forgotten.

'So when do I start?'

Willie nodded his approval. 'Keen, eh? That's the stuff, lad. I like keenness in a person. Apart from anything else it shows character. And I hope the son and heir of Willie Seaton would have that.'

Willie squirmed himself into a more comfortable position while Ian waited patiently for him to go on.

'I want you to learn as I did and my father before me, which means starting at the bottom. When you're finished there won't be a job on this estate, including mine, which you won't be able to do if necessary. Understand?'

'The hard way in other words,' Ian commented ruefully.

'Exactly.'

It was what Ian had expected. Thanks to his studies he was well versed in the theory. Now came the practical side of things. He had to admit he was looking forward to it.

'You start next Monday under Jock Gibson. Jock is getting on in years and it won't be too long until his retirement. When that happens you'll be the next estate manager.'

Ian thought of Jock Gibson, a dour Scot, though kindly underneath, if ever there was. He'd known Jock all his life.

'While you're working for Jock he's the boss and you do as he says. I don't want you trying to pull rank on him. Is that clear?'

'Quite clear, Pa.'

'It would be rude if nothing else and I can't abide rudeness. Never have.'

Ian recalled the several cuffs he'd received when a youngster for cheeking his father, incidents he still vividly remembered. There had been nothing token about those cuffs, they'd hurt like billy-o. Willie wasn't joking when he said he couldn't abide rudeness.

'And make sure you dress properly. You're going to get more than your hands dirty.' He added sarcastically, 'It wouldn't do to ruin one of those smart suits of yours now, would it?'

Ian laughed. The idea of him turning up for work under Jock wearing a suit appealed to him. He was almost tempted to do so just for a lark. Dear old Jock would have a fit.

'Indeed, Pa,' he replied in mock seriousness.

Willie took a deep breath. He'd been looking forward to this ever since Ian had been born. How proud Mary would have been, just as proud as he himself was. Darling, lovely, departed Mary.

'Any queries?'

Ian considered that. 'I don't think so, Pa. Except for remuneration of course.' That was said slightly tongue in cheek.

'Your allowance will continue as before. And consider yourself lucky, it's far more than the estate workers get.' Willie decided to tease his son. 'Though on second thoughts perhaps I should pay you what they earn. That way you'd really learn the value of money. That a ha'penny is hard come by.'

Alarm flared in Ian. Surely his father wasn't serious? 'Pa?' he queried anxiously.

Willie's eyes twinkled. 'Just a wee josh, son. You'll continue on with your allowance as I said.'

He finished his whisky, stared at the empty glass for a moment, then looked again at Ian and smiled. 'I believe I'll have another. It's not every day you welcome your son into the firm.'

Ian again did the honours.

'Your father tells me you're starting work on the estate this

Monday,' Georgina Seaton, Willie's second wife, said to Ian across the dinner table.

'That's right, Georgina.'

'Good.'

Willie indicated to a hovering maid to refill the wine glasses. Georgina covered the top of her glass with a hand, having had her quota. Ever mindful of her figure she took great care with what she ate and drank.

'I must say it's all very exciting,' she declared.

Rose Seaton made a small harumphing sound.

Ian raised an eyebrow. 'You wish to make an utterance, sister dear?'

Rose shook her head.

'Oh! I thought you might have.'

'Only that it was so quiet and peaceful when you were away,' she stated sweetly.

'I thought you missed me.' That dripping sarcasm.

'Dreadfully. It was so dull without you charging about the house. That and the general hubbub you always seem to cause when you're around.'

'Rose!' Willie admonished sharply.

'Yes, Pa?' she smiled, innocence itself.

'I'll have no such banter at the dinner table. It's most unseemly.'

Georgina secretly enjoyed 'such banter' as Willie called it. It livened things up. She glanced at Willie and not for the first time wondered what her life would have been like if Harry had lived. Harry who'd gone to war and never come back. Harry whom she'd simply adored. He'd been another lively one, just like Ian.

'Georgina?'

She roused herself from what had been only a few moments' reverie. 'Yes, Willie?'

'You had the strangest expression on your face. Are you all right?'

'Perfectly, thank you very much.'

'Not a tinge of indigestion, I trust?'

She laughed throatily. 'Not at all. I was simply reflecting on how delicious this lamb is. Mrs Kilbride has quite excelled herself. I must remember to compliment her.'

Rose, with a tendency to plumpness, agreed with Georgina about the lamb and considered whether or not to have a second helping. She envied Georgina her figure and Georgina's discipline regarding it.

'I thought we might play whist after dinner,' Willie announced. 'Or canasta perhaps.'

Ian and Rose both inwardly groaned.

'I was thinking we might play the gramophone,' Ian said.

Georgina would have much preferred the gramophone to whist or canasta. And several dances with Ian who was a marvellous dancer, unlike Willie who was terrible. Many a time Willie had succeeded in trampling on her feet.

'I think the gramophone is a splendid idea,' Georgina declared.

That didn't suit Willie at all. He'd had his mind set on a game of cards. 'How about we have some whist then the gramophone?' he suggested hopefully.

Georgina decided to humour him. 'Better still. That way honour's satisfied all round.'

Willie beamed at her, Georgina's heart sinking when she recognised a particular gleam in his eyes.

It was going to be one of *those* nights.

Kathleen Flynn glanced over at the mantelpiece clock. As was usual on a Friday Pat was late home from work. She knew where he was – the same place he went every Friday evening after being paid – the pub.

Kathleen sighed. How much, or little, would he bring back with him this time? And how drunk would he be? Mind you, she was lucky, a lot luckier than many in their street. Pat rarely hit her, while others she knew got a right battering each and every Friday night.

She didn't begrudge him his drink, it was the culmination of a hard week's graft after all. A man had to have something to look forward to. If only he wouldn't get carried away and spend so much.

Kathleen briefly closed her eyes. How she hated the eternal scrimping and scraping, half the time robbing Peter to pay Paul. How many Thursdays and Fridays had they been reduced to eating bread and dripping? Times without number.

Another half-hour she calculated. For Pat never left until after last orders.

Would he eat something or go straight to bed? You never knew with Pat. It never bothered him that when he did insist on going straight to bed without a wash he made a terrible mess of the sheets. He was a coalman after all. As far as he was concerned that was something for her to worry about.

'Why don't you put the kettle on?' Kathleen suggested to Bridie sitting opposite, her face in one of the books she constantly devoured.

Bridie blinked and looked up. 'Did you say something, Ma?'

'Why don't you put the kettle on?'

'Not for me, Ma, I don't fancy a cup right at the moment. Shall I put the kettle on for you though?'

Kathleen considered that. It seemed a waste to make a pot just for herself, tea being so expensive nowadays. Why, only the previous week it had gone up again, that and many other things. It was scandalous. How was a body supposed to get by on those prices! If only wages would go up as well, but there was little likelihood of that.

'No, I'll leave it for the now,' she replied.

Bridie nodded and returned to her book. *The Maid of Avalon* was a humdinger in her opinion.

Willie rolled off Georgina. 'That was wonderful, darling. Thank you.'

'It *was* wonderful, thank *you*,' she lied in the darkness.

As was his custom, after every session of lovemaking, he took her into his arms and held her close, savouring the perfumed smell of her.

'Happy?' he queried softly.

'Completely.'

'That's fine then.'

'And you?'

'You know I am. Just being with you makes me so.'

'It's the same with me.'

He released her. 'Goodnight then.'

'Goodnight.'

Georgina waited for him to turn on to his side, facing away from her, as he always did. She smiled cynically when that happened.

How predictable he was in bed, she thought. How utterly, awfully predictable. Sometimes she felt like screaming at just how predictable he was.

She drew in a slow, deep breath, trying to calm herself. Willie was the only man she'd ever slept with. Was all lovemaking like theirs? she wondered. She couldn't believe that to be so. Surely there had to be some satisfaction in it for the woman.

She'd asked him in the past to try and take longer which he'd genuinely tried to do. To no avail. Willie's clock was a fast one, hers slow. His alarm bell always went off long before hers was ready to ring.

She didn't love Willie, never had. Perhaps that had something to do with it; she didn't know. If only she had someone to talk to, to discuss the matter with. But that sort of thing was never spoken about in polite society, of which she was most definitely a member.

Willie began to snore gently, informing her he'd dropped off. Quickly, as again was *always* the case. Other nights he might toss and turn, but never after they'd made love.

She thought of Harry. What would it have been like with him? The same as with Willie, or different? That was something she'd never find out.

Willie had asked her if she was happy and she'd lied by saying yes. Truth was, she wasn't *un*happy. Dissatisfied perhaps. Frustrated was the word that came to mind. Frustrated that when they joined it didn't give her anything like the pleasure it gave him. It was as if she was forever trying to climb a mountain but never getting to the top, always being stopped halfway. Sometimes not even halfway.

She moved restlessly, knowing it would be some while before sleep claimed her. She was all on edge, a-jangle.

Should she or shouldn't she? She'd feel guilty after, a little soiled somehow. Guilty and ashamed.

It was only the previous year she'd discovered she could do such a thing. The idea had simply never entered her head until one particularly bad night after Willie she'd found herself doing it without thinking. And then . . . oh the glorious release, release that had made her gasp and shake all over.

How fearful she'd been afterwards that Willie might have realised, but he'd been asleep and known nothing.

Her hand crept downwards to find herself. She would, she decided.

Sean Flynn let himself into the house, pausing to listen just inside the door. As he'd expected the rest of the family were in the land of Nod.

He closed the door and then tiptoed through to his bedroom. He groaned as he began to undress. Christ, but he hurt. At least, as far as he could tell, none of his ribs was broken, but he'd be black and blue come morning.

He suddenly grinned, thinking of the other two. What a pasting he'd given them. He'd be sore tomorrow but not nearly as sore as that Proddy pair. Hell mend the bastards.

It had been a good night he decided, though he could have done without the rammy. And trust him to be on his own, for once caught without his pals around to help and back him up.

He hadn't meant to jostle the Prod, it had been an accident. But that hadn't stopped them waiting outside the boozer and jumping him.

'Effing Prods,' he muttered. 'Effing bloody Prods.'

He hated them.

Jock Gibson watched Ian stride towards him and smiled inwardly. He had a little treat planned for Ian's first day.

'Hello, Jock,' Ian greeted the estate manager.

'During working hours I think it had better be Mr Gibson,' Jock stated.

Ian swallowed. Jock had always been Jock for as long as

he could remember. Even as a wee boy it had been Jock. 'I understand.'

'That would be best in the circumstances, don't you agree?'

Ian nodded. 'Whatever you say Jo—, Mr Gibson.'

'Fine then.'

Ian rubbed his hands together. 'So where do I begin?'

'I thought with the pigs. You'll be helping mucking out. A filthy job I admit. But one that has to be done.'

'Of course.'

'The lads there are expecting you, so off you go. I'll drop by later to see how you're getting on.'

Pigs! Ian thought ruefully as he walked away. He'd never liked pigs. Nasty, unpredictable creatures.

His nose wrinkled in disgust as he approached the first pen and he got a whiff of what lay ahead.

Bridie came hurrying up to Teresa and the pair of them fell into step together.

'Another Monday morning and another week at the lemonade factory,' Bridie groaned. 'The thought makes me sick.'

Teresa grinned at her friend. 'Oh come on, it's not that bad.'

'Bad enough. It's the boredom that gets me down more than anything. Repetition, repetition, repetition. Bottles into boxes, bottles into boxes, bottles into boxes.'

'Well, if you're that cheesed off you could always ask the gaffer to shift you to another part of the factory. That would make a change if nothing else.'

'Fat chance of that. Do you not remember Sheena McLaughlan tried that last year and got told to get on with what she was doing in no uncertain terms?'

Teresa pulled a face. 'Oh aye, I'd forgot.'

'Packing is where I started and where I'll no doubt finish, whenever that might be.'

'When you find your Prince Charming you mean?' Teresa teased.

'I suppose so.'

They walked a little way in silence. 'Are you going to the dance next Saturday?' Teresa queried. 'Who knows, you might meet Prince Charming there.'

Bridie thought of the dance in question, a local affair held once a month. She had about as much chance of meeting Prince Charming there as she had of flying to the moon. Still, you never knew.

'I haven't decided yet.'

'There was a lad at the last one took my eye. But he never asked me up.'

'You never mentioned.'

Teresa shrugged.

'Nice, was he?'

'I've no idea as we never spoke. But he looked nice enough. The shy type I'd say.'

'Not too many of those round here,' Bridie commented. 'They're a forward lot by and large.'

'True enough.'

Bridie recalled the last dance they'd attended, the one Teresa was referring to. She'd been asked up far more times than Teresa, as was usually the case. Teresa was verging on being plain while she . . . well, she was hardly a ravishing beauty but folk did say she had 'looks'.

'It'd be a laugh,' Teresa went on.

'Hardly that,' Bridie commented wryly.

'Well, where else do you want to go? There's always the flicks, though you won't meet any fellas there. You don't get a lumber at the pictures.' Lumber meant meeting someone and being escorted home.

'I don't really fancy the flicks either.'

'You're becoming a right stick in the mud, so you are. I suppose you'd rather stay indoors on a Saturday night with one of your books.'

Bridie didn't reply to that.

A few minutes later her heart sank when the lemonade factory came into view.

'Here we go again,' Bridie muttered.

'Here we go,' Teresa agreed.

Chapter 2

'Well, I'll be damned!' Willie exclaimed. He was at the breakfast table sorting through the morning post.

Georgina glanced up from her kipper. 'Bad news, darling?'

Willie beamed at her. 'Quite the contrary. It's from an old chum of mine who served alongside me in the First Essex. He's going to pay us a visit.'

'That's nice.'

Rose was the only other person at the table, Ian having long since gone to work.

Willie re-read the letter then laid it aside. 'It'll be wonderful seeing Andrew again. He's a terrific chap.'

'You certainly sound enthusiastic,' Georgina commented.

'How old is he?' Rose queried.

Willie considered that. 'About the same age as me I suppose.' He suddenly chuckled. 'Far too old for you, my poppet.'

Rose coloured slightly. 'That wasn't why I asked at all.'

Willie regarded his daughter thoughtfully. He sometimes

regretted not having sent her off to school as he had Ian. Not that the various tutors hadn't done a first-rate job, they had. It was simply that she lacked a wider experience than might have been otherwise.

'Is this Andrew married?' Georgina enquired.

'Doesn't say. Certainly wasn't when in the army. I recall he was engaged at one point, to an Irish lass . . .' He broke off and shook his head. 'Sad business.'

'What happened?' a curious Rose asked.

Willie's expression became grim. 'She was killed and let's just leave it at that. Andrew was deeply hurt. Took it very badly indeed.'

This sounded intriguing, Georgina thought, wondering how the fiancée had been killed. 'So when's he coming?'

'Beginning of next month. He's not certain about the actual date yet but will write again when he is. In the meantime I shall write to him saying we shall be delighted to have him as a guest for as long as he wishes to stay.'

Willie paused, then said, 'Andrew is Drummond of Drummond whisky. We must get some of that for when he's here. Can't offer him another brand now, can we?'

'I'll speak to Mrs Coltart and see it's ordered,' Georgina declared. Mrs Coltart was the housekeeper who did all the ordering and buying for the household.

Willie leant back in his chair, breakfast temporarily forgotten. 'It's six years since I last saw him, I wonder if the old bugger's changed much.'

'Willie!' Georgina admonished, nodding in Rose's direction.

'Wouldn't it be fun if he'd gone bald or something,' Willie chuckled. 'That would upset him. He was always rather vain about his good looks. Bald and a paunch,' Willie chuckled further.

'You're being evil,' Georgina chided.

'Quite the ladies' man I remember. Had an easy way with them that I always envied. Myself and quite a few others.'

Pity he was so old, Rose reflected. This Andrew Drummond sounded fun.

'I'll write later today,' Willie announced.

'A gang of our own?' Noddy Gallagher repeated.

Sean nodded. 'Why not? There are enough of us, to get started anyway.'

'All Catholics of course,' Sammy Renton said.

Sean gave him a withering look. 'Of course, you eejit. That would be the whole point.'

Sammy grunted.

'I like the idea,' Mo Binchy declared thoughtfully. 'We could hardly rival the Billy Boys or the Norman Conks yet. But who knows, one day.'

Sean's eyes gleamed. 'I've even got a name for us.'

'Oh aye?' prompted Noddy.

Sean glanced from face to face. There were ten of them present, huddled over cups of coffee in an Italian café they frequented. All eyes were glued on him, something he was enjoying.

'The Samurai,' he stated proudly.

The response was blank stares.

'The what?' Bobby O'Toole queried.

'The Samurai,' Sean repeated.

'And what the hell's that when it's at home?'

Sean's expression became one of superiority. 'You're a bunch of ignorant sods, so you are. Samurai are Japanese warriors.'

'Is that a fact,' breathed Jim Gallagher, Noddy's brother.

'How come you know that?' Mo queried of Sean.

'I saw a picture all about them last year at the Poxy Roxy. They have funny haircuts and carry bloody big swords which they use to cut their enemies' heads off with. It was a rare film. I took Maeve Dunphy, you know her with the really big ones, and she got all upset with me.' Sean laughed. 'Said I was more interested in the film than I was in her.' He laughed a second time. 'And she was right too.'

'Will we have to carry bloody big swords?' Dan Smith queried, shivering at the prospect. This was frightening and exciting at the same time.

'Not to start with anyway,' Sean replied slowly. 'I mean to say, Japanese swords aren't exactly thick on the ground around Glasgow. Perhaps we can eventually lay our hands on a few though.'

'The Samurai,' Sammy Renton mused. 'It certainly has a ring about it.'

A murmur of agreement ran round the group.

'If we're going to be a proper gang then we'll need someplace to meet. If we gets lots of members then this café will hardly do,' Sammy went on.

Sean nodded. 'I've already thought of that too. You know that old condemned building at the end of Thistle Street. The one they've been going to pull down for years but never got round to it. Well, how about there?'

'Would it no be dangerous, I mean, it's condemned after all?' Mo Binchy queried.

Sean shot him a contemptuous look. 'Are you feart? Is that it?'

Mo went quite red. 'Don't call me feart. I'm nothing of the sort.'

'Well, I had a shufty round the other day and it's all shored up inside. There's nothing to worry about.'

'That settles that then,' Don McGuire stated emphatically.

Noddy Gallagher cleared his throat. 'If we're going to be a proper gang and all that we're going to need a leader. A heid bummer so to speak.'

Sean sat back in his chair and waited, not wanting to put himself forward, confident someone else would.

'That has to be Sean then,' Jim Gallagher duly obliged. 'If he agrees that is.'

'What do you say, Sean?' Bobby O'Toole queried.

'Is that what you all want?'

Another murmur of agreement ran round the group.

Elation swelled in Sean. The leader of his own gang, oh that was dandy indeed.

'So be it,' he declared.

'Would you care for a brandy, son?' Willie enquired of Ian, sitting slumped on a sofa.

'You appear done in,' Georgina smiled.

Ian nodded. 'I am. It's all this hard physical work that I'm not used to. It really takes it out of you.'

'You'll soon toughen up,' Willie commented, smiling also. 'Georgina dear, something for you?'

She shook her head.

'And what about you, Rose?'

'A sherry would be lovely, Pa. Thank you.'

Ian closed his eyes. He ached all over despite the hot bath he'd wallowed in for over half an hour. Toughen up, his pa had said. The sooner the better.

'I'm thinking of planning a trip to Edinburgh, darling,' Georgina informed Willie. 'I desperately need some new clothes.'

Desperately, Willie thought wryly. Why, she had wardrobes full of clothes.

'Can I come, Georgina?' Rose asked hopefully. Sometimes Georgina took her on these trips but on other occasions her stepmother preferred to go on her own.

'Of course you can, Rose. We'll stay for several days at least. How does that sound?'

'Exciting,' Rose beamed.

'And it'll be new clothes for you too.'

'Spiffing!'

Willie groaned inwardly. More expense! Honestly, those two thought money grew on trees. Still, if he was honest with himself he didn't really mind. He enjoyed indulging the pair of them. What was money for after all? As the saying went, you couldn't take it with you.

When he came to hand Ian his drink he found he'd fallen fast asleep.

'He's going to ask you up,' Teresa whispered excitedly. She and Bridie were at the local dance, sitting side by side on two of the chairs that lined the wall.

'Who?'

'Him coming over. The chap in the blue suit and swanky tie.'

Bridie quickly picked out the young man in question. He had a serious, determined expression on his face as he carved his way in their direction.

'How do you know it's me he's going to ask?'

'He's been watching you for some time now. I'm surprised you haven't noticed.'

Watching her indeed. She had another look at the chap whom she'd never seen before. There were lots of people present who were friends and acquaintances or whom she recognised as regulars to these dances. This was a new face.

The chap came to stand in front of them. 'Hello,' he

said, almost defiantly, to Bridie on whom he was focusing his entire attention. For some reason she found that a little disconcerting.

'Are you for up?'

The usual charming proposal, Bridie thought wryly. She slowly rose. 'That would be nice.'

'Right then.'

They took a position on the floor, the band struck up and he swept her into his arms. 'I'm Bob,' he stated.

'And I'm Bridie.'

He wasn't a bad dancer, she thought. Not brilliant but not bad either.

'Do you live round here?' he queried.

'Near by. And you?'

'Not that far away. Walkable, you understand?'

She nodded. 'I haven't seen you here before?'

'That's right. I usually go into town to the Locarno. It was a pal suggested we come tonight and I thought, why not for a change?'

'Good band,' she commented.

'Aye, fair enough. Not a patch on the ones at the Locarno, mind. They're something else. Ever been there?'

'You mean the Locarno? No, I'm afraid I haven't.'

'Maybe I'll take you some time.'

Bridie laughed. 'You are quick off the mark. What makes you think I'll stay up for a second dance far less go to the Locarno with you?'

'Because of my devastating charm and wit,' he flashed back in reply.

Bridie laughed again. 'I can tell you're the modest type.'

'Modesty never got you anywhere, that's my belief.' He suddenly gave her a huge smile. 'You're lovely, so you are.

A real cracker. But then you must have been told that hundreds of times before.'

'Are you taking the mickey?'

He detached a hand from her waist and waved it over his chest. 'Cross my heart and hope to die if I'm doing that. I mean it, you're a cracker all right. The best-looking lassie here tonight in my opinion.'

'Flattery will get you everywhere,' she replied somewhat coyly.

'That's what I'm hoping, Bridie. That's what I'm hoping.'

When he asked her to remain on for the next dance she, fascinated, agreed.

'Well, goodnight then the pair of you,' Teresa said to Bridie and Bob, Bridie having insisted that Teresa accompany them while Bob walked her home.

'Goodnight,' Bridie and Bob answered in unison.

Teresa giggled before turning and hurrying into her close – the entranceway into her Glasgow tenement.

Bridie and Bob, hand in hand, continued on their way.

'At last I've got you to myself,' Bob said.

What a character, Bridie thought. Despite his bumptiousness she rather liked him. And would go out with him if asked.

A few minutes later they reached Bridie's close which was lit with soft yellow gaslight.

'This is it,' she declared.

Bob glanced into the close then back at her, giving her another of his broad, disarming smiles. 'We can't stand here, shall we go inside?'

She'd already decided about that as well. 'All right.'

'We'll go through to the back close,' he said. 'There's more privacy there.'

Bridie wasn't so sure about that. The back close, an area out of sight of the rest of the close, was for serious snogging while a quick kiss was what she had in mind.

'I've only just met you,' she whispered.

'So what! I feel like I've known you all my life.'

And with that he tugged her in the direction of the back close.

'So how did it go?' Teresa demanded as Bridie joined her. It was Monday morning again and the pair of them were on their way to the lemonade factory.

Bridie's face hardened. 'If you're referring to that Bob, I stupidly went into the back close with him which turned out to be a terrible mistake. The man is an animal.'

They fell into step, hurrying on their way.

'What happened?'

'Before I knew it he had me pinned against the wall with his tongue so far down my throat I honestly thought I was going to choke. His hands were everywhere, and I mean everywhere. It was horrible.'

Teresa's eyes were wide as saucers. 'How awful.'

'It was, believe me. At one point I thought he was going to rip the front of my dress. Completely ruin it.'

'So what did you do?' Teresa couldn't wait to hear.

'He was far too strong for me to push off so when he finally got his tongue out of my mouth I told him if he didn't stop I'd scream the place down and then he'd have my father and brother to deal with. And that they were both real hard nuts.'

'So *did* he stop?'

'Sort of. He was full of apologies, saying he didn't know

what had come over him and all that guff. But even as he was telling me that he was still touching me. He even tried to get his hand up my skirt.'

'An animal right enough,' Teresa agreed with a nod.

'I'd only just met him, for God's sake. What did he take me for?'

'Some blokes,' Teresa sympathised, shaking her head.

'It was so unromantic, Teresa,' Bridie complained bitterly. 'There was no tenderness or affection. Nothing like that at all. Just sheer lust. He was like a maniac.'

'Well, that's the end of him.'

'You're darned tooting.'

'He seemed such a nicc chap too.'

'It only goes to show how you can misjudge people.'

'Aye,' Teresa agreed. 'Aye indeed.'

Georgina glanced out of the tea-room window at the castle dominating the Edinburgh skyline. She and Rose were having a break during their first day's shopping.

'My feet hurt,' Rose stated, emphasising that by pulling a face.

Georgina brought her attention back to her stepdaughter. 'Badly?'

'Oh, I'll survive.'

'I hope so. We've a lot more to do today.' She paused, then said, 'If they really are that bad you can go back to the hotel and we'll meet up again later.'

'Oh no!' Rose exclaimed in sudden alarm. 'Being here is such a treat I don't want to miss out on a moment of it.'

Or miss getting something, Georgina thought. Something she entirely understood.

Rose reached out and picked a cream cake from the

stand in the centre of the table. 'These are so yummy,' she declared.

Georgina frowned at her. 'Do you really think you should? It is your third after all.'

Rose averted her gaze. 'I said coming to Edinburgh was such a treat and this is part of it.'

'Hmmh,' Georgina mused, studying her stepdaughter. 'I do believe you're putting on more weight.'

'I'm doing nothing of the sort,' Rose protested.

'Oh yes you are, and you know it. You really should learn to curb your appetite, young lady. You'd have an extremely good figure if only you'd learn to look after it.'

Rose placed the cake on her plate and studied it. Should she or shouldn't she? It was such a temptation.

'You want to be popular with the young men, don't you?'

Rose nodded.

'Well, stuffing yourself full of cakes isn't the way to accomplish that.'

It was true, Rose reflected miserably. Trouble was she had such a sweet tooth, and a liking for food in general. If she ate the way Georgina did, like a bird, she'd end up starving all the time. Where was the pleasure in that?

'Of course some men do prefer plumper ladies, it can't be denied. But in my experience they're in the minority.'

That made Rose feel even more wretched. With a sigh she pushed her plate away. 'There,' she declared.

Georgina nodded her approval.

On the dot of eleven o'clock everything came to a halt for the morning break. Bridie reached for her flask. A cup of tea would be a welcome relief.

Teresa came hurrying over. 'Have you heard?'

Bridie frowned. 'Heard what?'

'The whisper has been going round since early on. A number of staff have been given the push. Nobody seems to know exactly how many yet.'

Bridie was shocked. 'The push?'

Teresa nodded vigorously.

Sally Dunn and Vicky Grieve, co-workers, joined them. 'What's that you're saying, Teresa? We couldn't help but overhear.'

Teresa repeated herself.

Sally and Vicky were as visibly shocked as Bridie. 'But why?' Vicky demanded.

'It seems salcs have been falling away over the past few months and as a result it's been decided to have a cut-back on staff.'

Bridie's flask and tea were forgotten. This was terrible news. The worst. For what happened if sales fell even further? More staff for the chop was the inevitable conclusion.

'Do we know who these people are?' Sally asked.

Teresa shook her head. 'Though I imagine we'll find out at dinner-time.'

Bridie loathed her job at the lemonade factory, but it was a job and a wage coming into the house. Who knows how long it would take her to find another job should she lose this one. They were hard to come by.

'It makes you think, doesn't it,' Teresa said.

'Aye,' Vicky breathed. It would hit her particularly hard to be laid off as she lived alone with a crippled mother.

They continued speculating amongst themselves until it was time to resume work.

'Co-al! Co-al!'

Pat Flynn scanned the surrounding tenements for the

cards issued by his firm which, when placed in a window, told him that coal was needed. He reined in Jasper, his horse, when he spotted one.

With a sigh Pat tied off then jumped to the ground. This particular customer, a Mrs Buchanan, was a new one, she and her husband having moved into the area only a few months previously.

He manoeuvred a bag on to the side of the cart then heaved it on to his back, a back protected by a thick leather pad.

Into the close he went and up four flights where he found Mrs Buchanan waiting for him with the door open.

'Just put it in the bin,' she instructed.

There was the usual swirl of dust as the coal thudded into the almost empty wooden bin situated inside the kitchen.

Pat shook out the bag. 'One or two?' he queried.

'Just the one. I'll go and get my purse.'

Pat's reply was a grunt.

Mrs Buchanan made to move away then stopped as though she'd suddenly remembered something. Turning again to Pat she smiled. 'I'm sorry to be in my dressing-gown. It's quite lazy of me at this time of the morning.'

Pat shrugged. 'Nothing new to me, missus. You see all sorts in this job. You'd be surprised.'

'I suppose you do.' She clutched the dressing-gown more tightly about her. 'I'll find that purse.'

Good-looking woman, Pat reflected when she'd disappeared from view. Lovely pins, from what he'd been able to see of them. An unusual face too, brown eyes and blond hair. You didn't come across that combination very often. How old? Early thirties, he judged. Strange there wasn't any sign of children. There was invariably some evidence knocking about. Maybe the Buchanans couldn't have any.

Mrs Buchanan returned with a ten-shilling note. 'I'm afraid this is all I have. Have you got change?'

'Oh aye, plenty of that.'

He delved into the leather bag that dangled from his waist and was soon giving her what she was due.

He noted the peculiar expression on her face and wondered about it. She seemed quite mesmerised.

'There we are then,' he declared when the transaction was complete.

'Thank you, Mr . . . ?'

'Flynn.'

'An Irish name.'

'Aye, we are that. Second generation in both my case and my wife's.'

'You're married then.'

'With three children. The oldest is nineteen.'

'Quite grown up.' She smiled.

'He is that.'

'And the others?'

She was chatty, he thought. 'Two lassies. Bridie and Alison.'

Mrs Buchanan nodded, while her eyes strayed briefly to his wrists. Something he didn't fail to notice.

'I'd better get on my way then,' he stated.

'Of course. I'm holding you back.'

'Not at all.'

And with that he headed for the front door.

'Bye!' Mrs Buchanan called out as she was closing the door.

'Bye!'

Odd woman, he thought as he remounted his cart.

Though exactly why he couldn't have said. Perhaps it was that peculiar expression he'd noted. And why glance at his wrists the way she had?

They were perfectly ordinary wrists as far as he was concerned!

Pat sat studying Kathleen who was busy darning socks. She hadn't aged all that well, he thought. Her hair was shot through with grey and pulled back in a tight bun from her lined face. She'd also put on considerable weight since their marriage. Her bosoms were far larger than they'd been then and sagging now where before they'd been tight and firm.

Well, what did you expect after having, and nursing, three weans? Of course that took its toll. Stood to reason after all.

He wasn't exactly a spring chicken himself any more. Far from it. And as for a lined face, years out in all weathers had left their mark. His hair was still jet black though, he reminded himself proudly. And lots of it. There was no thinning or receding he was glad to say.

'Penny for them?' Kathleen queried, glancing across at him.

'Eh?'

'Penny for them.'

He pursed his mouth and shook his head. 'Only day-dreaming, that's all.'

'About?'

'Nothing in particular. Just day-dreaming.'

And with that he picked up the evening paper from his lap and again immersed himself in it.

* * *

'Andrew!'

Andrew shut the car door and strode to meet his friend. The pair of them warmly shook hands.

'Welcome to The Haven,' Willie declared.

Andrew glanced over Willie's shoulder at the pile called The Haven and thought it even more magnificent than Drummond House. In fact in some ways it reminded him of . . . He swiftly put that memory from his mind.

'So how are you, old bean?' Willie queried.

'In the pink. And all the better for seeing you.'

Willie chuckled. 'Come on in and meet everyone. With the exception of my son Ian, that is. You'll meet him later.'

'Jolly good.'

Willie's arm went round Andrew's shoulders and they mounted the long line of stone steps that led them to the massive oak door.

Chapter 3

'I know it's early but how about a drink?' Willie queried, rubbing his hands together. 'It's not every day a chum I haven't seen for years turns up.'

The four of them were assembled in the drawing room, Willie having already made the introductions.

'Not for me, Willie. But a little soda water would be nice,' Georgina replied.

Rose thought of the conversation she'd had with her stepmother in the Edinburgh tea room. 'Same for me, Pa, thank you.'

'And what about you, Andrew?'

'Whisky if you have it.'

'I not only have it, I have Drummond.'

Andrew laughed. 'That would be excellent.'

Willie busied himself with the drinks. He'd also have whisky.

'Can I ask what brings you to this part of the country?' Georgina queried of Andrew.

'Business. I'm en route to visit a few people. I'm a great believer in the personal touch, can work wonders in my opinion.'

'I understand. Willie tells me this is your first time at The Haven.'

'That's right. I should have been before but . . .' He shrugged. 'Something always got in the way.'

'I hope this business of yours isn't too pressing,' Willie said. 'We're hoping you'll stay a few days.'

Andrew hadn't planned on that. The night yes, but not a few days.

'Oh please do,' Georgina urged.

Andrew considered. 'Do you have the telephone here?'

'We do indeed,' Georgina replied.

'Then I shall make several calls later today and give you my answer afterwards.'

'Splendid.'

What a handsome, dashing man, Rose was thinking. He certainly didn't look as old as her father, but considerably younger.

There was something dangerous about Andrew Drummond, Rose decided. That was apparent even on this short acquaintance. He wasn't a man to be trifled with.

Willie handed Georgina and Rose their soda waters then returned for the whiskies.

'Are you married now, Andrew?' Willie enquired. 'You never mentioned in your letters.'

A lopsided, slightly cynical smile twisted Andrew's mouth. 'No I'm not. That's just never happened.'

Willie regarded Andrew thoughtfully. 'Pity.'

Andrew, still smiling, shrugged.

Willie changed the subject. 'So what have you been

doing, apart from running your distillery that is? And which I'm sure you're being most successful at.'

Andrew accepted the glass Willie gave him. 'Not a lot, to tell the truth. The distillery takes up most of my time.'

'But you must do something else?' Georgina queried with a frown.

'A bit of this, bit of that. I shoot on occasion, and have even been known to use a fly rod.'

'And socially?'

'I used to receive quite a few invitations, but rarely nowadays. I simply never took them up.'

'You have changed,' Willie mused, sitting down beside his wife.

'I suppose so.'

'Willie says you were quite the ladies' man at one time.'

Willie shot his wife a warning look which she chose to ignore.

'I suppose I was,' Andrew confessed. 'But that was in my salad days.'

'Surely you'll have to get married sometime,' Georgina went on. 'You'll need a son and heir to pass the distillery on to.'

'There is that,' Andrew acknowledged. 'It is a matter I have given some thought. But until the right woman comes along . . .' He trailed off and had a sip of whisky.

'You were engaged once I understand. But your fiancée died.'

This time the look Willie gave Georgina was withering.

'That's correct.'

Georgina waited for Andrew to continue, but he didn't.

'I say, how are those sisters of yours?' Willie asked, again changing the subject. He was furious with Georgina for trying to probe.

'Fine,' Andrew replied. 'Charlotte married the local minister and they now have two children. They're very happy. Nell is also married with a brood of her own.'

'Good for them,' Willie enthused.

'Charlotte keeps an eye on the distillery for me when I go off on these occasional trips of mine. She ran it by herself for a while after Pa died and I was still in Ireland.'

'By herself!' Rose exclaimed. 'She must be an extraordinary woman.'

'She is. A very determined and resourceful lady. I have every admiration for her.'

'I thought I might give you a tour of the estate after lunch,' Willie proposed.

'I'd like that.'

'Not all of it of course. You'd have to stay a week for that. It is rather large.'

'And thriving I trust?'

'Oh, very much so.'

'He works ever so hard,' Georgina stated. 'Too hard at times in my opinion.'

'I'm afraid it has to be done. However, I'll soon have Ian to help and that'll take something of the burden off my shoulders.'

'Did you enjoy Ireland, Mr Drummond?' Rose asked.

'Andrew, please.'

Rose blushed. 'Andrew then.'

'Yes, I did. In retrospect that is. At the time I wasn't so sure.'

'I loved it,' Willie declared. 'Dublin is such an exciting city. It positively throbs.' He smiled at Andrew. 'We have a great deal of reminiscing to do.'

'Indeed.'

'Do you remember . . .'

'He's a very sad and lonely man,' Georgina said to Willie that night after they'd retired.

'That's the impression I got.'

'Fun though. I enjoyed his company.'

'I thought you did.'

Georgina paused in her undressing. 'What did happen to his fiancée, Willie?'

Willie glanced away. 'That's something I think Andrew should tell you himself. Which I doubt he will. You could see how touchy he is on the subject.'

'I'm intrigued, darling. Positively intrigued.'

'Then you'll just have to stay that way. I'm not willing to discuss the matter. Let's just say it was all bound up in The Troubles over there.'

'The Troubles?' she repeated, her tone innocence itself. She was probing again.

But Willie wasn't taken in. He knew his wife only too well. 'And that's an end to it,' he stated firmly.

Her curiosity was killing her. But when Willie spoke like that nothing would budge him.

He could be such an obstinate man.

Rose crawled beneath the sheets and lay back to think about Andrew Drummond. What a pity he was so old. Ten years younger and . . . Well, who knew.

Closing her eyes she conjured up a picture of him. Recalling the way he smiled, the habit he had of flicking back a lock of hair when it dropped over his forehead. The delicate hands that had a somewhat feminine quality about them. The only thing that was feminine about him.

With a sigh she opened her eyes again, knowing she was going to have trouble sleeping. Andrew Drummond had disturbed her in a way no other man, of whatever age, had ever done before.

'Andrew!'

He turned to find Rose tripping towards him. 'Hello.'

'Hello as well,' she said on reaching his side. 'Do you mind if I join you?'

'Not at all. I was just admiring those roses.'

She glanced at the roses in question. 'They are rather splendid, aren't they. Do you like gardens?'

He gazed about him. 'Very much so. I find them, especially when the flowers are in bloom, extremely relaxing.'

'Do you have one at your house?'

'A number actually. I take great delight in strolling amongst them whenever I can.'

Strolling alone, she thought. 'I should like to see them one day.' Now that could be construed as being forward, she chided herself.

'And so you shall. It was already in my mind to invite the family to Drummond House. To repay your hospitality for having me here.'

Andrew bent and smelt a rose. 'Beautiful,' he murmured.

As he was, she thought.

'I have a friend in Dalneil, that's the village where I live, who sits for hours in his garden when the weather's clement. It's his favourite place. Only a small garden, mind you, as he lives in a cottage, but he says it inspires him.'

'Inspires?'

Andrew smiled. 'Jack is a writer. And pretty successful too. He's had several plays on in the West End of London, one also in New York.'

'I say. How thrilling!'

'Jack almost went to see the New York production, but in the end didn't.' Andrew paused. 'Did I say see? I meant listen to, for Jack's blind.'

'How awful for him,' Rose sympathised. 'Has he been blind from birth?'

'No, it happened during the war on the Western Front. Your father and I were lucky in being posted to Ireland for the duration. Jack and my elder brother Peter were the unlucky ones. Peter was killed and Jack not only blinded but horribly scarred on the face.'

'Your elder brother. Does that mean he would have inherited the distillery?'

Andrew nodded. 'It was always his by right. I had a career in the army planned, but of course all that changed when Peter bought it. His death literally broke my father's heart. He dropped down dead when he received the official telegram.'

Rose covered her mouth. 'That's ghastly.'

'Peter was Father's favourite, between the pair of us I mean. I believe Pa always considered me the black sheep of the family.'

'Surely not?'

Memories came flooding back. 'Oh yes, I'm afraid so. And he was quite right. I was a bit of a bounder when younger. More than a bit when I come to think of it.'

That only added to his charm she decided. 'But you're a changed man now?'

Was he? Perhaps. Perhaps not. It was said that leopards never change their spots after all.

'That's for others to judge. Not me.'

Rose stared at his finely chiselled features, then glanced away as an emotion she'd never experienced before trembled inside her.

'Was Peter much older than you?' She was being crafty here. At least so she hoped.

'Two years.'

'And how old would he have been now?'

'Why, eh . . . Forty I suppose.'

Which told her what she wanted to know. Andrew was thirty-eight, twenty years older than herself. An insurmountable barrier? Not really in her opinion, though many would have thought so. Father had been wrong about Andrew's age, Willie being forty-four.

'Do you miss him?'

Andrew considered that. 'Yes I do. We were never very close, but he was my brother when all's said and done. Yes I miss him. Though I have to say Jack Riach has been far more of a brother to me than Peter ever was.'

'You're very fond of this Jack, aren't you?'

'Extremely. He and his wife Hettie have been good to me. I can drop by there any time and be welcome for a meal or whatever. Jack and I try to go once a week to the local pub together. We invariably have a good laugh.'

'I've never met a writer,' Rose stated. 'But then what do you expect being born and brought up on the estate. It's very limiting, you know.'

'You shall meet Jack and Hettie when you come to Drummond House, that's a promise.'

'Thank you,' she smiled.

'Hettie used to work for Jack when he farmed. A farm

he sold after he lost his sight and couldn't personally run it any more. He adored that place and yet he sold it. I can understand why.'

'And what did Hettie do for him?'

Andrew gave a small laugh. 'She was a dairy maid. A real down-to-earth country lass if ever there was. The pair of them are a strange combination, but it works. They idolise one another.'

'Would you care to walk for a while?' Rose asked.

Andrew frowned. 'I really should be getting back to the house. Your father will be wondering where I've got to.'

She tried not to show her disappointment. 'A short walk then? Just enough to stretch the legs.'

He conceded. 'A short walk it is. And during it you can tell me all about yourself.'

She laughed. 'I've already explained, there's very little to tell.'

Pretty girl, he thought. If a trifle overweight. Nice personality too.

They walked for longer than Andrew had intended.

'Now don't forget,' Andrew said to William. 'You'll come to Drummond House.'

'In the winter when things are quieter round here. You have my word.'

The two men shook hands.

'I really have enjoyed myself. Thank you all.'

'It was a pleasure having you, Andrew,' Georgina declared. They'd come out to see Andrew off, with the exception of Ian who was working.

Did he know her well enough? Andrew decided he did. Going to Georgina, he pecked her on the cheek. 'You've been most kind.'

'Not at all. As I said, it was our pleasure.'

He turned to Rose who was finding his departure a terrible wrench. Andrew Drummond had made a big impression on her. A very big impression indeed. She'd have given anything for him to be staying longer and couldn't wait for the proposed visit to Drummond House.

'Goodbye, Rose.'

'Goodbye, Andrew.'

Disappointment flooded her when he started towards the car. 'Don't I get a kiss as well?'

'I say!' Willie exclaimed. 'Where's your modesty, girl?'

Rose blushed deeply. 'I'm sorry. I didn't mean to offend.'

'You didn't offend at all,' Andrew declared gallantly. 'I'm the one at fault.' And with that he returned to Rose and kissed her as he'd kissed Georgina.

'Thank you, lovely miss,' he smiled, amused by her continuing blushes.

'Have a safe journey,' Willie said.

'I'm sure I shall.'

Andrew climbed into the Rolls and wound down his window. 'Here we go then.'

He started the car which purred sweetly into life. 'Toodeloo!' He waved.

It was with a heavy heart that Rose turned towards the house. It might have been a short acquaintance but she'd miss Andrew dreadfully.

Once inside she headed for her room, wanting to be alone.

Sean Flynn gazed about him, taking in the flickering candles illuminating the room of the condemned house they'd taken over as their own. There were ancient curtains on the window, closed to ensure their privacy, while a number of broken-down sofas and chairs provided seating. It was hardly the Ritz but suitable for their purposes.

'Home from home,' he breathed, which raised a laugh from the others present.

'Some home,' Don McGuire commented, raising another laugh.

Mo Binchy gingerly sat on one of the sofas, liberated from a dump, in case it collapsed under his weight. 'What now?' he queried.

Sean focused on him. 'How do you mean?'

'I mean, what now? Where do we go from here, O leader?'

'Less of your bloody sarcasm. Don't you know it's the lowest form of wit.'

'That's me,' Mo riposted. 'Real low life.'

Sean produced a cut-throat razor which he'd stropped before coming out. 'I think we should have a gang insignia. Our own mark so to speak.'

Sammy Renton frowned. 'What sort of mark?'

'I'll show you.'

Sean took off his jacket and dropped it to the floor. He then partially rolled up the left sleeve of his shirt. 'A cross right here,' he declared, indicating a patch just above his wrist.

Sammy swallowed hard.

'Done with that razor?' Noddy Gallagher queried.

Sean nodded.

That was greeted with a deathly silence.

'I'll go first,' Sean proposed. 'Once marked you're in the gang for life. And no one can be a gang member without it.'

'Christ,' Jim Gallagher whispered.

Sean did it quickly. One deep stripe was instantly followed by a second. Blood spurted from the cuts and ran down his hand.

Sean stared triumphantly at them. 'Who's next?'

There were no takers.

'Come on, you bunch of jessies. Who's next?'

Don McGuire came forward. 'See's that razor, Sean.'

When they left the house a little later all bore the mark of the Samurai on their left arm.

'Have you heard the latest?' a clearly worried Vicky Grieve queried of Bridie and Teresa as they arrived in the cloakroom where they hung their coats, exchanging them for the large white aprons they wore while working.

'What's that?' Bridie asked.

'The rumour is there's to be more sackings.'

Teresa swore. 'Are you sure?'

'It's only a rumour, mind. That's all I know.'

Bridie bit her lip.

'What'll I do if I lose my job?' Vicky choked. 'God help me if I do, what with my ma and that.'

This was a worry, Bridie thought. A real worry. 'Sales must have dropped again.'

'If the rumour's true,' Teresa added. 'It might just be a right load of rubbish. Someone said something that was overheard wrongly and passed on the same way. That could be all it is.'

'Aye,' Bridie agreed.

'Whatever,' Teresa went on. 'We'd better get moving. I for one don't want to be late on the floor with the rumour of possible sackings flying about. I don't want to give them any excuses to pick on me.'

The three of them quickly changed and hurried from the cloakroom.

Ellen should be along any minute now, Andrew thought, staring up at the ceiling. He was eager for her presence, and body.

It was Jack Riach who'd given him the idea one night when they were talking in the pub. Jack had been worried about his 'wellbeing', as Jack had called it.

Andrew had been amused when Jack had come out with the suggestion, further amused by Jack's embarrassment.

'What made you think of that?' he'd asked.

'I heard of someone else who'd come to the same arrangement,' Jack had lied in reply, not wanting Andrew to know that the arrangement had been between him and Hettie when she'd been his dairy maid.

'One of the servant lassies?' Andrew had repeated.

'Perfect, if you fancy one that is and she'll comply. You'd have to be careful in picking the right one. One who'll keep her mouth shut whether she agrees or not.'

Andrew had considered that a wise piece of advice.

He brought himself out of his reverie and yawned. What was keeping the damned girl? He wanted her and he wanted her now.

Andrew smiled in the darkness. Ellen Temple had been the only one he'd approached and a good choice it had been. He'd read her character correctly. Underneath that prim exterior lay a natural tart. And so it had proved.

A deal had been struck. An agreed sum paid once a month and the assurance that she'd be well taken care of should she fall pregnant.

How long had it been now? Just over a year, Andrew reflected. A year of having access to her body whenever he wished it. And a fine body it was too, a body she was enthusiastic in using. Just as she'd been enthusiastic about learning all the little tricks and refinements he'd taught her.

Andrew's ruminations were disturbed when his bedroom door opened and a shadowy figure slipped inside. The door was closed as silently as it had been opened.

The shadowy figure flitted to the side of his bed where Ellen dropped her dressing-gown to the floor. Still wearing her nightdress, which would soon be removed, she got in beside Andrew and snuggled up.

'I was beginning to think you'd gone off me. You've been back a whole week without giving me the nod until tonight.'

His hand sought out a breast. 'I haven't been in the mood, that's all.'

'Are you certain about that?' she queried anxiously.

'Absolutely.'

She sighed with relief. The last thing she wanted was to lose this added income. An added income that would one day release her from the life of service she so loathed.

Strictly business, Andrew thought, that was the nice thing about their arrangement. He didn't have to pretend to be romantic in any way.

'If you weren't in the mood before you certainly are now,' she whispered as his hardness pressed into her.

'Let's get you out of this,' he whispered in reply, always preferring her to be naked when in bed with him.

The nightdress was removed and tossed aside.

Kathleen Flynn shook Bridie's shoulder. 'Time to be up, lass.'

Bridie groaned as she came awake. She never liked

getting up in the morning. Especially when she had work to go to.

'I'm dead beat,' she declared. 'Alison has kept me awake most of the night.'

Bridie and her younger sister Alison shared a cavity bed in the kitchen. This was a peculiar Glasgow device, a bed set in a wall recess looking rather like a cave.

'Why's that?'

'She's got another cold. Hour after hour she was sniffing and snorting. And talk about being restless!'

'I'm sorry,' Alison wailed from underneath the covers. 'I couldn't help it.' She popped her head into view. Her eyes were puffed and streaming, her nose quite red.

Kathleen placed her hands on her hips and studied her youngest child. 'I don't know how you manage it, young lady. If it's not one thing that's wrong with you it's another.'

Alison clutched the bedclothes to her chin. 'It's not my fault, Ma. I don't ask to get ill all the time.'

'You manage it nonetheless,' Bridie retorted caustically.

Kathleen leant across Bridie and felt Alison's forehead. 'Aye, you've got a temperature right enough.'

'I'm sorry,' Alison repeated.

Bridie lay back and closed her eyes. She was so tired that for two pins she'd have taken the day off work. But that was something she daren't do. Fourteen people had now had the sack at the factory and she didn't want to be amongst the next batch if there was one. And if what she heard was true, that sales were still dropping, there could well be.

'You'd better get a move on, Bridie, before your father and Sean come through.'

Uttering another groan Bridie swung her feet out of bed.

It was the same every morning, Kathleen was up first, then Bridie so that she'd be dressed before her father and brother came through to shave and have their breakfast, which was invariably a cup of tea and thick slice of bread.

Bridie padded to the sink where she splashed cold water on her face. A quick dry and then back to her clothes which she began to put on.

'I feel like death warmed up,' she complained.

Alison was about to say, 'And you look it', then thought perhaps not in the circumstances. 'Can I have a hanky please, Ma?' she asked instead. 'I had to make do with my sleeve during the night.'

'Of course, lassie. Of course.'

'I just hope you haven't given me your rotten cold,' Bridie admonished her sister. That would be disastrous.

Chapter 4

Mrs Buchanan was waiting for Pat by her door. 'Good morning to you, Mr Flynn,' she smiled.

Pat's reply, weighed down as he was with a bag of coal, was a grunt.

'Come away in,' she said, leaving the door open as she followed him into the kitchen.

What a glamour puss, Pat was thinking as he filled the bin. She was all done up like a dish of fish.

'Just the one again?' he queried, shaking out the bag.

'That's right.' The smile so far hadn't left her face. 'Are you in a hurry, Mr Flynn?'

He frowned. 'Why do you ask?'

'I wondered if you had time for a bottle of beer. My husband left some behind when he went away and I never touch it. I will have a wee whisky on occasion, but never beer. Filthy stuff in my opinion.' She laughed, a tinkling sound.

Pat had never refused a free alcoholic anything in his life. 'That would be nice,' he replied, also smiling.

'Right then.'

She delved into a cupboard and produced a screwtop. 'I'll just get a glass to go with it,' she declared, handing him the bottle.

Pat wasn't fussed whether he had a glass or not. He watched her as she opened another cupboard. Classy piece right enough, he thought. She didn't half look smart in her warpaint.

'Dougal, that's my husband, is in the Royal Navy. When he goes to sea it can be for months on end.'

Pat accepted the glass from her. 'That wouldn't suit me at all,' he said, making conversation.

'Dougal loves it. Joined when he was only fifteen. He was at the Battle of Jutland you know.'

'Really.'

'Lost quite a few of his mates there. But he was fortunate to come through all right. That was the only action he ever saw. What about yourself, Mr Flynn, were you in the war?'

'Wasn't nearly everyone,' Pat replied softly.

'Did you see action?'

Awful memories crowded his mind. Vividly recalling that particular day when he'd come within a whisker of . . . 'Oh aye, I saw a bit.'

'Which regiment were you in?'

'The HLI. Highland Light Infantry. And a better bunch of blokes you'll go a long way to find.'

Pat had a long pull of beer. 'That's grand stuff,' he declared, wiping froth from his mouth. 'It sure hits the spot.'

Mrs Buchanan stared in fascination at the wrist of the hand he'd used, where thick tufts of hair jutted from under his cuff. Her mouth went dry thinking what the rest of him would be like. Should be like.

'Mrs Buchanan?'

She started. 'Sorry, I was lost in thought there for a moment.' The smile returned. 'Something I've got to do later,' she lied.

Pat topped up his glass, the smell of the heavy perfume she was wearing strong in his nostrils. It was a pleasant smell, very feminine. He couldn't remember the last time Kathleen had worn scent or perfume. He found himself comparing Kathleen and Mrs Buchanan. There was no contest, Mrs Buchanan won hands down.

'I'm Geraldine by the way.'

'Oh aye.'

She raised a well-plucked eyebrow in anticipation.

'Pat,' he said slowly. 'Short for Patrick of course.'

'Of course.'

He couldn't resist himself. 'My wife's called Kathleen. As Irish as Pat and Flynn.'

Geraldine's smile became slightly razored. She didn't reply to that.

Pat saw off what remained in his glass and then emptied the bottle into it. 'This is certainly going down well. I had quite a thirst on me. It's the coal you see, it gets in your throat.'

Offer him another? she wondered. And decided not to. She mustn't be too pushy. That might scare him off. 'How are the children?' she enquired.

'Och, the wee lass's got a bad cold. There's always something wrong with that one.'

'I'm sorry to hear so. Alison, isn't it?'

He nodded. 'That's right.'

She swallowed hard when a tuft of hair suddenly popped up from underneath his collar. Now she knew for certain. God, how she adored hairy men, the hairier the better. Hair covering their chests, their backs, their bottoms. Hair . . .

'Well, that's that,' Pat declared, laying the empty glass to one side. 'Thank you very much, Geraldine. It was most appreciated.'

'I'm sure you deserve a little treat.' The treat she had in mind wasn't beer.

'I'll see you next time then.'

When he'd gone she closed the door and leant back against it. In her mind's eye she was picturing Pat stark naked, hairy from neck to toe.

'Oh God,' she whispered, wishing not for the first time that Dougal wasn't a sailor and came home every night like most normal men.

But a sailor he was and she had to put up with it.

With certain exceptions that is.

Andrew laid the tray he'd been carrying on the table then placed Jack Riach's pint and whisky in front of him. It was one of their Friday nights out at the local.

'I've been meaning to ask for a while, how's your little arrangement going?'

Andrew stared at his friend whose eyeless sockets were covered with dark glasses. Although Jack knew an arrangement had been made, he didn't know the name of the lassie it was with. 'Fine.'

'That's good then. No problems?'

'None at all.'

Jack nodded. 'A man shouldn't be alone all the time, Andrew. It isn't good.'

'I'm not alone, Jack. I'm at the distillery every working day.'

'You know what I mean. I worry about you, old pal, rattling around in that big house all by yourself.'

'I'm hardly that. There are the servants.'

'Not quite the same though, is it. You need a proper companion, Andrew. In other words, a wife.'

Andrew sighed. 'Not that again.'

'Your Alice was years ago. In the past. We're in the present which has to be lived.'

Andrew conjured up a picture of Alice in his mind. Dear sweet Alice whom he'd started out wooing because of her wealth and then fallen in love with. Even now, after all this while, just thinking about her brought a lump to his throat.

'Apart from anything else, Andrew, you need a son and heir to pass the distillery on to.'

Andrew gave a low laugh. 'Someone else said that recently.'

'Oh?'

'Willie Seaton's wife. The chap I served alongside in Ireland.'

'Well, she's right. And so am I.'

'All in due course, Jack. All in due course. I'm sure the right person will come along in time. And I'm hardly decrepit yet.' He thought of his last session with Ellen. 'Hardly,' he repeated with a chuckle. Ellen could certainly testify to that.

'You want to get out and about more.'

'To where? Besides, when I get home most nights all I'm good for is having a meal, a few drams and then bed.'

'I don't believe that.' Jack held up a hand. 'I know you work hard, but the rest is a state of mind. You don't really want to do anything so you don't.'

'Nonsense.'

Jack picked up his pint. 'Is it?'

Andrew found himself thinking of Georgina Seaton. Now there was a woman he could be interested in. Pity she was already married.

Jack cleared his throat. 'Changing the subject. Can I ask your advice?'

'Naturally. What is it?'

'First of all, promise you won't laugh.'

'I swear. As if I'd laugh at a friend.' That was said tongue in cheek, as Jack was only too well aware.

'I'm serious about this.'

'Oh go on, Jack, you're blethering on like an old biddy.'

Jack took a deep breath. 'I've only spoken about this to Hettie, no one else, apart from you tonight that is. Nor will I.'

Andrew waited patiently.

'Do you think I'm up to writing a novel?'

Andrew had no compulsion whatever to laugh. If anything he was taken aback. 'What sort of novel?'

Jack cleared his throat. 'A love story actually.'

'I see,' Andrew murmured, and tasted his dram.

'Well. Do you think I'm being daft? Overreaching myself?'

'I don't think that at all. It would be a big departure for you, as I'm sure you appreciate. There must be a huge amount of work in a novel compared to a play.'

'I know,' Jack replied softly, and nibbled a thumbnail. 'I must confess, the whole idea rather frightens me. It's a tremendous challenge, but that in itself is exciting.'

'I do believe you've already made up your mind to have a go.' Andrew smiled.

'I have nothing of the sort!' Jack protested.

'No?'

Jack shook his head. 'I swear.'

He had really, Andrew thought. Jack just didn't know it yet. 'Well, I hope you go ahead. And, having a great deal of faith in you, I'm certain if you do you'll carry it off. So there.'

Jack groped for his whisky, wishing he had the same faith. '*Slainte!*' he toasted.

'*Slainte*,' Andrew responded.

Rose reined in her horse Trixie and, after a few moments, dismounted. She needed a breather after a good gallop.

'Come on, Trix, let's have a little walk,' she said, patting the mare's nose.

Trixie whinnied in reply.

As they walked Rose thought of Andrew Drummond, wondering what he was doing at that very moment. Work probably, it being a Wednesday morning. He was bound to be at the distillery. Unless he was off on another of his business trips, that is.

When they went to Drummond House she must ask Andrew to take her round the distillery and show her everything. Just the two of them if possible, she didn't want her father or Georgina playing gooseberry.

Was she being silly? she asked herself. Andrew hadn't shown any particular interest in her, not that sort of interest anyway. He'd been polite of course, and attentive, when they were together. But that was only manners.

She recalled the kiss on the cheek he'd given her as he was leaving and reaching up caressed the spot where his lips had touched her. She flushed slightly remembering her embarrassment at asking for the kiss. Shameless hussy, she thought, which made her smile.

'Andrew,' she said. How she enjoyed saying his name. 'Andrew.' A tremor ran through her as she said it a second time.

Winter seemed an eternity away, years not months. She knew it to be her imagination but the days were positively dragging by. Each so long it made her want to scream from frustration.

Oh to be in his arms, to have his lips on hers and not her cheek. For them to . . .

Rose shook her head. Enough of that, girl, she chided

herself. She shouldn't be having such thoughts. Not about Andrew or anyone else.

Remounting Trixie she continued on her way, trying unsuccessfully to get Andrew out of her mind.

God, but they were tedious, Georgina reflected. She loved her parents dearly but her yearly week with them was hell. No wonder her father was called Boring Bob behind his back. A nickname he'd had for as long as she could remember.

She gazed in distaste around the somewhat shabby room, shabby as was the rest of the house. A house that, in its entirety, could have fitted into the drawing room of The Haven.

Well, maybe not in its entirety, there were two floors to it after all, but it seemed that way.

'More tea, darling?' Margaret Galbraith queried.

'No thank you, Mum.'

'Bob?'

'A spot more wouldn't go amiss.'

Georgina stared at her father. A small, balding, waspish man, he looked exactly what he'd been in life, a clerk. He blinked back at her through wire-framed spectacles.

'Yes, Georgina. You wish to say something?'

'No, Father. I was just thinking.'

Bob knew Georgina disliked her visits there, which he could well understand. She'd become used to far grander things after all. Far grander things and people. But it was her duty to come, to visit her mother if nothing else.

Margaret took Bob's cup and refilled it. 'What do you intend doing tomorrow, dear?' she asked Georgina.

'I thought I might go shopping.'

That scandalised Margaret. 'But you've already been shopping twice, Georgina. You'll have bought up the whole of Perth before you're finished.'

Georgina laughed. 'Hardly!'

'Why don't you take your mother with you this time,' Bob suggested.

Georgina sighed inwardly. That was the last thing she wanted. If her mother went along all she'd get was a constant lecture on how expensive everything was and how much she was spending. Her spending horrified Margaret.

'Mum?'

'I'll stay at home if you don't mind, dear. I'd planned a spot of baking.' She beamed. 'Your father so enjoys my baking, isn't that correct, Bob?'

He nodded.

What a relief, Georgina thought. What a blessed relief.

'Georgina, this is incredible. How are you?'

Georgina, just stepping out of a cab, turned to stare at Andrew Drummond in surprise. 'Why, hello!'

'Here, let me,' he said, and paid off the driver. 'What are you doing in Perth?' he queried as the cab drove off.

'My parents live here. I visit them once a year. And you?'

'A little bit of business.'

'I see.' She smiled.

'So where are you off to?'

'Just the shops.'

'Looking for something in particular?'

She shook her head. 'Passing time, that's all. My parents are lovely, but not in long stretches. They tend to be rather . . . claustrophobic, shall I say.'

Andrew laughed. 'I understand.' He glanced about him. 'As we've bumped into one another, why don't we take coffee? It's about that time of morning.'

Something jumped inside her. 'That would be splendid.'

'There's a coffee shop not far from here that I sometimes frequent. We could go there.'

'What's it called?'

'Darling's.'

Georgina smiled. 'I know it well. An excellent choice.'

'Pity I sent away that cab,' he commented, looking to see if he could spot another.

'We can walk,' she protested. 'It's only a few minutes' stroll.'

Offer his arm or not? Not, he decided. 'Then shall we?'

Andrew's eyes lit up when the cake stand was placed on their table. 'French cakes,' he enthused. 'I adore those. Have ever since I was a nipper. Especially the chocolate-covered ones. Yummy.'

Georgina laughed. 'Do you have a sweet tooth?'

'Not really. But French cakes are an exception. I'd murder for one.' For a brief instant a strange glint came into his eyes.

'Coffee for two please,' he instructed the waitress who'd reappeared to take their order.

'Certainly, sir.'

'So, where are you staying?' Georgina enquired.

'I'm not. I motored down early and will motor back later on this afternoon when my business is concluded.'

'In that gorgeous Rolls-Royce.'

'Yes,' he murmured.

'You will have to give me a spin in it when we come to Drummond House.'

'I'd be delighted.'

He really was such a handsome man, she thought. Quite dishy as the younger folk would say. Far better-looking than Willie. Not that Willie was unattractive, far from it. But he wasn't in the same league as Andrew Drummond.

'How are things at The Haven?' he enquired politely.

'More or less the same. Nothing changes there very much. It can be quite humdrum actually which is why it's always such a pleasure getting to a city.'

'Even Perth,' he grinned. Perth might be lovely but it was hardly the most exciting of places.

'Even Perth,' she agreed. 'For the shops.'

'So tell me, I never did find out. How did you and Willie meet?'

She vividly remembered the occasion, a night that had completely altered the course of her life. 'At a small gathering held by mutual friends.'

'Here in Perth?'

She nodded. 'Willie and I struck it off right away. Well, one thing led to another and eventually to marriage.' She paused, then added reflectively, 'So many women of my generation never got a first chance, far less a second.'

Andrew frowned. 'Second chance?'

She hesitated, then went on. 'There was a chap before the war, his name was Harry. We were very much in love and intended marrying. Then the war happened and . . .' She sucked in a breath. 'Harry was killed in France.'

'I'm sorry,' Andrew sympathised.

'I thought I was left on the shelf, there being so few men to go round after the war. That's why there are so many spinsters of my generation.'

'And then Willie popped up and that was that,' Andrew smiled. 'He whisked you off the shelf and the pair of you lived happily ever after.'

'That's right.' It was too, she reflected. For she was happy, though only to an extent. She'd never loved Willie, not when she married him, or now. Fond of him, yes. Very fond. But that was as far as it went. Her feelings for him were nothing like those she'd had for Harry. Now that had been true love.

If only Willie could satisfy her in bed it might make a difference, but he didn't, and never would. She'd become reconciled to that. Even if he had she still wouldn't have loved him, but she might have felt more towards him.

What a catch Willie had been, a catch she'd grabbed with both hands when given the opportunity. Never in her wildest dreams had she imagined she'd end up mistress of a grand house like The Haven, or with a husband so wealthy. Harry, bless him, had worked in a bank as a teller. A good job, he'd often assured her. And he'd had aspirations. He'd be a manager one day he'd repeatedly said, it was only a matter of time and passing the appropriate exams.

Harry, whom she still achingly missed. Her biggest regret was that they'd never made love. Even when he was off to fight she'd still refused him, wanting to be a virgin on their wedding night. Well, she had been on her wedding night, only it had been Willie she'd given herself to and not Harry.

'He's a wonderful man,' Andrew declared, referring to Willie.

'Yes,' she agreed. 'Wonderful.'

Andrew wondered why the mood between them had suddenly changed. Before it had been light and jocular but within the last few moments it had become sombre.

'So now I know how you and Willie met.'

She was lucky, she reminded herself, damned lucky to have had that second chance.

Even if love was absent.

'Pooh!' Rose exclaimed. 'You don't half pong.'

Ian Seaton glared at his sister. 'Well, what do you expect

after a day like I've put in. It wasn't only hard graft but nasty smelly work, I can tell you.'

'You don't have to tell me, the smelly part is obvious.' Rose wrinkled her nose in disgust. 'Pooh!' she repeated.

Sometimes his sister irritated Ian beyond belief. 'Anyway, I'm off for a bath now,' he declared.

'And don't you need one.' Rose's derisory laugh followed him up the stairs.

'Well, well, well,' Sean muttered, and gave a small belch. He and the rest of the Samurai were out for a Saturday night booze-up.

'What is it?' Noddy Gallagher queried, noting Sean's expression.

Sean nodded across the horseshoe-shaped bar. 'Remember I mentioned those Proddy bastards who jumped me a while back.'

'Aye.'

'That's them over there.'

Noddy peered in the direction Sean had indicated. 'Which ones?'

Sean described the two in question.

'What's up?' Jim Gallagher asked on joining them.

Sean explained the situation.

'I don't think they're regulars here,' Jim mused. 'I've certainly never seen them before.'

Sean recalled with grim satisfaction that he'd beaten the Prods, though at no small cost to himself. He'd been sore for days afterwards. His hand went to the hard metal object he was carrying in his inside jacket pocket.

'It's time we started making a name for ourselves,' he declared softly.

'You mean as Samurai?' Jim queried.

Sean nodded. 'Exactly.'

'What do you have in mind?'

'Get the lads over here. This is a night those bastards are going to remember for the rest of their lives.'

Noddy swallowed hard, shivering at the look on Sean's face. It was frightening.

'Right,' Jim said, and moved off.

Sean's eyes strayed to the clock above the gantry. They'd wait till nearly closing time and then leave. In the meantime he'd ensure he wasn't spotted by the Prods.

One moment the Prods were laughing and joking between themselves, the next they'd been set upon and bundled into an alleyway.

'Give them a right doing,' Sean instructed, landing a heavy punch.

The Prods didn't have a chance, they were simply overwhelmed by numbers. When they were both on the ground the boot went in.

'Keep them conscious,' Sean yelled, his own boot flashing.

A Prod screamed in agony as the boot found its mark between his legs.

Sean stepped back and reached into his inside pocket. The cutthroat razor he produced had an ebony handle.

'Now hold the fuckers there,' he hissed.

The Samurai swiftly obeyed.

Sean straddled his first victim to smile evilly down at him. 'Remember me?'

The Prod didn't answer.

'Remember me, you bastard?'

'Fenian cunt.'

Sean laughed and made small circles in the air with the

now fully opened razor. 'Well, you're certainly right about me being a Fenian, and proud of it I am too.'

The pinioned Prod spat at Sean. 'That's what I think of you and your like.'

Cold fury erupted in Sean as spittle ran down the front of his shirt. 'You're going to regret that.'

'Stop it, Tom. Don't antagonise them any further,' the other Prod counselled.

'Is that your name then, son? Tom.'

'Up yours.'

'Tom what?'

'Tom Thumb.'

Sean laughed again. 'Quite the comedian, aren't you?'

Mo Binchy glanced anxiously at the entrance to the alleyway. 'Hurry up, there are always lots of polis around on a Saturday night. We don't want to get caught.'

'We won't get caught,' Sean replied.

He bent over Tom. 'We're the Samurai. Don't forget, pal.'

There was no reply.

Tom shrieked when Sean scored a deep cut down one side of his face. He continued shrieking as another furrow was added on the same cheek.

Two furrows on each cheek, then Sean sliced off a thumb.

'There's your thumb, Tom.' Sean leered malevolently, placing it on the lad's chest.

Tom didn't reply. He was out cold.

Then it was the second Prod's turn. Two furrows on each cheek, only he got to keep his thumbs.

Chapter 5

Willie found Ian standing by a window staring out over the autumnal landscape, his son clearly lost in thought.

'Am I intruding?'

Ian started and turned to face Willie. 'No, I was just . . . thinking I suppose.'

'Oh?'

Ian watched his father light a cigarette. 'About how much I love this place.'

Willie smiled.

'Always have done. I wouldn't want to live anywhere else. Not in a million years.'

'I know what you mean. It's the same with me, I wouldn't trade The Haven for any other place on earth.'

Ian nodded.

'How's the work coming along?'

'Fine.'

'Enjoying it?'

'Some of the experiences I could do without,' Ian replied ruefully. 'But on the whole it's . . . well, you could call it good fun.'

'Jock Gibson treating you all right?'

'He's a hard taskmaster right enough. But fair, you have to give him that. He's well respected and admired by all those under him. As I hope I'll be when in time I take over his job.'

There was a change in Ian of late, Willie thought. A resolve about him that hadn't been there before. And certainly a new maturity. 'So what's it tomorrow?' he enquired.

'I'm not sure. Mr Gibson hasn't said.'

Willie smiled inwardly at the use of the title Mister.

'There are some trees needing felling so it might be that.' Ian shrugged. 'On the other hand it could be any of a dozen things. I won't know until I'm given my instructions.'

'Would you say you've learnt a lot?'

'Oh certainly. But more importantly I've learnt how much more I've still got to learn.'

Willie chuckled, pleased by his son's progress. When he passed on, the estate would be left in good hands. Of that he now had no doubt.

'Was there . . . anyone special when you were away studying?' Willie asked casually.

'You mean a girl?'

'That's right.'

Ian shook his head. 'I met a few nice lassies I have to admit, but no one you would call special. Why?'

'You'll get married one day and I just wondered . . . Well, you understand.'

'When I meet someone like that you'll be the first to know. All right?'

'All right,' Willie agreed.

He moved to stand beside Ian. 'Talking of loving this

place, your mother certainly did. She said to me once that every day she spent here was a sheer joy.'

Ian smiled to hear that. 'I still miss her.'

'As do I, son. As do I. She was a wonderful woman with an enormous heart.'

Willie's face clouded with memory recalling Mary's death from influenza. Her last words, as he'd held her in his arms, were that she loved him. What a terrible loss that had been. He'd thought the anguish of her passing would kill him as well.

'I'm glad you've long since made up your differences with Georgina,' he said softly. 'As I explained a dozen times in the past, she was never trying to take your mother's place.'

'I understand that now,' Ian replied. 'It was stupid of me, and selfish, to expect you to go through the rest of your life alone.'

'You were young, lad, and deeply hurt. You saw Georgina as an intrusion on your mother's memory. But, as they say, life goes on. Even I had to accept that after a while. And you can't deny Georgina's been good for me, not to mention yourself and Rose.'

Ian thought he couldn't deny it. Georgina made Willie happy and that was what counted. 'Tell you what, Pa, why don't we go for a walk? Just the pair of us, together.'

Willie nodded. 'I'd like that. A lot.'

'We could go down to the churchyard and pay our respects?'

'We could do, Ian. We could indeed.'

A beautiful warmth pervaded Willie as they left the room. Moments like these were so precious.

Kathleen glanced round in surprise as a long-faced Bridie entered the kitchen. 'What are you doing home at this hour?

Why aren't you at work?'

'I got laid off, Ma.'

'Laid . . . Oh my God! Your father will be furious.'

'It wasn't my fault, Ma. Do you think I wanted to be shown the door? Hardly.' Bridie slumped into a chair. 'There were three of us got the push this time. And I was one.'

Kathleen, who'd been washing dishes, dried her hands on a towel. This was awful.

'Could I have a cup of tea? I need one.'

'Aye, me as well.' Kathleen busied herself with the kettle, her mind whirling.

'Pa can't blame me, Ma. It would be completely unfair if he did.'

Kathleen knew that to be true enough. But you could never be sure with Pat, all he would see was a wage not coming into the house. It would be just like him to fly off the handle.

'Teresa's still there. Though worried sick she'll be next.' Bridie shook her head. 'I simply can't understand why there's been such a slump in sales. Glasgow folk have aye been heavy lemonade drinkers.'

Bridie was still in a state of shock from her sacking. She'd guessed the moment she'd been summoned to the manager's office what lay in store for her. And her guess had been only too right.

'Well, you'll just have to get something else,' Kathleen declared. 'First thing the morn's morn you're out doing the rounds. And tonight we'll look in your da's paper to see if there's anything there.'

Bridie nodded her agreement.

'And I'll ask around when I'm out and about. There's always the possibility that someone will have heard of a job going.' A possibility, but not much of one, Kathleen thought.

* * *

Hettie Riach's eyes were filled with tears when Jack finally stopped talking. 'So what do you think?' he asked after a few seconds' hiatus.

'It's a smashing idea for a book, Jack. I . . .' She broke off, then smiled. 'It's about us, isn't it?'

'More or less. Though changed somewhat. I want a happy ending. The hero doesn't come back blinded and scarred in my story.'

She went over and knelt in front of him. Reaching up she gently stroked his cheek. 'You'll always be my hero. For ever and for ever.'

A lump came into his throat. 'It's funny how things work out, isn't it? If it hadn't been for the war and my wounds we'd probably never have got together.' He paused, then added, 'And what a loss that would have been.'

'For both of us, Jack. For both of us.'

'Are you certain? You don't regret anything?'

'No,' she whispered. 'I swear.'

He recalled the cocky gallant of yesteryear, the dashing figure who'd used Hettie as no better than a common whore. Paying her for their weekly rendezvous where he'd have his way with her. What a different man he was now from that person.

He grasped Hettie by the hand. 'You're the best thing that's ever happened to me, Hettie. God does indeed move in mysterious ways.'

'Your husband must have left quite a bit of this stuff behind,' Pat commented drily to Geraldine Buchanan. This was the fourth time he'd been invited to stay on and have a beer.

Geraldine dropped her gaze. 'To be truthful, Pat, I've bought the last couple in.'

He raised a bushy eyebrow.

'I enjoy the company you see. It gets so lonely being on your own.'

'I can imagine.'

'And being new here I haven't any friends in the area. Oh, the neighbours are polite enough, but that's as far as it's gone so far.'

'Where did you move from?' he asked.

'Paisley.'

He waited for her to go on, and when she didn't asked, 'Why was that?'

She had no intention of giving Pat the real reason behind their move. Dougal had found out about Charlie, the last man she'd been entertaining while Dougal was away. What a ruction that had been, Dougal storming round to Charlie's house and punching him. That evening Dougal had informed her they were moving, he didn't care where as long as it was out of Paisley. She never had discovered who it was had told Dougal or how that person had known about Charlie.

'It was to be closer to Dougal's parents,' she lied. 'Now it's far easier to pop over and see them than it was while we were in Paisley.'

Pat nodded that he understood.

'It's the evenings that are the worst,' Geraldine said. 'They just seem to go on and on when you're alone.'

Pat had another swallow of beer and didn't reply.

'I was wondering . . .' She trailed off and dropped her gaze again.

'Wondering what?' he prompted softly, pretty certain he knew what was coming next.

'Don't get the wrong idea but I was wondering if you'd care to drop by some night. We get on so well that we could have a right old laugh together. I'd lay in some beer of course, and whisky.'

Beer *and* whisky, both compliments of Geraldine. What a temptation. And the rest too, he thought. Get the wrong idea indeed! She must think him daft.

'I'd be ever so appreciative,' she said.

I'll bet you would, he thought, regarding her over the rim of his glass. In all his years as a coalman this was the first time he'd ever had an offer like this.

'Well, Pat?'

He decided not to commit himself right away. He had to think this through.

'How about I give you an answer next time I come up with your coal?'

She gave him an alluring smile. 'I doubt your wife would be pleased if you told her.'

'Pleased! She'd have a fit. No, Geraldine, if I do decide to come Kathleen won't be knowing anything about it. I can assure you of that.'

'It gets so lonely,' she repeated wistfully.

Randy cow, he thought.

'Any luck?' Kathleen queried as Bridie walked through the door.

Bridie shook her head.

'Where did you try?'

'Templeton's, the carpet people. They suggested I go back in a month when they might have something. Then I tried a big bread bakery in the Cowcaddens. There was nothing there either.'

Kathleen bit back her disappointment. She'd come to rely on what Bridie gave her at the end of the week, just as she relied on Sean. Little enough though it was in both cases. Damn Pat for being such a boozer.

Bridie sighed. 'I'll go out again tomorrow. Who knows?'

Who indeed, Kathleen thought.

'You on a committee!' Kathleen exclaimed in astonishment.

'Aye, me.'

Kathleen stared at Pat in wonderment. 'Would you credit it.'

'I was right proud I can tell you. It's quite an honour for the Union to ask you to serve on a committee.'

'What's the committee about?' Sean queried from where he was sitting.

'The taking care of widows and orphans,' Pat replied glibly.

Sean shook his head. 'Don't take offence, Pa, there's none intended. But it's hard to see you on a committee. You're not the type.'

Pat winked at his son. 'Hidden qualities, Sean.'

'What's a committee?' Alison piped up.

'A group of people who talk about things and then decide on them,' Pat informed her.

'Is it important to be on a committee?'

'Very, lassie. Indeed it is.'

'And what nights will this committee be held?' Kathleen enquired.

He played his trump card. 'Fridays.'

Kathleen's eyes lit up. That meant Pat wouldn't be going to the pub. What a blessing, not to mention saving of money. This was terrific news.

'It might vary of course,' Pat went on. 'But as far as I understand it will mainly be Friday nights.'

Kathleen couldn't have been more delighted.

'Well, are you proud of me, girl?'

Kathleen went to him and pecked him on the cheek. 'I am, Pat. I never thought a husband of mine would be on a committee. That's quite something.'

He laughed. 'You'll see me in a new light now, eh?'

'I will that,' she replied, pride swelling within her. Her man on a committee! He'd be running for Parliament next. On the Labour ticket of course.

Hook, line and sinker, Pat congratulated himself. The committee thing had been inspirational, so it had.

Inspirational.

Despite three large drams in the pub round the corner Pat was still nervous as hell. He'd never done anything like this before. He was quite unnerved.

Think of the beer and whisky, he reminded himself. Aye, think of those and get cracking. It's not as if she was ugly or anything, quite the opposite. And his for the taking.

He timidly knocked on the door and waited.

What a fool he'd been, Pat reflected ruefully. What a bloody idiot. They'd sat there drinking for hours and he hadn't made a move. Not a single one, not even to kiss her.

He closed his eyes, remembering the vision that had been Geraldine Buchanan. And a vision she'd been too. Dressed up to the nines, smelling like . . . well, no woman he'd ever smelt before.

When he'd left her disappointment had been obvious, though she hadn't said anything. It had been simply, with a big smile, I hope you'll come again soon, Pat.

Would he? He didn't know.

Imagine him being scared! It was a joke when you thought about it. Him, Pat Flynn, scared of a woman. Scared to get to grips with her. And yet he had been. He groaned.

'Pat?'

He opened his eyes to stare at Kathleen who was gazing at him in concern.

'Are you all right, Pat?'

'A wee bit of indigestion that's all. They had some sandwiches there that couldn't have agreed with me.'

'I must say you looked real smart when you went out to your committee. Collar and tie and everything.'

'Aye, well you have to.'

'And it all went well?'

'Didn't I say it did.'

'And you spoke?'

'Once or twice.'

He glanced over at Bridie whose head, as so often, was buried in a book. He couldn't imagine where she got her bookishness from. Certainly not him, or Kathleen. During their entire married life together he'd never known either of them open a book to read.

He yawned. 'I suppose I'd better get on through. Being on a committee makes you tired.'

'Especially after a hard day's work,' Kathleen added sympathetically.

'Aye, it does that.'

Bloody idiot, he thought, heaving himself out of his chair. But at least the beer and whisky had been good, and lots of it.

Ian, sitting on a fallen tree, opened the packet of sandwiches that had been made up for his lunch. He was starving, but then who wouldn't be, grafting the way he had that morning.

'What have you got the day?' Jimmy Carruthers asked in a friendly way. He was one of the four of them working together.

Ian peered inside the sandwich he'd taken from the packet. 'This one's egg.'

'I like egg,' Jimmy commented affably. 'I often have it myself.'

'What's yours?'

'Spread.'

Ian loathed spread, no matter what sort. Unscrewing his flask he poured himself some coffee.

As he hungrily munched, Ian reflected on the plans for the estate that had recently been forming in his mind, plans he wouldn't mention to Willie until he was manager.

The estate was well run, there was no denying that. But times change and Willie hadn't really moved with them. Ian didn't blame his father, that's the way Willie was. Someone straight out of the old school.

Ian continued eating and ruminating, finding the former satisfying, the latter exciting in the extreme.

'Let me get this straight,' Andrew said. It was another of his and Jack's nights at the local. 'The plot is about a domestic servant who's secretly in love with her employer, a young wealthy landowner. Right?'

'Right,' Jack nodded.

Andrew couldn't help but smile. 'And this landowner doesn't know until he gets back from the war?'

'That's correct.'

Andrew sat back in his chair and gazed at his friend. 'Why do I think this has a somewhat familiar ring about it?'

Jack feigned innocence. 'Do you?'

'It wouldn't be about you and Hettie by any chance?'

Jack had the grace to blush. 'Certainly not.'

'Are you sure? Your plays have been autobiographical after all, about your experiences in the trenches. So why not your book?'

Jack cleared his throat. 'Hettie was never a domestic servant.'

'She was your housekeeper when you first moved in to the cottage. And you employed her before that.'

'True.'

Andrew laughed. 'You never were a good liar, old cock.'

Jack had a drink of beer while he thought. Damn Andrew for seeing through his story. He'd wanted that to remain strictly between Hettie and himself.

Suddenly it dawned on Andrew where Jack had got the idea for the arrangement between him and Ellen. It wasn't something Jack had heard about at all; a similar arrangement had existed between Jack and Hettie. Of course! It made sense.

'I think it a good plot, as far as it goes,' Andrew said slowly.

'Do you?'

'But a bit thin so far, wouldn't you say.'

Jack shrugged. 'I've got to work out the details, flesh the whole thing out so to speak.'

'Can I make a comment?'

'Of course.'

'Your protagonist comes back safe and sound I take it. All in one piece?'

'Uh-huh.'

'It might be more poignant if he returned disabled to find out the servant still loves him despite that.'

Jack tensed. 'What sort of disablement?'

'How about an amputee? God knows, there are enough of those came home from France. A chap who'd lost both legs for instance.'

'I want a happy ending, Andrew.'

'To my way of thinking that is a happy ending. The chap reappears thinking his life is more or less finished. Only it isn't. I do believe you could do a lot with that.'

'Hmmh,' Jack murmured.

Andrew snapped his fingers. 'Of course!'

'Of course what?'

'What if . . . I'm no writer, mind. This is only a suggestion. Instead of the domestic simply being secretly in love with him, what if they'd had an affair before the war?'

Alarm flared in Jack. Had Andrew guessed about him and Hettie?

'He'd have to be a cad naturally, a real bounder who was just using her for his own pleasure, completely oblivious to the fact of her true feelings.'

Jack winced inwardly. For hadn't it truly been something like that?

Andrew went on. 'When he comes back, minus his legs, he's a totally changed man. No longer the cad and bounder. She helps him come to terms with his injuries and during this period he genuinely falls for her. Eventually they marry and Bob's your uncle!'

Andrew beamed across the table. 'That sounds pretty good to me.'

Jack sipped his whisky and didn't reply.

'Well, old cock?'

'It has potential,' Jack murmured.

'More than potential I'd say.'

'Maybe you should be writing this book and not me,' Jack commented drily.

'Hardly. Haven't got that sort of imagination.'

'Well, you were doing all right there for a few minutes.'

Andrew laughed. 'I was too, wasn't I? But no, writing is your province, Jack. Not mine.'

A cad and a bounder, Jack thought. That hurt.

'Anyway, I'll leave it with you,' Andrew declared. 'Only trying to help after all. That's what friends are for.'

Andrew threw his whisky down his throat. 'Drink up and I'll get a couple more drams in.'

'It's my round,' Jack said, reaching for his wallet.

Andrew stood. 'By the way, have you got a title yet for this epic?'

'I'm considering *An Apple From Eden*.'

'*An Apple From Eden*,' Andrew mused. 'I like it.'

'He suggested what!' an aghast Hettie exclaimed.

Jack repeated himself.

Hettie sat. 'Does he know about us? Have you ever mentioned that you used to pay me, Jack Riach?'

'I swear, Hettie, not a word.'

'It would be so embarrassing if he did know. Imagine if it got out that I'd taken money from you before the war. My reputation would be in tatters. Our reputation. Oh Jack!' she suddenly wailed.

'There's no question of that,' Jack assured her. 'Andrew never mentioned cash when we were talking. Only that the couple had had an affair and that the chap in question was a bounder who returns from the war completely changed as a person.'

That calmed Hettie a little. 'You swear you've never told him?'

'I just have sworn. Only two people know about you and me, and that's you and I.'

Hettie swallowed hard. 'I got the wind up there for a moment.'

'There's nothing to worry about, I promise.'

'I sincerely hope so.' But there was a niggle of doubt in Hettie's mind.

Sean strolled over to the lassie who'd caught his eye, a pretty piece with dark hair and dark eyes. She was wearing a long blue dress with a cream lace collar and turned-back cuffs that he thought rather becoming. Her shoes were black of the button-bar variety.

'Are you for up?' he queried.

She rose and smiled tremulously at him. 'Aye, fine.'

'Right then.'

He grasped her by the arm and steered her on to the floor. As the dance had been organised by the chapel he knew she must be Catholic.

'What's your name?' he asked as the band struck up.

'Muriel. And you're Sean Flynn.'

He glanced sharply at her. 'How did you know that?'

A combination of fear and awe came into her eyes. 'You're the leader of this new gang, I hear.'

'Aye, that's so. The Samurai.'

'Is it true you gave two Prods a real doing, marked them and cut off one's thumb?'

His chest expanded with pride. 'True as you're here the night.'

Muriel shivered, unable to believe that such a worthy had asked her to dance. 'You must be right hard,' she said.

He gave her a condescending smile.

So, people were talking about him and the Samurai. Word was getting round. It made him feel ten feet tall.

At the end of the final number he said – didn't ask but said – he'd take her home. Muriel was thrilled.

He acknowledged a conspiratorial wink from Noddy Gallagher as he swaggered, with Muriel on his arm, from the hall.

Chapter 6

'Come away in. I'd almost given you up.' Geraldine greeted a nervous Pat.

'Sorry I'm late. It was just one thing after another.'

'It doesn't matter. You're here now, that's all that counts.'

Geraldine closed the door again, her eyes gleaming. She was determined this wasn't going to be a repetition of the last visit which had been so dreadfully disappointing.

She ushered him through to the sitting room where she instructed him to take a seat.

'You look smashing,' he declared. Her dress was cream, the hem about six inches above her ankles. It was tied loosely at her waist by a strip of matching material.

'Why, thank you.'

That perfume, he thought. Erotic wasn't in Pat's vocabulary, but if it had been it's the word he would have used to describe the perfume and the effect it had on him.

'Dram?'

'Please.'

She moved sinuously across to a sideboard and opened it. He couldn't take his eyes off her buttocks when she bent over. They mesmerised him.

'Soda as last time?' she queried.

'Aye, that's right.'

She poured a small one for herself, a large one for Pat, adding soda to both. She then bent again to retrieve a bottle of beer from the same sideboard cupboard.

'There you are,' she smiled, handing Pat the bottle and his dram.

'Better service than the pub,' he joked.

Geraldine sat facing him and they proceeded to make small talk, she periodically getting up and refilling his glass.

Pat sighed, that well-known warm glow spreading through him. Oh, but this was grand. The very dab.

'I couldn't help but notice, and I hope you don't think me being rude, that you're a hairy man, Pat,' Geraldine said in what was almost a croon. 'Dougal's the same way. Hairy all over.'

'I'm certainly that,' Pat retorted.

Something twisted inside Geraldine's stomach. It was taking all her self-control not to throw herself at him and rip his clothes off.

'I adore hairy men,' Geraldine went on. 'I find them so . . . attractive.'

'Oh?'

'So attractive,' she repeated, a husk coming into her throat.

'I, eh . . . I don't ever really think about it. That's how I've been for most of my life. Ever since I sort of grew up like.'

Geraldine had another sip of whisky. 'Why don't you come and sit beside me on this sofa,' she suggested, patting the cushion next to her.

'Can I have another drink first?'

'Certainly, help yourself.'

Geraldine was ready to home in for the kill.

Bridie felt wretched. She'd been so close, so very close. Now she was home all she wanted to do was burst into tears.

'Well?' Kathleen demanded anxiously when she entered the kitchen.

'I had it, Ma. I know I did. And then he asked me what school I went to and that was that.'

Kathleen swore under her breath.

'The moment I mentioned St Xavier's his whole attitude changed. He went on with the interview as though my being Catholic didn't matter, but it did.'

'The dirty Protestant dog,' Kathleen muttered. The old Glasgow story, what school did you go to? Not are you Catholic or Protestant, but which school did you go to? How many Catholics had missed out because of that question. Catholics without number.

Bridie ran a hand over her face. 'It was a great job too. Good money. And then . . .' She broke off and sobbed.

'There there, lass,' Kathleen said, hurrying to her daughter and enveloping Bridie in her arms. 'It isn't the end of the world.'

'It's so unfair, Ma. Why should me being Catholic make any difference? It's whether or not I can do the job well that should count.'

'I know, Bridie. The world's a harsh place at times. And as you say unfair. But there we are. That's how it is and we just have to live with it.'

Bridie sobbed again.

'Shall I put the kettle on?'

'That would be nice, Ma.'

'And I have a wee packet of chocolate biscuits in. We'll have a couple of those each. But don't mention them to Alison or that greedy madam will scoff what's left given half the chance.'

Kathleen, heart heavy with Bridie's disappointment and the reason for it, held her daughter for another minute before releasing her.

'I thought I might write to Andrew Drummond and propose we visit next month. What do you think, Georgina?'

'That's fine by me, Willie, as long as you feel you can get away.'

Rose's face had lit up. At long last she was to get to see Andrew again. 'How wonderful!' she exclaimed, and clapped her hands together.

Georgina glanced over at Rose in surprise. Now why should her stepdaughter be so excited about going to see Andrew Drummond?

'I'll stay behind if you don't mind, Pa,' Ian declared. 'I don't want to disrupt my work here.'

Willie nodded his approval.

Disrupting his work had nothing to do with Ian's decision not to accompany the rest of the family. The real reason was that he didn't like Andrew Drummond very much. There was something disturbing about the man that bothered him. Something he didn't trust.

Rose was positively bubbling inside. How she'd been looking forward to this.

'You seem very keen, Rose,' Georgina commented quietly.

'And why not,' Rose prevaricated. 'It'll be lovely to go somewhere different, to get off the estate for a while.' Then, ingenuously, 'Surely there's nothing wrong with that?'

'Nothing,' Georgina agreed, still wondering.

Ian roused himself from his chair. 'If you don't mind I'm off to my bed. Today was a killer.'

'Not too much for you, brother?' Rose remarked sweetly.

He glared at her. 'Not in the least. It was tiring, that's all.'

Willie sighed. Did those two never let up? What annoyed him most was that it was all so unnecessary. Why couldn't they just get on?

'Goodnight, lad,' he said, forcing a smile on to his face.

'Goodnight, Pa, Georgina.' Ian drew in a deep breath. 'Goodnight, Rose.'

'Goodnight, brother dear.'

Rose went back to thinking about Andrew Drummond.

Willie glanced up from his paperwork when there was a knock on the door. 'Come in,' he called out. He was dreading this, it was so distasteful.

An ashen-faced Lizzie McTaggart appeared followed by Mrs Coltart, the housekeeper. Mrs Coltart's expression was grim in the extreme.

Willie leant back in his chair to stare at Lizzie through eyes that had gone quite cold. 'Well, Lizzie, what do you have to say for yourself?' he demanded.

'Oh please, sir, let me have another chance. I'll never do it again, I promise,' she blurted out.

'But it wasn't the first time though, was it, Lizzie? According to Mrs Coltart you've stolen quite a number of things.'

'Some of which were found in her room,' Mrs Coltart commented quietly.

Lizzie hung her head in shame.

'All small articles, knick-knacks and the like,' Mrs Coltart went on. 'Which she no doubt thought wouldn't be missed. But I knew they'd gone all right. It was only a case of finding the thief.'

There was a few seconds' silence, then Willie asked softly, 'Why, Lizzie? Why?'

Lizzie shrugged.

'That's hardly an answer.'

'I thought to sell them to make a wee bit extra,' Lizzie finally choked.

'Indeed.'

Lizzie swallowed hard. 'I know it was wrong. I'm sorry. Honest I am. Please don't sack me, I like it here. Everyone's so friendly.'

Mrs Coltart snorted. 'If you want my opinion, Mr Seaton, should you find a rotten apple in the barrel then throw it out. There's nothing else for it.'

'I could prosecute, you know, Lizzie. That might mean going to prison.'

A thoroughly frightened Lizzie reeled where she stood. 'Oh, Mr Seaton, you wouldn't do that. The shame.'

'Aye,' Willie murmured. 'Shame indeed.'

'My ma and da would be mortified. They'd disown me so they would. I couldn't bear that.'

Willie knew the McTaggarts, a fine upstanding, church-going family. Mortified they'd certainly be. As for disowning their daughter, that was a distinct possibility.

'Mrs Coltart, any further comments?'

'No, sir. I've stated my feelings.'

Mrs Coltart was right, he told himself. A rotten apple had to be discarded. Though, because of the parents, it pained him to do so. Lizzie had to be punished, there was nothing else for it.

'I won't prosecute,' he declared, which brought a gasp of relief from Lizzie. 'But I'm afraid I will have to let you go.'

'Oh please, sir,' she pleaded.

Willie shook his head. 'Nor will I give you a reference. That's out of the question.'

'But . . . but . . .' Lizzie stuttered.

'I simply can't, Lizzie. What if you should succumb to temptation again? That would reflect on me.'

'I think you're getting off lightly, my girl,' Mrs Coltart said to her.

'You have half an hour to pack your things and leave. Mrs Coltart, stay with her the entire time if you don't mind and escort her from the premises. When you've done that come back and see me here. We'll have to discuss a replacement.'

'Yes, sir.'

Thoroughly distasteful, Willie thought as he rocked forward and continued with his paperwork.

'Pat, is there something wrong?'

Pat tensed in the darkness. He and Kathleen were in bed. 'How do you mean?'

'It's been weeks now since . . . Well, it's just so unlike you.'

She meant lovemaking of course. The fact was he'd gone right off Kathleen since sampling Geraldine's delights.

'Are you ill in some way?' Kathleen further probed.

'No,' came the gruff reply.

'Well then?'

'I just haven't felt like it, nothing more.'

Kathleen considered that. It had certainly never happened before. During their entire married life Pat had been regular as clockwork where that was concerned.

'Now wheesht, woman, and go to sleep.'

He'd have to make an effort soon, he thought. Otherwise Kathleen might get suspicious.

He imagined Geraldine, picturing the pair of them together, and smiled. He still couldn't get over what it was like to be with her. Utterly fantastic. That body *and* free booze too.

Sheer bloody paradise.

'Hey, Sean, haud on a bit.'

Sean turned to see Bill O'Connell hurrying towards him. The pair of them were in a long stream of men leaving Barry's Iron Foundry after the day's shift.

Bill fell into step beside Sean. 'How's it going?' Sean asked.

'Real dandy. And you?'

'Couldn't be better. So what can I do for you?'

'I was wondering, Sean, you and me have known each other a long time now. Right?'

Sean nodded that was so.

'I've been hearing about this gang of yours. The Samurai, isn't it?'

'Correct. It's Japanese you know. That's what their warriors were called.'

'Is that a fact?'

'It is. I chose the name myself.'

'Real class, Sean. Real class.'

Sean smiled in appreciation.

'The thing is, I rather fancy joining. If you'd have me that is.'

Sean considered the request, and couldn't see any objection. 'The others have a say, mind. It's not just up to me.'

'But you could put in a good word like. Would you do that for me? I'd be hellishly obliged.'

'Of course I will.'

'Thanks.'

Sean thought with satisfaction this would be the fourth new member since the Samurai was formed. He had no doubt the others would be only too pleased to welcome Bill into the fold. Apart from anything else Bill was a right hard nut. He'd be a real asset.

'Tell you what,' Sean said. 'We're having a meeting the morrow night. You wait for me outside my close at half seven and I'll personally take you along. How's that?'

Bill beamed. 'I'll be there. You can count on it.'

'On the dot, mind. I'm not hanging about.

'On the dot,' Bill promised.

'There just isn't anyone available locally, Mr Seaton. I've asked everywhere,' Mrs Coltart announced.

'Hmmh,' Willie mused. If his housekeeper said that was so, then it was.

Mrs Coltart waited patiently for a reply.

'I suppose we'll just have to advertise,' Willie said eventually. 'We have done so before as you know. Though I have to say I prefer local lassies.'

'Shall I leave that to you then, sir?'

'Yes, I'll deal with it, Mrs Coltart. Thank you for what you've done.'

She left him to it.

Ellen squealed. 'That hurt!'

Andrew grinned to himself. Of course it had hurt, he'd intended it to. 'Are you complaining?' he queried, a hard edge to his voice.

'No, not at all,' Ellen replied hastily, thinking of the money.

'Now keep quiet. I don't want anyone to hear.'

Ellen gritted her teeth as Andrew continued with what he'd been doing.

'Can we get Mrs Black to call? I've lost weight and my clothes need taking in,' Rose requested of Georgina. Mrs Black was the wife of one of the estate workers and a first-class seamstress, her occupation before marrying.

Georgina studied her stepdaughter. Rose was quite right, she had lost weight.

Rose ran a finger along the inside of the waistband of the skirt she was wearing. 'See what I mean.'

Georgina nodded her approval. 'Well done you, Rose. I've noticed you haven't been having puddings of late.'

And she'd been doing without other things too, Rose thought with satisfaction. The effort had been worth it. And she intended losing more weight before their visit to Drummond House. She wanted to be sleek and svelte when she next met Andrew.

'I've taken a leaf out of your book.' Rose smiled at Georgina.

Georgina had a thought. 'I do believe it's time we went to Edinburgh again. Instead of having your current wardrobe redone we can replace it.'

'A whole new wardrobe!' Rose gasped. Pa wouldn't like that. She could almost hear his objections.

'Well, maybe not an entire new wardrobe,' Georgina replied, thinking that had been something of a rash proposal. 'But certainly quite a few items. It is your birthday coming up after all. I shall persuade Willie that what we get will be his and my present to you.'

Georgina smiled inwardly. She knew exactly how to get Willie to agree to this. She'd entice him in the bedroom, then, when he was all worked up, put it to him. It was a ploy she'd used countless times before and one which never failed.

And while in Edinburgh she'd also buy for herself. She wanted to look her very best when they went to Drummond House. Andrew Drummond rather fascinated her.

Shopping, it was the best tonic in the world and something she absolutely adored.

Sean was passing a junk shop when he caught sight of an article in the window that brought him up short. Moments later the door bell was pinging as he went inside.

The shopkeeper was old and fat with thinning hair, a long lock of which he had plastered across the top of his forehead.

'Yes, sir, can I be of assistance?'

Sean jerked a thumb in the direction of the window. 'There's a sword in there I'd like to look at.'

'You mean the Japanese sword, sir?'

'Aye, that's the one.'

Sean watched the shopkeeper move away. A Japanese sword in Glasgow! What a stroke of luck. He might have searched high and low for years before coming across one for sale. It was his lucky day.

'There we are, sir.' The shopkeeper smiled, laying the sword in front of Sean.

Sean wrinkled his nose. 'It's a bit rusty, isn't it?'

'Some rust, I grant you that, sir. But it will polish up beautifully.'

'That's as might be.'

Sean lifted the sword and pulled it slowly from its black enamelled scabbard. The rust was mainly confined to the hilt, with only a few spots on the blade.

'What's the asking price?' he queried.

'Thirty shillings, sir.'

Sean pretended to be shocked. 'You must be joking! What are you, a comedian or something?'

The shopkeeper inclined his head slightly. He was used to haggling. 'These are extremely rare,' he countered.

'So what? It's only an old sword when all's said and done. It's probably been lying in that window of yours for years.' Sean ran a hand over the scabbard. 'See what I mean!' he exclaimed when his palm came away covered in dust.

The shopkeeper grinned ruefully. 'It has been with me for a while, I admit. But that doesn't take away from its value.'

'I'll tell you what,' Sean said, sounding reluctant. 'I'll give you ten bob and I reckon I'm still being done.'

The haggling continued until at last a triumphant Sean left the premises having bought the sword for a pound. A pound he could ill afford but nonetheless a pound he considered well spent.

'Here, look at this, Bridie,' Kathleen said, tapping the newspaper she'd been reading.

'What is it, Ma?'

'A position as a maid on a big estate.'

Bridie rose from her chair and hurried across the room to stare over her mother's shoulder at the ad Kathleen was indicating. 'I don't know,' she demurred. 'Look where it is. It would mean leaving home.'

'Aye, that's so,' Kathleen agreed.

'What are the wages?' Pat asked.

'That's not mentioned,' Kathleen informed him.

He sniffed. 'A domestic servant. A bit of a comedown for a Flynn. Plenty of Irish folk have been domestics, but never us Flynns. We've always considered ourselves above that.'

'Beggars can't be choosers,' Kathleen commented quietly.

'Unemployment the way it is there are bound to be lots of applicants,' Bridie said.

'True enough,' Kathleen agreed. 'But it wouldn't do any harm to write. No harm at all.'

'And it is in the country,' Bridie mused, straightening up, thinking how wonderful it must be to live there. Trees, grass, animals no doubt. The prospect sent a little thrill racing through her. What a difference it would be to the life she'd known so far. The dirty grimy Glasgow streets, the filth, the squalor. Air that could make you choke when you breathed it in.

Suddenly she was filled with excitement, wanting this job badly. 'I'll write straight away and catch the morning post. There's nothing to lose after all except a sheet of paper, an envelope and a stamp.'

The country, Bridie thought again, eyes shining. Oh but wouldn't that be lovely.

'What's that you're carrying?' Sammy Renton queried when Sean strolled into the room of the condemned house where the others were already gathered and awaiting his arrival.

Sean held up the long brown paper-wrapped object. 'You'll never guess. It's a wee present from me to us all.'

'Is it a piece of fancy plumbing,' Mo Binchy joked, and guffawed.

'Or a year-old turd?' Dan Smith said, which raised a laugh all round.

'Very funny,' Sean retorted, and began unwrapping the object.

'Wow!' Bobby O'Toole exclaimed when the sword was

revealed. A sword that sparkled and was completely free of rust, Sean having attended to these matters in the privacy of his bedroom.

'Holy Mother of God,' an awed Noddy Gallagher whispered.

'It's the genuine Japanese article,' Sean proclaimed, brandishing the weapon.

'Is it sharp?' Bill O'Connell queried.

'As my razor. It would cut your head off quick as wink.'

'No thanks, Sean,' Bill hastily replied, fingering his throat. 'I'll go without that if you don't mind.'

That raised another laugh.

'Would anyone else like a demonstration of head cutting?' Sean teased.

The response was a chorus of refusals.

Sean waved the sword in front of him. 'Not bad, eh?'

'Where did you get it?' Jim Gallagher asked.

'A junk shop I happened to be passing. Cost me a quid.'

'She's a beauty,' Noddy Gallagher commented.

'It is indeed,' Sean agreed.

'Can I hold it?' Mo requested.

'Aye, sure.' Sean handed it over, Mo holding the sword gingerly while he admired it.

'I thought we'd put it in pride of place on the mantelpiece. What do you say?'

Sammy Renton nodded at Sean. 'That's a grand idea.'

'Will you take it outside anytime?' Mo Binchy enquired.

Sean's eyes gleamed. 'Who knows, Mo. Who knows?'

He grinned wolfishly. 'Maybe.'

'So, what's the big mystery?' Bridie demanded of Teresa, the latter having arrived at her house to urgently request they go for a walk together.

'I couldn't talk with your parents and sister about. What I have to say is confidential like.'

Bridie noted how twitchy her friend was. 'Well?'

'You know I've been going out with that chap Tony from work.'

Bridie smiled. 'And what a surprise it was when he asked you. You were quite taken aback from what you said.'

'I was. He'd never shown any interest before, and then suddenly, out the blue, would I like to go out? Darned tooting I would. I jumped at the chance.'

'So what's the problem?'

Teresa swallowed hard. 'Remember that dance we went to when the bloke mauled you in the back close.'

Bridie remembered only too well. 'Horrible it was. He was a right animal.' She stopped abruptly. 'Has Tony done the same to you?'

Teresa coloured. 'In a way, only in my case it wasn't a mauling, more of his being insistent.'

'Insistent?'

'Aye, you know.'

'You didn't let him touch you . . . *there*, did you?'

Teresa was now bright red. 'I did.'

'Oh Teresa, how could you!'

'It was easy enough at the time, Bridie. He's not a bad looker, and his kissing! I just melted. I didn't know whether I was coming or going, only that I liked it.'

Bridie shook her head. 'I'm ashamed of you, Teresa Kelly, I really am.'

Teresa almost changed her mind then about telling Bridie the rest. But she had to confide in someone, unburden herself. 'I'm afraid it went further than touching,' she stated in a quiet, cracked voice.

Bridie was aghast. 'You mean . . . ?'

Teresa nodded.

'All the way?'

'All the way,' Teresa repeated.

Bridie couldn't believe she was hearing this. It was awful. Apart from anything else, what if Tony opened his mouth and word got round?

'That's not the worst thing though,' Teresa went on, tears beginning to overflow.

Bridie knew with sudden certainty what was coming next.

'I've missed my monthly.'

Chapter 7

Andrew bustled into the drawing room where the Seatons were grouped together talking. 'Sorry I wasn't here to meet you but I got caught up at the distillery. A minor crisis that I had to sort.'

He was slightly dishevelled, a lock of hair having escaped over his forehead, which Georgina thought charming. Catching his eye she smiled.

'I see you've already been given a drink, good.' Andrew nodded his approval to Ellen who was also in the room.

'One for you, sir?' Ellen enquired.

'Please. A Drummond.'

'Well,' said Andrew, briskly rubbing his hands together. 'How was the journey?'

'Thoroughly enjoyable,' Willie replied. 'I must say your Perthshire scenery is quite beautiful.'

'Why, thank you. I've always considered it to be so.'

The long-awaited moment had finally arrived, Rose thought gleefully. She was in Andrew's company again.

And how wonderful that felt. A small flush of excitement crept on to her cheeks which she hoped no one noticed.

'Here you are, sir,' Ellen said, offering a silver tray to Andrew.

'Thank you, Ellen.' So prim and demure while on duty, he smiled inwardly. Well, he knew what the real Ellen was like, a different creature entirely.

Andrew held his glass aloft in a toast. '*Slainte.* And welcome to Drummond House.'

'To Drummond House and you, Andrew,' Willie responded.

Sean was alone in the condemned tenement, sitting gently caressing the sword on his lap.

What now for the Samurai? he wondered. Were they just a gang, a bunch of hooligans? Or could they be something else? Only what?

The other city gangs did nothing, at least not that he was aware of, except fight and create holy terror wherever they went. Surely there could be more to it than that.

And then he had the glimmerings of an idea. Profit. Was that it?

Not just a gang but some sort of business that made them money.

'Money,' he murmured aloud. 'Money.'

He continued caressing the sword, deep in thought.

'This saddle of lamb is really superb,' Charlotte, Andrew's sister, pronounced. 'Mrs Clark has excelled herself.' Mrs Clark was Andrew's cook who'd been with the family for years.

'I'll pass on your compliments,' Andrew replied.

'No need, I'll tell her myself later. I'll also ask her what she's done to make it different to any saddle of lamb I've ever tasted before.'

Andrew laughed. 'Oh come on, sis, you know Mrs Clark won't divulge any of her secrets.'

'She will to me,' Charlotte stated firmly. 'You see if she doesn't.'

How contented his sister looked, Andrew observed. Being a minister's wife and a mother suited her. He couldn't have been more pleased for her, she thoroughly deserved her happiness.

Charlotte was doing a splendid job of hiding the unease she always felt on returning to Drummond House. On the one hand it held so many wonderful memories of her childhood and growing up. On the other, it was in this house that her first husband Geoffrey had hanged himself.

Poor Geoffrey, what a changed man he'd been on returning from the war. So changed she'd hardly recognised him as the same person. She'd put it down to the war, of course, and tried to cope. And then the dreadful truth had finally emerged.

Geoffrey had lost his manhood to a German grenade. The torment he'd gone through because he was unable to be a proper husband, as he put it, to her. Torment and despair that had ultimately driven him to taking his own life.

She closed her eyes, recalling how it had once been between her and Geoffrey. Those golden, carefree days before the conflict, in stark contrast to the time afterwards. There were still occasions, usually late at night when John was fast asleep but she lay awake, when the nightmare vision of Geoffrey hanging there came back to haunt her.

She knew she couldn't blame herself for his suicide. She'd done everything in her power to assure him what had happened didn't matter. Except it had, very much so, to Geoffrey, God rest his soul.

Andrew was thinking how gorgeous Georgina was looking that evening. She was wearing a low-waisted dress in silk georgette. The bodice was cut straight and beaded in a swirly pattern. Thin straps with matching beading snaked across her shoulders. The skirt had soft gathers that fell into points at the hem.

Was it the stunning dress or something else that had brought such a twinkle to her eyes? he wondered. Again, he thought it a pity she was married. And to a friend at that. Forbidden territory. Beyond the Pale.

'I've never met a writer before.' Rose smiled across the table to Jack Riach.

'Me neither,' added Georgina.

Hettie gazed in admiration at Jack, sitting beside him as she always did, helping him with the meal.

'There's one thing I've been wondering about,' Rose said hesitantly.

'Which is?'

She cleared her throat. 'I hope you don't think this rude or insensitive of me, I don't wish to offend.'

Jack guessed the question. 'How does a blind man write? Is that it?'

'Yes,' Rose nodded.

'I'm also curious about that,' Georgina said.

Jack laughed. 'It's simple really. I dictate to Hettie who puts it down on paper. She then reads the dictation back to me and does any changes I wish to make. As I said, simple really.'

'Oh!' Rose exclaimed. Now why hadn't she thought of that. 'You must be a very clever man to write,' Rose went on. 'I envy you the ability.'

'He is clever,' Hettie agreed.

'I wouldn't say that,' Jack demurred.

'Come on, Jack, you're just being modest. You're a hero hereabouts. And I'm not referring to the war either. Getting not just one but *two* plays on the West End stage takes some doing,' John McLean stated.

'I was lucky,' Jack, becoming embarrassed, replied.

'Luck be damned,' Andrew declared. Then, to the rest of the table, 'Jack is about to start his first novel, aren't you, Jack?'

Hettie tensed.

'A novel!' Georgina exclaimed. 'I say. What's it all about?'

'I really don't want to talk about it,' Jack answered. 'Anyway, to be truthful, I'm not quite certain what it's all about myself yet.'

Fibber, Andrew thought. Jack knew well enough. He gestured to Heather, one of the maids, to refill their glasses.

Willie was thoroughly enjoying himself. The meal was splendid as was the company. He couldn't have asked for a better evening. And later, perhaps, he and Andrew could do some more reminiscing. Which might also be the chance to put the proposal he had in mind to Andrew – the reaction to which was uncertain.

'Do you keep horses, Andrew?' Rose queried.

'Of course.'

'Would it be possible to go out for a ride tomorrow morning?'

Andrew recalled another young lady who had also enjoyed riding. That was how he'd met her when her horse had bolted and he'd gone to the rescue. The start of what had become a love affair.

'That's fine, Rose. Tell the groom to give you Sophie. She's probably the best horse for you.'

'Thank you.'

When the main course was cleared away, dessert was offered. Both Rose and Georgina declined.

'Another?' Andrew queried. He and Willie were alone, the McLeans and Riachs having left long since while Georgina and Rose had excused themselves and gone up to bed pleading that it had been a long day.

'Please.'

Andrew fetched the decanter and crossed to Willie, recharging first Willie's glass then his own. They were reminiscing about their time in Ireland.

Willie hesitated, then said, 'It's been on my mind for a while now to go back there, you know. Take Georgina and Rose, make a holiday of it.'

Andrew sat. 'Really.'

'Not for too long, of course, a fortnight seems about right to me. The thing is, I'd love to see old Dublin town again and show Georgina and Rose the sights.'

'When shall you go?'

'In the New Year, certainly before spring when it all starts to get hectic again on the estate.'

Andrew pondered that. 'You might have a rough crossing at that time of year.'

'Possibly.' Willie laughed. 'At least we won't have to worry about damned U-boats and being torpedoed.'

'True,' Andrew mused.

Willie had a sip of whisky. 'Have you ever thought about returning?'

That startled Andrew. 'No, I can't say I have. When I left I . . .' He broke off. 'I certainly never envisaged a return.'

Willie swirled the amber liquid round his glass. 'May I speak openly, Andrew? As one friend to another?'

'Go ahead.' He leant back in his chair and waited.

'It worries me that you've never married. None of my business, of course, but it worries me nonetheless. I can't help thinking you may still be carrying a torch for Alice.'

Andrew continued watching Willie, and didn't reply.

'It seems to me that going back there might help. Lay the ghost so to speak.' Willie took a deep breath. 'If you wish me to shut up just say so.'

Andrew had a swallow of whisky. 'That's all right, old boy,' he said in a voice that was just above a whisper.

'Would I be correct about Alice?'

Andrew gave a self-mocking laugh. 'If anyone had told me before I met her that one day I'd carry a torch for a dead woman, any woman come to that, I would have roared in their face. And yet, that's precisely what's happened. I have met women over the past few years, but no one I could really get interested in. Not that way anyhow.'

Willie nodded that he understood.

'How did you manage it, Willie, after you lost your wife?'

'I don't know,' Willie replied slowly. 'I too thought I'd never be interested again, then I met Georgina and all that changed. I do believe Mary would have given her blessing to the union. In fact I'm convinced of it.'

'Perhaps there's a Georgina somewhere for me,' Andrew mused. 'Though I haven't come across her yet.'

Willie lit a cigarette. 'And Ireland,' he queried through a cloud of smoke. 'Why don't you come with us? We could travel as a foursome, myself, Georgina, Rose and you.'

Would it help? Andrew wondered. He simply didn't know.

'Can you leave the distillery for a couple of weeks?'

'That would depend entirely on Charlotte. She would have to take my place while I was away. But yes, given enough time to arrange things I'm sure I could.'

'Then you'll think about it?'

A number of seconds ticked by before Andrew finally answered. 'I'll think about it,' he promised.

Bridie was hovering by the front door when she heard the postman mount the stairs and then go on past. She turned away in disappointment.

'There should have been a reply by now,' she said to Kathleen on re-entering the kitchen.

'It might still come.'

Bridie shook her head. 'The people on the estate might at least have had the courtesy to answer my letter, even if it was to say I wasn't suitable or the position had already been filled.'

'That's the toffs for you. No manners whatsoever,' Kathleen declared angrily.

Bridie just didn't know where to try next for a job. Despair, which was never far away these days, filled her yet again.

Andrew, Willie and Georgina were emerging from the distillery when Rose appeared riding towards them.

'There she is now,' Willie said. He was cross with his daughter for not turning up when she should.

Rose reined in and slid to the ground. 'Is it over?' she queried.

'Yes it is,' Willie retorted. 'We waited and waited then finally went ahead with the tour when you failed to show. What happened?'

Georgina gave Rose a hard, disapproving look which Rose ignored.

'I'm afraid I got lost.' To Andrew she said, 'Sophie's a beautiful horse. We had a fantastic time together.'

'I'm pleased.' He smiled.

Rose hadn't got lost at all. For the past half-hour she'd been observing the distillery waiting for them to come out again. It was part of a plan she'd hatched the previous night after the arrangement to tour the distillery had been made.

Rose patted Sophie on the nose. 'Who's a lovely girl then. You are, Sophie.'

'You might at least apologise to Andrew,' Willie declared.

'I am sorry, Andrew. Truly I am. I was so looking forward to the tour and now . . .' She pulled a face. 'I've missed it.'

'Hardly your fault you got lost. Easy to do in strange surroundings. Another time perhaps.'

'Unless . . .' She trailed off. 'Probably not. I don't deserve it. I've caused you enough trouble as it is.'

'Hardly trouble, Rose. Unless what?'

'Do you think you could bear to take me round now? I'd be ever so grateful.'

'Rose!' Willie admonished. 'You can't ask that.'

Andrew laughed at her crestfallen expression. 'Of course I can, Rose. I'd be delighted to do so.'

Her heart leapt. The plan had worked. She'd get him to herself after all, just as she'd hoped.

'Could you take Sophie back for me, Pa. Please?'

'I suppose I'll have to,' Willie grumbled, grasping the reins.

'See you both later,' Rose called out as she and Andrew went inside.

* * *

'And this is the inner sanctum,' Andrew declared, throwing open the door.

It smelt of him, she thought. A most pleasant odour as far as she was concerned. She glanced around. 'Very workmanlike.'

'I'll take that as a compliment.'

'It was meant as one.'

'So tell me, Rose, what do you think of my distillery? You've seen it all now.'

'Wash stills, pot stills, wort and all sorts of other funny names. It all seems very complicated to me.'

He laughed. 'Not that complicated, I assure you. But it does take some learning which I had to do more or less from scratch when I returned from Ireland. My brother Peter was the one trained to take over, I had no experience of the distillery whatsoever. I soon learnt though, I was a willing pupil.'

He rubbed his hands together. 'Can I offer you a dram? I'm going to have one myself.'

That shocked her. 'Whisky! Women don't drink whisky.'

'My sisters do. They were brought up to it as are all the women in my family. It's a tradition with us.'

'How extraordinary,' she commented.

'How about a weak one with lots of water. Nor will I take offence if you don't like it, whisky is something of an acquired taste.'

'And *strong*,' she pointed out.

'That too.'

She decided to tease him. 'I hope you're not thinking of getting me tipsy in order to take advantage.' She fluttered her eyelashes. 'Are you?'

'Most certainly not,' he protested.

She turned slightly away. 'Who knows? I might even enjoy succumbing.'

The little minx was flirting with him, he thought. Well, well, well.

'You might,' he replied slowly, seeing Rose in quite a different light. She'd lost weight, he now noticed. It suited her. Made her more mature somehow.

And how fetching she looked in her riding gear. Underneath the hacking jacket was a plain white, broadcloth shirt undone at the neck, that tucked into fawn jodphurs which in turn were tucked into black leather riding boots. He wondered what sort of underwear she had on.

Rose felt herself flushing under his direct gaze. Damn! She could have done without that.

Andrew smiled inwardly on seeing the flush. 'I'll get those drams,' he stated, and strode past her.

Rose swallowed hard. What on earth had possessed her to say 'succumb'. God alone knew what he'd made of that.

'Here you are,' Andrew declared. 'Well watered down as promised.'

He held his own glass up in a toast. '*Slainte!*'

'*Slainte,*' she responded, and nervously had a sip. It took all her self-control not to screw her face up in a grimace. Whisky was foul! She'd never tasted anything so awful.

'The verdict?' he queried with a smile.

'Very nice,' she lied.

'I'm impressed.'

'Are you indeed?'

'Oh yes.'

She had another sip, thinking it as foul as the first. If his sisters could drink this stuff then so too could she, she told herself.

When they finally left the distillery her head was swimming.

Georgina, standing at their bedroom window, saw Andrew and Rose coming towards the house. To her surprise she found herself feeling jealous. She wished it was her out there with him.

'What are you staring at?' Willie asked.

'Andrew and Rose on their way back here. They must have enjoyed themselves, they're both laughing.' That fact increased her jealousy. Again she found herself thinking of Andrew in a way she shouldn't.

Georgina turned to Willie. 'Are you all right, my dear?'

It was now his turn to be surprised. 'Yes, fine. Why do you ask?'

She went to him and stroked his head. 'No reason.'

Women baffled him at times, Willie thought. They were creatures that quite defied understanding.

Teresa hurriedly left the breakfast table and rushed to the sink where she was violently sick. Her mother, Father having already left for work, stared on in astonishment.

'Teresa?'

Mrs Kelly went to her daughter and put a consoling arm round her shoulders. 'What caused that, girl?'

Teresa shook her head. 'I haven't been feeling well, Ma.' Which was true enough, she hadn't. There had been recurring bouts of nausea over the past few days.

Mrs Kelly placed a hand on Teresa's forehead. 'You don't have a temperature.'

Teresa picked up a cup and pumped cold water into it. She swilled out her mouth and then spat into the sink. 'That's better.'

'Perhaps you should stay home today.'

'No fears, Ma. I don't want to be given the push like Bridie. I'm going to the factory if I have to crawl on my hands and knees.'

Mrs Kelly could well understand the lass's predicament. There had been two more sackings since Bridie. 'Well, sit down for a moment or two while I clear out this sink.'

'I'm sorry, Ma. I couldn't help it.'

'There's no need to be sorry. If you're ill you're ill. Nothing more has to be said.'

Teresa staggered back to her chair and plonked herself down. She now knew without any shadow of a doubt she was pregnant. She might have missed only one period but all the dreaded signs were there. Up the duff. In the pudding club! If Ma found out, if Da . . . All hell would break loose.

And it had happened just the once, that was what was so unfair. It wasn't as if she'd been doing it with Tony for months on end. There had only been that single occasion in the back close. He'd tried since of course but she'd always managed to stop him.

'You are looking pale now I come to think about it,' Mrs Kelly commented from the sink.

Teresa didn't reply. She couldn't go on being sick in the morning. Her ma wasn't daft, she would soon realise what the situation was. She groaned inwardly. What to do? She'd speak to Bridie that evening, she decided.

'She really is the most beautiful car, Andrew. I think I shall try and persuade Willie to buy one,' Georgina said as the Rolls purred through the Perthshire countryside. Andrew was keeping the promise he'd made when in Perth and giving her a spin.

Andrew drew into the side of the road and switched off the engine. Rolling down the window he inhaled deeply.

'Shall we get out and stretch our legs?' she suggested.

'If you like.'

She waited for him to open her door.

'The Pass of Killiecrankie,' he declared when they were both standing together.

'Wasn't there a famous battle fought here?'

'Oh indeed. A lot of good men died that day.'

She gazed about her. 'There is a melancholic feel about the place. It sort of lowers, if you know what I mean.'

Andrew thought of that long-ago battle and tried to imagine what it must have been like to take part. For some reason an image of his brother Peter came into his mind.

'Can I ask you something, Andrew?'

He roused himself from his reverie. 'Of course.'

'It's personal.'

'Go on,' he said softly.

'I asked Willie what happened to your fiancée, but he wouldn't tell me. Said it would have to come from you.'

'I see,' Andrew murmured.

'Will you tell me?'

He closed his eyes for a moment, memories flooding back. Dreadful memories that didn't only include Alice.

'The Fenians murdered her, torched her house. She and her mother and father were burnt to death.'

Georgina covered her mouth. 'How ghastly!'

McGinty, Andrew thought grimly. At least the Fenian bastard had paid, him and his. An eye for an eye, a tooth for a tooth. He hoped the bastard was roasting in hell.

'And you've never got over it?'

Andrew ran a hand across his face, remembering . . . remembering . . .

'Andrew?'

He shook himself, returning to the present. 'Sorry. I was miles away.'

'With *her*?'

'Yes,' he said. 'I was thinking of Alice and what might have been.' He paused, then added quietly. 'A single night and it was all over. My future, hers, all gone.'

'A single night?'

'The one she died.'

Compassion filled Georgina. He'd obviously been very much in love. Suddenly the day wasn't so glorious any more.

Andrew sighed. 'But that's in the past. Gone for ever. Now is what's important, and tomorrow.'

She wanted to take him in her arms, hold him, comfort him. 'Yes,' she agreed.

He turned to face her, a crooked smile lighting up his face. 'And you?'

'Something similar. The war.'

'I see,' he murmured.

'Why . . . Why does it all have to be so difficult. So painful?'

He shook his head. 'I don't know. Perhaps that's what life is really all about. Pain. Pain and the way it affects you. The way you cope.' He shook his head again. 'I don't know.'

Georgina stared up over the Pass of Killiecrankie, imagining the clash of swords, the screams of wounded and dying men, the total carnage of battle. It was horrible.

The Pass of Killiecrankie was a spot Georgina would never forget after that day.

Two wounded souls had touched.

Silence descended between them.

'Willie has asked me to go to Ireland with you,' Andrew eventually said.

'Really?'

'He said it might help lay the ghost.'

'Of your Alice?'

'Yes.'

'I wasn't aware we were going to Ireland. I knew Willie was thinking about it, but not that we were actually going.'

'Well, it seems you are.'

'And shall you come?'

'Until now I wasn't sure, hadn't decided. But now I have. I will.' Again he thought of McGinty and McGinty's family. Revenge was fine, but in retrospect . . . It took away part of yourself, your soul. In the afterlife he'd pay for what he'd done. Of that he was absolutely certain.

Georgina shivered. 'It's cold.'

'We'd best be getting back.'

She laid a gloved hand on his arm. 'I'm sorry for what happened, Andrew. Truly I am.'

'So am I,' he replied softly. 'So am I.'

Chapter 8

Bridie and Teresa were having another walk together so they could speak freely. 'You're absolutely certain?' Bridie queried.

'I couldn't be more so. I was sick again this morning, that's the third time this week. Ma's beginning to look at me very strangely indeed, though so far she hasn't said anything. Besides the sickness and missing period I just feel different. It's hard to explain, a sort of . . . contented wellbeing that wasn't there before.'

'You'll have to face Tony about this, Teresa,' Bridie counselled. 'Tell him he must do the proper thing and stand by you.'

But would he? Teresa worried. There was no saying.

'When are you seeing him again?'

'This Friday. We're supposed to be going to the flicks.'

'Then speak to him on the way home. Explain the situation.'

The street was hardly the place to give a chap such news,

Teresa thought. It would have to be the back close where the deed had taken place.

'From what I know of Tony he's a decent lad. He won't let you down.' Bridie hoped she was right.

'What's wrong with you?' Ian Seaton demanded of Rose sitting in front of the drawing-room fireplace. 'You look miserable as sin.'

Rose snapped herself out of her reverie. 'Do I?'

'Worse.'

She'd been thinking of Andrew and her stay at Drummond House. It had all gone well enough but, to her disappointment, Andrew hadn't taken any special notice of her. Not in the way she'd wanted anyway. Now she wouldn't see him again before the proposed visit to Ireland some time in the new year.

'Well?' Ian queried.

'I suppose I'm just down in the dumps.'

'Oh. Any special reason?'

'No,' she lied.

'I know how you feel, I get that way myself occasionally. Though not too often I have to admit.'

That afternoon Rose had come within an inch of confessing her feelings about Andrew to Georgina, then at the last moment had decided not to. Some instinct had warned her that would be the wrong thing to do.

If only she could talk to someone though. Certainly not her brother, she wasn't going to hand him that kind of ammunition.

'Is there anything I can do to help buck you up?' Ian asked kindly.

'No, I don't think so.'

'How about a joke. Or some funny faces?' And with

that he contorted his features and squinted both eyes inwards.

'Idiot.' She smiled.

'See! It's working already.'

If only a few funny faces could sort out her troubles, she thought.

'Perhaps a board game then? I could dig out one of those we used to play as children.'

'No thanks, Ian. I'm not in the mood.'

'Oh well,' he sighed. 'Don't say I didn't try.'

'It's sweet of you and I appreciate it. But I'd really rather be left alone.'

'If you wish.'

'Thank you, Ian.'

At the door he paused and glanced back at his sister who'd gone into herself again. He closed the door quietly behind him.

Bridie was outraged. 'He said what!'

'Wanted to know if I was certain the child was his.' Tears welled in Teresa's eyes to go running down her cheeks.

'I hope you smacked him for that.'

Teresa shook her head. 'I was too taken aback, too hurt. I mean, how could he possibly think I might have been with someone else? What does he take me for!'

'And what about getting married?'

'He wouldn't entertain the idea, Bridie. Said he was too young and didn't earn enough money. He also said it was best we didn't see one another again.'

'He just . . . walked away?'

'More or less.'

Fury filled Bridie that her best friend had been treated in

such a manner. If Tony had been present *she* would have slapped him.

'Oh Bridie,' Teresa whispered. 'What am I to do?'

'Tell your folks I suppose. What else?'

Terror lit up Teresa's face. 'Pa will thrash me with his belt, and it'll be the thrashing of a lifetime. As for Ma . . . I daren't even think what she'll say. She'll be beside herself and go on about our good name being dragged in the dirt.'

'Surely your father won't thrash you, being pregnant.'

'Oh aye, he will. And I wouldn't put it past him to do it on my bare backside either. My pa's got a terrible temper.'

They walked a little way in silence, Teresa snuffling into a handkerchief.

'There is of course another way,' Bridie said eventually.

'How do you mean?'

'There are women who I've heard can get rid of it for you. I don't know any myself, but they are around.'

Teresa went white. 'That's a mortal sin, Bridie.'

'Aye,' Bridie agreed.

'I could never do such a thing, murder my own baby.'

'It is a grisly prospect right enough. But consider the alternative. I don't mean the thrashing or your ma having fits. Who'd marry a lassie with a bastard in tow? Not many round here. If any at all.'

'They'll call me tart and whore,' Teresa whispered, wishing with all her heart she'd never gone out with Tony, or let him . . . She shuddered.

'At least Tony's kept his mouth shut so far, that's to his credit, if little else is. And I can't see him bragging that he's got you in the family way. Not when he's abandoned you like he has. That would hardly put him in a good light.'

Murder her baby, Teresa thought, and shuddered again. A mortal sin if ever there was. If only she could wake up and find this was all a nightmare. What she wouldn't have given for that. Only she wouldn't be waking up, for although it was a nightmare it was real enough.

They arrived back at Bridie's close. 'Do you want to come up with me?' Bridie asked.

Teresa shook her head. 'No, I'll go on home.'

'And face the music?'

Teresa considered that. 'Not yet. Who knows? A miracle might happen. I could still lose it naturally.'

'Aye, there is that possibility.' Though unlikely, Bridie thought. Teresa was as healthy a young woman as you'd find. Still, as Teresa said, a miracle could happen.

'Oh Teresa,' Bridie murmured, and touched her friend gently on the cheek.

Teresa attempted a smile which was pathetic to see. 'At least things can't get any worse. There's at least that.'

'Aye, there's at least that.'

Bridie was humming as she washed up the breakfast dishes. Kathleen had gone to the communal toilet their family shared with the other two families on the landing.

Kathleen re-entered the kitchen. 'You'll never guess what.'

Bridie turned to her mother. 'What?'

Kathleen held up a letter. 'They've finally decided to answer your application.'

Elation filled Bridie for a brief moment, then died. 'Throw it on the table, Ma. I'll read it later.'

'It might not be bad news.'

Bridie shrugged. 'Some hope after all this while.'

'You never know. Come on, open it. If you don't I will.'

She picked up the tea towel and dried her hands. 'All right, give it here. May as well get it over and done with.'

It was from the estate right enough, Bridie saw from the postmark. Anyway, who else would it be from? She never received any mail.

Bridie unfolded the single sheet of paper and quickly scanned its contents. Colour mounted her cheeks.

'So?' Kathleen demanded.

'They . . .' She couldn't contain her excitement. 'They want me to go for an interview next Monday and they'll reimburse my expenses getting there and back.'

Kathleen laughed and clapped her hands. 'There you are. It wasn't bad news after all.'

Bridie simply couldn't believe it. She'd become convinced there wasn't going to be a reply to her application. Now she not only had a reply but an interview too.

'I wonder how many they'll be seeing or have already seen?' she mused.

'Aye, there is that,' Kathleen nodded.

'I'll have to get the money for the rail ticket and things, Ma. That's going to be a problem.'

'You leave that to me, lass. I'll see to it.'

She mustn't get too excited, Bridie told herself. It was only an interview after all, not a job offer. It could still all come to nothing.

Hettie answered the door to find Andrew standing there. 'Andrew! What a lovely surprise. Come away in.'

'I'm not intruding I hope?'

'When did you ever do that. You're welcome as always.'

Not for the first time he thought what a wonderful atmosphere the inside of the Riach cottage had. Warm, cosy and . . . full of love. It enveloped one like a blanket.

They went through to the sitting room. 'Where's Jack?' he queried, seeing the room empty.

'Upstairs putting wee Tommy to sleep. Telling him a story no doubt. Something horrible about pixies and goblins probably, Tommy adores those. The more bloodcurdling the better.'

'Is the lad well?'

'Never better. Now how about a cup of tea, or perhaps something stronger?'

'Whisky would be fine.'

'Then whisky it is.'

Andrew settled himself into a comfortable chair. 'I came to ask Jack's advice.'

'Oh?'

'You remember the Seatons who came to stay?'

'Of course. Nice people. It was a grand night.'

'Willie is planning a holiday in Ireland and wants me to go with him. Or them actually. I said yes, but now I'm having second thoughts.'

She handed him a glass. 'And why's that?'

'You know my fiancée was killed by the Fenians, Hettie. Ireland has bad memories and associations for me.'

'I see.' She sat facing him.

Hettie didn't know about McGinty and neither did Jack. Only he did. It was a secret he'd never divulged to anyone.

'Are you scared?'

That startled him. 'Scared? I wouldn't put it exactly like that.'

'Then how would you put it?'

He considered that. 'I'm not sure. There's certainly nothing to be scared of.'

'Except what's in yourself,' she said softly.

He smiled at her. 'How very perceptive of you, dear Hettie. Jack fell on his feet when he married you.'

'And so did I, Andrew. Most certainly so.'

'I envy the pair of you. In the nicest way of course. You're so very happy together.'

'I certainly can't deny that,' she agreed.

Hettie studied Andrew, seeing the loneliness that was in him. A loneliness he so often succeeded in disguising.

'Will you go?' she queried.

He closed his eyes for a second, then opened them again. 'It would mean going to the graveyard. I couldn't be in Dublin and not.'

'You're saying that would be opening an old wound.'

'Definitely, Hettie. Definitely.'

She sighed. 'Well, I don't know what to advise, Andrew. It seems to me only you can make up your mind whether or not you go. But . . .' She trailed off.

'But what, Hettie?'

'If I was in your shoes I would.'

He nodded.

'By the way, speaking of the Seatons. Jack says that lassie Rose is sweet on you.'

Andrew stared at her in amazement. 'Jack says?'

'Heard it in her voice. Don't forget that being blind Jack's other senses are heightened. He hears things, nuances if you like, that we sighted people often miss.'

Andrew recalled the day in his office when Rose had flirted with him. He thought it just a female lark. But perhaps there was more to it than that.

'I'm old enough to be her father,' he protested.

Hettie raised an eyebrow. 'She's pretty.'

'And *young*.'

Hettie didn't reply to that.

'Hmmh,' Andrew mused.

'Would the age difference worry you all that much?' Hettie queried softly.

'If it didn't me it certainly would her father.'

They both laughed.

'Willie would turn cartwheels if he thought I was interested in Rose. No no, the whole thing's preposterous. Completely out of the question.'

'I liked her,' Hettie stated. 'I liked them all, but particularly her. You could do worse, Andrew Drummond.'

'She's far too young,' Andrew repeated. 'Only a child.'

'You've a lot to learn about women I fear, Andrew. Oh, I know you may have had plenty of experience with them in the past, but you still have a lot to learn.'

It suddenly dawned on Andrew that Ellen Temple was only a few years older than Rose. But that was different. Quite different. And Ellen wasn't the daughter of a friend and ex-colleague.

'Oh come along, son, you've always got a few quid stuffed away somewhere. Lend it to me, it's only for a few days.'

Sean Flynn shook his head. 'Honestly, Ma, I'm skint. If I had it I'd give it to you.'

Kathleen wasn't sure whether to believe Sean or not. 'Are you certain? This is important.'

'I swear to you, Ma, on any saint you care to name, I'm totally and utterly broke.'

When Kathleen had gone Sean sat on his bed, angry with himself for not being able to help his ma whom he held in high esteem. Money, why did so many things always boil down to that? If only he was rich, able to afford whatever he fancied. My God, wouldn't that be something.

He thought of what it must be like being a toff. No hard graft for them, but a life of luxury. A big house, car, fancy women. Never having to worry where the next penny was coming from.

It could be worse, he consoled himself. He was in work, things would be ten times harder if he wasn't. Look at Bridie, she never went out nowadays unless it was searching for a job. Poor bitch. He pitied her.

He swore, then lay back on his bed. A big house, car and fancy women. The stuff of dreams.

Or more than that?

Kathleen stopped outside the pop shop, a place she loathed going into. It was so degrading and she always felt soiled after being in there.

'Why hello, Mrs Flynn.' The pawnbroker smiled at her when she was inside.

'Hello, Mr Gordon.'

'Your dad's watch again, is it?'

She hated when he said that, which he always did. For years now she'd wanted to slap Mr Gordon across the face. 'I'm afraid so.'

'A little financial difficulty I take it.'

How he got under her skin. 'I wouldn't be here if there wasn't.'

'Aahhh!' he sighed.

He loved the plight of the poor unfortunates who had to use him, she thought. Positively revelled in it. The man was an utter swine through and through.

Kathleen laid her father's watch on the counter. How often had it been here? she wondered. Times without number. 'The same amount,' she said.

Gordon considered beating her down a little, add a bit of zest to the day. Then decided to be magnanimous. 'Naturally.'

It would be enough, Kathleen thought. Bridie would have her train ticket.

'I'll be back to reclaim it next week,' she stated when the money had been counted out and safely deposited in her handbag.

'Of course,' Mr Gordon replied.

She had to force herself not to slam the door behind her. If anyone could make you feel small it was Mr bloody Gordon.

'That's wonderful!' Teresa exclaimed, having called in on Bridie and been told the news about the interview.

'I'm thrilled to pieces.'

Teresa's face fell. 'Except it means that if you get it you'll be away from here. What will I do for a pal?'

'I'm sorry, Teresa, there's nothing I can do about that. Besides, it's only an interview. There's no saying I'll get the job.'

That brightened Teresa somewhat. It wasn't that she didn't wish Bridie every success with the interview, she did. But on the other hand it would be awful to lose her.

'Monday morning you say.'

'Aye, that's right. I've already been to the station and bought my ticket. I'm raring to go.'

Pat came into the room. 'I'm off out then, hen,' he declared to Kathleen.

'He's on a very important committee,' Kathleen informed Teresa. 'What about that!'

'A committee,' Teresa repeated. 'I'm impressed.'

'Oh aye,' Kathleen went on proudly. 'My Pat's becoming somebody nowadays so he is.'

'What sort of committee?' Teresa enquired.

'To do with the Union,' Pat lied. 'Right then, that's me.'

'Wait and I'll walk you out,' Kathleen said. 'It's time I fetched Alison.' Alison was at a neighbour's playing with their daughter who was in her class at school.

'Aye, sure. But come on then, I don't want to be late. Looks bad.'

Kathleen hurried from the kitchen to get her coat, with Pat following her.

'So tell me,' Bridie said to Teresa when the outside door had clicked shut. 'Have you spoken to your folks yet?'

Teresa shook her head. 'I've been too feart. Anyway, the morning sickness seems to have stopped. At least for now. Which gives me some breathing space.'

'You're going to have to speak to them sooner or later.'

'I know. It's just . . . Well I keep hoping for that miracle to happen. I pray every night that it will.'

'And if it doesn't?'

Teresa thought of her father and his belt. And that would only be for starters. She hung her head.

Bridie took her friend in her arms and held her close.

'Jesus, you're good, Patrick Flynn,' Geraldine Buchanan murmured to him later that night.

He visibly swelled.

'It's like being rogered by a steel piston.'

Pat had never heard the word roger used in that context before but understood what it meant. 'Aye, well, there you are!'

She ran a hand over the forest of hair covering his chest. Dougal was good in bed but couldn't compare to Pat. What a find he was.

'Will you get me a drink?' he asked.

'Of course.'

'Whisky and beer. I'm thirsty as hell.'

She laughed. 'I'm not surprised after that performance. You were terrific.'

Kathleen never said that to him he reflected. She took it all as a matter of course. Nor was she as responsive as Geraldine who, on occasion, could make so much noise he thought the neighbours must surely hear.

Geraldine slipped from the bed and into her negligée, an exotic delight Dougal had brought her back from the Far East. It was made of pure silk and patterned with fiercesome dragons and brightly hued birds.

Pat watched her as she tied the belt round her waist. What a figure, he thought, smiling at the memory of what he'd just been doing to it.

'I'll just be a minute, lover,' Geraldine said, and left the room.

Lover! Pat sighed with satisfaction.

Bridie stared in awe through the window of the car that had been sent to meet her as The Haven came into view. It was like something out of one of those romantic novels she read.

And the grounds surrounding it, they defied description. She might have died and gone to paradise.

Bridie closed her eyes. Dear God, Holy Father, please let me get this job. Now I've seen this place I've never wanted anything so much in my life. I'll work ever so hard, I promise. They'll never find fault with me. Not in a thousand years.

She opened her eyes again to continue staring at The Haven. How many rooms did it have? She couldn't even begin to imagine. Oodles and oodles.

Bridie glanced down at her clothes in dismay, her church Sunday best. The black three-quarter-length coat suddenly looked old and shabby while the shepherd-checked tailored suit she had on underneath was hopelessly out of date and fashion.

She was only going for a position as maid she reminded

herself. They wouldn't expect her to turn up looking a glam puss or wearing the very latest style. No, no, she was adequately dressed and neat and tidy with it.

What would this Mr Seaton be like, she wondered, for it was he who'd written to her? Formidable no doubt. And posh as all get out. She must mind her P's and Q's right enough.

Excitement throbbed within her.

Mrs Coltart popped her head round the door. 'Can I have a word with you, sir?'

'Of course, Mrs Coltart.'

She came to stand before him.

'Now what can I do for you?'

'I've just interviewed the last girl for the maid's post, sir, and wish to talk to you about her as she's the one I'd like.'

Willie leant back in his chair. 'So what's the problem?'

'It's her religion. She's a Roman Catholic.'

'Aahhh!' Willie breathed.

'We've never had a Catholic here before, sir, and I don't know your feelings on the matter.'

'She's definitely the one you want, Mrs Coltart?'

'Definitely, sir. There were only four applications as you're aware and as far as I'm concerned she's the most suitable.'

'And why's that?'

'Her enthusiasm, sir. She was bubbling with it.' Mrs Coltart smiled. 'She'd never been outside Glasgow before and thinks the countryside is absolutely wonderful. She was full of it.'

Willie made a pyramid with his hands and frowned in concentration. A Catholic working at The Haven? He wasn't at all sure about that. It might lead to trouble. 'It *was* a poor response to my advertisement,' he murmured, still thinking.

'Very, sir.'

'I expected far more applications.'

'In truth, sir, so did I. But there were only the four.'

'What about the rest of the staff, would she fit in?'

'I believe so, sir.'

'Not only as a person but with the religious difference?'

'I still believe so, sir. If I'm wrong, and there was conflict, then the matter would have to be sorted.'

He nodded. 'Did you explain there isn't a Roman Catholic church hereabouts?'

'Yes, sir. She was disappointed but said she'd just have to put up with that.'

'Hmmh. What's her name?'

'Brigit Flynn, sir. They call her Bridie.'

Willie gave a soft laugh. 'You can't get a more Catholic name than that. Irish I presume.'

'Descent, sir.'

Willie took a deep breath. 'Leave this with me, Mrs Coltart. I wish to mull it over for a while.'

'Certainly, sir.'

Mrs Coltart left him to it.

Kathleen's eyes were fixed on Bridie as she eagerly tore open the letter that had just arrived. Seconds later Bridie squealed with delight.

'I've got the job, Ma. I've got it! I start the beginning of next month.'

Kathleen breathed a sigh of relief. 'Well done, lass. Well done.'

Her prayers had been answered, Bridie thought in exaltation. Thank you, God. Thank you.

Chapter 9

'We must be feeding this lassie too much,' Mr Kelly commented affably across the tea table.

Teresa went very still, a piece of sausage halfway to her mouth.

'Oh?' Mrs Kelly smiled at her husband.

'Look at her, she's putting on weight like billy-o.'

Mrs Kelly glanced at Teresa. 'I do believe you're right. I hadn't noticed.'

Teresa returned the piece of sausage to her plate and swallowed hard. She *had* started putting on weight though she'd been pretending to herself that she wasn't.

Mr Kelly chuckled. 'It's your good cooking, Ma. And her healthy appetite.'

Mrs Kelly was frowning. 'She hasn't been eating more than usual. So why should she suddenly start putting on weight?'

'It must be the cakes,' Teresa muttered.

'Cakes?' Mrs Kelly queried.

Teresa's mind was whizzing. 'Aye, a few of the lassies at

work take it in turn to bring some in. Cream cakes and the like. It's just a wee treat amongst ourselves,' she lied.

'She's always had a sweet tooth, Ma. You know that.'

Mrs Kelly nodded her agreement. That was true enough. She had a sweet tooth herself, simply adoring chocolate whenever she could get her hands on some.

Should she speak up now? Teresa wondered, quailing at the prospect. No, she couldn't, not after that cock and bull story about cakes. She couldn't see her father's belt from where she was sitting, but pictured it in her mind. The belt would be pulled free and . . . She shuddered inwardly.

Her da might appear the genial sort, always laughing and joking. But you crossed him at your peril as many, including herself, had found out. As though a switch had been flicked he'd turn from a nice, pleasant man into a raging monster. She'd seen it happen many times.

'Well, you'd better watch it, girl. We don't want you becoming a two-ton Tessie now, do we?'

'No, Da.'

'Go easy on those cakes.'

'I will, Da. I promise.'

'A funny thing happened at work today,' Mr Kelly declared, changing the subject, and the others listened attentively while he recounted the story.

She was running out of time, Teresa thought desperately. Who would've imagined she'd have already begun to show!

'What's a Samurai?' Alison Flynn piped up from the floor where she was playing with her golly.

'No idea, lass,' Pat replied from behind his newspaper.

'You know, don't you, Sean? You're the leader of that gang.'

Sean could have wrung his little sister's neck. 'Leader of a gang?'

Pat's newspaper slowly descended to his lap. 'What's all this then?'

'She's blethering, Da. Forget it.'

'I am not blethering,' Alison snapped hotly. 'Molly Molloy's parents were talking about it the other day when I was round there. They didn't know what a Samurai was either.'

'Son?' Kathleen queried softly.

'*Are* you in a gang, you stupid bugger? Do you want to get yourself marked or something? I thought you had more sense.'

Sean glared at his father. 'So what if I am. What's it to you? And don't call me a stupid bugger ever again.'

'Or what?'

'Stop it you two,' Kathleen said sternly. She then rounded on Sean. 'Are you?'

'Yes I am.'

'And its leader?'

He nodded.

'Holy fuck!' Pat swore, and dashed his newspaper to the floor. 'I can't believe I'm hearing this.'

'The Samurai were ancient Japanese warriors,' Sean explained to Alison.

Bridie, who'd been out to the toilet, breezed in, then came up short. 'What's going on?' she queried, looking from face to face. Something clearly was up. You could have cut the atmosphere with a knife.

'Your brother is the leader of a gang,' Kathleen informed her.

Bridie was incredulous. 'You must be joking. Our Sean?'

'Aye, our Sean,' Kathleen responded.

'Well, not for long,' Pat declared. 'I forbid you to belong to any gang, Sean, far less be its leader.' He leant forward. 'Do you hear me?'

'I'll do what I bloody well like. I'm not having you lay down the rules to me any more.'

Pat was immediately out of his chair. 'How dare you speak to me like that? I'm your father.'

'So what?' Sean replied insolently.

Kathleen also came to her feet ready to divert any trouble. 'Will you two give over. I'm not having any trouble in my house.'

'He started it,' Sean declared.

A frightened Alison had gone to Bridie and taken her hand. Bridie squeezed it reassuringly.

'It doesn't matter who started it. Enough is enough.'

Pat was staring daggers at Sean. 'You're going to finish with this gang. I want your word on that. Heaven's sake, do you know what the gangs get up to? You could end up dead or scarred for life.'

'That's right, son,' Kathleen agreed.

Should he lie, make a promise he had no intention of keeping? He didn't see the point. If he lied they'd only find out eventually.

'I'm old enough to make my own decisions. And I'm staying in the gang and I'm staying its leader.'

'Like hell you are!' Pat roared and, pushing his way past Kathleen, advanced on Sean who instantly leapt up.

'Don't hit him, Pat, don't hit him!' Kathleen pleaded, clutching at Pat's shirt.

He tore himself free and continued on towards Sean.

'Hit me and you'll regret it,' Sean spat.

Pat's fist flashed, smacking Sean on the shoulder. 'I won't be defied,' he shouted. 'I won't be defied!'

The blow was only a glancing one but enough to make Sean lose his temper. 'Right, you old fart, you've been asking for this for years!'

Kathleen screamed as the two men fell upon one another.

'Holy Mary mother of God,' a wide-eyed Bridie whispered. This was awful.

Alison whimpered and fled behind Bridie's skirt from where she peeped out.

A kitchen chair went crashing. Pat roared again when Sean's fist found its mark. Blood spattered from his nose.

Neither of them was pulling their punches, this was in deadly earnest. Another kitchen chair went clattering away.

Sean grunted, that had hurt. He lashed out in retaliation.

'Stop it! Stop it!' Kathleen shrieked, hitting them both.

Some mantelpiece ornaments, including a plaster madonna, went tumbling to the floor where they all broke.

Pat succeeded in getting Sean in a bearlike grip, the pair of them swaying to and fro.

Suddenly it was all over. Somehow Sean's head smashed into his father's chin knocking him unconscious. Pat's arms dropped away and when Sean released him he fell to lie sprawling.

Sean stood over Pat, sucking in deep breaths. 'You old fart,' he repeated.

'You've killed him!' an hysterical Kathleen gasped. Next moment she was on her knees beside the fallen Pat. Bridie, with a now crying Alison still clinging to her skirt, hurried over.

'Pat, Pat, speak to me,' Kathleen urged, slapping him lightly on the cheek. Pat's reply was a groan.

'He's not dead,' Sean stated.

'No thanks to you!' Kathleen retorted.

Bridie knelt beside her mother. 'He's just knocked out, Ma. He'll soon come round.'

'I'm off,' Sean declared and, wheeling about, strode from the room.

Pat opened one eye, then the other. 'What happened?'

Kathleen explained.

'Where is he now?'

'Gone out.'

Pat was secretly pleased. He didn't fancy another tangle with Sean. The lad had surprised him.

'Let's get you back into your chair,' Bridie suggested.

'Oh, Dada. Dada,' Alison wailed.

'I've been thinking,' Georgina said.

Willie looked over. 'Usually when you say that it costs me money.'

She laughed. 'How right you are. As it could in this instance.'

Willie sighed. 'Well?'

'Why don't we have a party on Hogmanay? Invite about a dozen folk or so. Maybe more.'

'What a smashing idea,' Rose chipped in.

'Who would we ask?'

'The McLarens I thought. Their daughter Moira isn't long back from Switzerland. It would be interesting to hear how it went over there for her.' Moira McLaren had been to a Swiss finishing school.

Ian grunted. He remembered Moira as a horrible little so and so. They'd never got on.

'Hmmh,' Willie mused. He rather liked the idea of a party. It was ages since they'd entertained properly. 'Ian?'

'Sounds all right.'

'We could also invite Andrew Drummond.' Rose smiled innocently.

That startled Georgina, inviting Andrew being the whole reason for her suggesting the party. Now Rose had saved her the trouble of mentioning him.

'He must be lonely in that house all by himself,' Rose

went on. 'Though no doubt he usually goes to his sister's on Hogmanay, or to his friend Jack Riach's. Coming here would be a change for him.'

Georgina eyed Rose shrewdly. Not for the first time she wondered about Rose's interest in Andrew. There again, Andrew *was* excellent company.

'I quite agree,' Willie said. 'It would be a change for him. And while here he and I could discuss plans for Ireland.'

'Settled then?' Georgina asked.

Willie nodded. 'You go ahead and do what has to be done. A Hogmanay party it is.'

Georgina smiled inwardly with satisfaction while Rose was trying hard not to show her excitement.

'That's brilliant,' Teresa said. 'I couldn't be more happy for you.' Bridie had just told her the news about her job.

'We're all delighted,' Kathleen declared. With the exception of Pat that was, for he was still scornful of a Flynn being a domestic.

'I start the beginning of next month,' Bridie beamed.

'I'll miss you.'

Bridie's face fell. 'I am sorry, Teresa. But you do understand.'

'Oh aye.'

'I'm going to love it there. You should see the house and grounds, they're fantastic.'

Teresa nodded. Catching Bridie's eye she glanced meaningfully towards the door.

Bridie was puzzled only for a moment, then got the message. 'Anyway,' she declared. 'I've been home all day and could use a breath of air. Do you fancy a walk, Teresa?'

'I do indeed.'

'I really am pleased for you,' Teresa said as they left the close.

'Thank you. Now what's all this about? Has that miracle happened?'

Teresa gave a hollow laugh. 'If only it had. No, I need your help, Bridie. The help of a pal.'

'Of course. Just say.'

'I've, eh . . .' Teresa broke off, she still couldn't believe she was going to be doing this. But in the end, what choice did she have? 'I've decided to use one of those women we spoke of and want you to come with me for support.'

Bridie frowned. 'What women?'

'The ones who . . .' She gulped. 'Give you an abortion.'

Bridie halted and stared at Teresa in consternation. 'Are you serious?'

'I'm afraid so. I couldn't face bringing up a bastard, Bridie. And as you pointed out, what man would marry me with one of those in tow? I'd be a spinster for the rest of my life.'

'But you were so against it.'

'I know. I know. Only I've changed my mind.'

'A mortal sin, Teresa. Don't forget that.'

Tears welled in her eyes. 'I'm not forgetting. But maybe God will be merciful. Understand my reasons and forgive me.'

They resumed walking, Bridie full of sympathy for her friend. It was a terrible decision to have to make. 'I thought you didn't know any of these women?'

'I didn't. And then, quite by chance, a name came up in conversation at the factory. She's called Mrs Quinlan and she's agreed to do it this Friday.'

'You've been to see her?'

'Well, I had to. You can't just turn up at her door and ask for it to be done there and then.'

Bridie was curious. 'What's she like?'

'I wasn't sure what to expect, some old crone perhaps. But Mrs Quinlan is as normal as can be. She's not even old. Late thirties I'd judge, maybe early forties.'

'What about money?'

'I've been saving up for a while now. Nothing much, just a wee bit put by every week for a rainy day.' She laughed again. 'Well if this isn't a rainy day I don't know what is.'

'How much?'

'Five quid. Paid up front on the night.'

'I see,' Bridie murmured. The last thing she wanted was to be party to this sort of thing, but she could hardly let Teresa down. Teresa certainly wouldn't have let her down if the positions had been reversed, not that they ever would have been.

'What time Friday night?' she queried.

Sean, Noddy, Jim Gallagher and Mo Binchy strolled into the ice-cream shop which was empty apart from the owner behind the counter.

'Hello, Mr Rizzio,' Sean said casually.

'Hello, lads. What can I do for you? Some nice cornets with raspberry sauce on top perhaps?'

'It's more what we can do for you.'

Rizzio's face became anxious. There was something wrong here. He could tell. 'Like what?'

'You get trouble from time to time, don't you?'

'Not really.'

'Well you could do. I'm certain of it.'

Mo Binchy pretended to slip, knocking over a large glass

bowl of wafers in the process. The bowl smashed on the floor sending wafers flying everywhere.

'Oh, sorry, Mr Rizzio,' Mo said. 'How clumsy of me.'

'Hey, you do that intentionally.'

Mo was all innocence. 'What a nasty thing to say.'

'You did. I no wrong.'

'An accident,' Sean smiled thinly. 'Amazing how they happen when you least expect it.'

Rizzio was becoming extremely uneasy. 'What this all about?'

Sean glanced around. 'Lovely place you've got here. It would cost a lot of money to do up again.'

'Do up . . .' Rizzio spluttered.

'You know how violent this area is. Fights break out all the time. If a big one happened in here it could wreck the shop. I can just see it, broken tables and chairs, ripped wallpaper, even your ice-cream machine there might get broken.'

Rizzio was appalled. That sort of damage could put him out of business.

'Mind you, it wouldn't if you were protected,' Sean said slowly.

'Protected?'

'Aye, by the Samurai. Have you not heard of us?'

Rizzio shook his head.

Sean produced his cut-throat razor, flicked it open and laid it on the counter in front of the now terrified Italian. Rizzio stared at the razor as though it was a deadly snake about to strike.

'We're the gang round here,' Sean stated. 'There are lots of us in it.'

'A gang,' Rizzio said, and swallowed hard.

'Some of the others are outside making sure we're not disturbed like. Understand?'

Rizzio nodded.

'Now for a small sum per week we'd make sure nothing happened here. We'd put the word out that if it did whoever was responsible would have us to deal with. And that wouldn't be healthy for the person or persons. Get my meaning?'

'Oh yes,' Rizzio breathed.

'So what do you say?'

'It's daylight robbery.'

'Not at all,' Sean replied smoothly. 'It's insurance, that's all. And that's how you should think of it.'

Mo Binchy put his heel on a piece of broken glass and scrunched it underfoot. Rizzio winced at the noise it made.

'Why me?' Rizzio queried.

'Why not? As I said, you've a good business here, it would be a crying shame to see it . . .' He broke off and shrugged. 'Well you know.'

'And what this . . . insurance cost me?'

The agreed sum had been two pounds a week. Sean now changed his mind thinking, what the hell! The man was almost shitting himself.

'A fiver.'

'A fiver,' Rizzio gasped. 'That no possible.'

'Oh yes it is,' Sean said, voice loaded with menace. 'Oh yes it is.'

'And what if I tell police?'

'That would be a terrible mistake on your part.' He picked up the razor. 'One you'd regret the rest of your life I assure you.'

Rizzio knew he was beaten. Sean's threats were no idle ones. You didn't make idle threats in Glasgow.

Rizzio nodded. 'I take your insurance.'

'Payment starts right now and someone will be round once a week to collect from now on. Clear?'

'Clear,' Rizzio mumbled, going to his till.

Number one, Sean thought triumphantly. The first of many.

Ian Seaton was in a bad mood. The weather that day had been terrible, little outside work had been done on the estate and those who had been outside had soon been soaked through. He still felt chill, despite the roaring fire and bath he'd had, and wondered if he had a cold coming on. He listened to the rain. Had it stopped at all since early morning? It was hammering against the window panes.

'Ian?'

He glanced over at Georgina. The pair of them were alone in the drawing room. 'Yes?'

'Can I speak frankly?'

He raised an eyebrow. 'If you wish.'

'You worry me sometimes.'

'Do I indeed. Why, Georgina?'

'You never seem to show any interest in women. It doesn't seem natural to me.'

He laughed, amused. 'Do you think I might be a nancy boy or something?'

Georgina coloured. 'Such things are known.'

'Well, you can put your mind at rest. I have no interest in that direction, nor have I ever dabbled as some chaps do at school. I'm quite normal.'

'I'm pleased to hear it.'

He leant forward. 'You didn't really think I was queer, did you?'

'No, but . . . well it does happen, even in the best of families.'

'I like girls well enough, Georgina, but you can't say they're exactly thick on the ground round here now, can you?'

This time she laughed. 'True enough.'

'I meant suitable ones of course. There are always the maids, mind you, but I hardly think either you or Father would be best pleased if I cast an eye in that direction.'

'No,' she agreed.

'Besides, I'm too busy at the moment learning about the management of the estate to worry about girls. I doubt I'd have the time to go gallivanting even if I wanted to.'

'I hardly meant gallivanting.'

'Call it what you will. Come the evening I'm far too tired to think of anything other than food and bed.'

'Fine then.'

Ian lapsed back into his own thoughts which brought an end to that conversation.

'This is it,' Teresa said, stopping outside a close. 'Mrs Quinlan is two flights up.'

'How do you feel?'

Teresa gave Bridie a pained smile. 'How do you think? I'm scared out of my brain.'

'Aye,' Bridie sympathised. 'I can well understand that.'

Teresa stared into the close which had cream tiles to halfway up its walls. Her stomach was knotted, her heart beating wildly. She'd have given anything not to have had to go in there.

'You can still change your mind,' Bridie said softly.

Teresa laughed hollowly. 'Can I? I don't think so.'

Bridie took her friend's arm. 'I'm with you. Just remember that.'

'And I'm grateful. Far more than you probably realise. I doubt I could do this on my own.'

'It's almost eight, Teresa. We should go on up.'

Teresa sucked in a deep breath. 'I just hope it doesn't hurt too much, that's all.'

Bridie failed to see how it couldn't.

For the umpteenth time Bridie glanced at the clock on the mantelpiece. It was over an hour now. What was keeping them?

She started when she heard a muted scream. Dear God! She suddenly began to sweat profusely, her armpits quickly awash, sweat coursing down her back.

And still the clock continued to tick.

'All done.' Mrs Quinlan beamed, ushering Teresa into the sitting room where Bridie was waiting.

Bridie caught her breath at the sight of Teresa, whose face was milk-white and strained in the extreme.

'Everything go all right?'

'Perfectly,' Mrs Quinlan replied, still beaming. 'Now I recommend you take her home and put her to bed where she should stay for the weekend if she's any sense. Come Monday morning she'll be right as rain.'

Teresa staggered over to Bridie and clutched her. 'Let's get out of here,' she mumbled.

'I'll see you both to the door,' Mrs Quinlan declared, still beaming.

'How was it?' Bridie queried as they slowly made their way down the stairs, Teresa holding tightly on to her.

'Don't ask. And don't ask how she did it. The answer to that would give you nightmares.'

Teresa began to cry and they stopped while Bridie searched for a handkerchief.

Teresa woke from what had been a deep sleep. Not fully awake, but a sort of peaceful state in between.

Her ma had been full of concern when Bridie had explained that she'd come over ill which was why Bridie had brought her home. Mrs Kelly had thanked Bridie profusely and then proceeded to take her through to bed which, at that moment, had been the most welcome sight she'd ever seen.

The pain had gone, she realised. That terrible griping pain that had been gnawing at her insides ever since . . .

'Dear God, forgive me please. And understand,' she muttered. 'I'll be a good girl from now on. It'll never happen again. I swear to you on all that's holy.'

Sleep was beckoning her again, blissful, blessed sleep. Sleep she desperately craved.

Was it her imagination or could she really hear a voice saying she was forgiven? Imagination surely. And yet it seemed so real somehow.

Forgiven.

She drifted off with a smile on her face.

Mrs Kelly answered Bridie's knock. It was Saturday morning. 'Hello, Mrs Kelly. I thought I'd call by and see how Teresa is. Maybe cheer her up a little.'

Mrs Kelly's face crumpled. She tried to speak, but couldn't. She tried again, and this time succeeded. 'Oh lass, oh lassie,' she croaked.

A sudden chill ran through Bridie, goosebumps breaking out all over her. 'What is it? What's happened?'

The crumpled face collapsed even further while tears sprang into what Bridie now saw were red-rimmed and puffy eyes.

'It's Teresa. She had a haemorrhage in the middle of the night and . . . and . . .' Mrs Kelly swallowed hard. 'And died.'

Chapter 10

'Turn round, girl,' Mrs Coltart instructed.

Bridie, wearing the black and white uniform she'd been issued with, did as she was bid.

Mrs Coltart nodded her approval. 'It'll do. Though when you have the chance you might take the hem up an inch. Can you do that, Bridie?'

'Yes, ma'am.'

'Well turn round again then.'

Mrs Coltart studied Bridie who'd arrived earlier that afternoon. 'The girl you're replacing was dismissed for theft and not given a character. I trust we'll have no such problems with you.'

'You won't, Mrs Coltart.'

'Right then. Now go and find Jeannie Swanson whom you're sharing a room with, she should be on the second floor, and she'll show you what to do. Stay with Jeannie till the end of the week by which time you should have learnt the ropes. At least as far as your current duties will be. Do you understand?'

'Yes, ma'am.'

'Then off you go.'

'Thank you, Mrs Coltart.'

Bridie went in search of Jeannie Swanson whom she found easily enough.

Bridie's eyes were popping at the amount of food that had been laid out for their supper. The table was positively groaning.

She accepted a tureen from the girl next to her and helped herself to thick pea soup.

The atmosphere in the servants' hall was warm, literally, and friendly. Everyone seemed most relaxed.

Mrs Kilbride, the cook, reigned at one end of the table, Mrs Coltart at the other. They kept their own counsel, but others were chatting amongst themselves. It was Mrs Coltart who'd said grace.

When the meal was finally over Bridie felt as though she must surely burst. Whatever else you could say about being a domestic, lack of food wasn't something you apparently had to worry about.

Not at The Haven anyway.

Bridie collapsed on to her bed, an iron affair that was surprisingly comfortable, having just completed her first full day, and groaned. 'My feet are killing me. As for my legs, they ache like billy-o.'

Jeannie Swanson, a thin stick of a girl with large, protuberant eyes, grinned at her. 'You'll soon get used to it, I promise you.'

'And getting up when we do. That's something else. I rose early in my last job, but that was a long lie compared to this.'

Jeannie started to remove her uniform. 'Apart from the moans do you think you'll like it here?'

'Oh yes. The rest of the staff are ever so nice and helpful.'

'Aye, they're a good bunch right enough. We all get on well so I hope you fit in.'

'I'll certainly do my best.'

Jeannie paused, then glanced curiously across at Bridie. 'Is it true what I hear? That you're a Catholic?'

Bridie nodded.

'We've never had one of those here before.'

'Is it likely to cause a problem, Jeannie?'

Jeannie considered that. 'I don't think so. We're all fairly tolerant, at least to the best of my knowledge we are.'

Bridie lay back on the bed, quite exhausted. 'Tell me about Mrs Coltart,' she requested.

Jeannie poured water from their jug into the bowl it had been sitting on. 'She's very fair. True she can be a Tartar at times, but only with those who've asked for it. Strict, mind, oh she is that. But as I said, fair with it.'

Jeannie washed her face which she then dried with the towel provided. There were two towels, one for each of them. The water in the bowl she slopped into a bucket.

'The only trouble with being here is that it's so isolated. When you get your day off there's absolutely nothing to do or anywhere to go.' They were given one day off a month.

'That won't bother me,' Bridie replied. 'I shall walk which will give me enormous pleasure. The countryside around here is so beautiful it quite takes my breath away.'

'Aye, it is that,' Jeannie agreed.

'Walk and read. If I can lay my hands on any books that is. I love reading.'

'The master has a library downstairs,' Jeannie informed her.

Bridie sat up. 'Really?'

'He must have thousands of books in it, at least it seems like thousands. All of them leather bound.'

'What sort of books?'

Jeannie shrugged. 'I don't know. I've never really bothered to look.'

A sudden gust from under the door caused their single candle to flicker wildly sending all kinds of weird and wonderful shapes dancing round the room's walls and ceiling.

'It's cold up here as it always is in wintertime,' Jeannie said, shivering. 'The sooner I'm in bed the better.'

Me too, Bridie thought and, getting up, also began undressing.

Jeannie slipped a flannel nightdress over her head and once that was on removed her underthings.

'Last one into bed puts out the candle,' Jeannie declared, diving under her covers.

A library, Bridie marvelled. She couldn't wait to see it.

'Goodnight,' she said slightly later, snuffing out the candle.

'Goodnight, Bridie. Sweet dreams.'

'And you.'

Pat reined in Jasper. The card was in Geraldine's window which meant she wanted a bag of coal. It also meant he'd be having a bottle of beer.

She was waiting for him on the landing, a nervous smile on her face. 'Hello, Mr Flynn. How are you today?'

Mr Flynn?

'Please come in, Mr Flynn. You know where the bin is.'

There it was again, Mr Flynn. And why was she acting so strangely?

'Dougal,' she whispered as he went past her.

No wonder she was nervous, her husband was back from

sea. There would be no bottle of beer today, or Friday night visits for a while. He inwardly cursed.

'I'll get your money,' Geraldine declared as he was emptying the coal into the bin, and hurried away.

Pat was shaking out the bag when he heard a man's voice, though he couldn't make out what the man was saying.

Geraldine reappeared. 'There you are, Mr Flynn,' she said, handing him the correct money.

'Thank you, Mrs Buchanan.'

Pat was leaving the kitchen when Dougal came into view. He was very tall and very powerfully built with hands the size of shovels. Not someone he would wish to tangle with, Pat thought. No indeed.

'Nice day for this time of year,' Dougal commented affably to Pat.

'It is that.'

Pat was consumed with jealousy as he left the Buchanans. All he could think about was what Dougal would be enjoying that night.

Something he'd come to regard as his.

'The committee work is finished for a while,' Pat announced to Kathleen later on.

'Oh?'

'We've done what had to be done. For the present anyway.'

'I see.'

He glanced across at Sean sitting morosely in a chair. He was wary of the lad ever since the fight, uncomfortable in Sean's presence. He was only too horribly aware that the balance of power in the house had changed, and that he was no longer top dog. In truth, his son now frightened him.

'But we'll be meeting again soon enough. Though I don't

know exactly when.' How long before Dougal returned to sea? he wondered. He had no way of knowing.

Pat shrank back a little as Sean suddenly came to his feet. 'I'm off out,' Sean declared to his mother.

'Will you be late?'

'No idea, Ma. I'll be back when I get here.'

Pat felt himself relax as the outside door clicked shut.

Rose stared at herself in her vanity table mirror. She touched both cheeks, thinking how good her skin was looking. She could now see bones where she hadn't before. Losing weight certainly suited her.

She smoothed down the sides of the envelope chemise she was wearing, the chemise of silk crêpe de Chine and the step-in style. It was neatly trimmed in front with rows of lace insertions, top and bottom edged with lace to match. Set off with rosettes, the chemise had silk ribbon shoulder straps.

Only two more weeks till Andrew arrives, she thought, a thrill of expectation running through her. He was coming for four whole days! Four days in which to try and get him to notice her the way she wanted him to.

'Andrew,' she whispered, and sighed. How she craved seeing him again. With all her heart and soul.

She coloured at the sudden thought of him standing there staring at her, his gaze feasting on her near nakedness. How vulnerable that made her feel. And excited.

In her mind's eye he was now bending down kissing first one bare shoulder, then the other.

'My darling,' he murmured.

A hand crept round to enfold a breast which he began to lightly caress. Her eyelids drooped at the sensations which tingled inside her. Sensations to die for.

Rose brought herself out of her reverie with a laugh. She

was being daft letting her imagination run riot like that. Quite silly really.

There again, who knew? The time might come when fantasy became reality. Beautiful, wonderful reality.

And it would, if she had anything to do with it. She was determined about that.

Oh yes.

'Jack?'

'Yes, Hettie?'

'Why are you looking so odd?'

He chuckled. 'Am I?'

'Your expression is very odd indeed.'

It was night and Hettie had just returned from putting Tommy to bed, which had taken quite a while as he hadn't wanted to go to sleep. And when Tommy wanted he could keep himself awake for ages, fighting sleep all the way.

'I was thinking about the book,' Jack stated.

'And?'

'I'm considering changing the ending. Not a happy one as I intended, but something tragic.'

'But you were so adamant . . .' She trailed off.

'Of course I haven't decided yet. I'm still toying with the idea.' Jack rose from his chair. 'I'm going out into the garden for a breath of fresh air.'

'But it's freezing out there. You'll catch your death.'

'Not if I put my coat on.' He hesitated. 'Tell me, Hettie, are the stars out tonight?'

'Yes.'

'A clear moonlit night with lots of stars?'

She smiled. 'Yes.'

'Aah!' he sighed. 'I love starry nights. Thousands of sparkling pin pricks shining down from heaven. It's a sight I've always found so uplifting. It makes you sing inside.'

Hettie laughed. Sing indeed! What a funny way Jack had with words at times. But he was a writer after all.

'Except during the war,' Jack said softly. 'Starry moonlit nights could be the most dangerous of all. It's the visibility you see. For both sides. An awful lot of good men went west on nights like that.'

Hettie could well imagine. 'Don't forget the coat,' she said.

'I won't. I promise.'

Once outside he lifted his face to the heavens. He might be blind but he could still see the stars.

Andrew was standing at his bedroom window gazing out, waiting for Ellen to arrive.

He was in a troubled mood. The proposed Irish trip still worried him. How was he going to react when there?

Well or badly? That was the question.

Alice, how he missed her. Dear sweet Alice whom he'd come to adore with every fibre of his being.

He closed his eyes. Remembering . . . remembering . . .

'Just our luck to be stranded in bloody Ireland when there's a war on,' Second Lieutenant Roberts complained to Andrew, as the pair of them were out riding.

Andrew was a far more experienced rider than Billy who'd only taken it up eighteen months previously. He glanced sideways at his friend not at all sure he agreed with those sentiments.

'Think of the promotions that will be going,' Billy went on. 'There are bound to be stacks.'

Only because of casualties, Andrew thought grimly. He

gazed about him. It was beautiful countryside, lush in the extreme. But he wasn't too keen on the climate; it rained even more than in Scotland.

'That Captain Kennington's a right bastard,' Billy said. 'I can't tell you how much I dislike him.'

Andrew smiled. He got on with Kennington well enough, it was simply a case of how you handled the man. Toadying, some people might have called it, but it worked and, as far as he was concerned, that was all that mattered.

'You rub him up the wrong way,' Andrew commented quietly.

'It's his attitude that gets me, supercilious swine.'

Andrew reined in on spotting another horse, the rider a woman obviously in distress.

'I say, look at that,' Billy exclaimed. 'The beast appears to have bolted.'

'She needs help,' Andrew declared, kicking his horse forward. Billy immediately followed.

Andrew urged his horse, a powerful gelding, into a gallop. Slowly he began to narrow the gap between him and the woman.

The young woman heard their approach and turned her head to stare at Andrew and Billy. 'Help!' she cried.

'Just hold on,' Andrew shouted back, thinking she could easily be killed or badly hurt if she came off at that speed. He was well ahead of Billy whose horse wasn't nearly as fast as his.

Yard by yard, aided by some clever manoeuvring on his part, Andrew gained on them till at last his horse and hers were neck and neck. Leaning across he managed to grab the bridle.

For a few moments it was a fierce clash of wills between them, then the horse began to ease back and gradually slow.

When the horse finally came to a halt Andrew leapt to the ground and grabbed hold of its reins. He then assisted the young woman down.

'Thank you,' she panted. 'That was truly frightening.'

'What happened?'

She gave a wry grin. 'I was stupid and arrogant enough to think I could control Midnight, which clearly I can't.'

Midnight was an apt name, Andrew thought. The animal was velvet black from nose to tail.

'Just let me catch my breath a minute,' the young woman said, placing a hand on her chest.

Billy came charging up, reined in and also dismounted. 'Everything all right?'

'I think so,' Andrew replied.

Midnight whinnied and threw his head, but Andrew had him firmly under control.

'Dashed large beast for a girl,' Billy commented.

'He's my father's horse,' the young woman explained. 'My own is unwell and I wanted a ride. A mistake with Midnight as you witnessed.'

Andrew stroked a neck that was flaked with foam. 'There there, boy. There there,' he crooned.

'I'm Alice Fortescue by the way,' the young woman said.

'Andrew Drummond, Second Lieutenant in the First Essex based at Dublin Castle. This is my chum Billy Roberts, also a Second Lieutenant with the same regiment.'

'Delighted to meet you, Miss Fortescue,' Billy declared, giving her a small bow.

'And I the pair of you. Who knows what the outcome might have been if you hadn't been on hand.'

'How far away do you live?' Andrew enquired.

'Several miles in that direction,' Alice replied, pointing off to their left.

'Well I think it best we walk the horses for a bit,' Andrew said. 'They all need a breather after that.'

Pretty girl, Andrew was thinking. He placed her in her late teens, possibly early twenties. She was dressed in a black hunting jacket below which flowed an ankle-length grey skirt.

'I lost my hat somewhere along the line,' she explained. 'It just blew off.' She shuddered. 'I don't mind admitting that gave me quite a scare. Father will be furious if he finds out.'

'Well, we won't let on, will we, Billy?'

Billy grinned. 'Find out what?'

Alice smiled. 'You're both very kind and gallant.' She pronounced the latter in the French fashion.

'As every army officer should be,' Andrew retorted.

The three of them laughed at that.

Andrew could see she'd got her breath back. 'Shall we get started then?' he suggested. 'I'll lead my own horse and Midnight.'

'Fortescue isn't an Irish name,' Billy commented as they got underway.

'The family is originally English. We came over here in the seventeenth century when we were granted lands for services to the Crown. Lands that succeeding generations have managed to enlarge considerably.'

'I see,' Billy nodded.

'We don't think of ourselves as English any more, but Irish through and through, albeit we're Protestants.'

That was interesting, Andrew thought. 'And what does your father do? If you'll pardon my inquisitiveness.'

'He runs our estate, which is quite a task I can assure you. He'll be out now, doing whatever.'

Damn it, Andrew thought, when it started to rain. A light

smir as the Scots call it which nonetheless soon had them soaking. Alice seemed oblivious to it.

They made small chat as they proceeded in the direction of Alice's house till eventually Andrew decided they could remount. Alice was instructed to take Billy's horse, the smallest of the three, while Andrew took Midnight.

'Is this your land we're on now?' Andrew enquired as they proceeded onwards, keeping the horses to a walking pace.

'Oh yes. Everything round here is ours.'

Andrew wondered just how rich the Fortescues were. Considerably, he reckoned. Though owning land didn't always equate with having money in the bank.

Andrew reined in Midnight when the Fortescue house came into view. Dear God, he thought, it made Drummond House look like a cottage! It was vast.

'Greystones,' Alice smiled to Andrew.

'Very imposing I must say.'

'Far too big of course, costs an absolute fortune to maintain. We only live in the central part, both wings have been shut off for years.'

'You're not a large family then?'

'No, only my parents and myself. They'd hoped for more children but weren't blessed.'

'I have a brother and two sisters myself,' Andrew informed her. 'While Billy here is one of five brothers of whom he's the youngest. That right, old thing?'

'That's right,' Billy confirmed.

'I'd have loved to have brothers and sisters,' Alice said wistfully. 'But it wasn't to be.'

'They're a dashed nuisance at times I can tell you,' Billy grumbled.

'True enough,' Andrew nodded.

'But you wouldn't be without them, surely?'

Andrew considered that. 'I suppose not. Billy?'

'I suppose not either. Though in the past, when I was growing up, they could make one's life a misery.'

'Well I'd still love to have someone,' Alice said.

They came on to a long drive that wound its way towards Greystones, the drive intermittently flanked by conifer trees. Then they were on to the driveway itself which, it seemed to Andrew, could have taken an entire regiment of cavalry.

They dismounted in front of terraced steps leading to a massive wooden door.

'Would you care to come in and dry out a bit?' Alice asked.

Andrew was about to accept when Billy produced his watch. 'I'm afraid that's impossible, Miss Alice. We really must be getting back.'

Andrew sighed. 'Duty calls I'm sad to say.' If Billy said it was time to get back then it was.

Alice's face creased with disappointment. She'd taken a shine to these two young, personable men. 'I can't thank you enough for what you did,' she said to Andrew.

'My pleasure, miss. In every cloud, what? It gave us a chance to make your acquaintance.'

A smile replaced the look of disappointment. 'You're most kind. Perhaps you'll call another day.'

'Perhaps,' Andrew replied.

He formally shook her hand after which Billy did the same. Then he and Billy remounted.

'Goodbye, Miss Alice,' Billy said.

'For now,' Andrew added.

They waved as they rode off.

Andrew brought himself back to the present with a shake

of the head. How clear it all was in his memory, that first day he'd met Alice. That day and many others. So very very clear.

He started when a hand was placed on his arm. 'Oh, Ellen, it's you. I never heard you come in.'

'Sorry, did I startle you?'

'No. Not really.'

Suddenly the last thing he wanted was Ellen in his bed. Not after what he'd just been remembering.

'I've changed my mind about tonight,' he said softly.

'I see.'

'Nothing to do with you, so don't worry. It's simply that I've decided to stay up and think about some things. Business matters.'

'In the dark?'

'I do my best thinking in the dark. Helps concentrate the mind.'

She hesitated. 'You're certain it's not me?'

'Absolutely, Ellen. Now toddle off.'

She gave him a quick peck on the cheek then quietly left the room.

The *last* thing he now wanted, he thought, taking off his heavy winter dressing-gown and climbing into bed.

He wondered what had become of Billy Roberts, they'd never kept in touch. He must ask Willie if he knew when he was at The Haven.

'Oh I'm sorry, sir,' Bridie said hastily and returned the book she'd been glancing through to its place.

Ian regarded her with amusement. 'Do you like books?'

'Oh yes, sir. I've always adored them.'

'And what was that one?'

'Dickens, sir.'

He raised an eyebrow. 'Have you ever read him?'

'Oh yes, sir. But I prefer Sir Walter Scott myself.'

Ian was amazed. A maid who read Dickens and Sir Walter Scott. How fascinating.

'It's a wonderful library, don't you think?' he smiled, making a gesture that took in the entire room.

'Oh yes, sir. That smell, it's unmistakable. Books, books and more books. It's a smell you only get in libraries and bookshops.'

'I see you're supposed to be dusting.'

'Yes, sir. I only stopped for a few moments. I swear.'

'The temptation was too much I take it.'

She coloured slightly. 'Yes, sir. I apologise, sir.'

'There's no need for that. We're not slave drivers after all. At least I hope we're not.'

'No, sir.'

He studied her, thinking how attractive she was. For a servant girl that is. 'You're from Glasgow I believe.'

'That's correct, sir.'

'It must be quite a change for you coming here.'

'It is, sir. A change for the better. The countryside is lovely. I plan long walks in it on my days off.'

'Indeed. And what about reading?'

Her face fell. 'That's the only problem, sir. I don't now get much time for that as you'll appreciate. And even if I had it's impossible for me to lay my hands on books. All mine came from the public library.'

'Which aren't exactly thick on the ground round here,' he commented wryly.

She grinned. 'Not exactly.'

'What's your name?'

'Bridie, sir.'

'It suits you. Sometimes people's names don't but yours most definitely does.'

He crossed to a large imposing desk, extracted a folder from one of its drawers, the reason he'd entered the library in the first place, and headed for the door.

'Goodbye for now, Bridie.'

'Goodbye, sir.'

She hurriedly resumed her dusting.

Chapter 11

'You remember Moira McLaren, don't you, Ian?' Rose smiled. It was the Hogmanay party and the drawing room was humming with conversation. In the end thirty invitations had been sent out, all of them taken up.

Ian's jaw nearly dropped open. My God! he thought. What a stunner. Where was the horrible little so and so he'd once known and thoroughly disliked? In Moira's case the ugly duckling truly had turned into a swan.

'Of course. How are you, Moira?' he said, extending a hand. The hand that briefly touched his was cool and elegant.

'I'm very well. And you?'

'Learning the estate business at the sharp end. Hard work, but enjoyable and rewarding.'

He took in her dress which was made of dainty all-over embroidered net, the skirt displaying graceful godet flare inserts of harmonising silk georgette crêpe that had also been used for a cascade scarf. A nosegay situated on the shoulder added a pretty touch.

Moira was thinking that he'd matured considerably. She warmed to him in a way she never had previously.

'I understand you're not long home from Switzerland,' he said.

'That's right.'

'And how was it there?'

She pulled a face. 'Boring beyond belief. But it did have its moments I suppose.'

'Wasn't it a finishing school?'

'The boredom nearly finished me off.'

Ian laughed.

'But now I'm back and that's all that matters.' She glanced around. 'Quite a do you've laid on. I've no doubt we're all going to have a wonderful time.'

'That was the idea. There'll be dancing later. Scottish dancing to an accordion. I do hope you'll have one, if not several, with me.'

'That would be jolly.'

'It's settled then.' He signalled to a maid carrying a tray of drinks.

'A little refreshment?' he proposed.

Rose smiled to herself. It was as though she wasn't there, Ian and Moira were so intently focused on one another.

Muttering an excuse she left them to it.

Georgina had managed to manoeuvre Andrew into a corner of the room where, temporarily at least, she had him to herself. The scent of the cologne he was wearing filled her nostrils. 'Well, Andrew, any young lady on the horizon yet?'

He found that somewhat direct, and wondered at the strange glint in her eyes. 'I'm afraid not, Georgina.'

'Maybe I shall do something about that.'

He regarded her quizzically. 'Who exactly do you have in mind?'

Myself, she thought. Though would never have dared say so. 'That's my secret, Andrew.'

'Secret, eh?'

She was teasing him now. 'I don't want any resistance on your part. I know what men can be like when they think something, or someone in this instance, is being pushed at them.'

'Hmmh,' he murmured, and had a sip of champagne.

Rose was watching them enviously, wishing it was she who was with Andrew. The two of them alone together.

'I say, Rose?'

She turned her attention to Alastair Dundee, a drippy lad who'd been mad on her for years. 'Yes, Alastair?'

It was a good five minutes before she could get away.

Bridie was helping lay out the buffet supper that Mrs Kilbride and the kitchen staff had been slaving over for days. There was enough to feed the entire British army, she thought as she placed a platter of smoked ham on one of the special trestle tables that had been brought in for the occasion.

Ham, venison, hare, rabbit, pork, beef, those were the meats. Then there were salads of all varieties, potatoes, bread, pickles and chutneys. The *pièce de résistance* was an enormous bowl of trifle dominating the centre of the buffet. Her mouth watered just looking at it all.

'Some feast, eh?' Jeannie Swanson commented, placing yet another platter alongside the one Bridie had just put down.

'I'll say.'

'I hate to think what all this must have cost.'

'A king's ransom,' Bridie said.

'Aye, no doubt.'

'Still, you have to admit, it does look gorgeous.'

'Oh, to be a toff,' Jeannie sighed.

'Rather than be a toff you'll be unemployed if you don't stop chattering and get on with it,' a well-known voice rebuked them.

Both girls swung round to find the housekeeper there.

'Sorry, Miss Coltart,' Jeannie gulped.

'I should think so. Now hurry up, there's still plenty more to be done.'

Bridie and Jeannie scurried away.

'Enjoying yourself?' Willie asked Andrew a while later.

'Very much so.'

'Get enough to eat?'

'Plenty, and more.'

Willie nodded his approval. 'Good.'

'Some interesting people here tonight. I had a marvellous chat with a chap called Ogilvie.'

'Oh yes,' Willie said. 'Richard Ogilvie. Bit of an explorer in his time. Did he mention?'

'Yes. I found his tales of Africa quite fascinating.'

Willie glanced around. 'Can't see Georgina anywhere. Seems to have vanished.'

Andrew couldn't spot her either. 'Probably a call of nature, old boy. Or caught up elsewhere.'

'Probably.'

Willie took out his pocket watch and snapped it open. 'About an hour to go.'

'The new year, 1925,' Andrew mused. 'I wonder what that will bring.'

'I wonder,' Willie repeated.

* * *

'Ladies and gentlemen, can I have your attention please!' Willie called out.

Gradually silence descended.

'Five minutes to midnight. Can you all please ensure that your glasses are charged.'

Bridie was one of those whose duty it was to see that this was the case.

Rose joined Andrew. 'It's hot in here, isn't it.'

'Bound to be with so many people present. Not to mention several fires blazing.'

There was a sheen of sweat on Andrew's neck which Rose found fascinating. She blushed at the sudden thought of licking it off.

'You all right?'

'As I said, it's hot.'

'You're not going to faint or anything, are you?'

She smiled. 'Of course not, silly. I'm fine, simply hot that's all.' In truth, if she was being honest, it wasn't only the heat of the room that was making her that way, but also the proximity of Andrew.

'Miss Rose, a top up?' Bridie queried, brandishing a bottle of champagne.

'Please.'

'And you, sir?' she asked as she filled Rose's glass.

'Thank you.'

When she'd done that Bridie moved swiftly on.

'That's a nice cologne you're wearing,' Rose remarked. 'I noticed it earlier.'

'I'm glad you like it.'

'More men should wear cologne I always think.'

'Yes, I quite agree. But it is a personal thing. Many men consider it effeminate.'

Something Andrew could never be accused of, Rose

thought. He was one hundred per cent male. His maleness positively oozed out of him.

'A minute to go!' Willie called out.

Rose knew what she was going to do, and thrilled inside at the prospect.

It was almost as if everyone in the room was holding his or her breath, Andrew thought, staring out over the assembly. There again, this was the biggest moment in the Scottish calendar. The English could have their Christmas, for the Scots it was Hogmanay. Seeing out the old year and ushering in the new.

'Ten . . . nine . . . eight . . .' Willie counted down.

Willie raised his glass aloft. 'A happy new year to ane an' a!'

The room erupted, well wishing, back slapping, handshaking and toasting going on everywhere.

'A happy new year, Andrew,' Rose said, gazing deeply into his eyes.

'And a happy new year to you, Rose.'

He bent to kiss her on the cheek, but at the very last instant she moved her face so that his lips landed on hers.

That startled Andrew, who only now remembered what Jack Riach had said about Rose.

Rose wished Andrew would put his free arm round her, but naturally that was out of the question. But it would have been lovely.

'Well,' Andrew murmured when their lips parted.

Suddenly embarrassed, Rose glanced away. She didn't regret having done that, not in the least. She only wished she could do it again.

The accordionist appeared and immediately struck up. It was now time for the dancing.

People moved away from the centre of the room to line the walls. The furniture had been rearranged the previous day so that there was now a large area where the dancing could take place.

Willie took Georgina's hand and led her on to the floor, quickly joined there by others.

The accordionist stopped, announced an eightsome reel, and then struck up again.

Ian was already up with Moira McLaren.

'Rose?'

Her heart leapt. 'If you're asking me to dance I'd love to, Andrew.'

'Then shall we?'

'Here you are, Bridie,' Miss Coltart said, handing her a schooner of sherry.

'Thank you, miss.'

'It's the only time of the year I condone drinking amongst the staff. But it is Hogmanay after all.'

'Yes, miss. Happy new year.'

Miss Coltart's face softened. 'And you, Bridie.'

There was still masses to do, the celebrations would go on for hours yet, so Bridie didn't linger over her drink.

At last, Georgina thought some time later, when she saw Andrew approach. She'd been waiting for him to ask her up, which he was now surely going to do.

'The whisky is all Drummond you'll be pleased to hear.' Willie beamed at Andrew.

'I should hope so.'

'Champagne is fine, but it gets tedious after a bit. Not like good old Scottish whisky, eh?'

'Never that.' Willie had quite a load on board, Andrew noted. Unlike himself who'd been taking it easy.

'I was wondering if you care to dance, Georgina?' he asked.

'I'd be delighted to.' She handed her glass to Willie. 'Take care of that for me, darling, will you? Andrew and I are about to trip the light fantastic.'

Andrew laughed. 'Hardly that.'

'We'll see.'

It was a rare event for Willie to get drunk, but he certainly was now. He sat heavily on their bed and ran a hand over his perspiring forehead.

'Went excellently I thought,' he slurred.

'Yes it did.'

He struggled out of his jacket and threw it aside. 'Wine and whisky, shouldn't mix them.'

'No you shouldn't.'

He beckoned to her. 'Come here.'

Georgina crossed to Willie who pulled her on to his knee. 'You were the belle of the ball tonight. Know that?'

'Was I?'

'Without a doubt. By far the best-looking woman there. I couldn't have been more proud.'

She hoped he wasn't going to kiss her, which he promptly did. His lips were sloppily wet which she found disgusting.

'How about a little . . . ?' He broke off and winked slyly at her.

Georgina laughed. 'You're in no fit state for that sort of thing, Willie Seaton. You wouldn't be able to manage it.'

'How do we know unless I try?'

'I know all right. Now the best thing for you is to crawl

into that bed and get some sleep. You're going to have a dreadful hangover in the morning.'

'Never!'

'Oh yes you will.'

She slipped from his lap. 'Here, let me help you with those trousers.

'Don't need any help,' he further slurred.

She stood watching in amusement as he struggled with his braces, eventually managing to pull them over his arms. 'You're right, it is difficult,' he confessed.

'Let me.'

She removed his shoes and socks, then assisted him out of his trousers. 'I'll hang this lot up,' she declared.

Willie wormed his way up the bed until his head was resting on the pillows. He closed one eye in order to try and focus, something he was suddenly having a problem with. 'Best-looking woman there,' he repeated.

Moments later he began to snore.

Bridie's last thoughts before she dropped off were about Teresa. As always she'd remembered Teresa in her prayers and asked God to forgive her.

She recalled the funeral and how awful that had been. As had the wake afterwards. During the latter Mrs Kelly had drawn her aside.

She'd denied knowledge of knowing anything. As far as she was concerned Teresa had died of a sudden haemorrhage, presumably the result of internal bleeding, and that was that.

Mrs Kelly hadn't believed her, but was willing to accept she'd keep her mouth shut about the real reason for Teresa's death. It was an unspoken pact between them to save Teresa's reputation and the Kelly family's good name.

Goodnight, Teresa, she said in her mind.

Then she was asleep.

Georgina sat staring at herself in her vanity mirror. Dare she? Dare she actually do it?

She pulled the duck-egg blue negligée she was wearing tighter about herself. She knew such things went on, were commonplace even in certain circles. It was wrong of course, terribly wrong. But oh so very tempting.

Willie snorted and turned over. Georgina glanced at him and thought of their lovemaking two days previously. Another failure as far as she was concerned. He'd left her so high up in the air it had taken ages for her to come down again. Nor, because of the circumstances, had she been able to give herself satisfaction.

Georgina drew in a deep breath, then slowly exhaled. She was tipsy, but not to the point where her thinking was muddled, not fully appreciating what she was contemplating. There would be no excuses come morning.

She smiled inwardly. Hardly come morning for it was already that. But it would be hours before anyone stirred in the house, apart from a few of the staff. The party had finished so late it would be noon before most were up and about.

Dare she? That was the question. She could make an awful fool of herself which would be terrible. There again, as the saying went, nothing ventured nothing gained.

And she was so curious. So very very curious.

Andrew came groggily awake, dimly aware that Ellen was sitting on his bed. Now why was that, he hadn't asked her to come? Then he remembered he wasn't home but at The Haven. His eyes snapped open.

'Sshhh!' Georgina whispered, placing a finger over her lips.

'Georg . . . what's wrong?'

'Nothing's wrong.'

'Then why the hell are you here?'

'I just wanted to . . . be with you.'

'Jesus Christ!' Andrew swore, pulling himself upright. 'Where's Willie?'

'Sound asleep, drunk as can be. It'll be hours and hours before he comes to.'

Andrew's mind was whirling. This was bloody dangerous. 'You'd better get back to him at once. On you go and we'll forget all about this madness.'

'Please don't be cross with me,' she pleaded.

'I'm not cross.'

'Yes you are.'

He studied her in the darkness. 'What do you mean *be* with me?'

'I should think that was obvious.'

'But you . . . you're Willie's wife and he's my good friend.'

'I know,' she replied softly, reaching out for his hand which he quickly snatched away.

'I thought you found me attractive,' she said. 'I've seen it in your eyes.'

'I do, Georgina.'

'As I do you.'

'That doesn't alter matters. I can't take advantage of a friend's wife. Only a bounder would do that.'

Georgina hung her head. 'It wasn't easy for me to come here. I knew I risked making a fool of myself.'

He softened towards her. 'You haven't done that.'

'No?'

'You've simply made a mistake, that's all.'

'I see.'

'Now you'd better leave.'

Georgina shivered. 'It's cold in here. Our room is far warmer.'

'Then you'd better get back there.'

'I don't want you to think I make a habit of this kind of thing. The truth is, I've only ever been with one man in my life, and that's Willie.'

Andrew wasn't sure whether to believe that or not. 'Why me then?'

'Because you fascinate me. I keep wondering what it would be like being made love to by you. I wonder all the time and have done ever since meeting you.'

Andrew swallowed hard. Dear God, he'd never realised. Forbidden fruit, he reminded himself. Beyond the Pale. 'I'm flattered, Georgina, honestly I am. If things had been different I wouldn't hesitate. If you were even someone else's wife, not a friend's. But I just couldn't.'

'I understand.'

Damn it, he thought. He was becoming aroused. If only she didn't smell so damned gorgeous. She moved slightly so that one of her breasts was silhouetted against the curtained window.

He swore again when she began to cry softly.

'You mustn't do that. You musn't,' he pleaded.

'I'm sorry.'

And then Georgina played her trump card. The one she'd hoped she wouldn't have to play. But having gone this far, why not?

Standing, she slowly undid the belt of her negligée, and held the garment open. 'I want you to see what you're missing before I go.'

It was too much. What a sight. What a glorious sight. His resistance crumbled.

Andrew banished Willie from his mind as, with a groan, he reached for her.

Georgina lay staring at the ceiling, not having slept a wink. Alongside her Willie continued to snore.

She couldn't believe what it had been like. The sensations she'd felt, the things Andrew had done to her. Again and again he'd brought her to fruition until she'd thought she must surely die from the sheer pleasure of it all.

She ran her hands over her breasts, they still throbbing, over her stomach and along her thighs. Thighs Andrew had so recently been between.

What an experience. One simply out of this world. And to think she'd been missing that all these years. Compared to Andrew, Willie was . . . well, pathetic. There was no other word for it. Pathetic.

That wasn't fair, she chided herself. She was being cruel. But it was true nonetheless.

Andrew. She wanted to shout his name aloud. A few short hours and she'd come to worship the man.

She shivered in recollection of how it had been between them.

Andrew was pacing his bedroom as he'd been doing since shortly after Georgina had left. How could he have been so stupid. So bloody weak willed! What he'd done was appalling.

One thing was certain, it must never happen again. If Willie ever found out it would destroy the poor bugger, and that was something he never wanted to have on his conscience.

He'd been all right until she'd opened her negligée. Then he'd been lost. Quite overcome at the sight of that voluptuousness.

Andrew stopped and ran fingers through his hair. Go home straight away? That's what he wanted to do. But what would he say to Willie, what possible excuse could he make? None he could think of.

Willie would be upset to say the least, wishing to know why he was going. What was wrong. Had he been insulted. What?

No, he had to stay and brazen it out. That was all he could do. And pray Georgina didn't pay him any more visits.

He glanced at the door which he'd already checked earlier. It didn't have a lock, worst luck. He'd have felt a great deal safer if it had.

Andrew threw himself into a chair. What he wouldn't have given for a glass of whisky right then. Several glasses. And now he was going to have to get dressed and go downstairs. How long before he had to face Willie? Not long he shouldn't think.

He must keep the guilt out of his face. He must.

Andrew swore viciously, bitterly regretting what he'd done. At least part of him did.

If only she'd been someone else's bloody wife!

He met Georgina first, bumping into her in the corridor. She was positively glowing.

'Hello, Andrew,' she beamed.

'Hello, Georgina.'

'There's some late buffet luncheon set out to tide us over to dinner. I've already had a plateful myself.'

'How's Willie?'

She chuckled. 'Like a bear with a sore head, which is

precisely what he has. An extremely sore head according to him.'

'Is he up and about?'

'Well, he is up, but I'm not sure whether he's about yet.' She dropped her voice. 'Andrew . . .'

'No,' he interjected quickly. 'It never happened, understand? It just never happened.'

'Oh, but it did,' she replied, eyes sparking.

He stared at her in dismay. 'Well, it won't ever again. I assure you.'

She touched him lightly on the arm. 'I thought you enjoyed it.'

'I did. But that's irrelevant.'

Now that she'd tasted the delights he had to offer she wasn't about to give them up. Oh no. Somehow, some way, Andrew would be hers. She'd decided that while dressing.

'I'd better get along,' Andrew said.

'Goodbye for now . . . lover.'

Andrew blanched, and moved on his way.

'You look very sombre.'

Andew turned to find Rose standing beside him. 'Do I?'

'Sombre to the point of being grim. Have you also got a hangover?'

Andrew shook his head. 'I feel right as rain.'

'Poor Father. He swears he'll never mix wine and whisky ever again.'

'I haven't seen him yet. Is he that bad?'

'Terrible. His eyes are all sunken and he cut himself shaving. He's feeling very sorry for himself.'

'He'll survive.' Andrew laughed. 'I should know. I've suffered a few hangovers in my time.'

'Were you very wild when younger?'

That surprised him. 'Why do you ask?'

'You have that air about you. I think you must have been very wild.'

'A bit,' he acknowledged.

'I think young men should be. It shows spirit. And every worthwhile man should have that.'

'I see. I take it you're an expert on these matters,' he teased.

'Perhaps I am.'

He didn't want to pursue this any further. 'I've been standing here looking out this window contemplating, strange as it may seem, having a drink. Would you care to join me?'

'There's nothing I'd like better, Andrew.'

'Then let's find one.'

Chapter 12

It was his first day back at work after the new year which didn't please Pat Flynn one little bit. He'd much rather have been home in front of a nice cosy fire than out here in the snow. He glanced up at a leaden grey sky from which millions of swirling snowflakes were falling. No signs of a let-up there he thought.

He reined in Jasper when he spotted one of their cards in a window. Another sale, one of many in an exceptionally busy morning. He'd have to return to the depot shortly and reload. At least that meant he'd get a cup of tea.

He was about to jump down from the cart when a couple appeared round a corner heading in his direction. It was Geraldine and Dougal, the pair arm in arm.

Dougal said something which caused Geraldine to laugh and pull herself even more tightly to him. She looked happy as Larry.

Pat turned his face away, not wanting them to see his expression. Jesus, but he was jealous.

'Why, hello, Mr Flynn,' Geraldine said as they came alongside.

'Hello, Mrs Buchanan. And you, Mr Buchanan.'

'Not the best of days for your job,' Dougal commented with a smile.

Pat shrugged. 'That's how it goes.'

Then they'd gone past, continuing on their way.

Pat glared after them. How long to go before Dougal went back to sea?

He wished to hell he knew.

'You what!' Jack Riach exclaimed. It was a Friday night and he and Andrew were in the local.

'You heard me.'

Jack sat back in his chair. 'I'm disappointed in you, Andrew.'

'I'm disappointed in myself. I feel rotten about it.'

'I should think so.'

Andrew had a swallow of whisky. 'You should have seen her though, Jack. She's got a magnificent body.'

'Which you simply couldn't resist,' Jack replied sarcastically.

'She was standing there naked, flaunting herself in front of me. I'm not made of stone, Jack. I'm only flesh and blood after all.'

'She's that good looking?'

'Believe me, she is.'

'And she just turned up in your bedroom out of the blue?'

'Out of the blue, Jack, I swear.'

'Had you been leading her on in any way? You know, flirting and that sort of thing?'

'No I hadn't. I did dance with her at the party of course,

well that was obligatory. She was my hostess after all. Manners dictated that I did. Not that it was a chore, quite the contrary.'

'How extraordinary,' Jack commented, feeling for his pint.

'I kept as much out of Willie's way for the rest of my stay there as I could. Out of his way and Georgina's. I ended up spending quite a lot of time with Rose.' Andrew hesitated, then said, 'You were right about Rose.'

'You didn't . . . not Rose as well?'

'Of course not!'

'I'm glad to hear it,' Jack replied drily.

'She is very pleasant to be with. In fact she rather reminds me of . . .' He broke off.

'Who, Andrew?'

'Nobody.'

Jack smiled. 'I can hear it in your voice, old boy. It's Alice, am I right?'

'Only a little. The occasional gesture, the odd inflection. What she does do is ride like Alice, there were times when, if I hadn't known better, I would have sworn I was back in Ireland and it was Alice I was watching.'

'Interesting,' Jack mused. 'Speaking of Ireland, how does all this affect your plans?'

'I did consider cancelling, but Willie would be terribly put out if I did.'

'So you'll still go.'

'Yes.'

'And what if Mrs Seaton takes it upon herself to visit you again?'

'She won't, I'm convinced of that. Hotels are too public, Jack. Besides, hotel bedrooms have locks on their doors. So I'll be quite safe.'

Jack chuckled. 'It's funny hearing you talk about being safe from a woman. Usually it's the other way round, or it used to be in the past anyway. They had to worry about being safe from you.'

'Aye, true,' Andrew said with a smile. 'But that was a long while ago. Before Alice.'

'Before Alice,' Jack repeated, and nodded his understanding. He couldn't imagine what it would be like to lose Hettie. The end of the world as far as he'd be concerned. Hettie had become everything to him. Hettie and wee Tommy.

Andrew had a swallow of whisky, emptying his glass. Following that with a pull from his pint. 'Anyway, I really want to go to Ireland now. I was in two minds for quite some time, not sure at all how I'll react. And I'm still not sure. But I've come to the conclusion that it'll be a good thing for me to go back. No matter what happens.'

'Well, it couldn't be going better,' Sean Flynn declared to the rest of the Samurai. They were gathered together in the condemned tenement.

He indicated the pile of money in front of him. 'Look at that, eh?'

'It's like taking sweeties from a baby,' Sammy Renton chuckled. 'A few words from you, Sean, a bit of a threat like, and they're falling over themselves to give us cash.'

Sean nodded, that was true enough. After Rizzio it had just got easier and easier as word got round. The shopkeepers not already on their list were almost reaching for their tills the moment he and some of the others walked through the door.

'So what are we going to do with it?' Bobby O'Toole queried, gesturing at the money.

'A divvy?' Dan Smith suggested hopefully. 'Then we could all go straight down the boozer and have a whale of a time.'

'That's a possibility,' Sean acknowledged.

'Do you have something in mind?' Jim Gallagher asked, guessing that he did.

'I have.' Sean paused for effect. He was getting the hang of this leader thing, he thought. 'I propose we use it to rent ourselves a proper place which we can fill with decent furniture.'

'A proper place?' Jim frowned.

'Aye, look about you. This house stinks and it's got rats in it. I hate rats.'

'We could get a cat,' Bill O'Connell joked.

'Bugger a cat,' Sean snapped in reply. 'A decent house with decent furniture. Now what do you say?'

'I still fancy a divvy,' Dan Smith grumbled.

'Shall we take a vote on it then?'

Dan Smith was the only one to vote against the house and furniture idea.

Ian was shown into a room where Moira and her mother were sitting. It was a Sunday afternoon. His eyes immediately sought out Moira's.

'Why, Ian, how nice of you to call,' Delphine McLaren declared.

'I hope I'm not intruding.'

'Not at all. We were just about to take coffee. Will you join us?'

'That would be lovely.'

'If you'd ring that bell pull for us then.'

Ian crossed to the indicated bell pull and tugged it. He then returned to the ladies and sat close to Moira. He'd have liked to sit beside her on the sofa but thought that a bit forward.

She'd expected this to happen, Delphine thought with satisfaction. She hadn't failed to notice how well Ian and Moira had got on during Hogmanay. Well, it certainly suited her purposes, the Seatons were an excellent family to marry into, should it come to that. Which she fervently hoped it would.

The three of them began making small talk.

'Is something wrong or worrying you, darling?' Willie enquired.

Georgina, at her vanity table brushing out her hair, glanced at him in the mirror. 'No, why do you ask?'

He shrugged. 'You haven't been quite yourself of late. In fact since the party.'

'I can't say I've noticed.'

'Distant somehow, detached.'

She carefully laid her brush on the table and turned to face him. Oh dear, she thought. Had she been distant and detached? She certainly hadn't meant to be.

'It's probably the time of year,' she smiled. 'I've never enjoyed winter as you well know.'

He gave an inward sigh of relief. It would appear he hadn't offended her in any way, which he'd thought might be the case. 'I wondered if it was me getting drunk on Hogmanay? I did apologise as you will remember.'

'No, silly. I wasn't put out by that. Most of the male guests were one over the eight when they left anyway, why should you be any different? Hogmanay is Hogmanay after all.'

She must be more careful in future she told herself. Truth was since new year's morning she hadn't been able to get

Andrew out of her mind, awake and asleep. Andrew, and their lovemaking. How she desperately craved for another bout of that. Craved so much there were times it made her teeth ache.

As for Willie, she hadn't exactly gone off him. No, that would be taking it too far. He was still the kind, generous man he'd always been, and still a most unsatisfactory lover. Perhaps she had been somewhat detached as Willie put it. Yes, she must be more careful.

'Anyway, Ireland is coming up shortly,' Willie went on. 'I'm sure a break away from here will do you the world of good. Buck you up, what?'

'I'm sure,' she replied, returning to her brushing.

She couldn't have been more sure about anything. For Ireland meant Andrew.

She didn't know how. But she'd engineer another bout of lovemaking between the pair of them.

She trembled at the thought.

'Come in, Mr Flynn,' Geraldine Buchanan said.

Mr Flynn, that meant Dougal was still there. Pat swore inwardly.

'You know where the bin is. I'll just go and fetch some money.'

Pat upended the coal bag into the bin. How much longer before that sod Dougal went back to sea? How much bloody longer!

Geraldine reappeared. 'And how have you been, Mr Flynn?'

'Fine, thank you.'

'All this snow gets you down, don't you think?'

He nodded, accepting a ten-shilling note from her. He delved in his bag for change.

'Thank you,' she said, accepting it.

'Goodbye for now then.'

She let him get to the door. 'Oh, before you go.'

He hesitated. 'Yes?'

Her face broke into a huge smile. 'Would you care for a bottle of beer, Pat?'

'Bottle of . . .' He broke off, had the cow been teasing him? 'Where's Dougal?'

'Gone away again. Two days ago. And it'll be a long voyage. He doesn't know where but he does know it'll be a long one.'

'You . . .'

Geraldine tinkled a laugh. 'I couldn't resist it, Pat. I simply couldn't. Your face when I offered you the beer was a picture.'

'This Friday?' he croaked.

'I'll be waiting.'

She bent to open a cupboard, provocatively sticking her bottom in the air.

If Pat hadn't been so filthy he'd have had her there and then.

'Hey, you, come here!'

The pimply-faced lad turned to face Sean and Mo Binchy. 'Aye, what is it?'

'You've been nicking off Harris's the newsagent's. Haven't you?'

'Fuck off.'

He made to move away but Sean grabbed him and spun him round. 'I'm talking to you, son. Where's your manners?'

'Who the hell are you?'

'We're the Samurai and we give Mr Harris protection. Do you understand?'

For a moment fear flickered in the youth's eyes. He'd heard of the Samurai. 'Protection?'

Sean produced his razor. 'That's right.'

Pimple face stared at the razor, then up again at Sean. His mouth had gone dry. 'I didn't know that,' he replied, still trying to give an outward show of bravado.

'Well, now you do. I'm giving you a warning. If it happens again we'll come after you, and when we find you . . .' Sean flicked his razor several times. 'Mince.'

There was no reply to that.

'Have I made myself clear?'

The youth, his assumed bravado ebbing away, nodded. He knew what the result of a razoring was like.

'Now hop it. Bugger off.'

The youth didn't exactly leave at a run, but it wasn't far off it.

Pat swaggered into the kitchen. 'Well, that's me off to my committee meeting,' he announced.

'You look very smart, Pa,' Alison said.

He beamed at her. 'Why, thank you, lass.'

'You do indeed,' Kathleen declared. 'I'm right proud to see you like that.'

If only you knew, he thought. If only you knew.

Bridie brushed snow off a fallen tree, making a space for herself, and sat. How stupid this was, how incredibly bloody stupid. She banged her gloved hands together trying to restore some warmth to them. She was frozen through.

A glance at the sky told her it wouldn't be long before it got dark. What then? She daren't even think of that.

She mustn't panic she told herself. That would be fatal. Once she'd caught her breath she must trudge on.

'Hello.'

Bridie started and swivelled round to find Ian Seaton staring at her, his expression one of puzzlement. She gasped with relief. 'Thank God!'

'What are you doing out here all by yourself?'

She rose from the tree. 'It's my day off and I went for a walk. Only somehow I got lost.'

'I see.'

'I've absolutely no idea where I am.'

He smiled. 'City girls shouldn't go wandering around the countryside alone. Especially not in weather like this. What if I hadn't happened along?'

She hung her head. 'I know. I've just been telling myself how stupid I've been.'

'How long have you been out here?'

She shook her head. 'Ages. And a lot of that time has been spent trying to find my way back again.' Bridie suddenly sobbed. 'I've been so scared.'

Ian went to her and took her into his arms. 'There there. It's all right now. You're safe.'

'You must think me a fool.'

'Not a fool exactly. Silly perhaps, but not a fool. As I said, city girls shouldn't go wandering around the countryside alone. Especially . . .'

'Not in weather like this,' she finished for him.

They both laughed, which brightened her considerably.

'Let's make a move then,' he said. 'Are you up to it?'

'I'll have to be. I'm certainly not staying here.'

She fell into step beside him. 'Where have you been?' she asked.

'There's a stretch of fence been blown down and I was sent out to see precisely what the damage was.'

'Lucky for me you were.' Bridie glanced about her.

'These trees are spooky.' They were passing through a large wood.

'Only if you're not used to this sort of thing. I find them rather comforting myself.'

'Comforting?' She found that hard to believe.

He nodded. 'Yes. But don't forget I was brought up on the estate and know it in all its moods and seasons.'

'It's very large, isn't it? The estate I mean.'

'Very.'

Somewhere an owl hooted, a melancholy sound.

'The trouble started when I left the path I was on,' Bridie explained. 'I wanted to explore. Except I explored too far and couldn't find the path, or any other path, again.'

'Next time I suggest you don't leave the path, or go beyond sight of the house.'

'Don't worry, I won't. I'll be extremely careful from now on.' Bridie shivered. 'I've probably caught my death of cold.'

'Have a bath when you get back.'

'I can't. We're only allowed one a week and I'm not due mine till next Tuesday.'

Ian had forgotten about those particular staff arrangements. 'Tell you what, I'll have a word with Mrs Coltart. I'm sure she'll make an exception in this case.'

'That's very kind of you.'

'It's the least I can do.' He smiled.

What a lovely smile, she thought, really noticing it for the first time. 'I shall always think of you as my knight in shining armour,' she declared.

That amused him. 'Why so?'

'Well, I was a damsel in dire distress and you came to my rescue. My knight in shining armour.'

He laughed, liking the idea.

'Perhaps I shouldn't have said that, me being a maid and you the son of the house. I didn't mean to be impertinent.'

'I know that, Bridie.'

'Thank you.'

He'd forgotten she read a lot, no doubt where her fanciful ideas came from.

They emerged from the wood into a field bounded on three sides by high hedges. 'The house is about half a mile from here. It shouldn't take us too long.'

Bridie was glad about that, she was exhausted.

'Have you ever read the story of Robin Hood?' he asked.

'Oh yes. It was terrific, though sad at the end when he died.'

'Then you know of Maid Marian.'

'Of course.'

He was teasing her now. 'That's how I shall think of *you* in future. If I'm the knight in shining armour you shall be Maid Bridie. As you said, you are a maid after all.'

'But not that sort.'

'No?'

If she hadn't been so cold she'd have blushed on realising to what he was referring. 'Well, yes I am.'

'So Maid Bridie you shall be.'

She wasn't going to let him get entirely away with that. 'And you will be Sir Ian of Seaton.'

'Done.'

Sir Ian of Seaton, that further amused him.

Kathleen was on her way home from 'the steamie' as the communal wash house was known. She was struggling under the weight of the weekly laundry.

It never seemed to let up, she thought. From morning to

night it was all go. Cooking, cleaning, ironing, on and on it went in a never-ending circle.

Sometimes she wished . . . But what was the point in wishing for something that would never happen? Her lot was housewife and mother with the drudgery that accompanied those roles. Drudgery that made you old before your time. Lined your face, ruined your figure, reddened and chapped your hands.

She sighed. A nice cup of tea when she got in. And a biscuit she'd put by. Then it was down to ironing before Alison arrived home from school.

At least it wasn't all bad, she reflected. Bridie was working for toffs and her man was on a very important committee.

Aye, it wasn't all bad.

Hettie had watched Jack get more and more fidgety with every passing day. From past experience she knew what that was leading to.

'Monday morning,' Jack suddenly said. 'We'll make a start then.'

'All right.'

He shook his head. 'I'm still not certain I can manage a novel though.'

'Well, you won't know until you try, will you?'

'That's true enough,' he grudgingly admitted, and gnawed a thumbnail.

'There's something I've been meaning to speak to you about, Jack. Do you think you could buy me a typewriter?'

'A typewriter,' he mused. 'I can do that without any bother. But don't you have to go on some kind of course to learn how to use one?'

'That's the proper way of doing it, but I can hardly go on a course in Dalneil.'

They both laughed, their village being a small one.

'So I thought I'd try and teach myself. It can't be that difficult. I shall simply persevere until I've mastered it.'

And master it she would, he thought. That was his Hettie for you.

'It would make it all so much easier, Jack. And more professional too.'

He nodded. 'A typewriter you shall have.'

Too late for this book, Hettie reflected. But if Jack did manage a full manuscript there might be others.

'Monday morning,' he repeated, and went back to gnawing his thumbnail.

Bridie snuffled into one of several hankies she'd had to borrow, feeling wretched beyond belief.

The bedroom door swung open, and moments later Jeannie Swanson breezed in carrying a tray. 'Your luncheon, madam,' Jeannie announced in an affected posh voice.

Bridie struggled to sit up in bed where she'd been sent by Mrs Coltart when the heavy cold had manifested itself. Mrs Coltart had said she was to stay there until better.

'What is it?'

'Chicken broth and freshly baked bread. Mrs Kilbride told me she doesn't want to see anything left when the tray is returned.' Jeannie set the tray in front of Bridie. 'And a book from Master Ian.'

Bridie's eyes lit up. Sure enough, there was also a book on the tray.

'How kind of him,' she breathed.

'Gave it to me personally. Said it should help keep boredom at bay.'

Bridie picked up the book and glanced at the title, delighted it wasn't one she'd already read. '*Fame*,' she murmured. 'By Micheline Keating.' A quick glance at the back informed her it was the story of a great actress who rose from the gutter, and of her daughter who eclipsed her triumphs. 'I say, it couldn't be better. Sounds like a cracking tale.' She frowned. 'I wonder where Master Ian got it from?' Not leather bound, it clearly wasn't part of the library downstairs.

'He explained that. Said his sister Rose bought it last time she was in Edinburgh. He also mentioned that Miss Rose reads a bit herself and will be happy to lend you more books in future.'

'How wonderful. When you next see the pair of them will you thank them for me?'

'I'll do that,' Jeannie replied. 'Now you get on with that soup before it gets cold.'

Bridie laid the book to one side and hurriedly attacked her meal. She couldn't wait to get started on *Fame*.

Jeannie laughed as she left the bedroom. She'd never seen Bridie so excited. The book would do her the world of good.

Willie lit a cigarette and sucked the smoke deep into his lungs, thinking how enjoyable a cigarette was directly after a meal.

'You've been seeing Moira McLaren, I understand.' Georgina smiled at Ian.

He glanced over at his stepmother. 'That's right.'

'Is it serious?'

Rose sniggered, which earned her a disapproving look from Georgina.

Ian shrugged, trying to be nonchalant. 'I've no idea. It's early days yet.'

'But you do like her?'

'I'd hardly be seeing Moira if I didn't,' he replied sarcastically.

'Pretty lass,' Willie commented.

'Good figure,' Rose added, and sniggered again.

'Rose!' Georgina admonished.

Ian glared at his sister. Trust Georgina to bring up the subject of Moira when Rose was present.

'When are you seeing her again?' Georgina queried.

Ian sighed. 'With all due respect, isn't that my business?'

'I'm only showing an interest.'

Being nosy more like, Ian thought.

'Have you kissed her yet?'

'That's enough, Rose,' Willie said quietly.

'Well, I too was only showing an interest, Pa.' She rounded again on Ian. 'So?'

'That's for me to know and you to wonder about.'

And having said that Ian got up and left the room.

Bloody prying women, he thought angrily.

Chapter 13

Andrew stood on deck staring out over the choppy sea. There it was, just discernible, the coast of Ireland.

He closed his eyes. Remembering . . . remembering . . .

'I don't believe it,' Billy Roberts exclaimed softly. 'I just don't believe it.' He and Andrew were sitting by themselves in the mess having a drink, and Billy had just glanced at the front page of that evening's newspaper.

'Don't believe what, old boy?' Andrew smiled.

'Wait a moment, let me read this through.'

Andrew sipped his whisky, wondering what had perturbed his friend.

Billy looked at Andrew, his expression grim. 'It's the Fortescues,' he said, voice tight.

'What about them?'

'They're dead!'

It was a joke, Andrew thought. Billy was pulling his leg. 'Oh yes? All three I suppose.'

'All three,' Billy nodded. 'Here, read for yourself.' And with that he passed the newspaper to Andrew.

The headline hit Andrew like a hammer blow. Greystones, their home, had been gutted by fire. He went white as he read through the report.

'I am sorry,' Billy murmured when Andrew finally stared up from the paper.

Andrew was in shock, his mind reeling. This couldn't be true. It had to be a lie. It had to be. Alice, *his* Alice dead!

'Let me get you a refill,' Billy said, and picking up Andrew's glass he hurried to the bar.

Andrew started re-reading the article. The tragedy had occurred the previous night according to it, the entire family and some servants perishing in the blaze. Other servants had escaped to raise the alarm, to no avail. Arson was suspected.

Alice! Dear sweet Alice whom he loved and was engaged to. Alice dead.

Billy was still at the bar as Andrew rose and stumbled from the mess. All he wanted was to be alone.

Alice dead.

It was impossible. Impossible.

He managed to hold back the tears until his room door was shut and locked behind him.

'Andrew?'

Andrew blinked, then turned to find Willie standing a few feet away. 'Oh, hello.'

Willie stared at him in concern. 'I say, are you all right?'

Andrew pulled out a hanky and pretended to blow his nose, but was actually wiping tears from his eyes. 'Perfectly.'

'You do look rather rough, old boy. Here, have a swig from this.'

Willie produced a hip flask which he handed to Andrew.

'Thank you, I don't mind if I do. It's damned chilly out here. Doesn't take long to get through to the bones.'

Andrew unscrewed the flask's top and took a deep swallow. He sighed. 'That's better.'

'I think I'll join you.'

Willie also had a swallow and then stowed the flask away again, into the depths of the heavy Crombie coat he was wearing.

'How's Georgina?' Georgina had succumbed to seasickness shortly after they'd got underway and had remained in her cabin ever since.

'No change there I'm afraid. She's convinced she's going to die.'

'Still that ghastly colour you mentioned?'

Willie nodded.

'And Rose?'

'Continuing to play nursemaid. Thank God she was with us. I doubt I'd have managed by myself. The female side of things, you understand.'

Andrew took a deep breath. 'Tell Georgina she won't have to suffer for much longer. I've just sighted Ireland. It shouldn't be too long before we dock.'

He pointed into the distance. 'There she is. The Emerald Isle.'

Willie guessed then why Andrew was looking so awful. Memories. Not pleasant ones either.

Willie snapped open his cigarette case and proceeded to light up. The smoke he exhaled was immediately snatched away by the wind.

'It'll be strange going back, don't you think?' Willie said, making conversation.

'Very.'

'I wonder if it's changed all that much?'

'I shouldn't imagine so.'

'I hope it hasn't. It would be nice if it's just as it was.'

Andrew wished Willie would stop prattling on and go away. He wanted to be alone with his thoughts.

'Does it bother you, me speaking like this?'

'Not in the least,' Andrew lied.

'Good. That's a healthy sign.'

They stood in silence for a few minutes while Willie continued to smoke. When Willie had finished his cigarette he threw the butt overboard.

'I'd better get below again and give Georgina the good news.'

'I'll stay on up here.'

'We'll meet up at disembarkation then.'

'Right.'

When Willie had gone Andrew returned to watching as the coast of Ireland loomed closer and closer.

The first thing Andrew did on reaching his hotel bedroom was unpack the two bottles of Drummond he'd brought with him and pour himself a stiff one.

Glass in hand he crossed to the window and gazed out over St Stephen's Green. A park he and Alice had strolled in on several occasions.

He thought of the following morning and what he intended doing. It brought a lump to his throat.

Andrew rose as Willie and Rose approached the table he'd secured for them. 'No Georgina?'

''Fraid not,' Willie replied. 'She went straight to bed and intends remaining there until tomorrow.'

Willie assisted Rose to a seat and then sat himself.

A wine waiter came over and they placed their order. Then they fell to studying their menus.

'I'm so excited,' Rose declared, finally laying her menu aside. 'It's the first time I've ever been abroad.'

'It'll widen your horizons.' Willie smiled at her.

She lowered her voice. 'Their accents are very odd. I can hardly understand what they're saying.'

Andrew laughed. 'You'll soon get used to it. I know I did.'

Willie glanced about him. He'd dined here many times in the past, always with fellow officers. It was Dublin's finest hotel with an excellent reputation. It had never crossed his mind for them to stay anywhere else.

Rose, still with a lowered voice, said, 'Doesn't it all smell so different to home. So very foreign.'

Andrew chuckled. 'That's because it is.'

She pouted. 'No need to be sarcastic, Andrew Drummond.'

'Who me?' he replied, pretending mock innocence. 'As if I'd do such a thing. Particularly to a beautiful young lady like yourself.'

Rose blushed. 'Thank you. If you're being serious that is.'

'Never more so, Rose, I assure you.'

At which point their conversation was interrupted by the arrival of a waiter to take their food orders.

'Can we go sightseeing after dinner?' Rose asked halfway through the main course.

Willie picked up a crisp white linen napkin and wiped his lips. 'I'm afraid not, darling. I can hardly leave Georgina.'

She'd known that's what he'd say. Her face appeared to

fill with disappointment. 'Sorry, I should have thought. Yes, of course you must. And I can't go out by myself.'

Andrew smiled, realising what her game was. 'How would it be if I took you?' he suggested.

The disappointment instantly vanished. She'd achieved what she'd been after. 'Would you, Andrew!'

'My pleasure to do so.'

'None of those dives and haunts you used to favour, Andrew,' Willie said with a frown.

'Dives and haunts,' Rose repeated, eyes wide. That sounded wonderful.

'Don't worry, Willie. I wouldn't dream of it. She's your daughter after all.'

'Precisely.'

Andrew thought of a little club he'd frequented in Baggot Street. Friendly, discreet and, in his opinion, perfect for Rose. He only hoped it was still there.

'Now don't drink too much of that champagne. Your father would be furious if I took you back tipsy.'

'I won't,' Rose promised.

Andrew turned his attention to the singer, an Irish woman with flowing black hair and piercing blue eyes, thinking she was very good. Not to mention attractive.

'Any idea what she's singing about?' Rose asked.

Andrew shook his head. 'I don't speak a word of the language. Though from the sound of it, it might be a love song of some sort.'

A love song, Rose thought. How romantic. 'You said to Pa you wouldn't be accompanying us tomorrow morning. Would it be rude to ask what you're doing instead?'

He took his time in replying. 'I'm going to visit an old friend. Someone very special.'

'That sounds mysterious. Is it a woman?'

He nodded.

Jealousy filled Rose. 'I see.'

Oh no you don't, he thought. You don't at all.

'A woman you obviously knew from before, I take it?'

'That's right, Rose.'

'And haven't seen since?'

'You are inquisitive, aren't you?'

'I'm sorry,' she apologised. 'I didn't mean to be . . .'

'Nosy?' he interjected.

She dropped her gaze. 'You're telling me to shut up.'

'Not at all. But shall we change the subject.'

'If you wish.'

'I most definitely wish.'

The singer finished her song and the audience broke into rapturous applause.

'Thank you for a fabulous evening,' Rose said to Andrew as they waited for the hotel lift to descend.

'You're welcome.'

She looked into his eyes and wondered at what she saw there. Something she couldn't fathom. Something that sent a shiver through her.

Once upstairs he walked her to her room. 'Well, goodnight, Rose.'

'Goodnight, Andrew. I hope you enjoy tomorrow.'

Enjoy? It would be far from enjoyable. He made to turn away.

'Don't I get a kiss?' Her heart fluttered at being so forward. She could hardly believe she'd just said that.

He turned back to her in surprise. 'Rose, I . . .'

He had to break off when her lips landed squarely

on his. Instinctively his arms started to go round her, then realising what he was doing he pulled them away again.

'Thank you,' she whispered when the kiss was over.

When he returned to his room he locked the door securely behind him.

The grave was well tended, which pleased him. As was her parents' one alongside. He'd wanted to bring some flowers but there had been none to be had anywhere. It was simply the wrong time of year.

'Hello, Alice,' he said softly. 'I've come to visit you. It's been a long time.'

And then he couldn't speak any more, his throat too choked for words.

He began remembering . . .

It was a combined funeral for Sir Henry, Lady Fortescue and Alice and the church was packed. Andrew was present with Billy Roberts there for support.

The hymn finished and they all sat. 'Now we will pray,' the minister announced.

Andrew didn't hear a word of the prayer. All he could think of was Alice and how much he desperately missed her. He still couldn't really take on board that he'd never see her again, that she was gone.

At the end of the prayer he looked up and the first person he saw was Seamus McGinty.

Was that the hint of a smile on McGinty's face? Surely not. It couldn't be. And yet . . . and yet . . .

Then Andrew recalled the conversation with Sir Henry when he had mentioned the two Protestant houses in West Cork being torched by Fenians. And the row Sir Henry had

had with McGinty and the fact McGinty had threatened him, a threat Sir Henry had dismissed.

Suddenly, and with absolute certainty, Andrew knew it was McGinty who'd torched Greystones. Or if he hadn't done so personally had been behind it.

Arson had been suspected but so far the police hadn't made an arrest. Their investigations hadn't come up with anything.

But Andrew knew who the culprit was.

Sitting there in church, consumed by grief and hatred, Andrew swore an oath to himself.

McGinty, the bastard, would pay.

An eye for an eye.

So it would be.

Willie had knocked on Andrew's door and, on not receiving a reply, gone looking in the hotel bar where he now found him. He hesitated on seeing Andrew's face.

'Can I join you or would you prefer being left alone?'

Andrew pointed to a chair. 'Sit down.'

Willie did and beckoned a waiter over. 'Refill?'

'Please. Just ask for Scotch, they don't stock Drummond.'

Andrew took a deep breath. 'So how was the day out?'

'Grand. I showed them Dublin Castle where we used to be billeted, which they thought quite impressive. And a few other places. We had the most splendid lunch in a fish restaurant we came across. The prawns were magnificent, every bit as good as I remembered them.'

Willie gave their order, then turned again to Andrew. 'How about you?'

'I went to Alice's grave.'

'Oh.' That explained Andrew's expression when he'd come into the bar. 'How was it?'

'Pretty awful to tell the truth.'

'That's understandable.'

Andrew locked his fingers together and twisted them. 'I was pleased I went though. Painful as it was.'

'Will you go again?'

'Oh yes. At least once before we leave. I'll also go to Greystones at some point.'

Willie nodded. 'Did visiting the grave . . . help in any way?'

Andrew considered that. 'It's too soon to say really. But I think so.' He paused, then added, 'Yes, I do believe it did.'

'Good.'

'I never went back after the funeral, you know. Couldn't bear to. Several times I almost did, but changed my mind at the last moment. If it was painful today God knows what it would have been like then.'

Willie was thinking of his dead wife Mary. He still went to her grave at least once a month, staying for ten or fifteen minutes on each occasion. It had become a ritual with him over the years. He never asked Georgina to accompany him, the visits were strictly private affairs.

Their drinks arrived and Willie signed for them.

'I intend getting drunk as a lord tonight,' Andrew declared.

'I see.'

'The other thing is I shall be having dinner in my room. It's all right talking to you here like this but I won't really be fit company for the ladies.'

'I shall make your apologies and say you're not feeling all that well.'

'Thank you, Willie.'

When Andrew went to pick up his glass he noted his hand was shaking.

Willie noted it too but didn't comment.

Andrew stared grimly at the burnt-out shell of what had been the McGinty farmhouse. It hadn't been rebuilt and he wondered if Greystones had.

So long ago and yet it was as though it was only yesterday. An eye for an eye he'd sworn. And so it had been. McGinty, the bastard, had paid in full for Alice and her parents.

Andrew slowly closed his eyes, remembering . . .

He'd bided his time, now the score would be settled. He was standing in front of the McGinty farmhouse in the early hours of the morning, three full jerrycans of petrol at his feet.

The house was dark, the McGintys, he presumed, fast asleep. It was an overcast night with no stars or moon showing. Perfect for his purpose.

He thought again of Alice, dead and lost to him, all because of the Fenian bastard inside.

He picked up two of the jerrycans and walked softly towards the house. Stopping at the door he opened both cans. Then, using a knee to assist, he began pouring petrol through the letter box.

When the two cans were empty he took them back to the third with which he returned to the door and letter box. When that can was empty he took a deep breath, struck a match, dropped it through the letter box, picked up the can and ran like mad.

There was an enormous *whoof!* behind him which brought a smile of grim satisfaction to his face. He placed the can beside the others and turned to watch.

It didn't take long. Seconds later he could see flames licking behind the front downstairs windows and then wisps of smoke began to appear.

Would the smoke get them or the fire? Andrew wondered. If neither he had an alternative.

There was the sound of a small explosion. Now what was that? Could have been any of a dozen things.

Then he heard a female scream. Mrs McGinty or the daughter? He couldn't tell. Whoever, someone was now awake.

A young woman appeared at an upstairs window and threw it open, staring out in blind terror. She clearly considered jumping, then changed her mind and vanished from view.

Andrew took out his service revolver just in case it was needed. Using his thumb he slipped off the safety catch.

He wondered if they'd try the rear door. Well, if they did they wouldn't have any luck there, he'd jammed it. If they did come out it would have to be at the front.

The daughter's name was Roisin and she was twenty-two years old. Andrew knew that from discreet inquiries he'd made. She was the McGintys' only child, just as Alice had been the Fortescues'. Roisin opened the front door and rushed out, her long hair ablaze.

Andrew took careful aim and shot her through the head. She tumbled to the ground, hair still ablaze, where she lay still.

The entire house was now an inferno. Through the open door Andrew could see banks of flames leaping and dancing.

Mrs McGinty was the next to emerge, coughing and spluttering, her nightdress burning at the hem.

'For Lady Sybil, you bitch,' Andrew muttered as he pulled the trigger a second time.

And then McGinty was there, stark naked, which Andrew considered, for some reason or other, an added bonus. McGinty stopped to stare at the bodies of his wife and daughter.

Andrew pulled the trigger a third time, only there was to

be no quick bullet in the brain for McGinty. Andrew shot him in the stomach.

McGinty grunted and slumped to the ground beside his wife where he writhed in agony, blood dribbling from his mouth.

Andrew went and stood over him, smiling at the knowledge of how excruciatingly painful that particular death could be. McGinty stared up at him through bulging eyes.

'It's for my Alice and her parents the Fortescues,' Andrew explained, wanting McGinty to know why he'd done all this.

'Protestant cunt,' McGinty croaked through a froth of pink-tinged bubbles.

'You're going straight to hell, and that's exactly where you belong. You're going to roast,' Andrew crooned in reply.

McGinty continued to writhe, all the while clutching where he'd been shot.

Then Andrew had an idea. He put his revolver away and grasped McGinty by the shoulders. McGinty, too weak to resist, groaned as Andrew dragged him towards the doorway.

The heat was almost too much for Andrew but he was determined to do what he intended. Sweat rolled down his face as he hoisted McGinty to his feet and pointed him at the door.

'No . . . no!' McGinty choked.

'And the roasting starts here,' Andrew declared, pitching McGinty inside.

McGinty screamed and continued to scream until it was all over.

Andrew collected the three jerrycans and tossed them through the door as well, then beat a hasty retreat.

He walked away, not looking back. Alice had been avenged.

And sweet revenge it was.

Chapter 14

Kathleen frowned. She was putting the weekly wash together and it seemed to her she'd caught a whiff of scent. Picking up the shirt Pat had worn to the last committee meeting she brought it to her nose.

She hadn't imagined it, there *was* a definite smell of scent. And a rather nice one too, she thought.

But how could Pat get scent on his shirt? There wouldn't have been any women at the meeting for him to accidentally rub up against. So where had it come from?

Kathleen stared at the shirt in consternation, unable to think of an explanation for this. How on earth had scent got on Pat's shirt!

She shook out the shirt and examined its front. Nothing untowards there. Neither on the collar nor body of the shirt. Turning it round she began examining the back.

Kathleen caught her breath when she saw the faint red smudge close to the left armpit. She smelt that too to confirm it was what it appeared, lipstick.

She went very cold all over. Scent on his shirt and a smudge of lipstick could only mean one thing. Pat, her Pat, her husband, was seeing another woman.

Tears welled into her eyes. Surely not, Pat and someone else. And yet there was the proof.

Still clutching the shirt she staggered to a chair and slumped into it. It seemed obvious there were no such things as the committee meetings, they were just an excuse for Pat to meet up with whoever the bitch was. What a fool she'd been. What a complete and utter fool.

Why? That was the question, why? Hadn't she been a good wife to Pat? As far as she was concerned she had. She hadn't been remiss in any way.

All right, their marriage was fairly humdrum. But they had been married for years and people like them didn't have exciting lives anyway. It was a constant day-to-day struggle just trying to make ends meet.

Another woman, it seemed . . . well, just impossible. It had never once entered her mind that Pat might stray. Men like him didn't, at least she wouldn't have thought so.

Kathleen sniffed, and wiped the tears from her eyes. What a hammer blow this had been. And so completely out of the blue. She was stunned to say the least.

What to do? Confront him with it later on? She wasn't sure about that at all. Apart from anything else it would be embarrassing and humiliating.

She stared again at the shirt. Then, on a sudden impulse, grasped hold of it with both hands and tried to rip it. But the material was too strong for her and refused to be ripped.

Not to be beaten Kathleen got out of the chair and crossed to the drawer where she kept a large pair of scissors. She didn't cut the material, but stuck the point of the scissors through it and ripped it that way. Not just once but several times. When she was finished she felt a whole deal better.

'Damn you Pat Flynn,' she muttered. 'Damn you to hell for a cheating bastard.'

'Is something wrong, Kathleen?' Pat enquired on returning home from work that evening. The atmosphere was icy cold.

'No,' came the terse reply.

'Ma's in a bad mood,' Alison declared.

'I am nothing of the sort.'

'Oh yes you are, Ma. You've been ever so grumpy since I got back from school.'

'Can I get you anything?' Pat asked.

She glared at him, wanting to smack him across the face. 'Just sit down and be quiet while I get on with tea.'

'What is it tonight?' he queried.

'Potted hough.'

Alison pulled a face. 'I don't like potted hough,' she complained.

'That's too bad, young lady. It's what I'm serving up. If you don't want any you can go without.'

Pat glanced at Alison and raised his eyebrows. Heaven knew what this was all about. It was obvious Kathleen was in a right old paddy.

'Get off me!' Kathleen hissed and pushed Pat away. They had just come to bed. The thought of him touching her made her want to vomit.

'Will you please tell me what's wrong? You've been in a hellish mood ever since I arrived home.' He didn't really want to make love to her but had thought it might ease the situation, whatever that situation was.

Kathleen didn't reply.

'Is it me? Have I done something? Or have I forgotten to do something?'

Kathleen turned her back on him. Let him get that from his fancy piece. He'd get no more of it from her.

'Kathleen?'

Again there was no reply.

'Buggeration!' he swore angrily.

'Another cup?'

Ian Seaton shook his head. He'd had more than enough.

'Me neither,' Moira McLaren smiled. The two of them were alone, on a Sunday afternoon with Ian paying what had become a regular weekend visit.

Moira glanced at the window, purposefully showing off her profile of which she was justifiably proud. 'I do hate winter,' she declared.

Ian shrugged. 'It's not that bad.'

'I much prefer summer. We'll go for picnics when that arrives. I know the most beautiful shady spot beside the river. It will be quite heavenly.'

Ian smiled, totally charmed by her. 'I'm looking forward to the first one already.'

Moira brought her attention back to Ian. 'Tell me about your week,' she requested. 'Was it terribly hard?'

'Oh, very.'

She didn't really wish to hear about his week on the estate which would undoubtedly be boring in the extreme, but she knew men enjoyed talking about their work, and themselves, which was why she'd made the request. She forced herself to sit and listen attentively, apparently hanging on his every word, as Ian prattled on.

* * *

Bridie sighed as she closed *Fame*, which she'd just finished. It had been absolutely smashing.

She glanced over at the sleeping Jeannie Swanson, smiling when Jeannie gave a soft snort. She then laid the book carefully aside and blew out the candle situated by her bedside.

When Miss Rose returned from Ireland she'd give her back the book and ask if she could please borrow another.

That night she dreamed of being a great actress.

'Hello, Bridie, how are you today?'

'Fine, thank you.'

He decided to tease Bridie. 'What, no title. I thought it was to be Sir Ian of Seaton?'

Bridie flushed slightly.

'And I was going to call you Maid Bridie.'

She was aware of being teased. 'So you were, Sir Ian.'

'Sir Ian,' he mused. 'You know I really do like the sound of that. A title in the family at last. Pa will be delighted.'

Bridie was suddenly anxious. 'Oh you won't tell him, please? It was only our little joke between the pair of us.'

She was a pretty little thing, Ian thought. Couldn't compare with Moira of course, but pretty enough. She'd make some lucky chap a dashed fine wife.

He chucked her under the chin. 'Don't you worry, Bridie. I shan't tell Pa or anyone else. As you say, it's our little joke between the pair of us.'

'Thank you.'

'Sir Ian?'

She smiled. 'Thank you, Sir Ian.'

'Bye, Maid Bridie.'

'Goodbye, Sir Ian.'

Laughing softly, Ian continued on down the corridor.

* * *

Sean gazed with satisfaction round the sitting room of the three-bedroom tenement house that they'd rented. Between them they'd painted it then decent second-hand furniture had been bought and installed.

'It's quite a wee palace,' he declared.

'Aye, it is that,' Bobby O'Toole agreed from the sofa where he was lounging.

'There's just one thing still to be done,' Noddy Gallagher said. 'And by you, Sean.'

'What's that?'

Jim Gallagher produced the Samurai sword from behind a chair. 'The nails are already in the wall, Sean. All that's left is for you to do the honours.'

Sean accepted the sword from Jim and crossed to the fireplace. Standing on the hearth he hooked the sword on to the nails.

'Looks even better here than in that other dump,' he declared to mutterings of agreement.

Sean rounded on the gang. 'I've been thinking. As time passes our numbers will continue to grow, no doubt about it. That being so we can't allow everyone in here, it wouldn't be long before we'd be packed like sardines.'

That got a laugh from several of the others.

'So from now on only present gang members are allowed to use this place. Me as leader, and you lot as lieutenants. Anyone who joins after today is just an ordinary gang member who defers to us, right?'

'Right!' came the delighted chorus of replies.

Lieutenant, Mo Binchy thought. Oh, that made him proud right enough. It really made him someone.

'Now I've got some other plans,' Sean announced.

He sat while the others prepared to listen.

* * *

Georgina placed her cup back on its saucer. She, Willie, Rose and Andrew were in a coffee shop where they'd stopped for a rest and refreshment. 'If you'll excuse me for a few minutes I want to drop by a chemist shop I noticed on the way in.'

'Chemist shop?' Willie repeated with a frown. 'Is something wrong, my dear?'

She patted him reassuringly on the hand. 'Nothing at all, Willie. I merely need a few articles.'

'Shall I come with you?'

'No, you stay here. I'm quite capable of going into a chemist shop by myself after all.'

'Of course you are.'

Willie hurriedly helped her with her chair as she got up. 'A few minutes only,' she repeated, and swept away.

'I'll come to your room around midnight tonight,' Georgina said quietly to a startled Andrew shortly afterwards. She and Andrew were walking a little behind Willie and Rose.

'Are you mad! What about Willie?'

'Don't you worry about Willie. I'll take care of him. He'll know nothing about it. I promise you.'

'You can't, Georgina. It's far too dangerous. What if you're seen, for God's sake!'

'I won't be. And even if I am who's to know I'm keeping an assignation.'

Andrew swallowed hard. 'No, Georgina. I want nothing to do with this.'

She thought of the desperate craving inside her, a craving only Andrew could properly satisfy. She had to go to bed with him. She just had to. Her whole body ached for it.

'Scared?' she teased.

'Damn right I am. I've told you, Willie's my friend.'

'And I'm your lover. Don't forget that.'

'You're nothing of the sort. Not in the real sense anyway. It was once and once only.'

Her eyes glittered with determination. Since marrying Willie she was used to getting what she wanted. 'Around midnight,' she repeated.

At half-past eleven Andrew switched off his bedside light, and lay back to wait. Damn and blast the woman, he thought. Damn and blast her to hell.

He closed his eyes, recalling the night of passion they'd had together. The voluptuous body that had so eagerly moulded itself against his. The sweetness of her mouth. The firmness of her breasts. The hot wetness that had . . .

He snapped his eyes open again. He mustn't give in. All right, so he desired her, but that wasn't the point. He had no intention of continuing their relationship. If Willie was ever to find out it would be the end of the man.

What he couldn't understand was how she would get away from Willie. Surely she wasn't just going to wait until he fell asleep and then take a chance he wouldn't wake to find her gone. That would be sheer insanity.

'Willie?'

There was no reply.

'Willie?' Said a little louder.

Again no reply.

Turning to him she grasped his shoulder and gently shook him. 'Willie?'

Still no reply or reaction.

Georgina smiled to herself. The draught the chemist had sold her had done its stuff. Willie was out for the count and would stay that way until morning. Three drops for a good night's sleep the chemist had advised. She'd put six into the cocoa she'd had room service bring, and insisted he finish before they went to bed.

She slipped from under the covers.

Andrew heard a small sound as the doorhandle was turned. Christ! she'd come after all. He'd almost persuaded himself she wouldn't.

There was a pause, followed by the soft rattling of the doorhandle being repeatedly turned, to no avail. The door was securely locked.

'Andrew?' Her voice was quietly urgent. 'Andrew?'

How long would she stay there? he wondered. Seconds only if she had any sense. He couldn't believe he was keeping a beautiful, and available, woman from his room. The callous Andrew of old would have had no compunction about letting her in, friend's wife or not.

'Andrew, I know you're in there. Open up.'

He took a deep breath, then ran a hand over his face. He was surprised to find his forehead damp with sweat.

'Andrew!'

Go away, he silently commanded. Go away, Georgina!

A furious and very frustrated Georgina did just that.

If looks could kill, the one Georgina shot Andrew next morning across the breakfast table would have sent him tumbling stone-cold dead to the floor.

Willie yawned. 'Sorry,' he hastily apologised. 'I'm still frightfully tired for some reason. Most unlike me after a full night's sleep.'

'You were very restless,' Georgina lied. 'That's probably the reason.'

'I slept like a log myself,' Rose informed them.

Andrew was feeling most uncomfortable, having already decided to beg off accompanying the Seatons that day. Instead he'd go to Greystones, his last port of call. And later, perhaps Alice's grave again.

'How about you, Andrew?' Georgina smiled thinly. 'Did you sleep well?'

'I did, thank you.'

'Good.'

Willie yawned again. 'Dear, oh dear, what's wrong with me?'

'Old age, Pa?' Rose teased.

He smiled benignly at her. 'Wait till it catches up with you, my girl, you won't be so flippant then.'

'You're not old, Willie,' Georgina snapped. 'You're in your prime.'

'Aaahh!' he sighed. 'If only t'were true.'

How cross she was, Andrew thought. But then that was perfectly understandable. Cross, and gorgeous with it. He addressed himself once more to his bacon and eggs.

Andrew stood at the ship's rail watching the Irish coastline recede into the distance. He knew, beyond the shadow of a doubt, he'd never return there.

'Andrew.'

He turned to find Georgina standing beside him. This was the first time they'd been alone since the night she'd come to his hotel bedroom.

'Hello, Georgina. Taking a turn on deck?'

'Something like that. Willie's having a nap so I came up for some fresh air.'

He sniffed. 'And fresh it certainly is. I've always liked

sea air, it's so bracing I find.' He was nervous about this, wondering what she was going to say.

'I've never been so embarrassed and humiliated in my life,' she stated.

'I told you not to come,' he replied softly.

'I felt so . . . cheap . . . so dirty.'

'I'm sorry about that.'

'You were inside, weren't you?'

'Yes,' he admitted.

'I knew you were. You could have at least let me in.'

'And then what?' He shook his head. 'No, what I did was for the best, believe me.'

Tears misted Georgina's eyes. 'You don't understand, Andrew. You don't at all.'

'No?'

'I don't wish to sound disloyal to Willie, which I suppose is laughable in the circumstances. I told you he was the only other man I've ever been to bed with, and that's true. The thing is, he just doesn't satisfy me. Not in the least. I never knew what it could really be like, what I've been missing all these years, until you.'

Andrew gazed out over the sea.

'I had more pleasure with you that night, Andrew, in that one night, than all the times put together that I've been with Willie.'

'He can't be that bad, surely,' Andrew said softly.

'It's the difference between day and night where you and he are concerned.' She coloured slightly. 'He doesn't have anything like the stamina you have, or the experience. You did things to me, made me feel sensations, I'd never dreamed of.'

She paused, then said meaningfully, 'Can you blame me for wanting more of the same?'

He couldn't, but wasn't going to admit to the fact. If only she wasn't Willie's damn wife!

'You must think me a shameless hussy talking like this.'

'Not at all, Georgina.'

'But I wanted you to understand, fully understand. And now you do.'

'I'm so sorry,' he said.

'Not nearly as much as me, I can assure you.'

He shouldn't say this, he really knew he shouldn't. But he'd taken pity on her. 'There are other men you know.'

She stared grimly at him. 'Other than you, you mean.'

'Yes.'

'Men I could . . . have an affair with.'

He was hating this. 'It seems a possible solution. Don't you think?'

Georgina bit her lip. 'I suppose so. Except I wouldn't know where to start. You just sort of wandered into our life and it went from there. My curiosity got the better of me.'

'In what way?'

'If there was a difference between men, or if they were all like Willie. The answer stunned me somewhat.' She hesitated, then went on. 'I don't regret anything, Andrew.'

He did, but didn't say so.

'If I do have a regret, and I surely do, it's that there can't be more of the same. More nights like the one we had.'

He could suddenly smell her, a smell he found terribly exciting. Closing his eyes for a brief second he pictured her as she'd been when she'd opened her negligée to him. A twitch, and then a stronger twitch. He was becoming aroused.

'I'd better get back.' Georgina smiled sadly.

'Before you go, what did you do to Willie before you came to my hotel bedroom?'

The sad smile became an amused one. 'A sleeping draught I got from the chemist. Willie went out like a light.'

He nodded. 'I thought it must be something like that.'

She fixed him with her gaze. 'There's still plenty left, Andrew. Any time I wish to use it.'

And with that she turned and left him.

Andrew stared after her. Get behind me, Satan, he thought. Get behind me.

Andrew pulled up in front of Drummond House and switched off the car's engine. He sat there for a few moments thinking how good it was to be home again.

As it was a Sunday Charlotte wouldn't be at the distillery so he'd drop by the Manse later to see how she'd got on. Not that he had any worries in that respect, Charlotte had run the business before he had after all.

He thought of Ellen; he'd summon her to his room that night. It might only be a fortnight but it felt as though he'd been away for months.

He needed a woman and he needed one badly.

Very badly.

Andrew sighed and rolled off Ellen. That had been quick by his standards. But was only an hors d'oeuvre as far as he was concerned. The main course would follow shortly.

'Are you all right?' he asked.

'I'm just trying to catch my breath, that's all.'

He laughed softly.

Ellen wasn't sure what Andrew's reaction was going to be to this, but it had to be said. She just hoped he wasn't going to be angry.

'Andrew.'

'What?'

'I'm getting married.'

He came on to one elbow. 'Who to?'

'George Forsyth. You know him.'

'Of course I know him. How long has this been going on?'

'A wee while. He proposed last week.'

'Well, congratulations, I suppose.'

'You're not cross, are you?' she queried anxiously.

He laughed again. 'Why should I be? It's only an arrangement between you and me after all.'

'It's a big chance for me. He came into that small farm when his father died. He needs a wife and I consider myself lucky that he's asked me.'

Andrew thought of George Forsyth. A personable young man if a bit of a clod. 'Do you love him?'

'He loves me. At least he swears he does.'

'That doesn't answer my question, Ellen.'

'No,' she whispered in the darkness. 'But I'll come to, given time. And I'll make him a fine wife. He wouldn't get better.'

'I presume this means you're going to leave?'

'That's right.'

'Well, I can only wish you all the very best, and I mean that. I'm happy for you.'

'Thank you.'

He was going to miss her, he thought, but was already wondering if there was anyone else in the household he could approach to strike the same arrangement. He couldn't think of anyone offhand.

He ran a hand over her naked thigh. 'It's none of my business, but have you and George . . . ?'

She turned her face away from him. 'Yes.'

Sharing a woman with George Forsyth he found quite

repugnant. He wouldn't have Ellen in his bed again. 'I think we'd better stop this after tonight, don't you agree?'

'If you wish.'

'I believe it best. So when's the wedding?'

'June.'

That was only a couple of months off. 'I'll give you a damned good present. How's that?'

'You're very kind,' she replied appreciatively.

He wouldn't have her to bed again, he reflected, but in the meantime she was lying here beside him. George Forsyth or not, it would be stupid to lose the opportunity. Who knew when he'd get another.

Ellen had well earned her money when she finally left Andrew's bedroom.

Willie laid down the last of the ledgers he'd been studying. 'You've done well in my absence, Ian. By which I mean you haven't mucked anything up. At least not as far as I can make out.'

'Thanks, Pa.'

Willie regarded his son. 'And how's Moira?'

'Fine. Tip top. I was there again on Sunday.'

Willie nodded his approval. He had high hopes of this relationship. 'We must have her and her parents over to dinner shortly. I'll speak to Georgina about it.'

'Sounds grand.'

'Right, you toddle off and get on with your other duties. The old man's back in charge.'

'Who in the hell can that be?' Pat grumbled when there was a knock on the outside door. He was tired after his day and, having had tea, had thought to settle down for a snooze.

'I'll get it,' Kathleen said, and hurried from the room. She knew precisely who it was.

'We've a visitor,' she announced on returning to the kitchen. 'Father O'Banion.'

'God bless all here.' O'Banion smiled.

Pat struggled to his feet. 'This is a surprise, Father.'

'And sure, isn't the world full of them,' O'Banion replied in his thick Irish brogue.

'Alison, you come with me. We're going out for a while,' Kathleen declared.

That further surprised Pat. 'You're not going out with the good Father here?' he protested.

'Ah, but you're the one I've come to see, Pat.'

'Me?'

'You indeed.'

Kathleen bundled Alison from the room, closing the kitchen door behind her.

Pat was mystified. Then he thought he had it. 'I know, it's because I haven't been to confession lately.'

'Not for some time I understand.'

Pat shrugged. 'You know how it is, Father. You miss once which becomes twice, and so on.'

'I'm sure God will understand when you explain that to him one fine day,' O'Banion replied, still smiling.

Pat blanched.

'Now may I have a seat?'

'Of course, Father. How rude of me. Please . . .' He indicated a chair. 'And how about a cup of tea? I'm afraid I've nothing stronger in the house.'

'No tea for me, Pat. But thank you all the same.'

Pat sat facing the priest. 'Now what's this all about, Father?'

* * *

The house was empty when Kathleen returned. A quick examination of her now empty purse, which she'd inadvertently left behind, told her where Pat had gone.

Pat, who'd been to a pub he didn't normally frequent, one that sold neither beer nor spirits but poured glasses of cheap red wine and strong cider, a lethal combination when drunk in tandem, as was the custom there, was roaring drunk when he arrived home.

'Don't wake the wean!' Kathleen pleaded when, wild eyed, he came bursting into the kitchen.

Pat grabbed Kathleen and pushed her out of the room and into their bedroom. 'How did you find out?' he demanded.

She explained about the scent and smudge of lipstick.

'And you went to the priest, you fucking bitch!'

'I . . .'

Kathleen got no further. Pat's balled fist flashed to crack against her cheek.

And that was only the start.

'What the hell happened to you, Ma?' Sean demanded next morning on seeing his mother's battered face.

A horrendously hungover Pat tensed. He'd returned the previous night before Sean had come home so his son knew nothing, nor had heard anything, of what had happened.

Kathleen dropped her gaze for an instant. 'It was my own fault, I was going to the toilet when I tripped on the stairs and fell the length of them. You can see the result.'

'It looks right sore.'

'It is, Sean. It is.' Not only on her face but all over her body, Pat had given her a humdinger of a leathering.

Pat turned away, filled with relief. If Kathleen had told the truth, who knew what the outcome might have been.

Chapter 15

Who knows how these things happen? Or why? The only thing certain is that they do.

Ian was going upstairs, deep in thought, when he met Bridie coming down. Their eyes met, locked, and in that instant they each saw the other quite differently. In that instant they fell in love.

Ian stopped in his tracks, flustered, while Bridie reddened. Their eyes remained locked.

'I, eh . . . I, eh . . .' Ian stuttered.

Bridie broke their gaze to study the carpet beneath her feet. She could feel her heart going nineteen to the dozen. She was as stunned as Ian.

'How are you today, Bridie?' Ian eventually managed to get out.

'Fine, thank you, sir,' she replied in a small voice.

'And a beautiful day it is too.'

'Yes, sir.'

His mind had gone from being suddenly numb to

whirling. He couldn't believe what he was feeling. He had a mad impulse to wrap her in his arms and hold her tight. Hold her tight then kiss her deeply.

Bridie swallowed hard. What she'd seen in that moment was the prince of her dreams come to life. This was for real, she told herself, not a story book imagining or a bit of banter between the pair of them. She'd called him her prince that day in the wood, and now . . . Now he actually was.

'I'd better get on,' Ian said, and brushed past her.

Bridie went around for the rest of that day in a daze.

'What's wrong with you?' Jeannie Swanson demanded as they were getting ready for bed.

'Nothing, why?'

'You look very strange.'

'Do I?'

'Very. Are you ill?'

Not ill, Bridie thought. But in love. Desperately so. So much she ached from it. She shook her head.

Jeannie shrugged. 'I see you've got another book to read.'

'Yes, I borrowed it from Miss Rose.'

'You wouldn't get me wasting precious sleep time on a book. We get little enough as it is.'

'I enjoy it,' Bridie replied simply.

'You'd have to, and that's a fact.'

Bridie smiled thinly and continued undressing.

A few minutes later she was snuggled up in bed with the candle flickering by her bedside. She opened her new book and attempted to start it, but all she could see was a jumble of words overlaid with an image of Ian.

Ian meanwhile was sitting on the edge of his bed trying to make sense of what had occurred, and utterly failing to do so.

It was ridiculous, he told himself. Preposterous! How

could he fall in love with a housemaid. The whole thing was laughable.

Except, if it was that, why wasn't he laughing?

'How's the book coming along?'

Jack Riach sighed. 'I wish I knew.'

'Oh?'

'The more I get into it the more lost I seem to be.'

Andrew frowned. 'Lost? I don't understand.'

'Neither do I really. You know the expression about being unable to see the wood for the trees, well that about sums it up. I'm in there somewhere, but just can't for the life of me get an overall picture.'

Andrew wasn't sure what to make of that. 'What does Hettie say?'

'That it's all right.'

'There you are then.'

Jack had a sip of whisky. How he looked forward to these Friday nights out with Andrew, always pleased when they came around again. 'It's just as difficult as I imagined it would be,' he declared softly. 'The scope is so much bigger than a play.'

'You'll cope.'

'I only hope so.'

'And how's Hettie getting on with her typing?'

Jack smiled. 'I love sitting there listening to her trying to learn the infernal machine as she now calls it. Tap tap tap tap tap, it's very soothing.'

Andrew smiled, not for the first time wishing he was in a relationship as good and strong as Jack's. How he envied him, in the nicest way possible.

'Have you heard from the Seatons?' Jack enquired casually, already knowing what Georgina had tried to do in Ireland.

Andrew shook his head. 'No.'

'Maybe just as well if you ask me.'

'I'm not.'

Jack laughed. 'I see.'

'No, you don't. The girl I had an arrangement with at Drummond House is leaving to get married.'

'Ah!'

'Damn and blast.'

'That would be Ellen Temple then.'

'You've heard of the impending marriage I take it.'

'Something of the sort. George Forsyth, I understand.' Jack chuckled. 'He'll keep her busy. A lusty lad is George by all accounts.'

It depressed Andrew to think of Ellen. She had been so . . . well, convenient. And not bad in bed either, once he'd taught her a few tricks. Tricks that had been taught him years ago.

'So what are you going to do now?' Jack queried.

'I'm not certain. I'll have to think about it.'

'There must be someone else in your employ who'd like the same arrangement.'

'Possibly. As I said, I have to think about it.'

'And in the meantime you're thinking about Georgina Seaton?'

Andrew gazed into his pint. 'To be truthful, Jack, the answer's yes. I haven't slept with Ellen since she told me her news. And frankly . . . you know how it is.'

'You always were a libidinous swine.'

'That's me,' Andrew agreed.

'And how about the young one, Rose?'

'I said before, I'm not interested.'

'Then why is it I don't believe you?'

Andrew sighed. 'Honestly, Jack, there are times when I think you can see into my very soul.'

Jack laughed. 'Being blind does have its compensations. Your voice gives so much away, Andrew. It's most expressive.'

'If she was older, then perhaps. But it's the age, Jack. That and . . . her being Willie's daughter.'

'Hmmh,' Jack mused.

'Despite the age difference we do get on rather well. We spent a considerable amount of time in each other's company when in Ireland.'

'You said. While you were keeping out of stepmama's way.'

Andrew saw off what remained in his whisky glass. 'Will you have another round?'

'I'd be delighted to, old boy. And several after that.'

Both men laughed.

Pat strolled into the kitchen. 'Well, that's it then. I'm off to my committee meeting.'

A tight-lipped Kathleen refused to look at him.

'Kathleen?'

'If you must,' she forced herself to say.

'Oh but I do. I most certainly do.' He knew he was being cruel, but couldn't stop himself. She should never have set that damned priest on him. That was going too far.

'I'll be home around the usual time,' he said.

Kathleen didn't reply.

'Bye, Pa,' Alison beamed.

'Bye, angel.'

He sauntered from the room and moments later the outside door snicked shut.

Kathleen swore inwardly. How could he do this, how could he? It was beyond her.

At least she'd stuck to the promise she'd made herself. Pat

wasn't getting any at home. Nor would he ever again. Let him go to his fancy piece. Hell mend the pair of them.

It was nearly midnight when a far from sober Pat left Geraldine Buchanan's. Hands deep in pockets he set off down the street.

It hadn't been as good as usual, and he didn't know why. Oh, there had been drink a-plenty with Geraldine looking just as desirable as always. And yet, if he was honest with himself, he hadn't enjoyed it, or her, nearly as much as he normally did.

Conscience? he wondered. Probably. It had been different somehow when Kathleen didn't know about him and Geraldine. Different and more exciting.

Pat shook his head. What was he complaining about? All the free bevvy he could get down his throat and a woman like that to boot. There was certainly nothing to complain about.

He stopped and closed his eyes for a few moments, feeling giddy. He hoped he wasn't going to be sick, waste of good alcohol that.

He opened his eyes again to stare up at a sky filled with stars, stars that all seemed to be staring directly down at him.

He suddenly shuddered and was filled with dread. God was watching, and judging him. He knew that. Just as he knew he was in the wrong. It frightened him.

Pat stumbled on his way.

'Are you working or having a wee day-dream to yourself?'

Ian started, then smiled somewhat foolishly at Jock Gibson whose approach he hadn't heard. 'I'm sorry. You're quite right. I was day-dreaming.'

'Oh aye?'

'A personal matter.'

'A personal matter is it!' Jock replied sarcastically. 'Could you not day-dream about that on your own time?'

'I said I'm sorry, Mr Gibson.'

Jock regarded him shrewdly. 'There's been something wrong with you these past few days. I've noticed it.'

Ian didn't respond.

'Anything you want to talk about?'

Ian shook his head.

'Well, if it's that personal and bothering you so much maybe you want to speak to your father.'

'No, I'll work it out myself.'

Jock nodded. 'Well, I want you to do a bit of logging later on so for Pete's sake keep your mind on the job when you've got an axe in your hand. I don't want you doing yourself damage.'

'I will and I won't, I promise.'

Jock grunted. 'See that you do.'

Ian watched Jock walk away. It had been Bridie he'd been thinking of, wondering about. He'd spoken to her again that morning in passing, nothing much, the usual sort of thing. Was it his imagination or had she seemed as ill at ease as himself? It had certainly appeared so. Ill at ease and most uncomfortable.

Again he'd had the mad desire to wrap his arms around her and then kiss her deeply.

'Silly bugger,' he muttered to himself, and got on with the task in hand.

How handsome he was, Bridie thought, standing at a window observing Ian trudge home from work. He paused for a second, and seemed to stare directly at her which caused her to blush. Hurriedly she turned away.

She mustn't think of this in a romantic sense, she told herself. She could no more have Ian Seaton than fly to the moon. He was of the landed gentry, way beyond her, she a working-class Glasgow lassie.

And yet . . . oh, but it was lovely to dream. If only things had been different. If it had been at all possible.

But it wasn't, she must always remember that. Ian would marry this fine Moira McLaren he was courting, or winching to use the Glasgow word. And what a beauty she was. A right looker and no mistake.

Bridie sighed. How had this happened to her? Falling in love with the master's son. It was daft when you thought about it. She had no hope there, none at all.

'Ian.' She said the word aloud. Tasting it, savouring it. A common enough name in Scotland, perhaps the most common, but now it had taken on a whole new meaning for her.

'Ian.'

She shivered.

Imagine being married to him. Sharing the days with him, and the nights. Her throat was suddenly dry at the thought of the latter. She and Ian in bed together. He . . .

It could never be. Would never be.

But wouldn't it have been wonderful.

'Are you taking the piss, son?'

Sean stared at Bob Mather, owner of The Sheugh pub. 'Not in the least.'

'Let me get this straight. I'm supposed to pay you protection money, is that it?'

'Insurance is a better word.'

Bob laughed. 'Away to fuck, you wee nyaff. Don't try to put the frighteners on me. I could eat you and this poxy lot with you for breakfast.' Bob stuck out a barrel chest. 'Do you know who in the hell I am?'

'Of course.'

Bob brought his face to within inches of Sean's. 'I don't think you do, son. I used to be the middle-weight champion of Scotland. One punch from me and you'd be flat on your arse and staying there.' He gestured at Mo, Noddy, Jim and Bill O'Connell. 'Same with these cunts. A single punch each and that would be that.'

'Are you all right, Mr Mather?'

The speaker was a barman wearing the traditional white jacket. 'Oh aye, fine, Tam.'

Another barman appeared from out back. 'Come over here, Alex,' Bob called out.

Bob turned again to Sean. 'This is Tam, he fought in the war. That right, Tam?'

Tam nodded.

'How many Jerries did you kill?'

'I don't know how many in all, but a definite six in hand to hand.'

Bob smiled at Sean. 'And you, Alex, how many did you kill?' he said over his shoulder.

'Like Tam, I can't say how many in all. But five in hand to hand.'

'Five,' Bob repeated, eyes glittering. 'And how did you do the last bastard?'

'I strangled the fucker.' Alex paused, then added softly, 'Very slowly.'

A tremor of fear ran up Sean's spine. This was a different proposition entirely to scaring an ice-cream shop owner and the like.

'And let me tell you this, sonny boy,' Bob went on, his tone chilling. 'These lads, and others like them, are always here. So you try any funny business and you'll find you've bitten off more than you can chew. Understand?'

Sean didn't answer.

Bob grabbed him by the lapels of his jacket. 'Do you understand?'

Sean swallowed. 'Yes.'

'Good.'

Bob released Sean. 'Now get your miserable arses out of my pub before I have them kicked out.'

'That was humiliating so it was,' Mo declared when they were outside, and spat on the pavement.

Sean glared at him.

'Well, it bloody well was.'

'Are we going back mob-handed?' Bill O'Connell asked.

Sean didn't fancy the idea of going up against the likes of Tam and Alex. He didn't fancy it one little bit. Not even with the advantage of a razor.

'Let it be for now, all right?'

Bill gave a sigh of relief. Nor was he the only one.

When they got to 'the place', as they now referred to it, Sean took himself off to a bedroom where he closed the door before lying down. A bed a number of lassies associated with gang members had already had experience of.

Sean knew one thing was certain. He wasn't going to be beaten. He was damned if he was.

But what to do? Aye, what to do?

'Sammy, I've a wee job for you.'

Sammy Renton glanced up at Sean. 'And what's that?'

'You've heard what happened at The Sheugh?'

Sammy nodded.

'Well, leave it a few days and then get yourself round

there. You must be casual like, I don't want you to arouse any suspicions, but try and find out if Mather has a family, and if he does what it consists of.'

'That should be easy enough,' Sammy replied.

'And I mean it when I say casual like. Even if it takes going back a couple of times. We'll pay for the drink.'

'Hey, why him?' Mo queried.

Sean gave Mo a withering look. 'Because they know you now. You'd be spotted the moment you walked through the door.'

'Oh!'

'Got it?'

'Aye, Sean,' Mo said sheepishly.

'Have you got a plan?' Jim Gallagher enquired.

'Maybe,' Sean replied thoughtfully.

She'd been pointed out to Sean by a classmate. He now went over to the lassie who was just leaving school with several of her pals.

'Are you Annie Mather?' he smiled.

The girl, whom he knew to be eight years old, stared suspiciously at him. 'What of it, mister?'

'I wonder if you'd do me a favour, Annie.' He produced an envelope from his pocket. 'Would you give this letter to your da.'

She gazed at the envelope, then up at him. 'Why don't you do it yourself?'

'The letter's urgent and I have to get off to work. I do shifts you see,' he lied, handing her the envelope which she reluctantly accepted.

'You're a good lass. Thank you very much.'

And with that Sean strode swiftly away.

* * *

'A letter?' Bob Mather frowned. This was strange indeed. 'From a man at the school gate?'

'That's right, Da. He said it was urgent.'

He took the envelope. 'You'd better get off and have your tea.'

'Can I go out to play afterwards?'

'Ask your ma. That's her department.'

Bob opened the envelope, pulled out the single sheet of paper it contained, and started to read. He went white.

The message was simple:

SHE'S A PRETTY LASS. IT WOULD BE A TRAGEDY IF SHE WAS TO BE RAZOR-SCARRED FOR LIFE.

'Is Mr Mather about, Alex?'

Alex glared at Sean and the others with him. 'Aye, I'll get him for you.'

Sean glanced up the length of the bar where Tam and another barman were staring at them. The look on Tam's face spoke of a desire for more hand-to-hand combat.

Bob Mather appeared. 'What do you want?'

'Twenty pounds a week. First payment now.'

Bob could hardly contain himself. 'Call yourself a man, threatening a wee lassie.'

'Your pride and joy I shouldn't wonder, being an only child.'

Bob's lips thinned until they almost disappeared. He didn't doubt for one moment that the threat in the letter was real.

He reached for his wallet.

They went straight from The Sheugh to an off-licence

where they bought whisky and screwtops of beer. Then it was back to 'the place' to celebrate.

Sean couldn't have been more chuffed.

'I enjoy walking so much,' Moira McLaren declared.

'So do I,' Ian smiled. That was true enough, he did enjoy walking. But he wouldn't have elected to go for one by himself on a Sunday afternoon, because he got enough of it during the week while working on the estate.

Moira slipped an arm through his. 'Mind?'

'Not at all.'

There was a feline look about her that day, he thought. She might have been a cat who'd just consumed a large bowl of cream and was now lying in front of a roaring fire.

He glanced about, ensuring they weren't being observed. Then stopped. 'I want to kiss you,' he stated.

Her answer was to close her eyes and pucker.

Her mouth was sweet, her scent strong in his nostrils. He could feel her breasts pressing against him.

'That was lovely,' she breathed when the kiss was over.

Lovely? It certainly hadn't been distasteful in any way. And yet there had been a certain nothingness about it. No fire, no real passion. At least none that he'd experienced. He wondered what it would be like to kiss Bridie.

Moira reached up and stroked his cheek with a gloved hand. 'A penny for them?'

'Nothing. I wasn't thinking anything at all,' he lied.

'You appeared to be.'

They resumed walking. 'My father and stepmother are very keen on us, you know.'

'So are my parents.'

'They all . . . seem to see us having a future together.'

'Do you, Ian?'

There was a few moments' silence before he replied. 'It is early days, Moira. Don't you agree?'

That disappointed her. 'I suppose so.'

'We don't want to make a mistake after all. Do we?'

'No,' she reluctantly agreed, for she was set on having Ian for her own.

He thought again of Bridie. How could he be talking like this, even if it was half-heartedly, about having a future with Moira when he was in love with another woman. It was absurd.

Moira shivered.

'Are you cold?'

'I am a bit.'

'We'd better start back then.'

They turned around and began retracing their steps.

'There will be toasted crumpets when we get in,' Moira stated.

'Yummy.'

'And coffee.'

'Just the ticket.'

Would he always love Bridie? he wondered. Or would that pass as quickly as it had happened? He had no idea whatsoever.

Moira, arm again through Ian's, pulled herself closer to him.

'Flynn!'

Sean stopped work. 'Aye, what is it?' The speaker was his foreman Neil Donaldson.

'I've been meaning to speak to you.'

'Well, now's your chance.'

Donaldson didn't like Sean, the bugger was too cocky

by half. Cocky and cheeky with it. 'It's about all these days off,' he said.

'What about them?'

'This can't go on, Flynn. It seems you're only here half the time.'

Which was true enough, Sean thought. He'd been busy with Samurai business.

'I've been ill. I can't help that,' Sean declared defiantly.

'That's as may be . . .'

'Are you calling me a liar?' Sean interjected aggressively.

Donaldson took a step backwards. 'Nothing of the sort.'

'You'd better not. Or else . . .' He left the threat unsaid.

'It's just . . . well I've got my boss to account to. And he's mentioned you on several occasions.'

'Has he indeed,' Sean smirked. 'I didn't know he was even aware I existed.'

'He does, believe me. The thing is, you've got to buck up, Flynn, or it's the sack I'm afraid.'

'The sack,' Sean mused.

'Aye, the sack.'

Sean made a sudden decision. He didn't need this poxy job anyway. His income from the Samurai was more than enough to live on.

'Tell you what,' he smiled. 'Why don't you take your job and stick it up your arse.'

Sean laughed as he strode away. He was finished with hard graft for ever. From here on it was the life of Riley for him.

'Up your arse!' he shouted back over his shoulder.

Chapter 16

Kathleen's eyes flew to the clock then back again to Sean when he strolled into the kitchen. 'Why aren't you at work?' she demanded anxiously, remembering the last time a member of the family had returned home unexpectedly.

'Because I've left. Told them what to do with their job in no uncertain terms.'

Kathleen's hand went to her mouth. 'You what!'

'You heard me, Ma.'

He crossed to a chair and threw himself into it. 'What a relief to leave that bloody hell hole. I've always hated it there.'

'But . . .' She was suddenly angry. 'What do you think you're playing at, Sean? You know how hard jobs are to come by these days. God knows when you'll get another.'

'I won't be getting another, Ma. I'm finished with all that.' He fixed her with his gaze. 'And don't you go worrying about the money I give you every week. You'll get that as usual.'

'But how can I when you're not working?'

He tapped his nose. 'That's for me to know.'

She guessed this was to do with the Samurai of which she'd been hearing dreadful tales of late. It was a subject never discussed in the house.

What was it all coming to? she wondered in despair. A husband who was seeing another woman, a son who was a gang member and now, it seemed, living off that. She shook her head and turned away.

'It'll be all right, Ma, I promise.'

Would it? She doubted that.

Sean clasped his hands behind his head and closed his eyes, thinking of those he'd left behind at Barry's Iron Foundry. A bunch of wankers, he thought. That's what they were, a bunch of wankers. Not like him. He was the clever one.

'Any chance of a cup of tea, Ma?'

'What time is this to put in an appearance?' Kathleen queried next morning when Sean entered the kitchen. 'It's gone ten o'clock.'

'No need to get up early any more, is there.'

Kathleen sighed. 'I suppose you'll be wanting your breakfast.'

'Aye, that's right, Ma.' He placed a ten-shilling note on the table. 'I fancy something a bit special this morning, to sort of celebrate like. Why don't you go down the shops and get some bacon and eggs. For the pair of us.'

'Bacon and eggs during the week!' she exclaimed, scandalised.

'A wee treat, eh.'

Kathleen eyed the ten-shilling note. 'Is that part of your lodging money?'

'No, it's extra. I can afford it.'

Kathleen reluctantly picked up the note, her mouth watering at the prospect of bacon and eggs. 'I only hope you can,' she said, crumpling the note in her hand.

Sean laughed as he crossed to the sink to get washed. The life of Riley he'd told himself, and that's precisely what it was going to be from here on.

'What is it? What's wrong?' Hettie demanded, having found Jack sitting alone with the most terrible expression on his face. She immediately went and squatted beside him.

He reached out and found her hand. If he'd been capable of crying he would have, but his tear ducts had gone along with his eyes. 'Oh Hettie,' he croaked.

He brought her hand to his mouth and kissed it, taking great comfort from that. 'I was thinking about the war,' he said softly.

'Oh.'

'There was one young chap, I don't even know his name but he couldn't have been more than seventeen or eighteen, who fell off a duckboard one day. Within seconds he was up to his waist in mud.'

Jack paused, and swallowed hard. 'I can still hear his screams as he continued to sink. We did all that we could but the mud had too strong a hold on him. If only we'd had a rope we might have saved him, but we didn't and there wasn't time to fetch one.'

'Oh, Jack,' Hettie murmured, and rubbed his hand against her cheek.

'When the mud reached his neck I couldn't look any longer and turned away. I stayed turned away until those awful screams were finally silenced. When I looked again there was nothing to show where he'd gone down. Nothing at all. He'd completely vanished.'

Jack shuddered. 'I think we feared the mud most of all. If we had to go we all prayed it would be quick and clean. A bullet through the brain, blown to bits in an explosion, that sort of thing. But the mud . . . that evil foul-smelling mud. God alone knows how many men it claimed.'

Hettie couldn't even begin to imagine what it must have been like. Horrendous beyond belief.

'It's a scene I'm going to put in the book,' Jack said. 'It'll help the reader understand why my hero changed so much between going off to the Front and coming back. That scene and others which haunt me.'

That night Jack dreamed it was he in the mud and not the young lad he'd told Hettie about. He woke with a great gasp, sitting bolt upright, to find himself covered in hot, sticky sweat.

When he explained to Hettie, who'd also woken, she took him into her arms and rocked him as she would a baby.

'Thank you, darling,' Willie said, and stroked Georgina's bare shoulder.

Another failure, she thought bitterly. All right for him, but for her? That was a laugh. She'd have to remedy matters later when he was asleep.

Willie sighed. 'We should have a child you know. One of our own.'

That startled Georgina somewhat. 'A child?' she repeated.

'Wouldn't it be nice?'

Yes, she thought, it would be. She'd always wanted a child. Ian and Rose were hardly the same thing. 'We haven't been blessed so far,' she replied. 'There's nothing I can do about that.'

'I appreciate the fact, Georgina. I merely mentioned that it would be nice if we ever were.'

She tried to imagine what a child of theirs would look like. Would he or she favour Willie or herself? Or would he or she be an amalgamation of both?

'I'd wish for another boy,' Willie mused. 'Not that I'd mind a lass, but if I had my preference it would definitely be a boy.'

'Why?'

'I've no idea. It would simply be my preference.'

A boy, she thought. Her son. Their son. 'What would we call him?' she queried.

Willie considered that. 'How about Willie after me? The name Ian was Mary's choice, that of her father.'

A little Willie she thought, and laughed inwardly.

'What do you say?'

'It would be fine, and appropriate.' She was pleased it was dark and Willie couldn't see her expression. 'And what about a girl?'

'You suggest.'

A girl, she wondered. What would she call a daughter? 'I don't know,' she said eventually.

'You must have some idea.'

'I've always rather liked Rebecca.'

'Rebecca,' he murmured. Biblical. 'Yes, I approve of that.'

Willie was in a chatty mood and it was ages before he finally dropped off leaving Georgina to do what her body was craving for.

During it she thought of Andrew Drummond.

* * *

'Can I come in?'

Andrew glanced up and there was his sister Charlotte who'd popped her head round the office door. 'Of course. It's lovely to see you.'

'As it's almost coffee time I've taken the liberty of asking for a cup.'

'Saves me the effort.'

Charlotte perched on the edge of his desk. 'So how are you?'

'In the pink.'

'Hmmh,' she mused.

'You sound unconvinced.'

'That's because I am. There's been something wrong with you lately. I've no idea what, but definitely something. It's been worrying me.'

Andrew shook his head. 'There's nothing wrong, Charlotte, I swear.'

'You've been very edgy, irritable. Snappy almost. John's noticed it as well.'

He knew the reason for that. After such a long time without he'd got used to having access to Ellen Temple. Now she was denied him he damned well was irritable. He hadn't realized it showed so much.

'Maybe it's just the time of year,' he lied. 'The changing of season, that sort of thing.'

'Could be.'

He leant back in his chair and ran a hand through his hair. 'I'm looking forward to summer. Let's hope it's a good one.'

Charlotte's gaze went to the second desk in the office, the one that had originally been her brother Peter's. She could see him sitting there, and her father Murdo where Andrew now was.

'Do you ever wonder what it would have been like if the war had never happened?' she asked softly.

'Occasionally.'

'Father might still be alive. Peter certainly.'

'And I'd no doubt have remained in the army. Probably off in India or whatever. At least a Captain by now, possibly even a Major.'

'And very grand you'd be too,' she laughed, teasing him. 'I can just imagine it.'

'Grand maybe, but not pompous I hope. You get a lot of that amongst the senior ranks.'

Charlotte suddenly glanced away, her mood completely changing. 'And I'd still be married to Geoffrey. He'd never have . . .' She trailed off, hanged himself being what she hadn't said. Poor, demented Geoffrey, unable to live with himself because he couldn't be a proper man any more.

'How different things would have been,' a sombre Andrew murmured.

At which point their conversation was interrupted by the arrival of coffee and biscuits.

'Do try and buck up,' Charlotte said as she was leaving.

'I will, sis.'

He kissed her on the cheek, and then she was gone.

Andrew returned to his desk, not feeling in the least like work any more. He thought of Georgina Seaton, something he'd been doing a great deal of recently. How tantalising that prospect was. Tantalising, and forbidden because of Willie.

He had a business trip coming up during which he'd have to pass relatively close to The Haven. He could arrange it so that he'd be there on the Friday coming back which meant he could spend the weekend with them.

He closed his eyes for a brief second, recalling Georgina in all her naked splendour.

'Christ,' he groaned.

He hadn't approached any other of the female members of staff at Drummond House due to the fact, on reflection, that he simply didn't fancy any of them. There was only one and she was a mere fourteen. He just couldn't bring himself to proposition a fourteen-year-old. He did have some scruples after all.

Or did he?

He decided he did. But did they still include Georgina?

Willie signalled to Bridie who was tending table. 'Can you pour some more wine please.' He smiled.

Ian was feeling acutely uncomfortable with Bridie and Moira in the same room, the McLarens having come for dinner. Moira was seated beside him wearing the most exquisite dark blue voile dress. It boasted clusters of fine tucks, hemstitching and narrow ruffles trimming the square collar. The front of the waist was set off with pretty pearl buttons, harmonising in shade with the colour of the dress. Moira looked quite stunning in it.

The evening was agony for Bridie who'd done everything she could to try and get out of serving at table. She positively hated Moira for being so beautiful. While she . . . well, was downright plain by comparison.

'More wine, Miss McLaren?' she queried on reaching Moira.

Moira covered her glass with an elegant hand. 'No thank you.'

Bridie, who'd been desperately trying to keep the daggers out of her eyes, moved to Ian.

'You, sir?'

'Please.'

'What do you say, Ian?'

Ian glanced at his father. 'I'm sorry, I missed that.'

As Bridie left Ian's side her uniform brushed against him sending a tingle through him. Again he wondered what it would be like to kiss her. Would there be a different reaction to that he'd had when kissing Moira?

Georgina was bored. She'd thought the evening would be rather exciting but it was turning out to the contrary. Probably her mood, she reflected.

The big news, and Georgina's stomach contracted at the thought of it, was that Andrew was coming in a fortnight's time to stay the weekend. Mind you, that was something of a mixed blessing. He'd be with them, but unavailable to her.

Damn! she inwardly swore. Those few nights were going to be absolute hell. Sleeping with Willie and Andrew so close. Lifting her glass she drank almost half its contents at one go.

Rose wasn't thinking of Andrew, but had been earlier. She thrilled at the prospect of seeing him again. Perhaps they could go riding, she'd enjoy that. Especially if it was just the two of them.

Delphine McLaren was pleased to see Ian and Moira getting on so well together. What a handsome couple they made, she thought not for the first time. And he such a catch! Things couldn't have been rosier as far as she was concerned.

Bridie finished her wine round and replaced the bottle on an antique silver and cork coaster. For an insane moment she imagined how glorious it would be to have an accident and pour some of the wine over Moira's dress which she envied dreadfully. Idiot, she berated herself. She'd probably get the sack for such an 'accident'. Or at least a severe ticking off.

* * *

Bridie glanced up in surprise as Ian entered the room. She was clearing away after dinner.

'Hello,' he smiled.

She nodded, thinking not for the first time that night how dashing he looked.

'Moira's lost a pearl button and thinks it might be in here,' he explained.

She set down the dishes she was holding. 'I'll help you search for it if you like.'

'That's kind of you.'

She felt a blush tinge her cheeks. 'If it fell off it's probably round where Miss McLaren was sitting.'

'Probably, if it's here at all.'

Their gaze held for several seconds. Then, embarrassed, she glanced away.

'I must say Miss McLaren looked awfully pretty tonight,' she heard herself declaring.

'Yes. I agree.'

For some reason she could have slapped him for that, wondering why he was staring at her in such a quizzical fashion. Her blush deepened.

'Is something wrong, Bridie?'

She shook her head. 'Nothing at all, sir.'

'Sir? What happened to Sir Ian of Seaton?'

She knew he was teasing her and wished he wouldn't. It was totally inappropriate in the circumstances. 'Not indoors, sir.'

'But we're alone, Maid Bridie.'

Those words sent a thrill through her. A thrill that seemed to tickle her insides. She tried to reply but maddeningly the words stuck in her throat. She thought of all the men she'd known in Glasgow, none of whom even began to compare with Ian Seaton.

'Let's search then, shall we?' he proposed.

They both crossed to Moira's chair and started looking, Ian going down on his hands and knees to peer under the table.

'It doesn't appear to be here,' he frowned.

What a lovely bottom, she reflected. All taut and hard and . . . This time her blush was what they call in Glasgow a real 'reddie'. She was beetroot.

'I hope it isn't lost,' Ian murmured. 'It might be difficult to match a replacement.'

'If it's in the house I'm sure we'll find it. It's bound to turn up in time.'

'No doubt,' Ian agreed, scanning the area around them.

Then Bridie spied the button glinting underneath the drawn curtains. God alone knew how it had got there.

She swiftly crossed and picked it up. 'Here we are,' she stated.

Ian beamed at her. 'Clever lass. Moira will be pleased.'

Bridie didn't give a fig whether Moira McLaren was pleased or not. But Ian was, and that mattered a great deal.

She went to Ian and handed it to him. For a brief moment their hands touched which Bridie found quite unnerving.

'I'd better get on,' she stammered. 'Miss Coltart will be wondering what's keeping me.'

'Just tell her what happened and she'll understand. I'd hate to get you into trouble.'

His concern touched her.

'Thank you, Bridie.'

'It was nothing.'

He smiled once more, his eyes fastened on her face. 'And don't go walking in the woods by yourself again.'

'I won't. I've learnt my lesson.'

He would have liked to stay and chat with her but that was impossible, the company was waiting. 'Goodbye for now then.'

'Goodbye.'

He left the room, shutting the door behind him.

Bridie briefly closed her eyes, thinking of Moira McLaren and Ian. She had to admit they made a handsome couple together and seemed well suited. She could only wish them well.

When she came to pick up the dishes she'd set down she found her hands to be trembling.

Andrew, who'd already been to bed and then got up again, paced the drawing room with a large glass of whisky in his hand. There was a fever in him which had nothing to do with any illness.

It was cold in the room, the fires having gone out, but he didn't notice it. All he could think of was Ellen Temple upstairs.

He swallowed his whisky and crossed to the sideboard where he poured himself another hefty one.

It was ridiculous, he thought, that he, a grown man, should be acting like this. It wasn't as though he cared for Ellen, he didn't. It was what she had to offer that was disturbing him.

He wouldn't go to her, he told himself. He damned well wouldn't. Surely he had more self-control than that.

Andrew slumped into a chair and ran a hand over his forehead. If he was honest with himself it wasn't really Ellen who was bothering him, but Georgina. She was who he really wanted. Ellen would only have been a substitute, had she been available.

A fortnight until he visited the Seatons, and then what?

Would he play Judas? He feared he would. In fact it was almost inevitable.

He swore, then swore again.

Moments later he was back at the whisky bottle.

'Is it me?' Geraldine Buchanan asked softly.

'Is what you?'

'That's wrong.'

'There's nothing wrong,' Pat replied just a little too hastily, and unconvincingly.

'Oh yes there is. It's as though you're with me and not with me at the same time.'

Pat shook his head. 'That's not so.'

She regarded him quizzically. 'Has something happened? Is that it?'

'Nothing's happened, Geraldine. I swear.'

'Then why the coolness?'

He didn't reply to that.

'Come on, Pat,' she urged.

He sighed, deciding it might be best to unburden himself. Though he was loath to do so. 'It's Kathleen, she's found out about us.'

'Ahh!' Geraldine breathed. That explained it. 'How?'

He told her about the scent and smudge of lipstick.

'Careless of me,' Geraldine replied.

'It doesn't really make any difference,' Pat went on.

But Geraldine knew it did. 'Is she aware you're here tonight?'

Pat nodded.

Poor bitch, Geraldine thought. 'Will she leave you?'

Pat barked out a laugh. 'Not a chance. Where would she go, and how would she keep herself? People like us don't leave one another. Only death separates us. Once wed we're bound together for the rest of our lives. That's just the way it is.'

There were those whom it didn't bother to commit adultery, Geraldine reflected, and she was one of them. She was able to completely divorce what she did with Pat from her relationship with Dougal. But clearly it wasn't the same with Pat.

'So what happens now?' she queried.

'We go on as we have, I suppose. I don't intend changing anything. No fears.'

Geraldine was curious. 'And what about Kathleen? Do you love her?'

Pat stared blankly back. 'What the hell has love got to do with it? She's my wife, and that's that.'

Typical Glasgow male, Geraldine thought. She'd often wondered what Dougal got up to when away. Those foreign ports he visited where women were always available. Did he indulge? She suspected he did. Nor did she feel jealous about that.

Geraldine ran a hand through the forest covering Pat's chest. How she adored hairy men, the hairier the better. And Pat was hairy. She didn't want to lose him. He was perfect for her when Dougal was away.

'Why don't you pour us both a drink,' Geraldine suggested. She needed one. That had been quite a session. Pat might be disturbed about his wife knowing but it hadn't physically affected his performance in any way.

Pat handed her a glass then studied her from beneath thick bushy eyebrows. 'You're class so you are, Geraldine. Real class.'

She smiled. 'Thank you.'

'I never thought I'd ever get to go with a woman like you. You're sheer bloody magic.'

'Am I indeed?'

'Oh aye. A real lady.'

'Hardly that, Pat. But I appreciate the compliment.' And she did. She found it touching.

'You're not to worry about this, Geraldine. If I have been . . . well, not quite myself it'll soon pass. I promise you.'

Sean strolled out of The Thirty Shilling Tailor wearing the new suit he'd had made and which he was extremely pleased with. Wasn't he the dandy, he thought with great satisfaction.

Now what to do with the rest of the day? There wasn't any Samurai business to attend to. The boozer of course. A few pints and a natter with whoever might be there.

What a lark this was. No more Barry's Iron Foundry, but him swanning about as if he was Lord Muck.

Another three pubs were paying them protection since The Sheugh, and more would follow. The story of Mather's wee lassie had got round which had put the fear of God into the other publicans. Not to mention shopkeepers and the like.

Who knew where this might lead?

'Rose, how are you?' Andrew smiled. 'It's lovely seeing you again.'

Not as much as seeing you, she thought. 'I'm fine, Andrew. And yourself?'

'Enjoying life, Rose. Enjoying life.'

Now what did that mean? Had he found someone? Jealousy stabbed through her to think he had. Jealousy and extreme disappointment.

Andrew was nervous and had almost decided not to come at the last minute. He'd actually parked the Rolls far down the drive, wondering whether or not to go on. But in the end lust, for it was no more than that, had got the better of him.

'You've lost weight,' Rose commented.

'Have I?'

'I think you have.'

She had too, he observed. What had once been a plump pigeon was turning into a right cracker. Her bust was fuller too, he noted. Or was that merely his imagination? He didn't think it was.

'How was your journey?' she queried.

'Nothing untoward.'

'I thought we might go riding later. Or perhaps tomorrow?' She'd been determined to get that suggestion in as soon as possible.

'Tomorrow sounds fine. I'd like that.'

Her eyes sparkled. 'Then it's agreed.'

'It's agreed,' he laughed.

'Well, if you'll excuse me I think I'll have an early night,' Ian Seaton declared, stifling a yawn that he'd faked. Truth was, he just didn't like Andrew Drummond's company. There was something about the man, something he couldn't put his finger on, that disturbed him.

'Goodnight then, son,' Willie said.

Ian rose, went to Georgina and pecked her on the cheek. 'Toodooloo!' he called out as he left the room.

Andrew had been trying to have a private word with Georgina since his arrival, and so far had failed. There had always been someone else around.

Willie glanced at the clock, then got up. 'I have to make a phone call. Shan't be long.' And with that he also left the room.

Andrew focused on Rose. If only she too would go. 'What time shall we start out tomorrow?' he asked her.

'I thought directly after breakfast.'

'That's fine by me.'

'What's all this?' Georgina queried.

'We're going riding,' Andrew informed her.

Rose held her breath, hoping her stepmother wouldn't ask to come. But Georgina didn't really like riding and was unlikely to want to accompany them.

Andrew saw off what remained in his glass, having already noted the decanter was empty.

'Would you care for another?' Georgina asked.

'Please.'

'Would you do the honours, Rose dear.'

Rose went to the decanter to discover it empty. 'I'd better ring for more,' she said.

Damn! Andrew inwardly swore.

Andrew began undressing. He'd begun to think he'd never get Georgina alone and then suddenly the opportunity had presented itself. A surprised Georgina had quickly agreed to visit him later. All he had to do now was wait.

Georgina was in a lather of excitement and desperately trying not to show it. Andrew wanted her, she could hardly believe it. She couldn't imagine what had made him change his mind. Not that she really cared. All that mattered was he had.

She joined Willie in their bedroom carrying two balloons of brandy. 'I thought we might have a nightcap.' She smiled.

He stared at her in amazement. This was most unlike Georgina. 'A nightcap?'

'I just felt like one. I hope you'll join me.'

Willie shook his head. 'I've had a bit of indigestion come on. I'd better not. But you go ahead.'

Her excitement evaporated. She hadn't banked on this. 'How about if I send down for some hot milk. Would that help?'

'I don't think so,' Willie replied, rubbing his stomach. A gleam came into his eyes. 'But I know what might.'

Georgina felt like screaming. Not tonight of all nights! Oh please God, no.

'I must say, you're looking particularly attractive, and seductive. Not that you don't normally, but even more so at the moment.'

Geraldine had a large swallow from the balloon without the drops in it. She could cheerfully have murdered Willie.

'Come on, join me,' she urged. 'Brandy is good for the stomach.'

He again shook his head. 'Not tonight. I'll give it a miss if you don't mind. Now why don't you come over here.'

How long was she going to be? a drowsy Andrew wondered. It was getting so late he was rapidly going off the idea. A good dinner plus lashings of wine and whisky were taking their toll. He felt his eyes drooping.

At long last Willie was asleep. But what use was that without the drops inside him? It was just too risky, just too damned risky to go to Andrew under the circumstances.

As usual she'd been left high and dry, her body aching for release. And Andrew who could more than effect that release was only a few doors down the corridor.

She'd take the chance, she decided. To hell with it. As

gently as she could she started to pull back her side of the covers.

'Georgina, darling, cuddle me.'

There it was. That was it. She was stuck for the night.

'Of course, Willie.'

'Aahh!' he sighed as her arms encircled him.

Chapter 17

'Race you,' Rose challenged.

'You're on!'

Rose quickly kicked her horse into a gallop and sped off with Andrew hotly in pursuit.

She laughed, thoroughly enjoying this. That and the fact that for once she had Andrew to herself. She urged Trixie to go even faster.

Rose could certainly ride a horse, Andrew thought in admiration. Again he was reminded that she sat a horse just like Alice had done.

They raced for all of five minutes before Rose reined in, unaware that Andrew had let her win.

'There!' she gasped as he came up beside her.

Andrew took in her blazing eyes and flushed cheeks, thinking how gorgeous she looked. Delicious in the extreme.

'Well done,' he congratulated her.

'Thank you, kind sir.' Rose slid to the ground. 'I think we'd better walk them for a bit. Don't you agree?'

He also slid down. 'Quite.'

They began walking the steaming horses, both of them on the inside. 'I'm so pleased you've come to visit,' she declared.

'Oh?'

'Don't be coy with me, Andrew Drummond. It doesn't suit you.'

'Well, I'm pleased to be here.'

'Pity it's only for the weekend.'

He shrugged. 'That's all I can manage, I'm afraid.'

'The trouble with weekends, those you enjoy anyway, is that they tend to fly by. At least that's my experience.'

'Mine too.'

Rose clapped Trixie on the neck, Trixie whinnying in response.

'I did a lot of riding in Ireland,' Andrew said slowly.

'Really?'

'The Irish are mad on horses. And damned fine breeders to boot. But you probably already know that.'

She glanced sideways at him, wishing he'd stop and take her in his arms. She shivered at the thought.

'Something wrong?'

'No.'

'Certain?'

'Absolutely, Andrew.'

They walked on a few paces. 'I dreamed of you last night,' she suddenly stated.

That surprised him. 'I'm flattered.' He'd done a bit of dreaming himself, but it hadn't involved Rose.

'It was ever so lovely.'

He wasn't quite sure what to reply to that.

'Don't you want to know what happened?'

'In your dream?'

'Of course, silly.'

'Then what happened?'

A strange look came over her face. 'I couldn't really tell you. I'd be too embarrassed.'

'*Now* who's being coy?'

She laughed. 'I suppose I deserved that.'

'So what did happen?'

'I said I can't tell you.'

'But it was *lovely*,' he repeated drily.

'Very much so.'

'If you're not going to tell me then why bring it up in the first place?'

'Because I wanted you to know.'

'You're a teasing minx, Rose Seaton.'

She laughed again. 'Perhaps I am.'

'Who should have her bottom spanked.'

She came to an abrupt halt and stared at him. 'What an awful thing to say.'

'Well, it's true.'

She turned away. 'Perhaps I wouldn't mind that. If it was you doing the spanking.'

He wagged an admonishing finger at her. 'Rose, you should be ashamed of yourself.'

'I've heard that some people do it all the time. To each other that is. It gives them pleasure.'

'And where did you hear such a thing?'

She shrugged. 'I can't remember.'

'Fibber.'

'I am not!' she replied hotly.

'Oh yes you are.' His gaze dropped to her rear, thinking . . . He hastily put that thought from his mind.

'Fiona Bell,' Rose declared.

'And who's Fiona Bell?'

'A friend. She also told me all sorts of other interesting things.'

'Like what?'

Rose didn't reply for a few moments. 'About the birds and the bees I suppose.'

Andrew couldn't help smiling. 'I see.'

'I tried to get Georgina to explain to me some years ago but she wouldn't. And of course I couldn't ask Father. He'd probably expire on the spot if I did.'

'But come on, Rose, you're a country lass. You must have seen animals.'

'Oh yes. But that's just basics. I wished to know . . . well, more than that.'

'Very enterprising of you,' Andrew commented drolly.

'Well, it is difficult. You must agree. I mean . . . well, there's the wedding night to consider. I want to be aware of what I should be doing.'

'Maybe you should leave that up to the chap?'

'And what if he knows nothing either? That would be awful. And quite unsatisfactory I should imagine.'

Andrew had a sudden thought. 'And was that what you were dreaming about last night?'

Rose went scarlet.

'Well?'

'Sort of,' she mumbled.

'You and me that is.'

Oh Christ, she thought. Her and her big mouth. Why hadn't she kept it shut. This must sound dreadful. 'You know I like you,' she said.

'And I like you.'

She took a deep breath. 'More than like, Andrew. Or like in a different way if you prefer.'

'Were we in bed together?' He was teasing her now.

'In a way.'

'What do you mean in a way? We either were or weren't.'

She turned to him, but wouldn't look him in the eyes. She was still bright red. 'You think I'm too young for you, don't you?'

'Yes.' That came out baldly, matter of factly.

'Well I'm not, Andrew Drummond. And it's high time you married. I've heard Pa say so on a number of occasions.'

'Have you indeed.'

'He worries about you.'

Andrew glanced up at the sky, a picture of Alice in his mind. 'I worry about myself sometimes. As for marriage, I've nothing against that where I'm concerned. In due course, I imagine, when the right woman comes along.'

'Which I'm not?' she queried in a small voice.

'Most decidedly not. You're the daughter of my friend, for God's sake.'

'So?'

'The age difference, Rose. Remember that.'

'I have thought about it, and it doesn't matter. You're not exactly decrepit, Andrew. And a lot younger than Pa. He may be your friend but I fail to see how that matters. If anything it's a bonus.'

'How do you make that out?'

'Wouldn't it be nice to marry the daughter of a friend? No remarks now, but it's almost like keeping it in the family.'

Good grief, the girl was actually proposing. Or suggesting he do. That stunned him. 'I think we'd better terminate this conversation,' he said.

'Why?'

'Because . . . it's inappropriate, that's why.'

'Is there someone else, Andrew?'

He shook his head. 'No.'

'I wasn't quite sure. There have been occasions when it seems to me there might have been.'

'Well, there isn't, I assure you.'

Forward? She didn't give a damn any more. This was far too important. 'Kiss me, Andrew.'

He stared blankly at her. 'I beg your pardon?'

'You heard. Kiss me.'

'I, eh . . . This isn't a party now, Rose.'

'I'm well aware of the fact.'

He studied her grimly. 'You really are the most precocious child.'

'I am not a child!' she retorted. 'I'm a grown-up woman. Now kiss me, damnit.'

What else could he do? 'All right.'

She moved into his embrace. 'And kiss me properly.'

'You mean passionately?' he teased.

'Precisely.'

When it was over her eyes remained closed.

'Rose?'

'Now do it again.'

He laughed. 'You are a glutton for punishment.'

'There was no punishment about that,' she sighed. 'None whatsoever. Now do it again.'

Georgina stood at her bedroom window watching Andrew and Rose cantering back from their ride out. She was still furious about the previous night, and deeply frustrated. There was only one night remaining during which she could get to Andrew's room. Somehow she had to, she simply *had* to.

What had made things worse was Willie wanting to make love to her. Of all nights for him to pick it had to be that one. What an acting performance it had been on her part. If awards were given for such things she would certainly have been honoured.

She sighed and moved away from the window, not wishing Andrew to see her.

How to get some of those drops down Willie's throat that evening? How!

And then she had another idea. One that sent prickles up her spine.

Andrew had bathed after his ride and was dressing when his bedroom door opened and Georgina entered. He stared at her in amazement.

'What is this?' he demanded. 'Are you out of your mind?'

She went straight to him. 'Maybe I am.'

'The servants, anyone could have seen you.'

'That was a risk I was prepared to take.'

'Well, I'm not,' he exploded. 'You'll have to leave at once.'

'No please, please. Don't send me away just yet.'

'Where's Willie?'

'Busy with estate business. He'll be tied up for quite a while. Hours probably.'

Andrew glanced at the door, nervous as could be. He certainly hadn't bargained for this.

Georgina wrapped herself around him. 'I'm sorry about last night, truly I am.' She went on to explain what had happened.

There was a wildness about her, Andrew observed. That and an abandonment which he found very erotic.

'I must have you, Andrew, I must,' she breathed huskily. 'You've no idea what I've been going through.'

He liked the idea that she was begging, that too was erotic. Despite himself he found he was becoming aroused.

He suddenly pushed her away. 'Not now, not like this, Georgina. It's out of the question.'

'Willie's away from the house, Andrew. He won't find out.'

Christ but she was tempting. A ripe peach just waiting to be devoured. His hand went to a breast which he gently squeezed. Georgina moaned in appreciation.

What a to-do, he thought. First the daughter proposing to him, and now the stepmother begging him to have her. His ego swelled.

'But the servants, some might come in,' he protested.

'They won't. Your room has been done while you were out riding, there won't be anyone till early evening when it's time to light your fire. We're quite safe.'

He was still in two minds about this. But he had to admit, it was exciting. 'We'd have to be quick,' he said.

She groaned. 'Not that, Andrew. That's the last thing I want.'

He swore inwardly, thinking it lucky the door had a lock on it. 'Wait here,' he said.

Georgina hurriedly began to strip.

Jesus, he thought later, Georgina asleep and cradled in his arms. That had been unbelievable. There had been nothing tender and loving about it, quite the contrary.

Georgina's eyes flickered open. 'Thank you, my love,' she whispered.

Her body was at peace, completely satiated. That had been even better than their first time together. She stretched languorously, every fibre of her being relaxed.

'Georgina, I don't wish to seem ungentlemanly, but you really must go. Willie . . .' He trailed off.

She marvelled again at what she'd been missing in life.

There was simply no comparison between Andrew and Willie. Any comparison would have been a joke.

'I'll try and come again tonight,' she whispered.

He wanted her to, that was the trouble, where common sense told him he should forbid it. They'd already taken a big enough risk as it was.

'If you do you must be very careful,' he warned.

'I will be. I swear.'

'If we get caught out there'll be all hell let loose. Not to mention the end of your marriage I should think.'

For the moment Georgina didn't care about any of that. All she could think of was Andrew and what it was like being with him. If only he was her husband instead of Willie. Oh, but that would be Heaven on earth.

'Now come on, you'd better leave,' he declared, disentangling himself and swinging out of bed.

Her expression was as though she was about to purr. 'Do I really have to?'

'You know you do.'

She sighed. 'I suppose you're right.'

'I am. Tempus fugit.'

Georgina sighed again. The last thing she wanted to do was get up. She could have stayed in his bed for ever. 'Andrew?'

'What?'

'Come here.'

He raised an eyebrow. 'Why?'

'I want to touch you while you're still naked.'

She squirmed on to an elbow exposing her breasts, breasts still flushed from their recent activities. Her eyes had narrowed almost to slits.

Andrew, against his better judgement, went to her and sat alongside. 'This won't do, Georgina. Not at all.'

She ran a hand over his groin, thinking, remembering, what pleasure that had given her. Exquisite pleasure. 'You're a lovely man, Andrew Drummond. I wish I'd met you years ago.'

'Do you?'

'Oh yes,' she crooned.

For someone who'd only slept with two men in her life she'd certainly learnt quickly, Andrew reflected. Not only quickly but had been the most eager of pupils. If there had been time . . . But there wasn't.

'Kiss me,' she said.

He couldn't help but smile. That was the second time today a woman had asked . . . no, demanded, he kiss her. It really was extremely flattering.

He bent and pecked her on the lips. 'There.'

'A proper kiss, Andrew,' she pouted.

But he knew himself only too well and what it would lead to. 'No,' he said, rising again. 'That'll have to wait.'

Georgina shivered in anticipation.

'What's wrong with you two?' Sean queried, as he and the rest of the family were having tea.

Kathleen glanced at him. 'I don't know what you mean, son.'

'Oh aye you do, Ma. The atmosphere in this house has been awful for ages. I'm getting sick of it.'

Pat kept his head down and got on with his meal.

'Well, Ma?'

Kathleen was tempted to land Pat in it, well aware of how scared he now was of Sean. 'You're imagining things.'

Alison laid down her knife and fork. 'I don't want any more. I don't like it.'

'Eat up,' Pat growled. 'Food's hard enough to come by as it is without wasting any.'

'What your da says is true,' Kathleen agreed. 'It's a struggle to make ends meet.' She thought of the extra money Sean was giving her and which Pat knew nothing about. That had been, and was, a right Godsend. Even so, it went against the grain to waste food.

'I still don't like it,' Alison complained, a hint of tears coming into her eyes.

'It's great scoff,' Sean declared. Picking up his little sister's plate and giving her a wink, he forked what remained of her meal on to his own plate. 'There, problem solved.'

'You spoil that lassie so you do,' Kathleen said disapprovingly.

'Aye well, what of it?'

Alison beamed at Sean who gave her a second wink.

Pat hated it now when Sean was home, although it was rare enough, mainly confined to mealtimes.

'Are you out tonight?' Kathleen asked Sean.

'It's Saturday isn't it. Of course I'm out. Me and the lads are going for a bevvy.'

Kathleen thought of the Samurai. 'You just take care, that's all. You know Glasgow on a Saturday night.'

Sean grinned wolfishly at her. 'No need to worry about me, Ma. I'll be safe as houses, and that's a promise.'

Pat belched. 'That was terrific,' he declared.

Kathleen thought of how he'd come home smelling of that woman again the previous night. No scent this time, just female smell. Lying there in bed with him snoring his head off it had disgusted her.

'So what about this atmosphere of late?' Sean persisted.

'There isn't any,' Pat replied quietly. 'It's your imagination, Sean.'

'Like hell it is.'

Pat cringed inside.

'So?'

Kathleen couldn't resist it. 'Ask your da.'

'Da?'

Pat picked up his cup of tea and had a swallow before replying. Sean was his mother's boy, always had been. If he found out about . . . It didn't bear thinking about.

'Your ma and I have had a few problems, that's all.'

'What kind of problems?'

Answer that, Kathleen thought.

'Och you know, the sort all married couples have.'

'Oh aye?'

Pat took a deep breath. 'I understand your concern, Sean, but this is strictly between your mother and myself.'

'Not when I've got to come home and put up with it, it isn't.'

'Can I be excused please?' Alison asked.

'Of course, pet,' Kathleen replied.

Alison got down from her chair. 'And can I go out to play?'

'On you go,' Kathleen said. 'Just make sure you put your coat on.'

Alison skipped from the room.

'What's wrong?' Sean demanded belligerently of Pat when Alison had gone.

'I told you.'

'Aye, but what sort of problems?'

Kathleen was enjoying seeing Pat squirm. It was a little bit of revenge.

'It's personal, Sean.'

'Is it indeed, Da. I just hope it isn't causing Ma any unhappiness that's all.'

Kathleen decided to let Pat off the hook. If the truth came out there would be another barney which she didn't want. 'We'll sort it, Sean. Now leave it alone, there's a good lad.'

He nodded. 'All right, Ma. Whatever you say.'

Pat heaved an inward sigh of relief. Thank God and all his angels for that. He rose. 'I'll get on with my paper. Haven't read the half of it yet.'

Sean stared at his mother, unconvinced by all this. If that old swine was giving her grief he swore he'd give Pat a right seeing to. One his father wouldn't forget in a hurry.

'If you're going out you'd better get changed,' Kathleen smiled to Sean.

'I'll be in late. You know what it's like.'

Pat immersed himself in his newspaper.

Pat glanced up from his paper as the outside door snicked shut behind Sean. He'd been worried there for a few minutes. That could easily have become nasty.

Kathleen was piling dishes up at the sink, preparing to wash and dry them. She didn't expect any help from Pat, for a Glasgow man that would have been unthinkable. Nor would she have welcomed his offering – he had his job, she hers.

Pat's gaze slowly traversed the room. How cosy it was, he reflected. And welcoming like. A real home and no mistake.

He thought of Geraldine's house. That was different somehow. He couldn't put his finger on why, it just was. Mind you, it wasn't his home, but there were some places you felt more relaxed in than others.

It was all rather showy there, he further thought, frowning. Not that he didn't like it, he did. And Geraldine was tremendous company, not to mention a damned good hostess, provider of beer and whisky. There was always plenty of that.

He wondered what it would be like living with Geraldine. It was fine and dandy making his Friday night visits, especially what they got up to during them. But could he actually live with her? The day-to-day thing, rubbing along together through thick and thin.

Kathleen began to hum, an old Scottish ballad that was one of her favourites, which made Pat smile. How often had he heard her quietly sing the same ballad? Times without number. He found it a comforting sound, the familiarity of it.

'Would you like another cup of tea?' Kathleen asked over her shoulder.

'No thanks. I've had enough.'

'Suit yourself.'

'But don't let that stop you.'

'It won't, Pat.'

He recalled their courting days. Nothing spectacular, more or less the same as everyone else round there, he imagined. The usual initial shyness, he trying to be the big man, she laughing up her sleeve at him. But still continuing to go out with him nonetheless.

They'd been through a lot together, he mused. Well, you didn't bring up three children and not have problems. Bad times, good times, and he had to admit, earlier on anyway before it had all begun to grind them down a bit, a lot of laughs.

He recalled her getting drunk one night. What a to-do that had been. He helping her stagger home, she apologising profusely with every wobbly step. The hangover in the morning when she'd sworn she'd never touch another drop ever again was something to behold.

And then there was the wedding night. He'd never forget that, it being the first time he'd ever seen a naked woman. There had been experiences before Kathleen mind, oh aye, but nothing really of any consequence. A few fumblings here, a few gropings there. Certainly not the whole hog.

Talk about a blushing bride, Kathleen had been that right enough. It had taken him ages, not that she hadn't been willing enough, to calm her down before he could do anything.

Had it been good? Well, all right, he supposed. But then what did you expect in that situation? He remembered cuddling up to her, holding her, listening to her sleep.

Pat sighed. He was enjoying being in that night, now that Sean had gone, that was. There was a great contentment about it. A rare experience for him of recent years when all he'd really wanted to do was put on his jacket, cap, and go to the pub but couldn't because there wasn't enough money to do so.

He closed his eyes, thinking of him and Geraldine the night before. Wonderful in its own way, and yet . . . There had been something missing. An ordinary something that he both missed and enjoyed.

Kathleen continued to hum, wondering about Bridie and how she was getting on. There hadn't been a letter for a couple of weeks now, but then Bridie, as herself, wasn't much of a letter writer. No doubt there would be one shortly.

Pat yawned. The meal had been a good one even if wee Alison hadn't like it. He felt full and satisfied.

'I might have that cup of tea after all,' he declared.

Kathleen turned to look at him. 'Oh?'

'Aye, if you don't mind.'

She shrugged. 'It's no bother.'

When she eventually came to him with his cup of tea he'd dozed off.

Having been keen to get to The Haven, Andrew was now eager to get away. His conscience was bothering him far more than he'd thought it would. And still there was later to contend with when Georgina might visit him again.

He wanted her to, and at the same time didn't. Why did life always seem to end up so bloody complicated!

'Another ride tomorrow?' Rose asked across the dinner table.

'Why not.'

She flushed slightly, delighted at having got him to agree.

Georgina was smiling at Willie, having devised what she considered to be a sure-fire plan for him to take the drops.

Her stomach knotted at the thought of a second session with Andrew.

Chapter 18

Mo Binchy was drunk, which was hardly surprising considering the amount of alcohol he'd consumed. There were four of them out for a bevvy together.

'It's your round, china,' Sean said to Bobby O'Toole, swallowing the remains of his pint.

'Aye, fair enough.' Bobby turned his attention to the bar, waiting to catch the eye of a barman. Being a Saturday night the pub was full to bursting and doing a roaring trade.

'I've been meaning to ask you something,' Mo slurred to Sean.

'What's that?'

'This bint you've been seeing, Muriel. And a lovely lassie she is too. You've taken her back to "the place" often enough, but how come you've never had her in one of the bedrooms?'

Noddy Gallagher laughed. 'That's true enough. How come, Sean?'

Sean, who was far from sober himself, focused on his

companions. 'How do you know I haven't when we've happened to be on our own?'

Mo tapped his nose. 'I can tell.'

'Can you now.'

'Oh aye. Without any disrespect, Sean, I think she'd be a right goer. You should be in there getting your end away.'

Sean didn't like this topic of conversation at all. Why hadn't he taken her into one of the bedrooms? The truth was, though he'd never have admitted it to the others in a million years, he was scared to do so.

'More haufs?' Bobby O'Toole asked over his shoulder. Haufs were whisky.

'Too right,' Jim Gallagher replied, and hiccuped.

Sean was suddenly angry, thinking it a right liberty for Mo to have put him in this position. He tried to act in what he considered to be a nonchalant manner. He could cheerfully have punched Mo.

'That one I had in a bedroom last week was something else,' Noddy declared. 'Talk about squeal, you'd have thought I was slaughtering a pig.'

The others laughed, but not Sean.

'You should have seen the tits on her,' Noddy continued. 'Big as bloody melons they were.'

Sean wished they'd change the conversation.

'That big?' Bobby queried, again over his shoulder.

'Massive. I stuck my face in them and slobbered like a baby.'

'When are you seeing Muriel again?' Jim asked Sean.

'Wednesday night. We're going to the flicks.'

'Why not give her a treat and take her to "the place" instead?'

'I might just do that,' Sean replied in an offhand manner.

'Would you like some FLs?' Mo offered, reaching for his wallet.

'No thanks, I've got my own,' Sean replied in a steely voice.

'Here you are, Sean,' said Bobby, handing him a hauf and a pint.

'Thanks, pal.'

Sean was seething inside. Mo and his big mouth, he could have seen them both far enough. Now he was committed, providing Muriel agreed that was. There again, she might not which would suit him just as well.

He didn't know why he should be so scared of doing what should come naturally after all. There was no reason for him to feel that way. He was perfectly capable.

Right then, he decided. He'd take Muriel to 'the place' and when there give her a right seeing to.

By God and he would.

'Hello, Maid Bridie, your day off again?'

She'd seen him approaching and wondered if he'd talk to her. Her heart was thudding. 'Yes, sir.'

'Oh, what's happened to Sir Ian of Seaton?'

She shrugged.

'Bad mood, eh?'

'Something like that.'

His expression became one of concern. 'Everything going all right in the house? Nobody's giving you aggravation, are they?'

She couldn't help but smile. 'No, nothing like that.'

Bridie thought of the sleepless nights she'd had since falling so hopelessly in love with Ian Seaton. Nights during which her imagination had often run riot. If only he'd been working class like herself instead of who he was. But that could never be. Wealthy and landed gentry he'd been born and that was how he'd stay. The gulf between them was insurmountable.

'Do you mind if I sit with you for a bit?'

That surprised her. 'Not at all.'

He joined her on the bench. 'So what have you been doing today?'

'Nothing much really.'

He raised an eyebrow. 'No more forays into the countryside?'

She knew he was teasing her. 'I didn't want to get lost again. That last time quite frightened me. Who knows what might have happened if you hadn't come along.'

'Who knows indeed,' he mused. 'When we'd eventually found you you'd probably have been stiff as a stone statue.'

What a frightening thought. Scary. To end up like that. She shivered.

'I'm sorry,' he apologised. 'Has that upset you?'

'A little,' she admitted.

'I'm sorry again.'

There was a few seconds' silence between them, then he said, 'I'm going out after foxes tonight. We've been having chickens taken recently due to the blighters.' His face darkened. 'I hate foxes. Destructive beasts.'

'Are there many round here?'

'Oh, quite a few. We try to keep them down as much as possible.'

Bridie wasn't certain about that. Foxes had always seemed rather adorable animals to her.

Ian laughed when she told him that. 'You're a town person, Bridie, not familiar with the ways of the country. Adorable looking or not, foxes are vermin and should be treated as such.'

'I suppose I am a town person,' she said. 'And I'm not learning much about the countryside either. Even though I've been here quite some time now.'

'Well, you hardly get much of a chance to do so.'

'No,' she agreed.

He had a sudden thought. A rather inspirational one at that. 'Would you like to come out with me tonight? After the foxes I mean.'

'Tonight?'

'That's right. I shall leave about ten.' He glanced up at the sky. 'It promises to be blowy later which should be ideal.'

'And why's that?'

'Foxes have acute hearing. Try to get close to them when the weather is still and you haven't a chance. But when it's windy they don't hear nearly as well which gives you a chance.'

Bridie found that rather fascinating.

'Well?'

'I don't know,' she replied slowly. 'I mean, how would I get away?'

'Your time's your own today. Who's to say where you go or get up to?'

Be with Ian alone, just the two of them as they were now. 'How long would we be out for?' she asked.

'A couple of hours.'

Oh, but she'd love that. Not the shooting of foxes, but to be with Ian.

What she didn't know was that he was thinking the same thing about her. He was also excited at the prospect.

'Bridie?'

She emerged from the shadows. 'It's me.'

He laughed softly. 'Any trouble sneaking out?'

'None at all.'

'Good.'

He felt different somehow when he was with her. A good feeling, the sort of feeling he might have been searching for all his life. In a way it scared him.

'Have you wrapped up well?'

'Just as you said.'

'It'll be cold out there.'

'I'll be fine, Master Ian. I promise you.'

He hesitated for a second. 'Why don't you just call me Ian. For now anyway.'

'All right,' she whispered, thrilled.

'Then let's go.'

Ian glanced up at the sky. As he'd predicted there was a wind blowing, but there were also the elements of a storm brewing. He wondered whether or not to go on.

'What's wrong?'

He explained to her.

'Oh.'

He could hear the disappointment in her voice and decided they would continue.

'It's so dark,' she breathed.

'There's a moon above.'

'It's still dark.'

He chuckled. 'Townie.'

'I can't help that.'

'No,' he agreed. 'You can't.'

They proceeded over the fields, she at his side.

There was a sharp crack of thunder which brought Ian up short. 'Hell!' he swore.

'Ian?'

He took a deep breath. 'It's all right, Bridie.'

'Are you sure?' Any moment now she expected some

horrible monster to come out of nowhere and attack them. Talk about spooky! Give her a town any day to this.

Thunder cracked again, followed by a brief flash of lightning. Ian knew he should abandon this, but didn't want to lose Bridie's companionship. He produced a squeaker and blew into it.

'What's that for?' she whispered.

'I'm trying to call up a fox.'

He blew into the squeaker again.

What an odd sound, she thought. If she'd been asked to describe it she wouldn't have been able to.

There was an answering bark from what seemed a long way off. Ian blew on the squeaker again.

Another lance of lightning followed by a thunder clap. And then it began to rain. 'Damn,' he muttered.

'Ian?'

'What?'

'I want to go back.'

He immediately broke his gun. It was over anyway. There wouldn't be any foxes that night. Not with this weather. 'All right.'

The moon had vanished, obscured by cloud. And the rain was rapidly increasing in intensity. Moments later it was hammering down.

Bridie thought of how far they'd come, she was going to be soaked through before she got back to The Haven. Even though she was with Ian she wasn't best pleased.

'I didn't think it would rain,' he apologised. 'Honestly I didn't.'

'Well, it is,' she replied almost tartly.

Suddenly the heavens were alight with lightning, flash after flash banging and booming. Bridie wished with all her heart she was in bed with the covers pulled over her head.

'There's a wee hut not far from here,' Ian said. 'We'll take shelter there and hope this passes over.'

'A hut?'

'Rather small I'm afraid. And full of stores. But at least it'll get us out of the rain.'

'You lead then.'

He considered taking her hand, then decided against it. He didn't want her getting the wrong idea. 'Come on then.'

It took them about ten minutes to reach the hut, stumbling through the terrible rain while overhead the lightning continued to flash and the thunder crashed.

'Christ!' Ian swore when they were finally inside. 'If I'd realised it was going to be like this I'd never have come out myself, far less brought you.'

Bridie was trying to catch her breath. 'That was awful.'

'I'm sorry, truly I am.'

'Not your fault, Ian. You weren't to know.'

'Oh, but I should have done. I should have read the signs better.' He propped his gun against a wall and wondered how long the storm would take to abate, if indeed it would before morning.

'You know what I'd love,' Bridie said.

'What?'

'A cup of tea.'

He laughed. He'd have preferred a whisky himself. 'I'm afraid I can't do that for you.'

Bridie was thinking of Glasgow and how different this all was. In a perverse way she was enjoying it.

'What now?' she asked.

'Wait, I suppose. And if it doesn't let up too bad on us.'

Bridie moved, and hit some sacks, almost falling over. There was a smell in the hut she couldn't place, but a nice one. For some reason it reminded her of Christmas.

Bridie suddenly giggled. 'Jeannie Swanson must be wondering where I am. She probably thinks I'm out with a secret . . .' Bridie broke off in confusion.

'A secret what?'

'I can't say, Ian,' she mumbled.

'Of course you can.' It was so dark in the hut he could make out only the merest hint of an outline.

'Lover,' she whispered.

The effect of that statement on Ian was electrifying. 'Lover?' he repeated.

She didn't reply.

'Bridie?'

'Yes?'

'Nothing.'

He cursed himself for being so cowardly. She was only a servant after all. No one to be afraid of. So why should he be afraid?

Because he didn't see her as a servant. He was in love with her, as a woman, that's why. Her station in life had nothing to do with it.

'Tell me about Glasgow,' he requested.

That surprised her. 'Glasgow?'

'Your life there before coming here.'

'What about my life there?'

'I don't know. All of it. Your home for example.'

Bridie had to smile. 'Well, if you can imagine something as different to The Haven as can be then that's it.'

'Was it a slum?'

Bridie was immediately indignant. 'I can't deny we live in a poor part of the city but our house is absolutely immaculate. My ma would be furious if she heard you suggest otherwise.'

He chuckled at her indignation. 'I wasn't meaning to

offend, Bridie, that's the last thing I intended. I was referring to the area you come from. Not your home conditions.'

She relaxed a little. 'Well we don't live in a posh part I have to admit. We're working folk, through and through. But my ma takes great pride in our house. Works her fingers to the bone to keep it neat and tidy so she does.'

'I believe you,' he said softly.

'And Da's a hard grafter. A coalman by trade. Out in all weathers.'

Ian smiled to himself. 'Sounds a bit like me and many others on the estate. We're also out in all weathers. So we have something in common there.'

Bridie hadn't thought of it like that. 'I suppose you do.'

'I don't exactly lead a life of indolence you know. But then you must appreciate that.'

'It's not quite the same, Ian. You're rich with a house that . . . well it's a palace. You don't want for anything whereas we . . .' She trailed off for a moment. 'It was a real problem when I lost my job at the lemonade factory. Not only because my wages weren't coming in any more but the fact that other work was so hard to come by.'

'I understand, Bridie.'

'Do you?' she queried, almost accusingly.

'Oh yes. I might have been born into a well-to-do family but that doesn't mean I'm not aware of what it's like for less fortunate people.'

She wondered what her ma and da would make of Ian Seaton. She hated to think. Especially where her da was concerned.

She was so vulnerable, he thought. So very vulnerable. Which wasn't the case with Moira. Moira had . . . a veneer about her. A class thing? He didn't know. What he did know was he much preferred the vulnerability. It made him feel extremely protective. And more of a man somehow.

'We can't stay here all night,' she said.

'Hardly.'

'And I'm freezing.'

He instantly took off his coat. 'Here, put this round your shoulders.'

'What about you?' she queried in concern.

'I'm made of sterner stuff.'

Bridie shivered, something that had nothing to do with the cold. Her mind was running riot.

'We'll leave it for a little while,' he declared. 'And then if there's no let up we'll simply have to make a dash for it.'

'Yes.'

'Again, I'm sorry I got you into this.'

'That's all right.'

'No it's not. I'm angry with myself. I'm supposed to be the countryman after all. You the novice about these matters.'

How kind he was, and thoughtful. She shivered again.

He listened to the rain rattling against the hut's roof, while outside it sounded like a firework display.

'I can hardly see you,' he said. 'Even though you're standing right there.'

'Nor me you.'

'Perhaps . . . and don't take this the wrong way. If I held you it might warm you up.'

Oh God, she thought. Please.

'Bridie?'

'I am cold.'

'Babes in the wood,' he joked. 'Just like them.'

His arms went round her and she pressed against his chest. He could feel her thudding heart.

'Sir Ian of Seaton,' she murmured.

'Maid Bridie.'

Then, throwing caution to the wind, not giving a damn, he pressed his lips on hers, she eagerly responding.

For the space of a minute or more it seemed that time stood still for the pair of them.

'You know, you're one of the best things that's ever happened to me.'

That shook Georgina, coming as it did so completely out of the blue. 'Willie?'

He beamed at her. 'It's true. When Mary died I thought . . . And then eventually you happened along. You make me very happy. I want you to know that.'

She averted her gaze, guilt and shame strong within her. 'Thank you.'

'I was very lucky. And still am.'

'And so was I,' she mumbled.

He went to her and knelt, something that further disconcerted Georgina. 'We make a good couple you and I, don't you agree?'

All she could think of was Andrew and the pair of them in bed together. What bliss that had been, what sublime ecstasy. And now here was Willie not only proclaiming his love for her but also his devotion. It made her feel so cheap.

'Any regrets?' he asked quietly.

She wished she was anywhere but where she was. How could she answer that? Certainly not with the truth. Willie was a dear sweet man, she couldn't hurt him. Though if he ever found out about Andrew . . . But he wouldn't, she assured herself. He wouldn't. She'd never let the cat out of the bag, and Andrew wasn't likely to.

'Don't be silly,' she smiled.

He took her in his arms and held her close. 'Darling Georgina,' he whispered.

They stayed like that for a few moments and then he released her, rising again to his feet.

'What brought that on?' she queried.

'I don't know. I simply felt like saying it.'

'And I'm glad you did,' she lied. 'Women need to hear such things and so many men don't do it.'

'I appreciate that. Which is perhaps why I did.'

She closed her eyes, remembering Andrew and their lovemaking. While with Willie . . .

'I don't have any regrets either,' she further lied.

'Are you sure?'

'What do you think?'

His smile was one of pure contentment. 'I was thinking, I know we've recently been to Ireland. But how would it be if we had a few days away together? Just the pair of us.'

Her heart sank. 'What about the estate?'

'Ian did such a splendid job I don't have any fears about leaving him in charge again. And it would only be for a few days. A long weekend perhaps.'

'That would be wonderful, Willie.'

'Let's call it a second honeymoon.'

'I'm looking forward to it already.'

'Good.'

She thought once more of Andrew. If only . . . Oh if only . . .

On reaching her room Bridie closed the door and started to strip out of her wet things. She was soaked to the skin.

When naked she vigorously towelled herself then slipped into her nightie and dressing-gown. Sitting on the bed she started combing her hair.

There hadn't been any let up in the storm so in the end they'd had to brave it. Not that she'd cared about the rain by then any more. Ian had kissed her. A dream come true.

He'd apologised afterwards, muttering he didn't know what had come over him. She had replied that it didn't matter. They'd then lapsed into an awkward silence, neither sure what to say next.

Bridie stopped combing and closed her eyes, recalling the kiss. She'd been kissed before but never like that. It was as though . . . She'd felt that kiss right down to the very soles of her feet.

She mustn't be taken advantage of, she thought. She wasn't going to end up at an abortionist's. Look what the outcome of that had been for poor Teresa.

She had to put this out of her mind, she told herself. It was something that had happened on the spur of the moment. Ian was a young man after all, hot blooded as they all were. She didn't mean anything to him, how could she?

Perhaps he'd sensed some of her feelings towards him and the kiss had been his natural reaction. Well, it was possible. Though she'd tried hard not to let those feelings show.

Tried, but possibly failed. She resumed combing, wishing he'd kissed her a second time, and a third, and . . .

'Och stop havering, Bridie Flynn,' she said aloud. It had just been one of those things. Nothing more.

Sean swore and swung his legs out of bed. He felt so bloody humiliated, not to mention embarrassed.

Muriel raised herself on to an elbow and stared at him. 'It doesn't matter,' she said.

'Of course it bloody matters,' he retorted angrily.

'You were just nervous, that's all.'

Nervous! That was a laugh. He'd been terrified.

'Maybe it was my fault,' she said placatingly.

'Aye, that's it. Must have been you.'

Muriel wasn't sure what to do in this situation. She'd never been with a lad who couldn't manage it before. It was a totally new experience for her.

Calm down, Sean counselled himself. And don't raise your voice. He didn't want the others in the next room to hear. He smacked a fist against a palm. 'Shite!' he muttered.

Muriel reached out and touched his back. 'Why don't we try again?'

He wrenched himself away. It would be useless to do so, he just knew it would. 'No,' he growled.

Muriel gazed at Sean, wondering what he might do next in this highly volatile mood. She put a hand to her mouth and worried a nail.

Sean thought of the other lads in the house. He couldn't admit to them what had happened. He'd be a laughing stock, his credibility straight down the pan.

He swung on Muriel. 'You'll keep your mouth shut about this. Understand?'

She nodded.

'Because if you don't I'll mark you.'

Her eyes grew large with fear. 'I won't mention a word, Sean. Believe me.'

'See that you don't.'

She swallowed hard.

Sean glanced down at what dangled between his legs, hating it for failing him. It had been like a dead thing, no reaction whatsoever. He couldn't believe it.

'Get dressed,' he instructed, and proceeded to do the same.

When she was ready he suddenly grabbed her by the throat. 'Mind what I said. If this gets out you're marked.'

When he released her Muriel sagged and sobbed.

'Right then,' Sean declared, pulling himself together. 'Big smiles and you all over me like a rash when we get through there. And let me do the talking.'

'Yes, Sean.'

'It was a big success, savvy? A belter. I'm a real stud.'

He was smiling broadly when they joined the others, Muriel clinging on to his arm.

'Wo-hey!' Mo Binchy called out.

'Wo-hey!' Sean repeated, his smile becoming even broader.

Muriel felt like throwing up.

'What have you done to yourself?' Bridie exclaimed in alarm as Ian came through the front door, a large blood stain on his trousers.

'I got careless and cut myself,' he explained. 'My fault, no one else's.'

Bridie, en route from one task to another, instantly went to him in concern. 'Shall I send for the doctor?'

Ian shook his head. 'No, it's not as bad as it looks. A gash that's all.'

She stared into his face. 'You look in pain.'

He shrugged. 'As I said, a gash that's all.'

Bridie immediately took charge. 'Well, it has to be seen to. We'd better get you to the kitchen and Mrs Coltart's medical box.'

That was what he'd intended and why he'd returned home. The gash certainly needed attention if it wasn't going to turn septic. He smiled when she took his arm. 'Nurse Flynn, is it?' he teased.

Bridie disregarded that, worried about him. This wasn't a time for jocularity. 'If you lean on me I'll help you there.'

He didn't really need help but rather liked the idea of leaning on Bridie. He winced when he started to move again.

'I don't want to get blood on the floor,' he declared.

'Your leg is far more important than that. Blood can always be mopped up.'

There was an authority about her which appealed to Ian. In a way it rather reminded him of his mother. 'This is very good of you,' he said as he hobbled along.

'Nonsense.'

It was one of the few occasions in the day when the kitchen was deserted. 'You sit there,' she instructed, pulling out a chair. She considered trying to locate Mrs Coltart, who might have been anywhere in the house, then decided to deal with the matter herself. She was entirely capable after all.

'Pull up your trouser leg and let me have a look,' she commanded.

He did as he was told. Bridie made a face when she saw the wound, a nasty ragged tear. 'How did you do that?'

'With an axe, would you believe. I'm lucky it wasn't worse.'

She couldn't have agreed more. It was the work of a few moments to pour some hot water and pick up a newly washed cloth.

'You're being very kind, Bridie.'

'Don't talk rot. I'm only doing what any of the others would do.'

He noted how tender her touch was. Firm, yet tender at the same time. Despite the discomfort he was in he was actually enjoying this.

'Maybe it should be stitched,' she murmured.

'It's not bad enough for that. Once bound it'll heal well enough.'

She glanced up at him thinking how brave he was. A real man in her opinion. 'It'll probably leave a scar.'

He shrugged again. 'That doesn't bother me. A small scar is neither here nor there.'

'Hold on a sec,' she said, and went to find a pair of scissors which she used to snip away hair covered in congealed blood.

How lovely she smelt, he reflected. A most enticing smell. He wanted to bend down and touch her but of course didn't.

'There,' she declared at last. 'That's as clean as I can get it.'

'Thank you.'

Rising, she crossed to where Mrs Coltart's medical box was kept, usually used for accidents in the kitchen, and returned with it. From the box she produced a roll of bandage and bottle of iodine.

'This is going to sting,' she said, taking the stopper off the bottle.

He smiled, a smile that quickly turned to a grimace. 'Ouch,' he whispered through gritted teeth.

'I warned you.'

He dragged in a deep breath which he slowly exhaled. She hadn't been exaggerating when she'd said it would hurt. He wanted to jump up and hop around but felt he couldn't do so in front of her.

The iodine applied, Bridie now began to bandage the wound, pulling the bandage tight. There were small brass safety pins in the medical box which she used to fasten the bandage off.

'All done,' she finally announced.

Ian flexed his leg a little. 'You've done an excellent job, thank you.'

'I think you should go and lie down for a while, don't you?'

He considered that a good idea. 'I believe I will.'

She nodded her approval. 'Shall I take you up?'

'I'm sure I can cope.'

'It's no trouble, honest.'

He was tempted, but decided against it. Now the gash had been dealt with he should manage under his own steam. 'I'll be fine, I assure you.'

For a few moments their eyes met and there was something between them, an intimacy.

'What's all this then?'

That sudden intrusion startled the two of them. They turned to discover Mrs Kilbride framed in the doorway. Ian swiftly explained.

'Dear me,' Mrs Kilbride sympathised.

'My own fault,' Ian repeated as Bridie began putting things away again.

He came to his feet. 'Bridie here has been splendid. I couldn't have been better looked after.'

Mrs Kilbride beamed, obviously pleased to hear that.

'Now if you'll excuse me. At Bridie's suggestion I'm going to lie down for a while. The leg is throbbing somewhat.'

'Shall I send you up something, a cup of tea perhaps?'

Ian shook his head. 'I'll have a stiff whisky, that'll do me a lot more good than tea.'

He was at the door when he turned to stare directly at Bridie. 'Thank you again, Bridie. I appreciate what you did.'

She didn't reply, but a faint smile danced on her lips.

Chapter 19

Kathleen woke to find Pat flailing about in bed. 'Pat, what's wrong?'

He didn't reply, his arms and legs continuing to thrash wildly.

'Pat?'

He suddenly sat up, said something she couldn't make out, then fell back again.

Dear God, she thought. When she touched his shoulder it felt red hot.

Kathleen lit a candle, then caught her breath when she saw Pat's face. His eyes were open and staring, sweat streaming down his forehead and cheeks. He looked like a man demented.

'Pat, can you hear me?'

Again there was no reply.

She shook him. 'Wake up. I want to speak to you.'

He turned his head to stare at her, but his eyes were unseeing.

'Holy Mary Mother of God,' she whispered. What was all this? He was in a dreadful state and no mistake.

She had to think, she told herself, forcing herself out of the deep sleep she'd been in. The first thing to do was get Sean. She needed help.

'What . . . what is it?' Sean mumbled a few moments later.

'Your da's been taken ill. Come on through.'

'Ill? Pissed more like.'

'It isn't that. He wasn't out tonight. And he was fine when he went to bed.'

Sean groaned. 'Bloody hell!' Trust the sodding old man. 'Aye, all right, Ma. Just give me a sec to collect myself.'

Kathleen hurried back to Pat who was now dribbling at the mouth. She had a thermometer somewhere, she remembered. Maybe she should take his temperature.

She placed a hand on his forehead, which frightened her. He seemed to be literally burning up.

'I'm here, Ma,' Sean yawned.

'Come and take a look at this.'

Sean crossed to the bed and gazed down at Pat. 'Jesus wept,' he muttered.

'You'll have to run for the doctor, son. This is serious.'

Sean shook his father as Kathleen had done, only more vigorously. 'Da? Da, wake up!' He knew when there was no response that his mother was right. Here was a job for the doctor.

'I'll get round there right away,' Sean declared, and vanished from the room.

Kathleen started to cry, this was awful. What was wrong with him, what was wrong? She wrung her hands praying for the doctor to turn up as quickly as possible.

Pat briefly returned to his senses. Slowly he focused on

Kathleen sitting by his bedside, her expression one of grave anxiety. Christ but he was boiling.

He opened his mouth to speak but nothing came out. No sound at all. And then he was drifting off again. A great black hole beckoned, a hole into which he was falling.

Dr Robertson shook his head, this was beyond him.

'Well, Doctor?' Kathleen demanded, Sean hovering in the background.

'To be honest with you, Mrs Flynn, I don't know what's wrong. So what I'm going to do is go home and read up some books and then come back again in a few hours.'

'Have you no medicine you can give him?' Sean queried.

Robertson considered that. 'Not really. Until I know what the problem is I can't treat it. If I gave him the wrong thing now it might do more harm than good.'

'Some bloody doctor,' Sean muttered ungraciously.

Kathleen rounded on him. 'Sean!' she admonished. 'The doctor's doing his best.'

Robertson shrugged. He was used to this sort of behaviour. It often happened. A natural enough reaction in the circumstances. So many people expected him to turn up, give the patient a pill, and hey presto! Well, sometimes it just wasn't like that.

'In the meantime all I can suggest is you keep him covered. I don't want him catching a chill on top of everything else, and see if he'll take some water.'

Robertson stood up, then regarded Pat quizzically. This really was a poser. He'd never seen anything quite like it. 'As I said, I'll be back later.'

'Thank you for coming at this hour, Doctor. It can't be any fun having to get out of your bed in the middle of the night.'

He wanted to laugh at that. It was an ongoing part of his life he'd never got used to. As for Betty his wife . . . she'd become stoic in the extreme about the telephone ringing in the early hours, or, in this case, a bang on the door.

'I'll be on my way then.'

Kathleen saw him out.

'Would you like a cup of tea, Ma?'

'Oh thanks, son. That would be lovely.'

'I'll put the kettle on.'

Kathleen brought her attention back to Pat. At least the flailing of limbs had stopped. And his eyes had shut. In fact he was now so still he might have been . . .

Kathleen shuddered. What if he died? What then? It didn't bear thinking about.

Pat could hear voices, one of which he recognised as Kathleen's. That gave him enormous peace of mind. He somehow felt safe with her close by.

Kathleen, his wife of so many years. The woman he'd married and who'd borne his children. The woman who was almost an extension of himself.

He knew he'd be all right as long as she was there. Kathleen would take care of him. Wouldn't let him down.

Not as he'd let her down.

The heat had gone out of Pat's body, and now he began to shiver with extreme cold. Kathleen piled the spare quilt on top of the bed, and when that didn't help climbed in beside him and held him close, giving him her own body heat.

It was possible what he had might be contagious, but she wasn't bothered about that. All she wanted was for him to get better again.

'Pat,' she crooned. 'Oh Pat.'

The smallest of smiles crept on to his face.

* * *

'It's hospital for him I'm afraid, Mrs Flynn,' Dr Robertson announced.

'What about those books you went home to read?'

'Didn't shed any light I'm afraid. I'm still stymied. Mr Flynn needs to be seen by a specialist in my opinion.'

'Can I go with him?'

'To hospital?'

'Aye, that's right, Doctor.'

'Of course you can. If you wish.'

'I do.' Then simply, 'He's my man.'

Robertson nodded that he understood.

Half an hour later the ambulance, which Robertson had already ordered, arrived.

Sometime during the journey to the hospital Pat lapsed into a coma.

Ian stopped and sat on a grass-covered tussock. He was on the moor which formed part of the estate. He should be getting on, he thought, there was so much to do. But, as so often of late, all he could think about was Bridie.

He ran a hand through his hair and sighed. It was madness really, he told himself for the umpteenth time. Falling for a servant. Daft beyond belief.

Except he hadn't asked to fall in love. It had simply happened. An event over which he had had no control.

He smiled, recalling the kiss in the hut. How responsive she'd been. And how sweet her mouth. A mouth he yearned to taste again.

Then his mind turned to Moira. That's where his future lay. Or if not with Moira, then some girl like her, of her class and standing. Anything else was a nonsense.

Moira would be a good wife, he thought. And they made a

handsome couple together, everyone said so. There was only one drawback. He didn't love her.

Liked her, yes. Respected her, yes also. And she was certainly beautiful, a real knock out. Far prettier than Bridie.

But it was Bridie he loved, there was no getting away from that. And damnable it was too.

Damnable!

Getting up he continued on his way, trying – and failing – to put Bridie out of his mind.

Kathleen was waiting in a side room while Mr Durie the specialist was with Pat. She glanced again at a wall clock, wondering how long this was going to take. Mr Durie had already been with Pat a good half-hour.

The seconds continued to tick slowly by.

Kathleen stood up the moment Mr Durie, accompanied by Dr Robertson, entered the room. Her expression clearly denoted how worried she was.

'Well, Mrs Flynn.' Durie smiled. 'I've examined the patient and had some tests made. Hopefully we'll know more when we have the results of those tests.'

'So you still can't say what's wrong with him?'

'I'm afraid not, Mrs Flynn. To begin with I suspected meningitis, but that was soon discounted. Then I . . .' He broke off. 'I won't go into all the details, merely that I haven't yet been able to diagnose the problem.'

Disappointment filled Kathleen. She'd been sure Durie would have made a diagnosis by now and they'd know what was what. 'I see,' she murmured.

'Now I suggest you go home and have some rest. You can come again this evening at visiting time.'

Kathleen stuck out her jaw. 'I want to be with him, Doctor. All the time he's here.'

'That isn't possible, Mrs Flynn,' Durie replied sympathetically. 'Hospitals have rules which can't be broken.'

Kathleen's defiance immediately vanished and she crumpled in on herself. 'I'm sorry,' she apologised as she began to weep.

Robertson went to Kathleen and put an arm round her shoulders. 'What I'm sure we can do is let you have a little time with him before you go home. Five or ten minutes say.' He glanced at Durie who hesitated, then nodded.

'So how about that?'

'Thank you, Dr Robertson.'

'There might be a risk involved should you touch him so I'd prefer you didn't. Not for now anyway. Understand?'

Kathleen nodded. 'Anyway, if I'm going to catch anything from Pat I've already done so. I was in bed with him for most of the night don't forget. And I got back in again and cuddled him when he became cold.'

Durie wondered if he should keep Kathleen in for observation 'And how do you feel, Mrs Flynn?'

'Beside myself.'

He smiled. 'I meant physically.'

'Tired. Worried. Nothing else.'

That seemed normal enough. 'I'd like to check you over just in case. Then you can visit, Mr Flynn.'

Kathleen had no objection to that. 'There's one thing I want to ask you, Doctor. And I'd appreciate it if you're frank with me.'

'What's that, Mrs Flynn?'

'Could Pat die from whatever he's got?'

Durie took a deep breath. 'Then frank I'll be. Your guess is as good as mine right now. But I have to admit there is that possibility. He is in a coma after all.'

Kathleen made a choking sound and turned away from the two men so they couldn't see her expression.

Sean was at 'the place' which he had to himself. He was staring at the money belonging to the Samurai. It was kept in a steel box which was now open on his lap. Recently the gang numbers had swollen to thirty-five members but only the originals shared out the cash they brought in every week. Cash that kept growing and growing in quantity as they expanded their operations. Fourteen pubs were now paying them protection plus a great many shops. The gang was rolling in it.

'All thanks to me,' Sean said aloud, and smiled. Yes, the whole thing had been his idea, the gang, the protection, everything. To his way of thinking he was due more than he'd been paying himself.

The others would never know, he reasoned. They got their divvy every week and that was that. What was left over was kept right here in the money box, no one knowing how much there actually was apart from him.

'Fuck it!' he swore softly. It was his right.

He counted out thirty pounds and slipped the notes into his pocket. He then shut and locked the box before returning it to its hiding place.

King of the castle! That was him right enough. He felt no qualms whatsoever about stealing from his friends.

They were all dummies anyway. Not like him.

Mail to the staff was always given out over breakfast. A delighted Bridie accepted the letter from Mrs Coltart and, on recognising her mother's writing, eagerly tore it open an began reading the contents.

She went pale. 'Dear God in Heaven,' she muttered.

Mrs Coltart, who'd just sat down, glanced over at Bridi who was only two places away. 'Something wrong, Bridie?

Tears sprang into Bridie's eyes. 'It's my da. He's . . . he' . . .' She swallowed hard. 'He's ill and maybe going to die.

The chatter round the table ceased.

Mrs Coltart regarded Bridie steadily. 'Does the letter sa what's wrong with him?'

Bridie shook her head. 'They don't know but he's i a coma.'

She glanced at the letter again, tears spilling on to th pristine white and heavily starched table cloth. 'My m wants me to go home and see him just . . . just in case.'

'Understandable,' Mrs Coltart murmured.

Bridie gave Mrs Coltart a pleading look. 'Can I?' sh whispered.

On brief reflection Mrs Coltart came to the conclusio this was a matter for Mr Seaton to decide. 'Can I have tha letter?' she asked.

It was passed to her. 'Wait here and finish your breakfas Bridie. I shan't be long.'

Finish her breakfast? How could she do that? It wa impossible.

Jeannie Swanson, sitting next to Bridie, squeezed he arm while the rest of the table, including Mrs Kilbrid remained silent.

As chance would have it Ian was with his father when M Coltart came in. 'Sorry to bother you, sir, but something come up.'

Willie and Ian had been deep in conversation about ma ters regarding the estate, the pair of them in disagreeme over one of them. Willie was subsequently in a rather testy mood.

'Yes, what is it, Mrs Coltart?'

She explained the situation.

'Poor lass,' Ian exclaimed in concern.

'Here's the letter, sir,' Mrs Coltart said, handing it to Willie who swiftly scanned it.

'I thought whether or not she was allowed to go should be your decision, sir.'

'You must let her go, Pa, you must,' Ian urged.

'Must I indeed?'

'Well I certainly think you should.'

Ian was right of course, what he would have done anyway. 'I presume she'll want to leave straight away?' Willie said to Mrs Coltart.

'In the circumstances that would make sense, sir.'

'Right then, see to it. She can have as long as she likes, within reason that is.'

'With pay, sir?'

Willie considered that for a moment. 'Yes, with full pay. And I shall also take care of her train fare. See she's given sufficient funds out of petty cash, Mrs Coltart.'

'You're very generous, sir.'

Willie didn't reply to that.

Mrs Coltart was turning to leave when Ian had an idea. 'I think I'll drive her to the station myself.'

Mrs Coltart paused to hear the outcome of this exchange.

'You?' Willie queried in astonishment. 'But you've got work to be getting on with.'

'It won't take that long, Pa. And I'd like to. She's a nice girl, and hard working as I'm sure Mrs Coltart will testify.'

'She is indeed, on both counts,' Mrs Coltart stated quietly.

'So is it all right, Pa?'

Willie shrugged. 'Suit yourself. As long as you make up the time when you return.'

'I will, Pa. I promise. Now I'll go and bring the car round.'

Ian accompanied Mrs Coltart from the room leaving a puzzled Willie staring after his son.

Now why was Ian volunteering to drive a member of staff to the station when there were others who normally did that sort of thing?

'Hmmh,' he mused. Could it be there was something between Ian and Bridie Flynn, something he knew nothing about? It wouldn't be the first time after all that there had been a relationship, purely on a sexual basis of course, between the two classes. Could that possibly be it?

No, he was letting his imagination run away with him. Ian wasn't that sort. It just wasn't part of his nature. At least he didn't think so.

And Ian had Moira, he wouldn't jeopardise that. Surely not! Not for a little dalliance with a maid.

Everyone looked round when Mrs Coltart came back into the kitchen. 'All right, Bridie, go and get packed. You're on the first train home. And you're being driven to the station by Master Ian himself no less. So get a move on, girl.'

Bridie hastily rose. 'Thank you, Mrs Coltart. Thank you.'

'It's Mister Seaton you want to thank. Not only for giving you paid leave but offering to meet the cost of your train fare into the bargain.'

'Ooh!' Bridie breathed, that was a huge bonus.

'Now hop to it. You don't want to keep Master Ian waiting. He's a busy man.'

'Right then,' Bridie said, and, excusing herself, rushed away.

Mrs Coltart caught Mrs Kilbride's eye and they both nodded. This only confirmed yet again what they'd often said to one another. Mr Seaton was a gem of an employer. They didn't come any better. And it looked as though Master Ian was taking after his father in that department.

'Are you close to your dad?' Ian asked Bridie as the car moved away from the house, her case lodged in the boot.

Bridie hesitated for a few seconds. 'I suppose so, sir. Though not as close as I am to my ma.'

'I see. And it's Ian when we're alone.'

'Yes, s . . . Yes, Ian.'

'We don't have to rush by the way. I checked the timetable before leaving and there won't be a train for a while. I'll wait with you at the station to make sure you get safely aboard.'

'There's no need to do that, Ian. I don't want to put you out any more than I have to.'

He grinned. 'I insist. As Jock Gibson the estate manager says, if a job's worth doing then it's worth doing well. And he's right. So put you on the train I shall.'

'You're very kind. Driving me yourself and that.'

'Not particularly kind, Bridie. It's something I want to do.'

She glanced sideways at him, then again at the road stretching ahead. 'About that night in the hut, Ian.'

'Yes?'

'I'll never mention it to anyone.'

'I know that, Bridie.'

There was silence between them, then Bridie said, 'Can I ask you a question?'

'Go right ahead.'

'I've been wondering . . . why did you kiss me?'

Tell the truth? He couldn't do that. Not all of it anyway. 'Because I find you very attractive, that's why.'

She tried to digest that. He found her attractive! 'You wouldn't ever . . . try to take advantage of me, would you?'

Ian sighed. How did he answer that one? More than anything else he wanted to take advantage of her, as she put it.

'Because I wouldn't let you. Not you or any other man. Not even if it cost me my position.'

'Don't worry, Bridie, I won't.'

'Thank you, I appreciate that.'

Again silence descended between them. 'Miss Moira's very beautiful,' Bridie said eventually.

If he'd been more worldly wise Ian would have heard the jealousy in her voice. 'I suppose so,' he admitted reluctantly.

There was no supposing about it, Bridie thought. Moira McLaren was gorgeous. The bee's knees. 'Are you . . . going to get married?'

Bridie gulped, what an impertinent question to ask. It was none of her business whether they were or not. But part of her desperately wanted to know.

Now it was Ian's turn to glance sideways at her. 'It's a possibility.'

'Ah!' she breathed.

'Why?'

Bridie shrugged. 'Just curious, that's all.'

'And why should you be curious, Bridie Flynn?'

Oh God, she thought. Because it would break her heart, but she wasn't going to tell him that. 'Women usually are about such things,' she prevaricated.

'Indeed.'

'Oh yes.'

He suddenly felt the almost overwhelming temptation to

pull the car off the road and kiss Bridie. Hold her close. Breathe in her smell.

'And what about you, will you get married one day?' he queried instead.

'I hope so.'

'He'll be a fortunate lad who marries you.'

She flushed slightly. 'Thank you.'

'I mean it.'

She wanted to reply that Moira was fortunate too, more than so. But didn't.

'How is your reading coming along?' Ian enquired, changing the subject.

Much to Bridie's relief.

'There she is,' Ian declared, having spied steam in the distance. The train was right on time.

'How are you getting home from the station?'

'Tram of course. It's too far to walk. Especially with a case to carry.'

'Will you do me a favour?'

Do him a favour! She'd have done anything for Ian Seaton. Well, almost anything. 'If I can.'

Ian pulled out his wallet from which he extracted a five-pound note. 'Take a taxi home on me.'

Bridie stared at the note. 'I can't accept money from you, Ian.'

'Why not?'

'It wouldn't be right. I mean . . .' She broke off in confusion.

He laughed softly. 'It would give me pleasure for you to accept it, Bridie. Honestly. And there aren't any strings attached, I swear.'

'But . . . a whole five pounds!'

'Taxi there and back when you return. Plus a few pounds to spend as you will.'

She regarded him coldly. 'This isn't payment for that kiss I hope?'

He was outraged. 'It most certainly is not. All I was thinking is that in your present state it would be far nicer for you to go by taxi than tram or omnibus.'

Bridie softened. It would be nice. If for no other reason than she'd never ever been in a taxi. Talk about swank! She could just imagine what the neighbours would think when she drew up outside their close. It would be all round the street within minutes.

'Go on,' Ian urged. 'Please.'

'No strings attached?'

'My word of honour.'

She hesitated for only a few seconds longer. 'Now you're being more than kind.'

'Just don't let on to anyone at The Haven that's all.'

'I won't.'

'They might misunderstand. Read into it what isn't there.'

'I understand.'

'Good.'

She slipped the fiver into her coat pocket.

'And, Bridie.'

'Yes?'

'I sincerely hope your father gets better.'

'Thank you, Ian.'

He wanted to touch her, run his fingers down her face. But daren't. There was a hollowness inside him, a sense of loss, at her impending departure.

Bridie stood as the train was now approaching the station. Ian did likewise.

He glanced up and down the platform, they were the only ones there and that's how it seemed it was going to remain.

Bridie wondered how she was going to say goodbye. Shake his hand?

The train tooted just before drawing alongside in great gushes and whooshes of steam. When it eventually stopped Ian led her to a compartment and opened the door.

'In you go then,' he smiled, following her so he could put her case on the overhead rack.

'Thanks again for everything, Ian,' she said rather awkwardly.

'Don't mention it.'

He was about to leave the compartment when, on a sudden impulse, he turned and hastily pecked her on the cheek.

'You take care, Maid Bridie.'

'I will . . . Sir Ian.'

He leapt onto the platform and shut the compartment door. They both stood staring at each other until, with a jolt, the train continued on its way.

'Goodbye, my love,' Ian whispered to himself.

Chapter 20

Bridie let herself in with her key. She laid her case down and went through to the kitchen where she found her mother dozing in a chair.

'Ma?'

Kathleen's eyes blinked open, then delight flooded her face. 'Bridie!'

'I'm back as you asked, Ma.'

Kathleen flew into Bridie's arms and they hugged one another tight. 'Thank the Lord,' Kathleen whispered.

They disentangled themselves. 'How's Da?'

Kathleen shrugged. 'The same I'm afraid. And they still don't know what's wrong with him. A second specialist was called in and he's as mystified as the first.'

Her mother had lost weight, Bridie noted. And there were new lines on her face. Deep lines as though cut with a knife. 'When can I see him?'

'Tonight. We'll go together.'

Bridie nodded, then glanced about her. How good it was

to be home, everything just as she remembered it. 'So how have you been coping?'

'Surprisingly Sean's been very good. Helps me out in all sorts of ways. Mind you, he has the time now that he doesn't work.'

'Doesn't work? Has he been laid off?' This was news to Bridie, Kathleen never having mentioned it in any of her letters.

'Would you like a cup of tea?'

'You sit down, Ma, I'll do it.'

Kathleen sank back into the chair she'd just been dozing in. 'You might as well know, he left Barry's of his own accord. Simply walked out.'

'But why?' Bridie was appalled.

'He doesn't have to work any more. Doesn't need the money. He . . . eh . . .' This was difficult. 'It seems he gets money from that gang of his, the Samurai.'

Bridie frowned as she ran water into the kettle. 'How does he do that?'

'Don't ask, girl. I don't. I've heard stories though. The sort that would make any decent mother weep.'

'That bad, eh?'

'Worse, lass. It appears he's turned into a kind of . . .' She swallowed, finding the word hard to say. 'Gangster.'

'Jesus,' Bridie breathed.

'Him and the others, his chinas, up to all sorts. He's bound to land in jail if he's not careful. But you know Sean, he's not one to be told.'

Bridie knew that only too well. She had a strange relationship with her brother, she reflected. There were many likeable things about him, but even more dislikeable ones. He'd always rather scared her if she was honest. Her da had always been able to control him until that fight which she'd realised had been a turning point. That night the young Turk had taken over from the old.

'Does he pay you now? For his lodge I mean.'

'Oh aye, same as before. Only now I get wee extras. And right handy they come in I can tell you.'

'Where's he now?'

'Search me, Bridie. The pub most like. He spends a lot more time in there than he used to. Well, he's got more money now than he had when at Barry's.'

'I'm pleased to hear he's been a help. Now what about Alison?'

'She's at school as you probably realise. She's been in to see her da, I thought that best. When she was there I told her he was sleeping, not that he was in a coma. She doesn't know how serious it all is.'

Kathleen choked and turned her head away. 'I don't know what I'll do if he dies, Bridie. Even if it has been difficult between us for a while.'

'Difficult?'

The kettle now on, Bridie came and sat facing her mother.

Kathleen's shoulders heaved. 'I shouldn't tell you this, but . . .' She trailed off.

'Ma?'

Kathleen had to force herself to speak. 'He's been seeing another woman.'

That rocked Bridie. 'You're joking!'

'I'm not. He confessed when I confronted him with the evidence.' She didn't mention the terrible beating he'd given her.

'And what evidence was that, Ma?'

Kathleen told her.

Bridie couldn't believe this. Her father with a fancy

piece, a bit of fluff, on the side. 'Do you know who she is?'

Kathleen shook her head. 'The excuse to visit her was that he was going to a union committee meeting. I was so proud that he was on a committee, only to find out it was all a lie.'

Bridie knelt in front of Kathleen and took her into her arms. 'How awful for you, Ma.'

'You've no idea, lassie. It was as though the world had ended. I've always thought your da and I had a good marriage. Oh it's had its ups and downs right enough, but that's only natural. But for him to go with someone else. That was a bitter pill and no mistake.'

'Oh Ma, I'm so sorry.'

'Not nearly as much as me, lass. I keep thinking I must have failed him in some way. Though how I don't know.'

Bridie released her mother. 'I can't believe you've failed him in any way. You always seemed so . . . happy together.'

'That's what I thought. But it would seem we were both wrong.' Kathleen sighed and closed her eyes. 'I even had Father O'Banion speak to him, but that didn't do any good. He just went on as before.'

'Does anyone else know?'

Kathleen shook her head. 'Just me, you and Father O'Banion. And you musn't say anything, mind. I'd die of shame.'

'I won't, Ma. You can trust me.'

'Aye, Bridie,' Kathleen smiled. 'I can that.'

Kathleen got up. 'I've a few wee biscuits in. Some of them chocolate. Shall we spoil ourselves?'

Bridie laughed. 'Why not.'

Bridie gasped when she saw her father. How old he looked,

and thin. Gone was the roistering Irishman she remembered.

'Dear God,' she whispered.

'Not a murmur out of him since he went into the coma,' Kathleen said.

Pat's face, normally a healthy pink verging on the ruddy, was white and waxen. There were streaks of grey in his hair where there had been none before.

'What do you think?' Kathleen queried in a soft voice.

'He looks terrible.'

'Aye, true enough.'

'And shrunken.'

That too was true, Kathleen thought. If Pat did recover, and please God he did, he'd never be the same man again.

'I usually talk to him,' Kathleen explained. 'I don't suppose it does any good, but I usually talk nonetheless.'

'About what, Ma?'

'Oh, anything and everything. Gossip on the street, remembrances from when we were younger, how Alison's doing at school. That sort of thing. Now you're here why don't you have a go?'

Kathleen sat on the chair by the bedside and Bridie pulled up another. 'Hello, Da, it's me. Back to visit you. What's all this nonsense then?'

Of course there was no reply.

'Would you like to hear about the place where I'm working? It's some house I can tell you. The biggest mansion you could imagine.'

She told him everything about The Haven, with the exception of her falling in love with Ian Seaton.

Geraldine Buchanan stared out of her window at the

coalman below heaving a bag on to his back. Surely that wasn't Pat?

A few minutes later the man was at her door. 'Come away in,' she smiled, and ushered him through. 'You're new.'

'Aye, that's right. On this round anyway.'

'It's usually a Mr Flynn who delivers.'

'Pat, you mean, poor sod's in hospital lying at death's door.'

'Death's door?' Geraldine stammered in reply.

'He's got something terribly wrong with him and they don't know what. He's in a coma.'

'How . . . did that happen?'

The coalman regarded her quizzically. 'A friend of yours, is he?'

'No no, nothing like that. I'm simply concerned, that's all. He's always such a pleasant, cheery chap.'

'They've no idea how it happened. Took him in the middle of the night apparently and en route to hospital he went into a coma. That's all I can tell you.'

'I'll get your money,' a stunned Geraldine said, and hurried off.

When the man had gone Geraldine poured herself a stiff drink. Pat in a coma, at death's door!

As the saying went, you never knew the moment till the moment after.

'What's wrong with your face the night?' Noddy Gallagher enquired good-humouredly of Sean. They were in the pub with Bill O'Connell and Don McGuire.

Sean glared at him. 'Why don't you mind your own fucking business.'

'Sorry,' Noddy hastily apologised. 'Didn't mean to offend annat.'

Sean picked up the whisky in front of him and threw it down his throat. He was in a black anger over what had happened earlier. Or to be precise what hadn't happened.

He'd taken Muriel back into the bedroom and tried again, only to fail a second time. She'd been placatory, but that hadn't washed with him. It had to be the bitch's fault. Had to be. There was nothing wrong with him as he could testify most mornings when he woke. Or on other occasions.

He'd smacked her one, knocking her right off the bed, which had made him feel better. Once outside he'd told her to piss off, he never wanted to see her again. He'd smiled watching her scuttle away like some frightened rabbit.

He'd get another bint and that would make all the difference. That weekend at a dance perhaps. Nor would he have any trouble, they all knew who he was. All he'd have to do was crook a finger at whichever bird took his fancy and she'd come running.

'Oh Christ!' Bill O'Connell swore softly.

'What's wrong?' Don McGuire queried, seeing Bill's expression of extreme apprehension.

'Sean,' Bill hissed.

'Aye, what is it?'

Bill nodded to some young men who'd just come into the pub and sauntered over to the bar. 'Do you know who they are?'

Sean glanced at the newcomers and shook his head. 'Haven't a clue.'

'They're Tong.'

Sean involuntarily sucked in a breath. 'Are you sure?'

'Sure as damnit. I've got an old pal runs with that lot. He introduced me to some of them once. And several of those are there.'

Sean quickly counted them. Eleven in all, while they were only four. Hardly good odds if a ruction started.

'What are we going to do?' Bill asked anxiously.

'Do? Ef all. They're entitled to come in here if they want. They're not causing us any harm.' Sean turned to Noddy. 'It's your shout. You'd better get the round in.'

'Aye, right away, Sean.' Noddy hastily vacated his seat.

'They don't look so tough to me,' Don McGuire declared bravely.

Sean shot him a contemptuous glance. 'Well, they are, if their reputation is anything to go by. Hard men, one and all.'

Sean noted several of the Tong surreptitiously looking in their direction. Shit, he thought. This could well be trouble.

About five minutes later one of the Tong strolled across to stand by their table. He was smiling affably. Though that didn't fool Sean any.

'Which one of youse is Sean Flynn?'

Sean stared into the palest and coldest blue eyes he'd ever seen. 'I am.'

'Oh aye. Well, I'm Big Bill Bremner. Maybe you've heard of me?'

Sean nodded. Big Bill Bremner was the leader of the Tong. He could now see why he was called Big Bill. The man was only slightly over five feet tall, if that. In Glasgow it's well known that the smaller the man the more dangerous he can be. And Big Bill was no exception. He had a reputation for violence and mayhem as long as anyone's arm.

'So you're the Samurai,' Big Bill chuckled.

'A few of us.'

'Doing well I understand, though in a rather unconventional way if I may say so.'

Sean bit back an acid retort. He had no wish to antagonise the bastard.

'All Micks as well.'

Sean had no idea how this was going to turn out. He was just glad he had his razor in his pocket. If he went down it would be fighting.

'That's right.'

Big Bill's gaze swept the foursome. 'The map of Ireland written over all your faces.'

Sean didn't reply to that.

'An awful wee gang I understand. We've got hundreds.'

Again Sean didn't reply.

'I hope you don't mind us coming into your territory like?'

Sean was hating this, feeling humiliated. But he wasn't going to start anything, not when it was eleven against four. He shrugged. 'Suit yourself.'

'Aye, that's right. I usually do.'

A pale-faced Noddy picked up his pint and had a sip. He had trouble swallowing.

'Maybe you'll come up our end of town one day?'

That was clearly a challenge. 'Maybe.'

'I'd like that.'

Sean had no doubt Big Bill would. Should they be so stupid, in their present strength it would be a massacre. 'As you say, Big Bill, one day.'

Big Bill finished his drink and placed the empty glass on the table. 'Interesting meeting you blokes.'

'Likewise,' Sean replied.

'I'm sure.'

The affable smile returned. 'I'll be seeing you.'

Sean nodded.

'Cunt,' he swore quietly when Big Bill was out of earshot. 'Cunt.'

'I thought I might visit my parents for a few days,' Georgina announced to Willie.

'But it's not that time of year!' he protested.

'I know that, but I just fancy going. A change of scenery would do me the world of good.'

An understanding smile came on to his face. 'You mean you want to go round the shops.'

She pretended confusion, as though she'd been found out. 'That will be nice I have to admit.'

Willie disliked it when Georgina went away. He felt lonely, even though there were others in the house. 'If you wish.'

'Just for a few days as I said, not longer.'

That mollified him a little. 'I'll miss you of course.'

She went to him and pecked him on the cheek. 'Good. Then you'll appreciate me even more when I get back.'

'I always appreciate you, Georgina. Never think I don't.'

Guilt stabbed her at what she had planned. Or hoped to plan. 'And I appreciate you, Willie. You're a loving, adoring husband whom I love with all my heart.'

He beamed on hearing that. 'Give me a proper kiss,' he requested as they were alone.

Female Judas, Georgina thought, as their lips met.

Andrew opened the letter and scanned its contents. His eyebrows slowly rose.

'Well well,' he muttered, laying the letter aside. How about that! Whatever else you could accuse Georgina of it wasn't being shy in coming forward.

Go or not? He wasn't sure.

Of course he was, damnit. He bloody well would. Wild horses wouldn't keep him away.

He desperately needed a woman and this one was available.

Jack Riach ran a hand over his forehead, while facing him Hettie waited for him to continue dictating.

'Damn!' he swore.

'What's wrong?'

'I can't . . .' He shook his head. 'I don't know what comes next. It's a blank.'

'Then I suggest that's enough for today, Jack.'

'I suppose so.'

He lapsed into a brooding silence.

'Would you like a cup of tea or coffee?'

'No thank you.'

Hettie stared at him, his face creased with thought. 'Let it go, Jack. Put it out of your mind for now.'

He took off his dark glasses and rubbed his eyeless sockets which, for some reason, were hurting him. 'It's the war, Hettie, the bloody war. Remembering it for the plays was bad enough, but this, being a novel and far longer, is worse. A great deal worse.'

'I think you're doing awfully well so far, Jack.'

'Do you really?'

'Yes. And I wouldn't lie to you. I'd never do that.'

Hettie hesitated, then said, 'The bits about you and me are so true to life, Jack. When you dictate it's as though you were speaking and I was replying.'

'What an idiot I was in those early days,' he mused. 'Young, selfish, full of myself. It took a German grenade to knock all that out of me and see things . . .'

He broke off to laugh mirthlessly. 'To see things as they truly are.'

Emotion welled within Hettie. 'Oh, Jack!'

'Still no regrets? About you and me, that is.'

'Never. And don't ever ask me again. You already know the answer.'

And then he had it. Painful a recollection as it was. 'Pen at the ready, Hettie?'

'Of course.'

'Now what was that last line . . . ?'

'Kathleen.' The voice was hoarse and very faint.

She started, her attention having wandered. 'Pat?'

His eyes were open, recognition there. She quickly grasped his hand and squeezed it.

'What happened?'

'You've been very ill.'

The faintest of smiles played over his mouth. 'I don't know where I was but I often heard you there.'

'I've been with you as much as I've been allowed, Pat.'

'Dreams,' he murmured. 'So many dreams.'

'But now you're back with us, Pat. That's all that matters.' She began to cry.

'Don't, lass. Don't.'

'I can't help it. I'm so happy.'

He closed his eyes for a second, then opened them again. 'Did I also hear Bridie?'

'Aye you did. She came home to be with us.'

'I've been that ill?'

Kathleen nodded.

'What was it?'

'They never found out. They couldn't diagnose you.'

'Difficult as always, eh?'

'That's you, Pat.'

He felt dreadfully weak, and somehow detached, as though he wasn't even part of the real world. 'I love you, Kathleen,' he said.

She stared at him.

'I know I've been rotten to you, but that's over now. I swear it. If I get through this I'll never be unfaithful to you ever again.'

'Oh Pat,' she whispered.

'I don't know what possessed me. But in my dreams I came to realise what I risked losing. And, Kathleen, I don't want to lose that. Not you and me.'

So much emotion was clogging her throat she couldn't speak.

'Will you forgive me. Please?'

Kathleen nodded.

'Jesus, but I don't deserve you. You're one in a million, Kathleen Flynn and I the lucky man who has you.'

She bent over and kissed him on the mouth, a mouth dry as parchment. 'I should call the doctor.'

'Not yet. I want you to myself for a bit. Just the two of us.'

'All right then.'

He gazed at her, drinking her in. Remembering the dreams that had been about the pair of them. Good dreams. Warm dreams. Dreams that had made him realise how stupid he'd been.

He wasn't going to come, Georgina thought in despair, having been dawdling over her meal waiting for Andrew to put in an appearance. Oh well, there had always been the chance he wouldn't be able to make it, or simply didn't want to. He of course hadn't been able to reply to her letter, that would have been far too risky.

She sipped at her wine, a rather nice Mâcon. But the pleasantness of it was lost on her.

'Is madam finding everything satisfactory?'

She smiled at the hovering waiter. 'Yes, thank you. The meal is excellent.'

The waiter bowed and moved away.

For the umpteenth time Georgina glanced round the dining room of the Saltire Hotel where she was booked under an assumed name. There was still no sign of him.

Eventually she finished her main course and ordered a dessert that she didn't want but which would give her an excuse to linger longer.

The dessert was a chocolate concoction with cream on top. Delicious, she thought when she tasted it. And extremely fattening.

And then suddenly he was there, talking to the *maitre d'*.

Andrew glanced up and down the corridor to ensure he wasn't being observed, then discreetly tapped on Georgina's door. He smiled, recalling how she'd let him know which room she was in by dropping her key as she passed him on her way out. He, naturally enough, being a gentleman, had picked it up for her, the only words passing between them being 'thank you, sir'. As Georgina had said in her letter, they had to be most careful. She in particular, as being a native of Perth she was known to many people there.

The door opened and he slipped inside. The door instantly closed again.

'Hello,' he smiled.

'Hello.'

He took in the long free-flowing pink silk negligée she was

wearing over a matching nightdress. She seemed to shimmer in the light.

'I say,' he murmured appreciatively. 'You look absolutely ravishing.'

'It was more *being* ravished that I had in mind,' she retorted, marvelling at her boldness.

He laughed. 'You certainly don't mince your words. I like that in a woman.'

She melted into his arms. 'I was so scared you wouldn't make it, my darling.'

'Well I did and here I am.'

The taut hardness and sheer masculinity of his body sent shivers coursing up and down her spine. While the cologne he was wearing and which she remembered so vividly made her head swim.

'I laid in a bottle of whisky for you should you wish a drink,' she said.

'Later I think.'

'Good.'

He lightly ran a hand through her hair, then down over her shoulders and back, finally letting it come to rest on the swell of her buttocks. Georgina moaned.

'You make me go all liquid inside,' she whispered.

'Do I?'

'Oh yes. A sort of fiery, molten liquid that's quite indescribable.'

He liked that as well.

'And what do I do to you?'

He nudged her with his groin. 'That.'

This time she groaned.

'Why don't I make myself comfortable?' he suggested.

'Here, let me help you.'

Slowly, starting with his tie, she began undressing him.

Andrew watched her in amusement, relishing the power he had over her. A power he'd had over many women. He'd decided during his meal what course their love-making would take. He had a few surprises in store for Georgina Seaton, surprises taught him years previously by a professional.

When he was finally naked she pressed herself against him again and began to rub herself up and down his body.

'Let's get into bed, darling,' she proposed.

'Not yet.'

His hands, which had been motionless while she had undressed him, started to move. Touching, caressing, fondling.

In the end, which was what he'd intended, Georgina was pleading with him to take her.

It was a night to remember.

Chapter 21

Mr Durie, the specialist, straightened up from Pat's bed, Pat watching him anxiously. There were two nurses also in attendance.

'You're doing extremely well, Mr Flynn,' Durie pronounced. 'I'm delighted with your progress.' He shook his head. 'I only wish I knew what's been wrong with you but that remains a medical mystery I'm afraid.'

'Will I get it again, Doctor?'

Durie gave a thin smile. 'I simply can't answer that. But my guess, and that's all it is, based on years of professional experience I would point out, is I don't believe so.'

Pat heaved a sigh of relief. 'When can I go home?'

'Ah! A good question. Certainly not this week. I want to keep you in for a while to recuperate and for observation. How do you feel?'

'Weak,' Pat confessed.

'Natural enough. I wouldn't have expected anything else after what you've been through. Any headaches?'

'None, Doctor.'

'And within yourself? Deep down that is.'

Pat considered that. 'The same but different I suppose.'

'Different?'

Pat dropped his gaze to stare at the bedclothes. 'You'll laugh.'

'No I won't, Mr Flynn. I assure you.'

Pat glanced at the two nurses standing po-faced in the background, wishing they weren't there. They made this more difficult somehow.

'It's as though I've had some sort of religious experience. I know that sounds daft but there you have the truth of it.'

Durie smiled. 'Interesting. And something I've heard said before.'

'Really?'

'Yes, Mr Flynn. It's more common than you might imagine.'

Durie pondered for a few moments, then said, 'I'm convinced you're well on the way to recovery. You're a lucky man.'

Pat thought of Kathleen. Yes, he was a lucky man and not just to have survived the illness.

Durie picked up Pat's notes from the bottom of the bed, studied them briefly, then, taking out a pen, added a few additional comments.

'I'll see you again tomorrow, Mr Flynn,' Durie declared, replacing the notes.

'Thank you, Doctor.'

'And don't worry. I'll have you home as soon as possible.'

'Thank you, Doctor.'

'In the meantime try and move your bowels. You haven't so far.'

Pat blanched. The idea of using a bedpan was anathema to him. He intended holding out as long as he could before that humiliation. A bottle was one thing, but a pan!

Bridie was standing at the kitchen window staring out over the back courts and tenements that lay beyond. It was odd, she reflected, this was all she'd known for most of her life and yet now, somehow, she felt a stranger here.

How dirty it all was, and squalid. She watched some wee boys playing 'kick the can', the clatter they were making reverberating round the back courts. One of the boys had a great tear in the rear of his shorts so that his bare bottom was peeping out.

She thought of The Haven and Ian Seaton. Now that her da was on the mend it was high time for her to return there. She'd leave the following day, she decided. There was an early train, she'd catch that.

'Ian,' she murmured wistfully.

'Is there something wrong with you?'

Ian turned to face his sister. 'No, why?'

'You've seemed quite out of sorts recently.'

'Have I?'

'Grumpy to say the least.'

It was because of Bridie, he thought. He couldn't wait to see her again, be in her company. 'You haven't appeared quite yourself either.'

Rose immediately became defensive, the accusation too close to the mark. 'There's nothing wrong with me that I'm aware of,' she lied.

'No?'

'I'd know if there was.'

He saw the beginnings of a blush tinge her cheek and

arrived at completely the wrong conclusion – that it was that time of the month for her.

'Anyway, I've got things to do,' Rose declared, and swept from the room.

If Ian had been out of sorts on account of Bridie then she'd been the same way because of Andrew.

When was she going to see him again? she inwardly raged as she hurried on her way.

'How's Mr Flynn?' Geraldine Buchanan asked the coalman who'd taken over Pat's round.

He shook out the bag he'd tipped into her bin. 'Coming along handsomely from what I hear.'

Relief washed through her. Thank God for that. 'Any news of him coming back to work?'

'He won't be doing that for a while, missus,' the man replied. 'I think I said to you the poor sod was at death's door. You don't recover from that overnight.'

'No, of course not.' Geraldine smiled understandingly.

Again the coalman wondered at her concern for Pat. It seemed odd somehow. More than it should have been. There again, it was none of his business. And certainly not to be remarked on back at the yard.

'Thank you, missus,' he said on giving Geraldine her change.

As she'd done on his previous visit, Geraldine poured herself a large drink when the man had gone.

'Bridie?'

And there he was, at long last. 'Hello.'

'How's your father?' Ian queried anxiously.

'Recovering, I'm happy to say. He's hoping to get home before too long.'

'When did you get in?'

'Late last night.'

'I see.'

He found himself staring deep into her eyes, eyes that were attracting him as though he was a piece of iron being drawn to a magnet.

'I missed you.'

That startled Bridie. 'Did you?'

Ian was suddenly covered in confusion. 'Yes,' he whispered.

And how she'd missed him, dreadfully so. 'How's Miss McLaren?'

'Moira? She's fine. Why do you ask?'

Bridie shrugged. 'I don't know.'

He hadn't heard the jealousy in her voice before, now he did. Could it be . . . could it possibly be?

'I went there on Sunday as usual.'

Bridie's face tightened slightly. 'Did you have a good time?'

He had and he hadn't. It had been pleasant enough, though, if he was truthful, boring. Moira had chattered endlessly on.

Ian shrugged. 'I suppose so.'

Suppose so? What kind of answer was that? 'I must be getting along,' Bridie declared. 'I've a lot to do.'

'Of course. Don't let me keep you.'

Ian wheeled around and walked quickly off, leaving Bridie staring after him.

'More wine?'

Moira McLaren shook her head. 'Not for me, Ian, thank you. I really have had sufficient.'

Ian refilled his glass and then lay back to stare at a

beautiful summer sky. He and Moira were having a picnic by the Coothie Burn which ran through the estate. She was resplendent in a white cotton dress, perfect for the occasion, and large, floppy-brimmed, straw hat.

'Do you remember my cousin Elspeth White?' Moira enquired casually. 'I'm sure you've met her.'

Ian had to think for a moment. 'Oh yes.'

'She got engaged last week.'

'Good for her,' Ian smiled.

'To a veterinary surgeon she only met quite recently. It was love at first sight apparently.'

Ian closed his eyes, enjoying the sun beating down on him. He yawned. 'Excuse me.'

Moira tinkled out a laugh. 'That's all right.'

'It really is the most soporific day. If I'm not careful I'll fall asleep.'

She frowned. 'Not with me here I hope you won't.'

He immediately came on to an elbow. 'Sorry, that must have sounded awful. It's simply that between the combination of heat and wine I find myself wanting to drop off. Nothing to do with you, Moira, I assure you.'

That mollified her a little.

'I must say you look gorgeous today,' he declared.

'Why, thank you, kind sir.'

She did too, he thought. Crackingly so. Any man would be proud to have her as his girl friend. He had another sip of wine and listened to the drone of bees.

Moira studied Ian. 'Elspeth is two years younger than me, you know.'

'Is that a fact?'

'And now she's engaged to be married. I quite envy her really.'

Moira continued to watch Ian's face.

A sudden chill thought came into Ian's mind. This wasn't just making conversation. Moira was hinting that they too should get engaged. He said nothing.

'I understand he's bought her the most beautiful ring.'

Ian continued not to reply.

'The wedding is set for next year in the spring. And he's hinted to her that they'll go abroad for the honeymoon. Imagine!' Moira sighed. 'How romantic.'

'Yes, isn't it,' Ian replied quietly.

'I'd love to go abroad for my honeymoon.'

Ian's heart was sinking fast. What had been a very pleasant afternoon had suddenly gone extremely flat. He sipped more wine.

'It'll be a big wedding of course, hundreds there. I wonder if she'll buy a dress or have one made.'

'You must ask her.'

'Oh I will. I shall certainly have my wedding dress made, and those for the bridesmaids.'

Ian swallowed the remains of his glass and refilled it. 'I sometimes fish in this burn,' he stated, changing the subject. 'I've caught some marvellous trout in it.'

Moira's forehead creased. 'Have you indeed.'

'Oh yes.'

'I've never understood what men see in fishing. It seems quite boring to me.'

'Tranquil more like. For much of the time. And then a lot of excitement when you get a bite, not to mention land your fish.'

'Paris I should think,' Moira declared defiantly.

'Paris?'

'For the honeymoon. You can't get more romantic than that.'

'I don't suppose you can,' Ian replied vaguely.

'I've heard such a lot about Paris. The Left Bank, that sort of thing.'

Ian thought of Bridie, the woman he loved. What a situation to find himself in. A situation he had to do something about if he was to retain his sanity.

Moira's lips thinned. 'Wouldn't you like to go to Paris? I believe the food is out of this world.'

'France has never really attracted me,' Ian replied.

'No? How peculiar.'

He briefly closed his eyes. Decisions were going to have to be made soon. And they weren't going to be easy ones.

'I think we should be getting back,' he said briskly, coming to his feet.

Her disappointment clearly showed. 'So soon?'

'We have been here a good while.'

'But I was enjoying myself.'

As had he, until she'd started on about engagements and marriages. He'd been prepared to stay for several hours more until that had started. Talk about putting a dampener on the day.

'Ian.'

'Yes?'

'Come here.'

Christ, he thought. She wasn't going to let up. 'What for?'

Anger flitted across her face. 'Because I'm asking you to.'

He tried not to show his reluctance as he went to her. 'Now what can I do for you?' he queried, taking her in his arms. Hypocrite, he thought to himself.

'You could kiss me for a start.'

'Now that would be a pleasure.'

'Are you sure?'

He managed a smile. 'Of course. Isn't it always?'

Their lips met and he felt nothing. Nothing at all.

'Hmmh,' he murmured when it was over.

She raised a hand and traced it across his cheek. 'Is something wrong?'

'Why should there be?'

'I'm not sure. You don't seem particularly enthusiastic, that's all.'

'No?'

'Or is it my imagination?'

'Your imagination, Moira. A man can't be at white heat all the time you know. It's not like that.'

'I thought . . .' She trailed off.

'What?'

'We have been seeing each other for some time.'

He laughed softly. 'Hardly that. A little while perhaps.'

'You do like me, don't you?'

'Why would you be here if I didn't? Of course I do.'

'We get on so well together.'

Again he thought of Bridie. That extra something that was there when he was with her. That something which excited him in a way Moira never had.

'Yes,' he murmured.

Her doubts disappeared. 'I'm so fond of you, Ian. Truly I am.'

Fond, now there was a word. There again, he'd never declared feelings stronger than that to her so why should she to him?

'And I of you, Moira.'

He kissed her a second time, then disentangled himself. 'I'll pack up.'

Moira never took her eyes off him while he was doing that. He was acutely aware of her stare.

Sean barged into the pub and beckoned the barman over. 'A pint and a hauf,' he said tightly.

God but he needed a drink, a bucketful of the stuff. He'd had another failure back at 'the place'. A smashing wee lassie called Babs whom he'd picked up a fortnight previously.

He'd got her stripped and into bed, then set to. Except, as with Muriel, nothing had happened. Not a bloody thing.

He stared down at the counter, wondering what was wrong with him. Why? The question raged in his mind. Why! Why! Why!

'There you are, Jimmy,' the barman declared, placing his drinks in front of him.

Sean tossed a pound note on to the counter. Then, in one quick motion, he swallowed his whisky.

She'd had a lovely body too, beautiful tits, even better than Muriel. And she'd been keen, no problem there. He'd thought at one point she was going to devour him. So why hadn't he reacted as he should have done?

An awful thought came into his mind, one that both shocked and alarmed him.

Don't be stupid, he told himself. Nah! There was nothing of the nancy boy about him. He'd never fancied men, the very idea made him want to throw up.

A chap came to stand beside Sean, accidentally nudging him. Sean immediately rounded on the chap with a snarl. 'What's your fucking game, eh?'

Alarm flashed on to the chap's face. 'Sorry, I didn't mean it. Honest. I apologise.'

For a moment Sean considered having a go at the chap, giving him a seeing to, then thought the better of it. The bloke had apologised after all. You couldn't ask fairer than that.

He took a deep breath. 'Think no more about it, pal.'

The chap nodded, his relief obvious, wishing he'd never come into that particular pub or been so clumsy. There was that about Sean which he found extremely menacing. Once he'd paid for his drink he moved away to a table at the far side out of harm's way.

Sean was thinking again about Babs and worrying about himself. Afterwards he'd put the frighteners on her as he had on Muriel. She'd keep her yap shut knowing what would happen to her if she didn't.

Why? he asked himself for the umpteenth time.

Why?

Pat sighed. 'I can't tell you how good it is to be home.'

'Come on, get yourself sat down. Remember the doctor told you you've still got to get plenty of rest.

Pat allowed Kathleen to assist him to his favourite chair and sank gratefully into it. 'I know we came by ambulance and all I had to do was get into it and then climb the stairs when we arrived but it hasn't half taken it out of me,' he declared in a weak voice.

'Well, you've been lying in bed all this while so what do you expect?' Kathleen rubbed her hands together. 'Now how about a nice cup of tea? The sort you can stand a spoon up in.'

'That would be terrific.'

He watched her as she filled the kettle and put it on. Truly it was good to be home, that was no lie. To be home with Kathleen.

The outside door banged shut and Sean came in. 'I thought we'd got shot of you for ever,' he joked.

'No such luck I'm afraid, son.'

Sean studied his father. 'You look like shit.'

'Sean!' Kathleen admonished. 'Language please.'

'Sorry, Ma. But he does.'

Pat ran a hand over his face. He knew exactly what he looked like and Sean was right. But time would deal with that.

'You never once came to see me,' Pat said to Sean.

'Don't like hospitals. They give me the creeps. Ma kept me informed of your progress.'

Pat didn't press the point, he knew better.

'What's for dinner?' Sean queried.

'Lamb chops. A special treat for your da.'

Pat raised an eyebrow. 'They're expensive.'

Kathleen glanced at Sean, then at her husband. 'I did mention Sean's been giving me extra. Well it's been quite a bit extra recently. We can afford them.'

Sean gave a thin, almost wicked, smile. 'That's what comes of being a success in the world, eh?'

Pat refrained from commenting on that, well aware where Sean's money was coming from. He didn't approve, not one little bit.

Pat suddenly felt old. Old as could be.

'Kathleen?'

'What, Pat?'

They'd just gone to bed together.

'I want to say something.'

She didn't reply.

'I really do love you, Kathleen. I told you in the hospital and I meant it. Can we start again?'

'What about her?' Kathleen queried in a tight voice.

'I said, it's over. I'll only see her one more time and

that's to finish it between us.' On returning to work he intended asking for his round to be changed. That would make it easier if he didn't have to deliver Geraldine's coal any more.

Pat put an arm round Kathleen and gently pulled her close. 'I'm not up to . . . well you know what. But can we just cuddle?'

She turned to face him and they embraced.

'It'll be just like it used to be,' he whispered. 'Only better. I swear.'

A warmth of contentment welled through Kathleen. Contentment and peace.

'When I'm up and about properly I want to go and take confession,' Pat said. 'I want to do so very badly.'

'I'm delighted to hear that.'

'And I'll have a special word with Father O'Banion. I want him to know everything's fine between us again and also ask him about those dreams I had while in the coma.'

'Father O'Banion will be pleased.'

'Aye, he will.'

'Now get some sleep, Pat, you need it.'

'It'll be the best night's sleep I've had since it happened. And you know why? Because you'll be beside me.'

Everything had come right again, Kathleen reflected. Surely nothing as bad as Pat's affair and illness would ever blight their lives in the future.

Surely.

'So tell me about your book,' Andrew said to Jack, as they enjoyed their weekly visit to the pub. 'I haven't asked you for a while.'

Jack shrugged. 'As always Hettie thinks it's fine. That's all I can say.'

'Well, I'm sure she's right.'

Andrew gazed about him. The pub was quieter than usual and he wondered why that was. It was a beautiful evening outside, the dying sun ablaze on the horizon.

He turned his attention back to Jack. 'I shall be expecting a free copy when it's published you know.'

Jack smiled. '*If* it is published.'

'I'm sure it will be. You're a natural when it comes to writing, Jack. You've proved that.'

'Plays perhaps, but a novel?'

Jack had a sip from his pint. 'If it is published I'm going to dedicate it to your brother Peter. We were great pals he and I.'

Andrew glanced down at the table. He and Peter had never been the best of friends, in fact they'd quite disliked one another. 'That's nice,' he replied.

'One day I'll visit his grave "over there". I'd like that.'

'You'll pull the novel off if I know you, Jack.'

Jack sighed. 'I wish I had as much faith in myself as you and Hettie have in me. You're pillars of support.'

'And rightly so in my opinion.'

'She's a gem that girl. A real gem,' Jack said in a soft, loving voice.

'She is indeed. As I've said so often in the past, I envy you.'

'And as I've said to you in the past, Andrew, you should get married. You don't want to be rattling around in that big house all by yourself. It's positively unhealthy.'

'That's what Charlotte says. She's always going on at me about the same thing.'

'And she's right. As am I.' Jack paused, then said, 'What about Rose Seaton?'

'What about her?'

'Exactly, what about her?'

'Jack, you know I've been sleeping with her stepmother.'

'Which I heartily disapprove of as you're aware.'

'I disapprove of it myself. But there we are.'

'There's something you're not telling me, Andrew. I can hear it in your voice.'

'Can you indeed.'

'Oh yes. So what is it?'

'Her age, Jack, and the fact she's Willie's daughter puts any relationship out of the question.'

'Scruples, eh? Georgina being Willie's wife didn't stop you there,' Jack commented drily.

Andrew blanched. 'That's below the belt.'

'As no doubt what you two get up to when alone together.'

Andrew had to laugh at that.

'Well?'

Andrew decided to confide in Jack. 'Do you remember the last time I went to The Haven, the Seatons' house?'

'I recall.'

'Well, Rose and I went out riding, just the pair of us, during which she near as damnit proposed to me. Or, to put it another way, tried to get me to propose.'

Now it was Jack's turn to laugh. 'Did she really!'

'She's serious, Jack, believe me.'

'Oh I do, I do. And?'

'And nothing. I wasn't having any.'

'Pity,' Jack mused. 'I have a hunch, and it's only that, she'd be ideal for you.'

'Nonsense. Besides, I don't want people thinking of me as a dirty old man.'

'But you are, Andrew, you are. And always have been. If not old by our standards then certainly dirty.'

Andrew grinned. 'I'll take that as a compliment.'

'Take it any way you like. It's true.'

There was a hiatus between them, then Jack said, 'I think you should reconsider the whole matter of Rose.'

'And Georgina?'

'She's already married. Regardless of what's passed between you, leave it that way.'

'Well, I certainly have no intention of trying to pinch her off Willie.'

'There you are then.'

'I'll get another round in,' Andrew stated, and crossed to the bar.

When he returned the subject of the Seatons was mentioned no more.

Chapter 22

Bridie laid down the book she'd been attempting to read. This was the second book she'd borrowed from Miss Rose that had failed to engage her attention.

Not that there was anything wrong with the books. She simply couldn't get into them and that was that.

She ran a hand over her face and gave a soft sigh. What was wrong with her? This had never happened in the past. Books, any book, had been devoured. Especially those with a romantic flavour as this and the last one had.

She closed her eyes for a brief moment, then opened them again. She knew what the trouble was, of course she did. Fiction didn't grip her any more because of reality. In other words, Ian.

Her shining knight no longer existed on the page but in the very house where she lived. Printer's ink had given way to flesh and blood.

'Sir Ian of Seaton,' she murmured, and shivered. Her own knight in real life.

Well, almost her knight, for there could never be anything between them. But how wonderful to pretend there might.

Jeannie Swanson snorted in her sleep which made Bridie smile. Dear Jeannie, what good friends they'd become. She'd have loved to confide in Jeannie, but that was impossible. Her love for Ian was her secret and would have to remain so.

Strangely, though it had been a hard day, she wasn't tired. Sleep would be a long time in coming.

'Ian,' she said, and shivered again. There would never be another love in her life, she was convinced of that. She was one of those people who fall in love once and once only.

Perhaps she should try for another position, she thought. Already knowing she wouldn't. She'd stay as close to Ian as she possibly could for as long as she could.

Moira McLaren, now there was the lucky one. The lass whom Ian would eventually marry. What she'd have given to be in Moira's shoes. Anything, absolutely anything.

She closed her eyes again, remembering how he'd kissed her, and what she'd felt. Heaven come to earth that had been. Sheer unadulterated bliss.

She laid the book aside and snuffed out the candle flickering by her bedside, plunging the room into darkness.

When she finally did fall asleep it was to dream, as she'd known she would, of Ian Seaton.

Willie was standing at a window watching Rose riding in the distance. The lassie must be mad, he thought. She was riding like one demented. If she wasn't careful she was going to come an awful cropper.

He bit his lip, wondering why it was she'd been so strange of late. And strange she'd certainly been. Moody for a start, and petulant. Taken to abruptly leaving their company for no apparent reason or excuse. It was worrying, extremely so.

He'd speak to her, he decided. It was long overdue. Or should he have Georgina do that? She might be better suited to the task than him.

No, he'd do it. He was her father after all. As such perhaps he could get through to her.

Willie took out his cigarettes and lit up, inhaling deeply. Part of the problem was she didn't have a boyfriend. Though why that should be so he couldn't think. She was pretty enough, and personable. You would have thought she'd have caught some lad's eye.

Of course living on the estate didn't help, though there were always a number of opportunities for her to socialise with her own kind.

Only the previous week she'd received an invitation to a summer ball which, to his amazement and annoyance, she'd turned down saying she wasn't really all that interested. You'd have thought, being young and healthy, she'd have grabbed the chance. But no, not Rose. She'd elected to stay at home that evening.

Was she ill in some way? Could that be it? If she was it certainly didn't show. If anything she was the picture of rude health.

So what was it? For it seemed to him something had to be wrong. Perhaps a holiday might do the trick. Though, on reflection, he could hardly send her on her own. Rose and Georgina together? No, he wouldn't do that. He didn't want Georgina being away for the length of a holiday.

He knew he was being selfish in wanting Georgina to be with him, but that's how it was.

He'd think of something. And in the meantime have a

chat with her, a heart to heart. See if he could find out what was what.

Ian glanced at his alarm clock, and groaned. Ten minutes past two and he still couldn't sleep. All to do with Bridie of course, he simply couldn't get her out of his mind. She was haunting him.

Every time he saw her about the house it was as if his heart stopped. An exaggeration? No, that was exactly what it was like.

Bridie Flynn, housemaid. The girl he'd fallen head over heels for.

'Shit,' he swore.

The thing was, should he do something or not? He was going to look a proper idiot if he made a play for her and she rejected him.

There again, why make a play in the first place? To what end? There wasn't one.

'Damn,' he muttered, and started striding up and down.

It had become a joke between Moira and himself. At least on his part. She was still as keen as ever.

Fond, she'd said. And didn't that just about sum it all up. He was fond of her, and she of him. But what basis was that for a marriage? Not nearly enough in his opinion. Though he knew there were those who would have disagreed with that.

Moira was certainly beautiful, that was beyond dispute. And of a pleasant nature, again beyond dispute. But what chance would they have together when he was in love with another woman? Precious little in his opinion.

There it was then, he was going to have to break it off with Moira. There wasn't anything else he could honourably do.

Pa would be disappointed to say the least. Willie had set his heart on their union. As indeed had Georgina.

But damn it all, it was his life and he had to do what he considered right. And marrying Moira McLaren wasn't. Not by a long chalk.

That decision taken he felt a whole lot better. He'd do what had to be done the following Sunday when he visited the McLarens, then tell Willie and Georgina afterwards.

He felt as though a great weight had been lifted from his shoulders. Atlas without the world bowing him down could not have felt more free.

He wondered what Bridie wore in bed, and how she looked when fast asleep. He also wondered . . .

He pulled his dressing-gown more tightly about him as he continued pacing. Although it was summer the night was chill.

He wondered if there would be a row with his pa when he announced his news. Probably, he decided gloomily. He'd have a couple of swift drams before the encounter.

Willie would try to dissuade him, no doubt about it. But he'd stick to his guns. It was over between him and Moira McLaren, he was determined about that.

And God knows how she'd take it. He could expect tears and probably a tantrum. Not something he was looking forward to. Not in the least.

Andrew stared at the letter, recognising the handwriting. No doubt Georgina was trying to set up another tryst.

He discovered he was correct on reading the two sheets of scented notepaper the envelope contained. Willie was going to London on business and various personal matters for a week. Why didn't he drop by during that time, pretending to be unaware that Willie was absent, and stay the night? Or better still, longer. The tone of the letter was a pleading one.

Andrew laid the notepaper in front of him, then rocked back in his chair.

It would be easy for him to get away sometime during the dates mentioned, and another session, or sessions, with the lovely Georgina certainly appealed.

And then there was Rose.

Bridie was halfway down the stairs carrying a tray, Miss Rose having decided to have breakfast in her room, when it happened.

Somehow she slipped and, uttering a startled cry, went tumbling downstairs, the tray and breakfast things flying everywhere. She landed at the foor of the stairs with a jarring thump, banging her head in the process. For the space of a few moments she lost consciousness.

Ian heard the cry and, not knowing who'd made it or why, dashed to help. 'Christ!' he swore when he saw it was Bridie.

He swiftly knelt beside her as she was coming round. 'Oh, my poor darling,' he said. 'Are you hurt?'

Darling? She hazily wondered at that.

Ian grasped her under the arms and hauled her into a sitting position. 'Can you hear me, Bridie? Have you broken anything?'

'I . . . I . . .' She broke off, confused. Broken anything? She didn't know.

'Oh darling Bridie,' he whispered in concern. 'You must be all right. Please say you are.'

There it was again, darling. What was going on? 'I think . . . I think . . . Dizzy, that's all.'

'Let me check you for broken bones.'

He gently felt first one leg, then the other. 'Nothing amiss there,' he declared when there was no reaction from her.

He did the same thing again with her arms, hastily removing his hand when she suddenly yelped.

Bridie gingerly rubbed the spot. 'It's just bruising. I'm certain of it.'

She flexed the arm. 'See. I must have landed on this one.'

'What happened?'

She grinned sheepishly. 'I wasn't paying attention to where I was going and the next thing I was doing a flying act.'

He smiled back at her. 'Can you stand?'

'I'll try.'

He assisted her upright where she swayed on the spot. 'Everything's going round and round,' she whispered.

'It's bed for you, my girl.'

'But my duties!' Bridie protested.

'Bother those! Someone else can do them. It's up to your bed and then I'll send for the doctor.'

'Oh you can't do that, Ian.'

'But I can, and will. No can't about it. Is everything still going round and round?'

'Yes. Only not as badly as it was.'

'Try to walk. And don't worry, I'll be holding you.'

They gradually made it up the stairs and eventually to her bedroom. 'That gave me ever such a fright,' she stated.

'I'm not surprised. You were fortunate not to have broken anything.'

'I really don't need the doctor, Ian.'

'Yes you do. And I'll have no more argument. Now you

can get yourself into bed. I hardly think it proper I help you with that.'

She felt her face colour. 'No.'

'I'll root out Jeannie Swanson and send her to you. In the meantime you stay here. Right?'

'Right,' she agreed meekly, thinking how masterful he was. She liked that.

'I'll be off then. But back later to see how you are.'

'Thank you, Ian.'

He couldn't help himself, the urge was overwhelming. Bending, he tenderly kissed her on the forehead.

Bridie stared wonderingly after him as he hurried from the room.

'Well?' Ian demanded the moment the doctor emerged.

Dr Duthie was an old man close to retirement, his hair white tinged with yellow, as was his thick moustache. Ian was one of the countless children he'd delivered into the world.

'There's nothing to worry about,' Duthie pronounced. 'She's got a wee bit of concussion that'll give her a headache for a day or two. But apart from that she's right as rain.'

Ian gave an exhalation of relief. Thank God for that! 'Thank you, Doctor. If you'll just send in your bill as usual.'

Duthie's eyes twinkled. 'Oh aye, I'll do that all right, Ian. You can count on it.'

Both men laughed.

'Come in!' Bridie called out some minutes later when there was a tap on her door.

Ian entered. 'The doctor says you've got a headache.'

'It's not too bad. I'll survive.'

He saw now what she wore in bed. A plain nightdress without frills or fripperies of any kind. It became her.

'You've been very kind,' she said, a puzzled frown on her face.

'Think nothing of it.'

'Jeannie came and got me changed as you can see. She was terribly upset.'

Not nearly as much as he'd been, Ian thought. Why, Bridie could have been killed. A broken neck could easily have been on the cards. It didn't bear thinking about.

'I've spoken to Mrs Coltart,' he stated. 'Who was extremely sympathetic. You're to stay off until you feel up to resuming work.'

'Thank you.'

'Don't mention it.'

Unable to hold his gaze, quivering inside, Bridie glanced away.

'Right,' said Ian. 'I'll get on. I've got lots to do today. But I will call back again this evening. Just to see how you are.'

'You mustn't trouble yourself,' she protested.

'It's no trouble, Bridie. None at all.'

The quivering was increasing in intensity. 'Fine then,' she mumbled.

He cleared his throat, desperately wanting to remain but of course that was impossible. 'Goodbye for now,' he said a slight choke in his throat.

'Goodbye, Ian.'

He hesitated for another moment, then abruptly left.

He could hear them, Sean thought. He could actually hear

them. The bitch was shouting so loudly she might have been an animal being slaughtered.

'Sounds like Mo's giving her a right old slagging,' Bobby O'Toole sniggered.

Dan Smith lit a cigarette then blew a perfect smoke ring at the ceiling. 'I wish it was me in there.'

'Me too,' Bill O'Connell nodded.

Sean closed his eyes. He'd always got on well with Mo Binchy, the pair of them were good chinas. But right then he hated the bastard.

'Are you all right, Sean?'

Sean opened his eyes again and stared at Jim Gallagher. 'Aye, fine. Why?'

'You look a bit odd.'

Sean could just imagine it. Mo on top, the girl squirming beneath, her face contorted with passion. Mo doing to her what he couldn't. A hard core of anger erupted inside him, anger at himself and his inadequacy.

Sean jumped to his feet. 'I fancy a pint. Anyone else coming?'

'You don't have to ask twice,' Dan Smith replied getting out of his chair.

The lassie, Sean hadn't caught her name, gave a great cry of exultation and pleasure.

'Bloody hell!' Bill O'Connell exclaimed, turning to face the wall beyond which was the bedroom where the couple were.

Sean strode quickly from the room and house. He'd had enough. More than enough.

'Hello again,' Ian smiled. He was holding a large bunch of flowers from the garden.

'Are those for me?'

'They are indeed. Like them?'

'Oh yes,' she breathed. No one had ever given her flowers before. She was thrilled to bits.

Ian crossed and gave them to her. 'Jeannie can put them in something when she comes up later.'

Bridie sniffed the flowers. 'They smell gorgeous.'

'I picked them myself.' He looked about him. 'They might help brighten up this room a little. It's somewhat dingy to say the least.'

Bridie laid the flowers on the bed beside her.

'So how are you feeling now?'

'A lot better.'

'And the headache?'

'Not as bad as it was. I shall return to work tomorrow.'

Ian frowned. 'You'll do no such thing. That was a terrible fall you took. You'll stay in bed for another day anyway and no arguing.'

'But . . .' She broke off when he held up a hand.

'Those are orders, Bridie. You'll remain in bed.'

Again she thought how masterful he was. 'If you say so, Ian.'

'I do.'

She glanced down at the bedclothes. 'It's very good of you to come and visit me again. I just hope it doesn't cause the rest of the staff to gossip. You know what it's like.'

Ian hadn't thought of that. Hmmh, he mentally mused.

'Ian?'

'What?'

'Can I ask you something?'

'Of course,' he beamed.

Bridie took a deep breath. This was hard. She only hoped she wasn't about to make a fool of herself. 'Why did you call me darling?'

That both startled and confused him. 'Did I?' He knew damn well he had but was pretending innocence.

'Twice. At the bottom of the stairs.'

He turned away so she couldn't see his expression. A word sprang to mind, the word Moira had used. 'You must know I'm fond of you, Bridie. Very fond indeed.'

She allowed a few seconds to elapse before saying, 'And you kissed me. In here.'

Should he confess, confide in her? He couldn't. He simply couldn't. 'Can you keep a secret, for now anyway?' he queried, noting that his voice was shaking a little.

'If you wish.'

'Until Sunday that is. Then everyone will know.'

'You have my promise, Ian. Whatever you tell me is strictly between the pair of us.'

How adorable she looked, he thought. He wanted to take her in his arms, hold her, breathe in her scent, kiss her.

'I shall be breaking it off with Moira McLaren this Sunday. She and I are finished.'

Bridie's eyes opened wide. 'But why? She's so beautiful, Ian.'

'That's as may be. I certainly can't deny it. But . . . Well she just isn't right for me.'

'I see.'

'Moira and I would be a mistake. For a while I thought differently. But now I know better.'

Bridie was rocked by this news. As everyone else in the house was, she had been convinced Ian and Moira would get married. She didn't know what to think.

'What will your father say?'

Ian gave a wry smile. 'He won't be best pleased. He had his heart set on the union. As indeed did my stepmother.'

'When will you tell them?'

'Sunday evening after dinner.'

'I don't envy you.'

He barked out a short laugh. 'I don't envy myself. All in all it should be quite a day.'

Bridie knew she shouldn't ask, but she couldn't help herself. 'Is there . . . someone else?'

Oh Lord, he thought. He didn't want to lie to Bridie, but how could he possibly tell her the truth? 'Yes,' he admitted, surprising himself with his honesty.

Bridie stared at him. 'Would I know her?'

'Yes,' Ian said very softly.

The quivering she'd experienced earlier returned. Don't be stupid, she told herself. It couldn't be her. Though if only . . .

'You still haven't said why you called me darling,' Bridie mumbled.

Ian took a deep breath, then another. It had been wrong to come here, dreadfully wrong. If he wasn't careful he was going to compromise himself. It would have been different if she hadn't been a housemaid, a working-class lass from Glasgow. And yet, despite all that, the truth remained. He loved her.

'I'd best be going,' he declared abruptly. 'I'm glad you like the flowers.'

'As I said, they're gorgeous.'

'And no work tomorrow,' he said sternly. 'I shall be furious if you even attempt it.'

'I won't, Ian. And your secret's safe with me.'

'Goodnight then, Bridie.'

Their eyes held. 'Goodnight, Ian. I shall be thinking about you on Sunday and hoping it all goes well.'

'Thank you.'

He didn't want to leave. That was the last thing he wanted. What he did want was to stay with Bridie. Not just then, but for ever.

The door snicked shut behind him.

Ian's face was hard as stone when he left the McLarens. What he'd just endured was far worse than he'd imagined.

Moira had been bad enough, but her mother, Delphine! That had been a nightmare. Her verbal abuse was still ringing in his ears.

He desperately needed a drink. No, more than one, several to restore his equilibrium. He'd never forget Moira clinging to him as though that would change his mind. Or the pure venom in Delphine's eyes when she'd been told the news.

He didn't dare glance back in case Moira was at a window which he suspected she might be.

'What!' Willie exclaimed, coming to his feet from the chair he'd just sat in moments before.

They were in Willie's den where he had requested they retire. The den was hardly used by Willie nowadays and hadn't been since he'd married Georgina, Willie much preferring her company to being on his own.

'Broken it off, Pa.'

'But why for God's sake?'

'We weren't right together, Pa. It wouldn't have worked.'

'Stuff and nonsense,' Willie snorted. 'You made a lovely couple.'

Ian sighed. 'Can I help myself to a dram?'

Willie waved a hand. 'Do as you please.'

'You, Pa?'

'May as well.'

Ian crossed to the decanter and glasses sitting atop a bookcase.

He poured out and handed his father a stiff measure. 'There you are.'

'I don't understand. I really don't.'

'Let me put it this way, Pa, how did you feel about Mother when you married?'

Willie studied his son. 'Go on.'

'Were you in love with her?'

Willie's expression softened. 'Very much so.'

'That's how I want to be when I wed. In love with a woman who's equally in love with me.'

Willie's expression softened even further. 'I understand.'

'I don't love Moira, Pa, and never will. Nor does she love me.'

'Did she say that?'

Ian shook his head. 'She didn't have to. I just knew. I was a good match, Pa, and that's a very different thing from love. Oh, we might have rubbed along together but what sort of life is that?'

Willie didn't reply.

'You've been lucky, twice. First with Mother and then with Georgina.'

'Yes,' Willie agreed, nodding slightly. 'I certainly have been.'

Ian saw off his dram and went to pour himself another. He wondered where Bridie was in the house and what she was doing. In the kitchen probably, he decided, with the staff having their meal.

'She's very beautiful, Ian.'

'Indeed she is. But I've learnt a few things along the

way, Pa, and one is that beauty isn't everything. Far from it. Don't you agree?'

Willie regarded his son with new respect. 'I do.'

'Moira's rather shallow which isn't what I want at all. She'd bore the pants off me before long as sure as eggs are eggs.'

Willie smiled. 'Possibly.'

'There's no possibly about it, Pa. Take Georgina for instance, whatever anyone may think of her she's hardly boring. She certainly seems to keep you on your toes and up to scratch.'

'I can't disagree with that,' Willie commented wryly.

'And another thing, they say look at the mother and see how the girl is going to turn out. Well, I saw a side of Delphine McLaren today that I thought most distasteful. You should have heard her, voice hard as iron, almost spitting like a snake.'

Willie laughed. 'Delphine does have a reputation for having a bit of a temper.'

'Bit of one! I'd call it a lot more than that.'

'And getting what she wants. You put a spoke in her wheel which she wouldn't have liked, or appreciated, at all.'

'You can say that again.'

'Georgina will be disappointed,' Willie mused. 'She was as much for this as me.'

'I'm sorry about that. But I won't be changing my mind as far as Moira McLaren is concerned. And that's final.'

'I believe you, son,' Willie replied quietly.

Willie thought of his first wife Mary, and Georgina. Ian was quite right. Marriage without love wasn't worth the candle.

Chapter 23

Sean was doing the rounds collecting protection money, and very nicely the gang was doing too. Every month saw an increase in their take, with that little bit extra, which they were unaware of, to him.

He was coming out of a greengrocer's when Sammy Renton came hurrying up.

'Hey, Sean!'

Sammy's face was flushed and he was gasping for breath when he stopped beside Sean. 'I've been looking for you everywhere. Have you heard?'

Sean frowned. 'Heard what?'

'Wee Pete Murray's fallen foul of the Tong.' Pete was one of the younger members of the Samurai, a lad no more than fifteen.

'How do you mean, fallen foul?'

'A number of them set on him and gave him a hell of a beating. He's been taken to hospital.'

Sean immediately thought of Big Bill Bremner. 'What did Pete do?'

'The stupid bugger was in their territory when they grabbed him for being there. They dragged him into a close and that was that. He didn't have a chance.'

Pete should have known better, Sean thought. 'How bad is he?'

'Pretty bad. They gave him a right kicking.'

'Was he marked?'

Sammy shook his head. 'Nothing like that, just a kicking. What are we going to do?'

'You mean in retaliation?'

'Aye, that's right.'

Sean took a deep breath. This needed thinking about. And seriously. 'Tonight at eight. We'll meet at "the place". Pass the word.'

'I'll do that, Sean.'

'Which hospital?'

'The Southern General.'

'I'll go and see him.'

Sammy beamed. 'He'd appreciate that, Sean. He thinks you're the next thing to God.'

Sean tried not to show the pleasure that statement gave him. Next thing to God! Wasn't that something.

'Eight o'clock,' he repeated.

'Aye, Sean. I'll pass the word.'

'Now off you go. I've got things to do.'

Sean's next port of call was a pub where he sat in a corner ruminating. Was there more to this than appeared on the surface? He wasn't sure.

'We can't let this go,' declared Don McGuire hotly. 'The Tong would think us a bunch of jessies.'

'Aye, we should give one of their lot the same treatment,' said Noddy Gallagher.

'I'm not so certain about that,' murmured Jim, Noddy's brother.

Sean focused on Jim. 'Why so?'

'The stupid bastard shouldn't have been where he was. He knows the rules and broke them.'

Sean nodded. 'I agree.'

'They'll still think we're a bunch of jessies,' Don repeated.

Brainpower wasn't exactly one of Don's assets, Sean reflected. Don was a hothead through and through.

'Mo?'

'There's hundreds of them. What could we do except get massacred? It would be four to one if not more.'

Bill O'Connell was in a blue funk about taking on the Tong. He was fervently praying this would come to nothing.

'Pete's got internal injuries,' Sean said quietly. 'There's even the possibility he might die.'

Bill blanched. Holy Mary Mother of God!

'And what if he does?' That was Bobby O'Toole.

'You tell me,' Sean retorted.

Bobby puffed on a cigarette, no keener than most there to go up against the Tong, knowing it would be certain suicide. 'It was his fault,' he mumbled.

'Anyone disagree with that?' Sean queried.

No one did.

Sean closed his eyes. He'd already made up his mind before coming to the meeting that they wouldn't do anything, but it was important everyone had their say.

'Well, Sean?'

His eyes flicked open. 'We let it pass. That's the sensible thing to do. Pete was in the wrong, as Jim says. He's paid the penalty and let's leave it at that.' Sean paused. 'Agreed?'

'Agreed,' was repeated throughout the gathering, with the exception of Don McGuire.

'Don?'

'Agreed,' Don said reluctantly.

'That's settled then. We forget it.'

Pete Murray survived, though he was never quite the same again. A blow to the head had seen to that. For the rest of his life he was referred to as 'daftie'.

Rose was bored, wondering what she could do, when Andrew was ushered into the drawing room. 'Andrew!' she exclaimed in delight.

'Hello, Rose.'

'This is a surprise,' she said, coming to her feet.

'I was more or less passing and thought I'd call in to see how you all were.'

Her eyes were sparkling. 'Pa's away I'm afraid.'

He pretended disappointment. 'Really?'

'In London. Some dreary business or other.'

'Which is why I'm in the area. Business that is.'

How wonderful he looked, she thought. Absolutely scrumptious. 'Will you take tea or coffee?'

'Coffee would be nice.'

She hurried over to the bell pull. 'How are you?'

'In the pink, as they say. And you?'

'The better for your company.'

She hadn't changed, he thought with satisfaction, thinking of the lectures he'd had from Jack Riach. Well, not lectures exactly, more friendly advice.

She'd matured somewhat, he observed. There was a difference to her tone of voice and the way she carried herself. He rather liked it.

Penny, one of the maids, appeared, and Rose ordered coffee and biscuits to be brought.

'Please sit, Andrew,' she smiled after Penny had gone.

'Thank you.'

She sat facing him. 'You're looking terribly well.'

'As are you.'

'I didn't . . . well, let's just say this is a pleasant surprise.'

'I'm sorry Willie's not here.'

'But you'll stay of course. The night, I mean.'

'I'm not so sure now,' he pretended to prevaricate.

'Oh please!'

Alice, there it was again. Not just the way she sat a horse, but Alice.

'Where's Georgina?'

'Oh somewhere about the house or grounds,' Rose replied airily. 'I don't really know.'

'She hasn't gone to London with Willie then.' What a glib liar he was, he thought.

'No.'

'Then I shall have the company of the pair of you.'

Rose fervently wished Georgina had gone to London which would have meant she'd have had Andrew all to herself.

'Will you stay?'

He shrugged. 'I'm not sure that's appropriate with Willie away. It might not seem proper.'

'Oh, stop being a fuddy duddy. Of course it's proper. I shall be furious if you don't.'

He arched an eyebrow. 'Really?'

'Yes,' she stated firmly. 'I shall. So stay the night you will.'

Andrew had to smile at her determination. If only she

knew the real reason for his visit she might not be so insistent.

'So what have you been up to?' he asked.

It was half an hour later when Georgina appeared. 'Andrew! I've just this moment been told you're here.'

He rose and gave her a small bow. 'Rose has been entertaining me. We've had a wonderful chat.'

That annoyed Georgina. 'I'm so pleased.'

'Andrew's staying the night,' Rose enthused.

'That's nice. It'll be lovely having company. Rose has told you that Willie's away, I presume?'

'Yes.'

'He'll be sorry to have missed you.' Georgina's insides were fluttering at the thought of what lay ahead later. She could already imagine herself in Andrew's arms, his strong body thrusting against hers. How she'd dreamed of it, fantasised about it.

'I see you've had coffee.' She smiled.

'Yes we have.'

'So how about something stronger? I could use a sherry myself.'

'How unlike you!' Rose exclaimed. Georgina was usually abstemious where alcohol was concerned.

'A little treat now and again is quite acceptable,' Georgina answered a trifle condescendingly. 'Especially when we have such a nice, unexpected guest.'

'I'm flattered,' Andrew declared. 'Shall I do the honours?'

'Please.'

Rose had been hoping Georgina would have kept away longer, she'd been having such a good time with Andrew alone. She wondered how she could get him on his own again.

Both women had sherry, Andrew whisky, which he was delighted to see was Drummond.

'Now then, Georgina,' he said, resuming his chair. 'What's new?'

Ian was done in. It had been a particularly hard day with a great deal of physical work involved. All he wanted was a bath, some food and then bed.

He came up short when he spotted the Rolls parked in front of the house. 'Damn!' he muttered to himself, recognising the car as Andrew's. He could well have done without this.

He let himself in quietly, pausing momentarily when he heard voices, one being Andrew's. He'd have to suffer the bugger through dinner, he thought. But he would excuse himself as shortly afterwards as was acceptable without being rude. Again he wondered why he didn't like Andrew. There was just something about the man.

Upstairs he stopped when he spied Bridie's rear view going in the opposite direction. His first impulse was to run after and talk to her. An impulse he resisted.

Ian sighed when she disappeared round a corner. What torture it was not being able to pursue her the way he would have liked, to court her as he had Moira. It was absolute agony.

Agony.

Rose woke with the most terrible pain in her stomach. It was quite excruciating.

She'd have to go to the toilet, she decided. This wasn't something for the pot under the bed, it was far more serious than that.

She groaned as she got out of bed. What had brought this

on? She had no idea. It certainly couldn't have been dinner, which had been delicious. Mrs Kilbride was scrupulous about her kitchen hygiene and what she used.

Rose slipped into her dressing-gown and padded to the door. She felt terrible.

She was halfway to the toilet when she heard the sound. A sound which at first mystified her. It was coming from her Pa and Georgina's bedroom.

Suddenly she went beetroot red, recognising it for what it must be. The noise of extreme passion.

Then anger flamed inside her. For who else could be with Georgina than Andrew? 'Bastard!' she hissed through gritted teeth. 'Oh, you rotten bastard!'

And to think she'd never guessed. What a fool she'd been. A blind, stupid fool.

Tears blinked into her eyes as she continued to listen, all sorts of images going through her mind. The kind of images that made her want to vomit in disgust.

How could Georgina betray her father like that? Willie who loved and adored her with every ounce of his being. If there were any vestiges of youth left in Rose they vanished there and then. The harsh realities of life had finally claimed her.

And Andrew, whom she loved, being with Georgina. That hurt. Oh how that hurt. Like a knife plunged straight into the heart, plunged and twisted.

She quietly sobbed, her discomfort temporarily forgotten in the light of this revelation. The plans she'd had disappeared like so many birds released into the sky. Rose rubbed a hand over her forehead, willing herself to continue on to the toilet, and yet somehow unable to do so. And still the sounds went on, all from Georgina.

How long had this been going on? she wondered. Not

that it really mattered. All that did was that it had been. Poor Pa, poor cuckolded Pa. If she was weeping it wasn't only for herself but him.

For a moment she thought of rousing Ian, then decided against it. God alone knew what he would do. She wouldn't have been surprised if he took a gun to Andrew. Took it and used it.

No, this was something she must never speak about. Something she had to keep strictly to herself. If Georgina wanted to play the slut then so be it. Pa would never find out from her. Not in a million years.

As for Andrew, damn him to hell! He was loathsome beyond belief.

Ian had already gone out when Rose joined Georgina and Andrew at breakfast. She felt terrible after an awful night. If she'd slept she hadn't been aware of it. Andrew and Georgina on the other hand were both as perky as could be.

'Good morning, Rose,' Georgina beamed.

She stared at her stepmother, hating her. 'Good morning.'

'Good morning, Rose,' Andrew echoed.

As for him! 'Good morning,' she somehow managed to force in reply.

Georgina frowned. 'Are you all right?'

'Why do you ask?'

'You seem a little peaky.'

'Do I?'

'Pale,' Andrew commented, concern in his voice.

Rose sat and waited to be served. The last thing she'd wanted was to join them for breakfast but thought it would have looked odd if she hadn't. 'Kippers please,' she said to Penny the maid who was in attendance.

'It's a gorgeous day outside. Absolutely wonderful,' Georgina gushed.

'I noticed,' Rose replied, a trace of acid in her voice.

'I think we should go for a long walk,' Andrew proposed.

'I thought you might be in a rush to get back to Dalneil,' Rose answered.

Andrew couldn't have felt better. His session with Georgina had been first class. By God, but she was a quick learner. And enthusiastic with it. Their lovemaking had just gone on and on.

'I'll be happy to do that.' Georgina smiled at Andrew.

Bitch! Rose thought, jealousy tearing at her. After breakfast she intended returning to her room and staying there in the hope that Andrew would have left by lunchtime.

'I wonder how Willie's getting on in London?' Georgina mused. 'I might try and telephone him later at his club.'

But not to tell him what you were up to last night, Rose thought grimly. Oh no, you wouldn't do that, lady. Bitch!

'Did you have any particular plans for today, Rose?'

She glanced dyspeptically at Andrew. How she wished it had been her in that bedroom with him. She he was making love to. She making those sounds of pleasure. Sounds that had been ringing in her ears for most of the night.

'Reading.'

'Reading!' he exclaimed.

'That's right. I enjoy it.'

'I didn't know that.'

She had no appetite whatsoever. She'd have to toy with

the kippers, eat just a few mouthfuls. 'When are you leaving?' she queried abruptly.

Georgina glanced sharply at Rose, not appreciating her tone. 'That's hardly something to ask a guest,' she declared.

Rose didn't reply.

'I thought I might stay another night,' Andrew stated. He was regarding her quizzically, wondering what was wrong. This wasn't the Rose he was used to.

Again she said nothing, but her heart was in her boots. Another night so he and Georgina could be together again. It made her want to spit.

'Should I leave today?' he queried slowly.

Georgina stopped eating to stare at Andrew in dismay. What was this business about leaving today? That had already been agreed between them.

'Suit yourself. Do as you wish,' Rose declared, pretending, or at least trying to, that she didn't care what he did.

'Then I shall stay if you don't mind.'

'I don't.'

What on earth was going on? Georgina wondered. Why this sudden hostility on Rose's part? It was positively oozing out of her. It was as though . . .

Georgina went icy cold inside. Rose couldn't know. How could she possibly? And yet it was as if she did.

Andrew was thinking the same thing, wishing now he'd never come to The Haven. For what if Rose did know and said something to her father! He dreaded to think the outcome of that.

'Is something wrong, Rose?' Andrew asked quietly.

'Wrong? No, why should there be?'

'You seem a trifle . . . upset.'

'Can't imagine why. There isn't a reason.'

Relief washed through Andrew, as it did Georgina who resumed eating.

When Rose's kippers came they tasted like cardboard in her mouth.

After breakfast, as she'd promised herself, she returned to her room where she cried for the rest of that morning.

'I'll leave Willie if you wish.'

Andrew and Georgina were out walking in a meadow with a fading summer sun high overhead. 'Leave Willie?'

'If you wish, Andrew. I want to be with you, not him.'

Andrew thought of Willie, and Ireland where they'd met and been colleagues together. He'd been a rat in his life, he had no illusions about that, but simply couldn't do that to a pal. Though he had to admit it was tempting. A temptation he mustn't succumb to.

'No,' Andrew stated baldly.

Georgina's face fell. 'But we're so good together. A natural couple if ever there was.'

'That's true. But the answer's still no. I won't hurt Willie like that. What I've done, we've done, is bad enough. But for him to find out and then lose you! It would finish him. And you know it would.'

'But what about me?'

Andrew thought of Alice. 'It seems we never get what we truly want in life, that it's all a compromise. If things had been different . . . Except they're not. You have a good marriage, a man who dotes on you. Isn't that enough?'

'No,' she whispered. 'I need more than that.'

Andrew knew then he'd never sleep with Georgina again, that it was all over between them.

'I need you, and what you do to me in bed,' Georgina added, still in a whisper.

'I'm sorry,' Andrew said. 'I truly am.'

She stopped and turned to face him. 'Don't I mean anything to you?'

'Of course you do, Georgina. But there are things which are right and others that are wrong. If you did leave Willie and came to me it wouldn't work.'

'But why?'

'Because Willie would always be between us. A ghost haunting us until the day we die. Believe me, that's how it would be.'

Georgina sucked in a deep breath. 'You're saying good-bye, aren't you?'

'Yes.'

Her body jerked the way a fish does when gaffed. 'Oh please, Andrew, please. I want you so much.'

'We've had a good time together, Georgina, let's just leave it at that. A fond memory.'

'Memory,' she choked.

'That's right.' He took her hand. 'No regrets, eh? Let's never have those.'

She'd never regret Andrew, she thought bitterly. What she would regret was this conversation and his breaking it off between them. If only she hadn't suggested leaving Willie the relationship might have gone on for who knew how long. But suggest it she had and this was the consequence.

'Georgina?'

'I'm fine,' she replied, forcing a smile on to her face.

Should she try and make him change his mind? she wondered as they resumed walking. But she already knew she wouldn't. There had been a finality and determination in Andrew's voice which told her any such effort would be useless.

Never again to experience what she had the previous night, she thought in despair. She simply couldn't believe that to be so. And yet it would be.

Andrew made his excuses and left directly after luncheon.

A puzzled, yet pleased, Rose watched him drive off. Georgina couldn't bear to.

Kathleen glanced over at Pat sitting facing her, reading the evening paper as he usually did at that time of night. Sean was out, Alison playing dollies between them.

'Pat?'

'Aye, what is it?' he answered without looking up.

'It's Friday night. Why don't you take a wee dauner down to the pub? It'll do you good.'

He stared at her in surprise. Kathleen actually proposing he go to the pub! Now there was a turn up for the book. He shook his head.

'Don't worry about money. I'll give you some. Sean was more than generous this week.'

'No, Kathleen. I won't bother.'

She laughed softly. 'Pat Flynn turning down a chance to go to the pub. I don't believe it.'

'Aye, well there you are.'

'I don't understand, Pat.'

He sighed and laid his paper aside. 'An explanation is it, woman?'

'I'm curious.'

Pat closed his eyes for a moment, then opened them again. A smile lit up his face. 'The real reason I don't want to go, Kathleen me darlin', is that I'm perfectly happy to be here with you. I don't need the pub, or the people there any more, or anything like that. Just you and I together in our own wee house is all I ask for.'

Alison had stopped playing to gape at her father.

Kathleen dropped her gaze, touched in a way she'd never been touched before. 'Thank you, Pat,' she whispered.

'No, my angel, thank *you*.'

He picked up his paper again and resumed reading while Kathleen dashed a tear from her eye.

There were times when life truly was worth living, she reflected. They might be few and far between, but there were times.

'It was the waiting that was the worst I think,' Jack Riach said quietly to Hettie. 'The waiting, knowing you were about to be ordered to go over the top and all that entailed.

'The rest was bad enough. The hours, the days, months, you spent thinking, remembering what it had been like before. And what it had now become. And all the time men, chums, disappeared. Killed most of them, wounded the lucky ones. The nightly bombardments that shook the dugout, the whizz bangs and "Jack Johnsons".'

Jack broke off into a brooding silence.

'Would you like a cup of tea?'

He shook his head. 'I sometimes wonder if it isn't worse for me being blind.'

'Why so?'

'Perhaps I remember more than most. Perhaps the images and sounds stay more real in my memory than they do for sighted people. I don't know. But I think I might be right.'

Hettie closed the notebook she'd been writing in and laid it by. 'I would say that's enough for today. You've done your quota.'

'And still I haven't got the end. But it'll come, I know it will.'

'I'm sure, knowing you.'

Jack sighed. 'All those chaps, Peter Drummond amongst them, all gone. Blown to buggery or worse. I still miss Peter like the devil. He was the best friend I ever had, or ever will. Excluding you, of course.'

'There's Andrew.'

Jack smiled wryly. 'Andrew's a friend, but not like his brother Peter. He and I were as close as two men can platonically be.'

'Tommy's at school,' Hettie said.

Jack frowned. 'So?'

'Why don't we go upstairs? I fancy a cuddle.'

The frown was replaced by a smile that curled the corners of his mouth. 'I can't think of anything nicer.'

'Neither can I. And no more talk about the war. Agreed?'

'Agreed.'

He might not talk about it but it was always there, always with him, he thought as, hand in hand, they mounted the stairs.

And that's how it would always be.

Chapter 24

Rose sat listening to her father and Georgina chatting animatedly to one another, Willie having returned from London earlier that day. Ian was dozing in a chair after another hard day's physical work.

She studied Georgina's face which showed no sign whatsoever of her betrayal. All it did show was pleasure at having Willie home again.

If only her father knew what had gone on while he'd been away, he wouldn't be so delighted with Georgina's company then. Quite the contrary.

Georgina reached across and patted Willie's hand as he gazed adoringly at her. Willie couldn't wait till it was time to go to bed and every so often his eyes slid sideways to where a clock was quietly ticking.

Well, Georgina's secret was safe with her, Rose reflected. For a number of reasons, not least the effect it would have on Willie should he find out his wife was an adulteress.

Jezebel, Rose thought. Bitch! And to commit that

adultery with Andrew, the man *she* loved. That was the hardest thing, the cruellest cross to bear.

It was going to be difficult, damnably difficult, but she had to try and forget Andrew Drummond. Though it would break her heart to do so.

How could she possibly retain any aspirations in that direction when he'd . . . She drew in a deep breath. Done that with Georgina.

Willie turned to her. 'You're very quiet tonight, Rose.'

'Am I?'

'You've hardly said a word all evening.'

'Maybe that's because I couldn't get a word in edgeways.'

He laughed. 'Georgina and I have been rattling on I suppose.'

'Just a bit.'

'Natural after all. I have missed her a great deal and I presume she has me.'

'You know that to be true, Willie.'

Rose had an almost overwhelming urge to leap across the room and slap Georgina's face. Slap it as hard as she possibly could.

'So what have you been up to?' Willie enquired of Rose.

'Nothing much. The usual.'

Willie nodded. 'Have you been riding?'

'Several times. I shall go out again tomorrow morning, providing the weather permits.'

'A pity Andrew hadn't stayed on. He might have gone with you.'

Rose swallowed hard. 'Perhaps.'

'Yes, that is a pity,' Georgina concurred.

Rose couldn't resist it, Georgina not having given any

reason for his sudden departure. 'I thought he *was* going to stay for another day.'

For a brief moment something flickered in Georgina's eyes, then was gone. 'He decided he'd better get home after all. Some matter he'd temporarily forgotten about.'

Suddenly Rose couldn't stand it any longer, the sheer hypocrisy of it all. Her own as well as Georgina's.

She stood up. 'I think I'll go for a walk in the garden.'

'At this time of night!' Willie exclaimed. 'It's pitch black out there.'

'I still want to go.'

'Then you'd better wrap up warm,' Georgina said. 'The nights are drawing in.'

'I'm not a child, Georgina,' Rose snapped in reply. 'I'll wear what I consider appropriate.'

Georgina stared at Rose in consternation. 'I didn't mean to offend. Of course you're not a child. On the contrary, you're quite the young woman.'

And one who hates you, Rose thought. 'I shan't be too long.'

'So you broke it off,' Jack repeated, and sipped his pint.

'That's right. She wanted to leave Willie and I couldn't have that.'

'Well, well,' Jack murmured.

'I take it you approve.'

'Oh yes.'

'The damn thing is she was right when she said we made a good couple, a natural one. That's exactly what we made. And that body! Oh, Jack, you wouldn't believe it.'

'Except she's someone else's wife,' Jack replied drily. 'Wonderful body or not, she's someone else's wife and someone who's a pal.'

'I know,' Andrew said dejectedly. 'That was the swine of it.'

'How did she take the news?'

'She put up a good front, I'll give her that. Though I could tell how hurt she was. I have to admire her self-control as my breaking it off was the last thing she expected.' Andrew paused, then added, 'It was the last thing I expected as well. But what else could I do?'

'You did right,' Jack assured him. 'If you'd strung her along it would only have got worse.'

'And what if she'd told Willie about our affair? That would have been ghastly.'

'You mean, to try and force your hand?' Jack thought about that. 'I suppose it was entirely possible. Mind you, dear boy, have you considered this, she might still.'

'Christ,' Andrew swore. 'I hadn't.'

'Something for you to ponder on.'

'I don't have to. If she leaves Willie thinking she's coming to me then she's mistaken, very much so. That's the least I could do for Willie.'

'Pity he's such a terribly nice chap, isn't it,' Jack commented, again drily.

'Aye, a pity. If he hadn't been . . .' Andrew shrugged. 'Well, who knows.'

'Indeed.'

There were a few moments' silence between them, then Jack said, 'So how about Rose?'

'She was fine. Though a bit testy over breakfast I have to admit. I actually wondered if she'd guessed about Georgina and myself.'

'Could she have done?'

'I don't see how, Jack. She was well tucked up before I went to Georgina's room.'

'Well, perhaps either you or Georgina gave the game away while she was present. It could be she noticed a look or expression and put two and two together.'

Andrew shook his head. 'No, that's hardly likely. I'd lay odds against it. Both Georgina and myself were extremely careful. Even when alone together.'

'Then maybe it was due to frustration.'

'Frustration?' Andrew queried, reaching for his whisky.

'She did lay her cards on the table after all and you haven't done anything about it.'

'I told her it wasn't on because of her age and being Willie's daughter.'

Jack laughed softly. 'But did she believe you? That's the thing. Anyway, women who lay their cards on the table and get rebuffed tend not to take the matter kindly.'

'That's possible,' Andrew mused.

'Will you see her again?'

'Who, Rose?'

'That's who we're now talking about, isn't it?'

'Oh I should imagine so. But not for a while. I shan't be returning to The Haven in a hurry so that Georgina can come to terms with how things now stand.'

'I still think you should marry Rose. I really do. Don't forget I heard her voice and she adores you. You could do a lot worse than that.'

A picture of Alice drifted into Andrew's mind. Dear sweet Alice whom he'd fallen in love with. But she was dead and gone, he'd never see her again in this lifetime.

'I'll get another round in,' Andrew declared, abruptly terminating the conversation.

Ian glanced up and down the corridor. It was a work day but he'd contrived to get back to the house on an excuse.

He took a deep breath. This was ridiculous, utterly ridiculous. But he was going to do it nonetheless.

Unobserved, the staff about their duties elsewhere, this part of the house deserted, he swiftly opened the door and slipped inside, hurriedly closing the door again behind him.

He gazed about, drinking in every last detail of what he considered a rather miserable room. Bridie's room.

There was her bed, neatly made, nightdress folded on top. The same nightdress she'd been wearing when he'd brought her the flowers.

'Bridie,' he whispered.

Was it his imagination or could he actually smell her? He believed he could. Especially when he moved to her bed and stood beside it.

Ian ran a hand over his slightly damp forehead. The woman was driving him insane, every fibre of his being craving for her. He exhaled slowly, balled his fists then released them again.

He thought of Moira McLaren. How she'd become a distant memory in such a short time. It was as though she'd never existed, or at least their relationship. She might be beautiful but she paled into insignificance beside Bridie. Bridie who, for him, shone like a bright star at night. Bridie, who made his pulse race every time he saw her.

'Madness,' he muttered. 'Sheer madness.' How had this happened, how? He didn't know, only that it had and was torture.

Her case was under the bed and he briefly contemplated opening it to see what was inside. No, he decided, that was going too far. A real violation of her privacy. Coming into her room was bad enough, the case would be too much.

He mustn't stay too long, he reminded himself. That

would be folly. How could he possibly explain being in a member of staff's room? He couldn't.

Picking up her nightdress he held it to his nose, the scent of her now strong in his nostrils. He drew it deep into his lungs, savouring it.

Enough, he thought. Enough. Replacing the nightdress, carefully arranging it as it had more or less been, he wheeled about and left the room, striding on his way.

'Bloody idiot,' he muttered to himself. 'That's what you are, a bloody idiot. A complete fool.'

For the rest of the day her scent remained with him.

Mo Binchy, and the girl he'd been sleeping with, Shelagh, Sean now knew her name to be, came off the dancefloor and up to the table where he was sitting. There were ten of them on a Saturday night out at the Trocadero, one of Glasgow's largest dancehalls situated in the centre of the city.

Mo was flushed, partly due to the heat of the place which was stifling, but mostly from the alcohol he'd consumed before getting there.

'I want to speak to you, Sean,' Mo announced, his arm circled round Shelagh's waist.

'Aye, go ahead.'

'In private like.'

There were three other members of the Samurai at the table. 'Can you fellas give us a couple of minutes.'

'Of course, Sean. Anything you say.'

Sean liked that. Anything he said! By God, it was great to have power and respect. The feeling was almost . . . sexual.

Mo and Shelagh sat when the others had moved away. 'We made a decision tonight and I want you to be the first to know,' Mo said.

Sean didn't reply, waiting for Mo to go on.

Mo glanced at Shelagh, who giggled, then back at Sean. 'We've decided to get married.'

That surprised Sean. 'Really?'

'Aye, really. A quick engagement and then the deed itself. What do you think?'

Sean wasn't sure how to answer that. The lassie seemed personable enough, though hardly anything special. But if it suited Mo, then so be it. 'I suppose congratulations are in order.'

Mo beamed. 'I was hoping you'd say that.'

'Thank you,' Shelagh said in a rather reedy voice.

Not his type at all, Sean thought. Far too mousy with a lousy figure. Very little on top that he could make out.

'The thing is,' Mo continued, 'would you be my best man? I'd be honoured . . .' He paused for a moment. 'We'd both be honoured if you'd be that.'

Sean felt expansive. Why the hell not! And it was his right to be asked as the leader of the Samurai after all. 'Of course I will. Consider that a promise.'

Mo reached over and shook Sean by the hand. 'You're a pal, Sean, through and through.'

Sean signalled to the others who'd been at the table that they could return, and soon they too were offering their congratulations.

It was a little later that Bill O'Connell had a word in his ear. 'I've just been dancing with a bird who says she fancies you rotten. Wants to know if she can be introduced.'

'Is that a fact.'

'Good-looking piece too.' He nodded his head. 'That's her over there in the pink dress. You can't miss her, she's ogling you.'

She was pretty too, Sean thought. Quite a cracker.

And with a decent figure, unlike Mo's Shelagh. Should he get her up?

Then he remembered Muriel and Babs and what had happened with them. No, he decided. He daren't risk another humiliation. That would be too much to bear.

He suddenly felt sick inside.

The girl was smiling fit to burst, her eyes an open invitation. He knew she'd do a turn if he wanted it. If not that night then shortly.

He dropped his gaze, breaking eye contact. She'd just have to go on fancying him, that was all. He wasn't going to do anything about it.

'Sean.'

He glanced round at Bobby O'Toole. 'What is it?'

'Look who's here and watching us. Second pillar on the left.'

Sean sought out the named pillar and there standing directly in front of it staring hard at them was Big Bill Bremner, leader of the Tong.

'Shit,' Sean swore softly.

'Do you think he's after a barney?'

'I've no idea, Bob. None at all.'

Sean doubted Big Bill was on his own, that was highly unlikely. The question was, how many of the Tong were with him?

'What shall we do?' Sammy Renton queried.

'I don't know. Hang on tight I suppose and see what happens. One thing's for certain, I'm not leaving with my tail between my legs just because he's here. Apart from anything else it would be a terrible mistake. Believe me. Show weakness and they'll be straight at your throat. For the fun of it if nothing else.'

'Christ,' Sammy muttered.

Sean glanced at Mo who'd gone back on the dancefloor with Shelagh, then at the lassie who'd told Bill O'Connell she'd fancied him. Her expression was one of clear disappointment.

He touched the hardness that was the razor in his inside jacket pocket, and wondered what Big Bill and his people might be carrying. He found he was sweating.

He left it a couple of minutes then looked over again at the pillar. Only now there was no sign of the man.

What did that mean? An ambush when they left the hall? It was a possibility.

A possibility that in the end proved unfounded.

Jeannie Swanson got into bed and pulled the covers up to her chin. 'I'm whacked,' she declared.

Bridie smiled. 'I'm a bit that way myself.'

'The apple tart we had tonight was lovely, don't you think?'

'Hmmh,' Bridie murmured.

'I can't cook much myself. I burn things when I try.'

Bridie laughed softly. 'That must be because you're not paying attention.'

'I find it so boring. That's probably why I'm no good at it. What about you?'

'Oh, I can get by. None of your fancy dishes, mind. Straightforward cooking and baking. My ma taught me.'

Jeannie sighed. 'My ma died when I was wee. There were six of us lived with my da. My older sister Tina used to do the cooking, only she wasn't all that clever at it either. Da was always complaining. Until he took up with my auntie Margaret that was. She'd been married but widowed in the war. She came to live in our house just before I got the job here.'

Jeannie turned on to her elbow to face Bridie.

'There's something I've been meaning to ask you.'

'And what's that, Jeannie?'

'Why don't you read at night any more? It's ages since I last saw you with a book in your hand.'

It was too, Bridie reflected. 'I sort of lost interest,' she replied.

'*You*, Bridie Flynn! I find that hard to believe.'

'Well it's true.'

'But why?'

Bridie shrugged. 'Who knows? These things happen.'

'I must say I'm surprised.'

Bridie wasn't. What fun was there reading about fictional heroes when her own hero was under the selfsame roof? Sir Ian of Seaton, her very own shining knight.

'I'm tired,' Bridie declared. 'Do you mind if I blow out the candle?'

'Go ahead.'

Bridie left her bed, crossed to where the candle was burning brightly, and did just that.

'Goodnight, Bridie.'

'Goodnight, Jeannie.'

'Sweet dreams.'

Bridie smiled in the darkness. That's what it had become, day-dreams as well as those she had in her sleep.

All of Ian Seaton.

Andrew was fed up, another evening by himself with a bottle of Drummond. He really had to do something about it. He was rapidly becoming a melancholic.

Andrew sipped his whisky and wondered if he should stroll down to Jack and Hettie's. They always welcomed him no matter the time and were such good company.

Rose, he thought. What about Rose? It was still too soon to visit The Haven again. He had to give Georgina time.

God, how he hoped Georgina hadn't said anything to Willie. Or didn't in the future. For both their sakes as well as Willie's.

He cursed himself for giving in to the woman in the first place. He should have resisted, refused to play her game.

Some hope, he smiled wryly. Women had always been his great weakness. If it hadn't been one of them, it had been another.

He got up from his chair and started to pace. No, he wouldn't go to Jack's he decided. The pub? No, he wouldn't do that either. It was all right being there with Jack but on his own was rather different. As the owner of Drummond's he didn't want to be seen propping up the bar by himself. That would only lead to talk.

He gazed around the room, memories of happier times flooding his mind. Not that he was unhappy, he wasn't. Just lonely and bored.

Rose, he wondered how she'd fit in here. Probably very well. And he was sure the staff would take to her after the initial surprise in the difference in their ages.

No no no, that simply wasn't on. She was far too young for him. Though . . . How had Jack put it? She adored him, Jack had heard it in her voice and where voices were concerned Jack was invariably right. Something he found rather scary.

Not for the first time he thought how he envied Jack the lovely home life he had. What a support and companion Hettie was, and then there was wee Tommy whom they both doted on.

He recalled what it had been like when he, Peter, Charlotte and his younger sister Nell had been young.

The house had reverberated with laughter. And fighting of course, for which brothers and sisters didn't fight?

Laughter and fighting, it brought the place alive. Whereas now, it was like a morgue.

He thought of Ellen Temple with regret. He missed her, and what she'd had to offer. Well, Ellen was now married to that clod of a husband and lost to him. As was the comfort she'd brought.

Jesus, he prayed Georgina didn't blab to Willie. Georgina whom he wished was there with him. It wouldn't have been so dull and dreary with her around.

He stopped pacing by his glass, drained it and crossed to the decanter for a refill. That was something else, he thought. He was drinking far too much nowadays. But drink was company and consolation, both of which he needed.

He knew then what he'd do. Take the Rolls out and go for a drive. It didn't matter where, just a drive.

Pathetic, he thought. That's what you've become, Andrew. Bloody pathetic.

Where was the young blood he'd been in Ireland? Gone for ever. Aged by years and responsibility. But what times those had been. Wonderful times, exhilarating times.

He swallowed his whisky and poured himself yet another.

Ian knew where he'd find Bridie, and sure enough there she was blackleading a grate. He paused in the doorway, she as yet unaware of his presence. Was he doing the right thing? He didn't know, and a large part of him didn't care. He was following the dictates of his heart.

He walked quietly over and halted behind her. 'Hello Bridie.'

She started. 'Hello, Master Ian.'

She had a smudge on her forehead that he found most appealing. 'How are you this morning?'

'Fine. Just dandy. And you?'

'Not too bad.'

She hesitated, unsure whether to continue with her work or talk. She decided to take her cue from Ian.

'Can you get away for a while this evening?'

That startled her. 'Get away?'

'That's right. For a half-hour or so.'

She thought about that. 'I suppose so. After our meal.'

He nodded. 'Good. Meet me in the stables. I want to speak to you.'

Now she was totally confused. 'About what?'

'Things,' he replied enigmatically.

Bridie stared at him, remembering Teresa. 'I'm not sure,' she stammered.

'Please?'

His pleading look was one she couldn't refuse. 'About nine. I'll make some sort of excuse if I have to and disappear for a bit.'

'I'll be waiting, Bridie.'

She watched him leave the room, completely mystified as to what this was all about. Meet him in the stables?

No matter what she felt for him he'd better not try anything, she thought. He'd just better not. He'd get a right flea in his ear if he did.

Ian was sitting on a bale of hay with a hurricane lamp dimly lighting the stables when she arrived. He immediately rose. 'Thanks for coming, Bridie.'

She didn't reply, nervous in the extreme.

'Why don't you sit down,' he proposed, indicating the bale.

She did, wondering yet again what this was all about. Please God he wasn't going to try and seduce her. She couldn't have borne that, it would have been far too hurtful.

'Was it easy to get away?'

Bridie nodded. 'I said I was off to my room and as Jeannie's busy she won't know that I haven't gone there.'

'Good.'

Ian took a deep breath. This was proving far more difficult than he'd anticipated. 'I took the liberty of bringing along a bottle of wine and a couple of glasses. Would you like some?'

Was he trying to get her drunk, was that it? Her opinion of Ian Seaton, knight in shining armour, plummeted. 'No thank you.'

'Then would you mind if I did?'

'Go ahead.'

Ian poured himself a glass from the already opened bottle, then sat on another bale a little distance away. It was a beautiful atmosphere, he thought. Soft and yellow with shadows dancing on Bridie's face. He felt an enormous sense of peace come over him.

'Well,' he said, and sipped his wine. In fact he'd already had quite a bit of wine that evening in preparation for their tryst.

Bridie dropped her gaze to stare at the floor.

'How's your father?'

That surprised her. 'A great deal better, thank you. He's started work again.'

'No after-effects?'

'Not according to the letters my mother has written.'

'Strange the doctors not being able to diagnose what was wrong with him.'

'He was very ill, Ian. Believe me, I saw him. He was at death's door.'

'I'm sure,' Ian replied hastily. 'I didn't mean to imply anything otherwise.'

She smiled, new confidence coming into her. 'What's this all about, Ian?'

'I wanted to talk to you.'

'Oh?'

He saw her expression and realised what she was thinking. 'Just talk, Bridie. I promise you.'

She believed him and immediately relaxed. 'Go on then.'

Ian was wretched and heady at the same time. Was he doing the right thing or just being a fool? But how could he be a fool feeling as he did?

'The truth is, Bridie, and I won't beat about the bush, I've fallen in love with you.'

She gaped at him, mouth hanging open.

'What do you say to that?'

Chapter 25

Bridie was stunned, completely and utterly. For the moment she couldn't think of anything to reply. Ian in love with her! It couldn't be right, it couldn't be so.

'Well?' Ian queried, now somewhat agitated. He'd made a mistake, he thought. He should never have declared himself. He wished he'd never set up this meeting.

'I . . . I . . .' Bridie trailed off.

'I'm sorry if I've offended you. I just wanted you to know.'

Ian had a large gulp of wine. God this was awful. If he'd been a magician he'd have waved his wand and disappeared.

'In love with *me*?'

'Yes,' he whispered.

'But . . . how?'

'I don't know. It just happened, Bridie.'

It *was* an attempt to seduce her. Had to be. And yet . . .

His tone was anything but insincere. It rang of truth. 'I'm . . . lost for words.'

'I can understand that. It has come somewhat out of the blue.'

And then she remembered his kissing her and what that had been like. 'Don't have me on, Ian, please.'

'I'm not, Bridie. On my oath.' He crossed his heart. 'May the good Lord strike me down if I'm lying.'

Tears welled into her eyes. It was a dream come true. No, more than that. 'I too have a confession to make.'

There was someone else, he thought. Damn! He should have known. A chap back in Glasgow probably.

She stared at Ian through eyes shining with tears, her heart pounding within her chest. 'I love you too,' she stated.

It was now his turn to be rocked. 'You do?'

She nodded.

'I never guessed.'

'I've done my best to keep it from you. I mean, what chance had I with you? Our stations in life are so different. And then there was Moira McLaren whom you were going out with. I can't . . . couldn't compete with her. Miss McLaren's beautiful whereas I'm ordinary.'

He slowly smiled. 'You're hardly ordinary, Bridie. At least not to me. In my book you knock Moira into a cocked hat.'

'I do?'

'Oh yes,' he whispered. He wanted to go to her, take her into his arms and hold her tight. But guessed correctly, for the moment, that such a move would be a mistake.

Bridie put her hands together and rubbed a thumb. This was all so bewildering. It was as though one of the novels she'd read had come to life. He loved her? Prince Charming actually loved her. She felt like Cinderella.

'I don't know what to do about it,' Ian said.

'How do you mean?'

'Exactly that. I don't know what to do.'

'Because I'm a servant?'

He flushed slightly. 'Yes.'

'I understand. It's not very practical, is it?'

He shook his head.

'Yet you love me and I love you. There was a day on the staircase when we looked at one another, and that was that. I was head over heels.'

He stared at her in wonderment. 'It was the same for me. The same day on the staircase.'

'Really?'

'It must have been the same day. The French have an expression for it, a *coup de foudre*. The Italians call it "the thunderbolt". Our eyes met and that was that.'

'Yes,' she breathed.

He laid his glass aside, rose and said, 'I'm coming over to you. Is that all right?'

'If you wish.' Again she thought of Teresa. 'No funny business, Ian.'

'There won't be,' he assured her.

He crossed to her bale and kneeled. 'You're crying.'

'With happiness.'

That tore at him. 'I feel like that as well. All sort of . . . He flushed again. 'Mushy inside.'

She smiled. 'It's the same with me.'

He took her hands in his. 'You and I are meant for one another, Bridie. We were destined.'

She gazed deep into his eyes feeling she could drown in them. 'We're both going to have to think about this, Ian.

'I agree.'

'There's one thing you must understand.'

'Which is?'

'I won't . . .' She gulped. 'I won't go with you unless we were married. Nor will that change.'

That disappointed yet pleased him at the same time. 'You are attracted to me?'

'Of course, silly. I think you are ever so handsome.'

He lifted her hands to his mouth and tenderly kissed them. He was filled with . . . what? Something he'd never experienced before. Something spiritual, though still very much of the flesh.

'I can't stay very long. I must get back before I'm missed,' Bridie heard herself saying.

'Do you have to?'

'They might wonder where I am.' Nonsense of course, she was supposed to be alone in her room. But enough was enough for the time being.

'Then let them.'

'No, Ian. I have my job to think about. I don't want to lose it.'

'You won't that, Bridie. I promise you.'

'Then my reputation.'

'Or that either.'

'Sir Ian of Seaton,' she murmured.

'Maid Bridie.'

Just being with him was so very special, she thought. Detaching a hand from his she reached up and stroked his cheek. He closed his eyes as she stroked.

'Maybe this isn't a good idea,' she said.

His eyes snapped open.

'I'm still a servant after all. And you're who you are. It's an impossibility, Ian. I hate to say that, but it is.'

'Nothing's impossible, Bridie. My father has often said that to me.'

'I think this is. It's a wonderful dream, Ian, but impossible in the end. You must see that?'

He did, but didn't want to accept the fact. How could he marry a servant, particularly when it was their house she was a servant in?

'Will you meet me again?' he pleaded.

'You mean here?'

'If you will.'

There was nothing she wanted more. 'Yes.'

'When?'

She thought about that. 'Monday would be best.'

'Then Monday it is. Same time?'

She nodded. 'And, Ian, I meant what I said about funny business. None of that.'

'Can I kiss you?'

'If you like.'

He raised her to her feet, then his lips were on hers, his tongue eagerly exploring her mouth.

For the pair of them it was sheer ecstasy.

Pat Flynn was scanning the windows on either side of the road on the lookout for the firm's cards when Geraldine Buchanan suddenly appeared round a corner.

He mentally swore when he spotted her. What in the name of the wee man was she doing in this area? He whooaed Jasper to a halt at her approach.

Geraldine, eyes glittering, stopped beside his cart. 'Hello Mr Flynn. How are you?'

He touched the peak of his cap. 'Fine now, Mrs Buchanan. I've been ill.'

'I heard.'

'I'm not delivering your coal any more as they changed my round.'

She didn't reply to that, just continued staring at him.

Pat lowered his voice. 'I meant to come and see you when I was better, but couldn't be sure your husband wouldn't be there. And what excuse could I offer for knocking on your door without a bag of coal on my back?'

Liar, she thought. He was lying in his teeth. She was damned if she was going to say how much she'd missed him and their evenings together.

'I understand, Mr Flynn.'

He relaxed a little. 'I'm sorry.'

'That's all right.'

'No I mean it, I truly am.'

She shrugged. 'Fine.'

Geraldine stood her ground waiting for more of an explanation. She considered she was worth that.

'And how are you?' he asked.

'Never better.'

'Who told you I'd been ill?'

'Your replacement mentioned something about it.'

'I nearly died according to the doctors. It was touch and go for a while.'

She raised an imperious eyebrow. 'What exactly was wrong with you?'

'They never did find out. It was something mysterious they couldn't diagnose.'

'I see.'

'I, eh . . . won't be visiting again,' he mumbled, just loud enough for her to hear.

'I guessed that.'

'It's nothing to do with you.'

'No?'

He shook his head. 'Something happened to me in hospital. Something that changed me. It's my wife . . .'

He broke off and sucked in a deep breath. 'I realised how lucky I was and how much she meant to me. That's the long and short of it.'

Geraldine believed him. She could hear it in his voice and read it in his face. In a way she was jealous. It wasn't that Dougal didn't love her, he did. But how could she truly love him if she was prepared to have affairs? Simply sex? Maybe Or perhaps there was more to it than that. Perhaps she was someone never meant to be faithful.

'Then I'll wish you all the very best, Pat.'

'And I you, Geraldine.'

She hesitated, then said, 'I was worried about you. really was. I want you to know that.'

'Thank you.'

'I just wish you had found some way of coming round and telling me to my face. You left me feeling such . . . slut.'

He blanched.

'Goodbye then, Pat.'

'Goodbye, Geraldine.'

Pat drove on, his feelings mixed. But he'd never stra from Kathleen again. Never in a thousand years.

The dreams had seen to that.

'Wake up, girl!'

Bridie started. 'Sorry, Mrs Coltart.'

'You were away with the fairies right enough. Standin there staring into space as though you were having a vision Were you?'

She had indeed. Herself and Ian together. 'No,' sh lied.

Mrs Coltart studied Bridie. 'Your work's fallen awa these last couple of days. Is something the matter?'

'No, Mrs Coltart. I'm sorry.'

'Then you'd better give yourself a shake. I won't have slacking in my household. Simply won't have it, hear?'

What was wrong with the lassie? Mrs Coltart wondered as she continued on down the corridor. Slacking was most unlike Bridie.

Ian leapt to his feet the instant Bridie appeared. 'There you are! I was beginning to think you weren't coming.'

'It was difficult to get away, Ian. The meal was delayed and I couldn't exactly leave before it was over. They'd all have thought that extremely strange.'

'Of course.'

Bridie was nervous, though she'd been constantly thinking about this and waiting for it since their last meeting.

'I brought another bottle of wine,' Ian said. 'Can I tempt you?'

Bridie went to a bale and sat. 'I've never drunk wine. Where I come from it's all whisky and beer.'

'In which case you must have some.'

'But only one,' she stated firmly. She wasn't about to get drunk. It wasn't that she didn't trust Ian, but under the influence of alcohol who knew what she might succumb to? It wasn't a risk she was about to take.

'Here,' Ian smiled, handing her a brimming glass.

'I've often wondered what wine tastes like. Since arriving at The Haven that is.'

'Then have a sip.'

She did. 'It's nice and warming.'

'That's called Châteauneuf du Pape, my favourite. I'm glad you approve.'

Bridie had another sip. It really was nice, and as she'd said warming.

He frowned. 'You look worried.'

'I'm still trying to take on board what's happenec Between you and me that is.'

He nodded. 'Me too.'

'You were being truthful, weren't you?'

'My word of honour, Bridie,' he protested quickly. wouldn't lie to you, or anyone else about something like that

She gazed about her. 'What an odd place for us to mee I know nothing about horses.'

'I do ride myself, though not a great deal. Rose is the or who's keen.'

'Yes, I've seen her out and around on a number occasions.' Bridie had an alarming thought. 'She's n about to suddenly come in, is she?'

'I doubt it very much. Nor the groom. As far as they' concerned the horses are bedded down for the night.'

How lovely she looked, Ian mused. There was somethi about her that drew him the way a moth is drawn to light.

Bridie had another sip of wine thinking she could get like this.

'Can I come and sit beside you?'

She nodded.

He did. 'And hold your hand?'

'Wait till I finish my wine.'

'Of course.'

'I've already told you about my life in Glasgow,' Brid said. 'So why don't you tell me about yours at The Hav and while you were away studying.'

'It's boring, Bridie. Believe me.'

'I'd still like to hear.

Ian began to speak and the minutes slipped all t quickly by.

* * *

Autumn had finally arrived, Georgina reflected gazing out of her bedroom window. Willie had already dressed and gone about some estate business so she was on her own.

Georgina left the window, crossed to the fire that had been lit earlier and sat in front of it. She'd miss breakfast that morning, having no appetite whatsoever.

There was no doubt about it, she thought. None at all. And, according to the dates and her own instincts, Andrew was the father.

She gently rubbed her stomach, thinking of the life growing inside. Her child. Hers and Andrew's.

Andrew stared at the envelope knowing who the letter was from having recognised the handwriting. He sighed. No doubt a proposal from Georgina suggesting they get ogether again.

He thought she'd understood when he'd said it was all over between them. Understood and accepted the fact. Apparently not.

He slowly slit open the envelope.

I wish I could take you to a dance,' Ian declared.

Bridie stared at him in astonishment. 'A dance?'

'Yes, why not. I'd enjoy that.'

She laughed. 'I think I would too.'

'I'd take you in my arms and we'd trip the light fantastic s they say.'

Bridie shivered slightly, imagining it.

'Or a ball, which is just a fancy dance with food. I'd buy ou the prettiest gown there was and you'd be the belle of he ball.'

She laughed again. 'Hardly that. Especially if Miss Moir McLaren was present.'

'You'd be the belle of the ball to me, Bridie, which i all that would count. I wouldn't be able to take my eye off you.'

Nor she hers off him, she thought. How at ease the were together nowadays, and how she looked forward t these meetings in the stables. In a way they'd become he whole life. And Ian, true to his word, had never spoilt then by trying any funny business for which she was immensel grateful.

Ian suddenly frowned. 'Andrew Drummond has writte to Pa saying he's paying us a visit. I don't like that man.'

'But why? He's always pleasant, to the staff anyway.'

'I don't know, Bridie, but I neither like nor trust hir He always reminds me of a snake.'

She found that highly amusing. 'Why a snake?'

'Sort of slippery and slimy. At least that's my opinio of him.'

'Well, I can't say he's ever struck me that way. And h always leaves a decent tip. There's certainly nothing mea about Mr Drummond.'

'He's rich you know. Owns a whisky distillery.'

'So I believe.'

'He and Pa were together in Ireland, served in the sar regiment. That's where Pa met him.'

'I can't remember if I mentioned but my father fought i the war with the Highland Light Infantry, the HLI. No there's a famous regiment.'

'They are indeed.'

'Sometimes, when he's in his cups, he'll mention od things about the war, but not very often. He's alwa extremely upset after he has.'

'Understandable,' Ian nodded, thinking how lucky he was not to have been caught up in that carnage. Thank God and all his angels he'd been too young.

'What's wrong with Mrs Seaton?' Bridie asked.

'Wrong?'

'She certainly hasn't been herself of late. The staff have been talking about it. Several times she's nearly bitten someone's head off for nothing at all.'

Ian pulled a face. 'There's nothing wrong with her that I'm aware of.'

'Don't repeat this but Mrs Coltart is most concerned. I overheard a conversation between her and Mrs Kilbride in which she said how difficult your stepmother had been recently.'

Ian thought about that. 'Now you mention it she has been a bit tetchy. And off her food. Not that she eats a great deal at the best of times but she's been picking like a sparrow these last couple of weeks. Pa ticked her off only he other night.'

'Maybe she's ill?'

'Or it could be female problems.'

Bridie blushed. 'Ian!'

'Sorry if that offended you. It wasn't meant to.'

'Well . . . it did and didn't. I just don't like that sort of hing being mentioned. Not in mixed company anyway.'

'Then I shan't again.'

'Thank you.'

Perhaps Georgina was ill, Ian mused. For not only was she ff her food and tetchy but decidedly pale into the bargain.

'If I learn anything I'll let you know.'

'And it'll be strictly between us,' Bridie promised. 'I'm ot one for gossiping and certainly not where my employers re concerned.'

'Good for you, girl.'

She adored it when he called her girl. There was an intimacy about the way he said it that never failed to give her a thrill.

'I've been doing a lot of thinking about you,' Ian stated slowly.

'Oh?'

'Well, *us* really.'

'And?'

'I love you and you love me, right?'

She nodded.

'Well, we can't go on as we are, meeting up in the stables whenever we can.'

She studied him curiously. 'What else can we do? I'm me and you're you. As we've already agreed, considering our different stations in life, an impossible situation.'

'I wonder,' he brooded.

'Ian, you know it is. You'll meet someone else in time, someone suitable and forget all about me.'

He shook his head. 'No matter what happens, Bridie, I'll never forget you. Nor do I think we should dismiss our love so lightly.'

'Lightly! I'm hardly doing that.'

'Well, it seems as though you are.'

She took his hand in hers and squeezed it. 'I assure you, Ian, that isn't so. But as I said, it's an impossible situation.'

'Perhaps not,' he breathed. 'Perhaps not.'

Rose was doing her best not to glare at Andrew sitting across the table from her. She'd hardly said half a dozen words during the entire luncheon, letting Georgina prattle on which she had done most effectively.

Willie sighed and laid aside his napkin. 'You'll have to excuse me, Andrew, but I have a few more hours of work. Things that just have to be done today.'

'I understand, old boy.'

'I'm sure Georgina and Rose will be able to entertain you.'

'You'll have to excuse me as well,' Rose declared, rising as her father had done. 'But I've developed a splitting headache.'

'Poor dear,' Georgina sympathised.

'So if you don't mind I'll go to my room and lie down.'

'Of course,' Georgina nodded, secretly delighted as she'd been wondering how she was going to get Andrew on his own.

Georgina smiled at Andrew when Willie and Rose had gone. 'I thought we might go for a stroll?' she suggested.

'That would be nice.'

'Then shall we get our coats. It's rather nippy out there.'

Andrew came to his feet and helped Georgina from her chair. He guessed this to be a ploy so they could speak together.

'It's a pity you can't stay the night,' Georgina said as they moved away from the table.

'Yes, it is,' he lied. He'd never had any intention of staying the night and had only come to The Haven because of the urgent pleading in Georgina's letter. He was also curious about 'the news' she had for him. Now that sounded rather mysterious.

'So,' he said when they were well out of earshot of the house. 'What's this all about?'

Georgina was suddenly nervous. 'Thank you for coming.'

Andrew didn't reply to that.

'The thing is, Andrew, I'm pregnant. And by you.'

He came up short, stunned. 'Pregnant?'

'That's right.'

'Are you absolutely sure?'

'Absolutely.'

Andrew, without a hat, ran a hand through his hair. 'You've rather caught me by surprise,' he confessed.

'It was always a possibility.'

'I appreciate that . . . but . . .' He broke off to stare into the distance. 'How do you know it's mine?' he asked softly.

'The dates, Andrew. It has to be you. Please don't ask me to go into the details of why I'm so sure, but I am.'

A baby, Christ Almighty! No wonder she'd been so mysterious about 'the news'.

'How far gone are you?'

'Work it out for yourself. It happened the last time we were together.'

He took a deep breath. 'Let's keep walking. It might look strange if we were seen standing still talking for too long.

'How do you feel about this?' he queried.

'Delighted. I'd given up the hope of ever conceiving. I don't think any woman feels truly fulfilled until she's had a child.'

'Hmmh,' he muttered. 'I presume you haven't told Willie.'

'About you or being pregnant?'

Andrew swallowed hard. 'About being pregnant.'

'No, I wanted to speak to you first.'

He almost didn't want to ask the question. 'Why Georgina?'

'Because I thought it might alter matters between us.'

'You mean about you leaving Willie and coming to me?'

'Yes.'

They walked a little way in silence before he eventually replied. 'It doesn't, Georgina. I'm sorry, but there you are.'

'I didn't think it would somehow. But I wanted to give you the opportunity. Just in case.'

'It's the same as it was, Georgina. I don't want to hurt Willie.'

'And yet you slept with me.'

'I was wrong to do that, terribly wrong. But the flesh was weak, I'm afraid and you were willing. Or to be truthful, more than willing. Downright eager.'

It might be true but she could have done without hearing that. It was both humiliating and degrading.

'Will you now pass the baby off as Willie's?'

'What else can I do if you won't have me?'

'I won't, Georgina. I want you to believe that and not come up with some crackpot notion that by leaving Willie I'll take pity on you because of the child. I won't, I assure you.'

'You can be a hard bastard, can't you, Andrew Drummond?' she almost hissed.

'When I have to be, Georgina. When I have to be. And this is one of those instances.'

Georgina closed her eyes for a moment, remembering how it had been with Andrew and what it was like with Willie.

'I'll be godfather if you wish?' Andrew smiled.

If they hadn't still been in sight of the house she'd have slapped him.

Chapter 26

They were having aperitifs before dinner and Willie was in an expansive mood. To his irritation Ian found himself in conversation with Andrew. He was pleased Andrew was leaving directly after their meal.

'Excuse me,' Georgina said in a raised voice, rounding on everyone. 'But I have an announcement to make.'

Andrew tensed, guessing what was coming next. Please God, for Willie's sake, she didn't name him as the father.

Georgina hooked an arm round Willie's and gazed deeply into his eyes. She might have been a woman totally in love.

'Yes, my dear?' Willie smiled.

'I had considered telling you this when we were alone but on second thoughts decided to share it with the family at the same time. And our good friend Andrew of course.

She paused dramatically. 'I'm expecting a baby.'

Andrew drew in a deep breath and held it, wondering if she was about to drop the second bombshell.

'A baby!' Willie exclaimed.

'That's what I said.'

'By all that's . . .' Willie threw back his head. 'Wonderful!'

'I thought you'd be pleased.'

'Pleased! I'm far more than that. Oh, my darling, my sweet, sweet darling.' He pulled Georgina into an embrace and kissed her.

'Well,' Ian murmured, taken aback. This was a bit of a shock.

Rose flew at Georgina and pecked her on the cheek. 'Congratulations! I'm delighted for the pair of you.'

'And so am I,' Ian added, not quite sure if he was or not. A baby at Willie's age, even Georgina's, seemed a little obscene somehow.

'And congratulations from me,' Andrew beamed. Crossing to Willie he shook him warmly by the hand. 'You old dog, you.'

'This calls for a celebration,' Willie declared, eyes glinting with moisture. 'Jeannie, can you go and fetch some champagne.'

Jeannie Swanson, who'd been handing round canapés, nodded, quickly got rid of the plate she was holding, and rushed from the room. She couldn't wait to tell the rest of the staff.

'How?' Willie queried of Georgina, totally bemused.

Georgina had the grace to blush. 'I think you know how, Willie.'

He was suddenly covered in confusion and glanced guiltily at first Rose then Ian. 'I didn't mean that literally. But . . .'

'It just happened, angel,' Georgina interjected sweetly. 'The way these things do.'

'Of course.'

'Congratulations, Pa,' Ian said, extending a hand.

'Thank you, son.'

'An addition to the family,' Ian mused. 'How about that.'

'How about it,' Willie enthused. He'd said to Georgina they should have a child and now they were going to. It was almost as though God had been listening.

Georgina was steadfastly refusing to meet Andrew's eye, as she'd been doing since they'd met up that evening. Despite her outward show of love and affection to Willie she felt sick inside.

Willie glanced over at Andrew. 'And you must be godfather, Andrew. I insist.'

The look Georgina suddenly shot at Andrew for the briefest of seconds was like an arrow directed straight at his heart.

'I shall be honoured, Willie. Thank you.'

Willie turned again to Georgina. 'When, eh . . . ?'

'We'll discuss the details later, darling. If you don't mind, that is.'

'No no, I fully understand.'

Mrs Coltart appeared carrying a tray on which was the bottle of champagne and appropriate glasses. Now she knew why Georgina had been out of sorts recently.

'May I offer my congratulations, madam,' she said, placing the tray on the sideboard.

'You may, Mrs Coltart. And thank you.'

'And to you, sir.'

'Thank you, Mrs Coltart. Will you see the staff get a drink. I think they should.'

'I shall, sir.'

A baby brother or sister, Rose was thinking. How scrumptious. She absolutely adored babies.

'I'll do the honours,' Willie declared, detaching himself from Georgina and going over to the tray. Seconds later the cork popped and the champagne was flowing.

'A toast,' Andrew proposed when the glasses had been charged and handed round. 'To the newest member of the Seaton family. May his or her life be a long and happy one.'

The wine tasted like gall in Georgina's mouth.

Andrew was deep in thought as he drove back to Drummond House in the Rolls. What a day that had been and no mistake!

Georgina pregnant by him, what a heart stopper. Thank God she'd kept her mouth shut about who the true father was. It would have been a disaster if she hadn't.

The expression on Willie's face when she'd made her announcement was one he'd never forget. He shuddered to think what the expression would have been had Georgina chosen to divulge their secret.

He couldn't have been happier for Willie whom he liked enormously. Willie's joy had truly been a sight to behold.

And he was to be godfather. That both amused and pleased him. He only prayed the child took more after its mother than it did its father. It might be tricky if not.

And what was wrong with Rose? She'd avoided him during the entire day. Something was definitely wrong, but what? All he could put it down to was his not proposing. It could only be that.

Surely.

* * *

'It's for you, Sean,' Kathleen declared, coming into the kitchen followed by Noddy Gallagher.

'Hello, Noddy,' Sean said.

'Aye, hello. I was wondering if I could have a word.'

'Of course you can.'

Noddy glanced over at Pat sitting in his chair and then Alison playing in front of the fire. 'In private like if you don't mind.'

Pat frowned. Gang business no doubt. It was bad enough that Sean was involved without bringing it into his house. He didn't like that one little bit. In fact he downright resented it. Not that he'd say anything mind, at least not to Sean. There was no fear of that.

'Come through to my bedroom, we'll talk there.'

Kathleen's expression was also one of disapproval. It worried her dreadfully that Sean was running with a gang. She'd tried to speak to him about it on several occasions but he'd cut her short declaring he'd do as he bloody well wanted and that was that. On the other hand, she had to admit, though reluctantly, the money he was bringing in was more than helpful. Why, only the previous week, even though Pat was grafting again, he'd upped his lodge once more. Whatever else you said about Sean you couldn't accuse him of not taking care of his family. He was a saint where that was concerned.

'So what is it, Noddy?' Sean queried, closing his bedroom door behind them.

'It's Mo, Sean. The Tong got to him.'

Sean, with Noddy alongside, strode down the ward. How he hated hospitals. He'd never have admitted it but they frightened the hell out of him.

They found Mo at the top of the ward, his face swathed

in bandages. 'You've been in the wars then, Mo,' Sean said, sitting on the single chair provided.

Mo's eyes, filled with pain, fastened on him. His eyes and mouth had been left uncovered. 'Hello, Sean. Good of you to come. You too, Noddy,' he mumbled.

'So what happened?'

Mo swallowed hard. 'Me and Shelagh were in town doing a wee bit of shopping like in Sauchiehall Street. When we'd finished I suggested a drink in the State Bar. You know, that pub in Holland Street?'

'I know it,' Sean confirmed.

'Well, we went downstairs and were having a right old chinwag when it started. As it turned out there were three members of the Tong at the next table.'

'Had they followed you?'

'No, they were there when we arrived. I didn't know they were Tong but they recognised me after a while. They started taunting me, Sean, me and the gang. Said we were all a bunch of fucking poofters.'

That instantly enraged Sean, touching a sore point. His eyes became diamond hard. 'Did they indeed.'

'Aye they did. Poofters, nancy boys and shirt lifters. Said they were surprised to see me out with a lassie.'

Sean fought to control his anger. 'Did they tell you they were Tong?'

'As soon as they recognised me. Though how they did that I don't know. I'd never seen any of them before in my life.'

'What happened then?'

'It all got a bit heated, them threatening and that. Poor Shelagh was terrified out of her wits.'

'I can imagine. Go on.'

'Christ, my face itches,' Mo groaned. 'All I want to do

is scratch but they warned me not to. The doctor that is. Sadistic bastard and no mistake.'

'I said go on, Mo.'

Mo paused, and took a breath. 'I thought there was going to be a barney there and then. I mean, no one calls me a poof and gets away with it.'

Sean winced.

'Then those two big buggers they have at the bottom of the stairs, do you remember them? Huge sods dressed in long black coats, who keep an eye on the place, came over and told the Tong to leave.

'The Tong protested it was all my fault but the coats were having none of it. After a few minutes' argument the Tong were escorted upstairs and shown the door. I, stupidly, thought that was the end of it. I should have known better. Anyway, I eventually got Shelagh calmed down and we had another drink. Then, still very shaken, she said she wanted to go home.'

Noddy was listening to all this in grim silence, thankful it wasn't he who'd gone into the State Bar at that particular time. Three, armed with razors, against one was no joke.

'So up the stairs we went, me carrying the shopping, and out on to Holland Street.'

Mo halted, then swore viciously. 'As I said, I should have known better. They jumped us out of an alleyway. I hadn't a chance against three, Sean. Not with Shelagh there to worry about. I got one good kick in and then I was down and they were at me. Shelagh was screaming her head off as they did their cutting, then they were off like three bullets.'

'Shit,' Sean muttered. 'How bad is it?'

Mo took another deep breath. 'I said the doctor was a sadistic bastard. I doubt his stitching was all that neat and careful. He was sewing me up as though I was a joint in a fucking butcher's shop.'

'How bad, Mo?'

'There are more than twenty marks, Sean, some very deep. I'm going to . . . I'm going to . . .' Mo's head dropped and he sobbed. 'Look like a monster for the rest of my life.'

Sean's hands clenched, then slowly unclenched. 'I'm sorry, china,' he whispered.

'So am I, Sean. So am I. It means the end of Shelagh and me of course.'

'Maybe not.'

'Don't try and kid me, Sean. What lassie, especially having been through that, would want to be tied up to the nightmare my face is going to be? No no, I've lost her all right.'

'Has she been to see you?'

'Nope. Nor do I expect her to. She's gone, Sean. And I can't say I blame her.'

'Och, maybe that's not the case, Mo.'

Mo almost grinned under his bandages, but it would have been too painful. 'If you were a lassie would you want someone with a face like I'm going to have? I doubt it very much.'

Sean felt for Mo, he truly did. 'How long are you in here for?'

'No idea. Until it heals I suppose. But maybe they'll let me home before then. The doctor says he's worried about infection, though, according to him, they've done all they can to safeguard against that.'

'Can you describe these Tong?' Sean asked quietly.

Mo thought about that. 'Not really. They were just ordinary Glasgow keelies. Nothing that would distinguish any of them. Though I'd know them if I see them again. Oh aye, I'll know them all right.'

Sean had to think about this, digest what he'd been told. 'Shall I have a word with Shelagh?'

'Don't, Sean. Please. Just leave her be.'

'All right then, pal. Now is there anything I can get you?'

'Oh aye, there is indeed. How about a new face?'

'Do you think it was intentional?' Bobby O'Toole asked.

They were at 'the place', Sean and his lieutenants gathered together to discuss what had happened to Mo Binchy. Sean's expression was a dark scowl.

'I don't know,' Sean replied. 'According to Mo it was a chance meeting where one thing led to another.'

'I think they're taking the piss,' Dan Smith said. 'I mean, this is the second time they've had a go. Don't forget Pete Murray.'

'I'm not,' Sean growled.

'They're getting out of order,' Sammy Renton declared.

'And treating us like clowns,' Don McGuire added.

Sean had a gulp from his screwtop. Poofters they'd called the Samurai! Nancy boys and shirt lifters. His stomach knotted with the anger that had been with him since Mo had uttered those words.

He closed his eyes for a few moments, conjuring up a picture of Big Bill Bremner. He'd come to hate that cunt.

'So what do we do?' Jim Gallagher queried.

'What would you do, Jim?'

'I've no idea. Brains aren't exactly my department.'

That raised a laugh, though not from Sean.

'I'm not sure yet,' Sean mused quietly. 'I don't want to rush into anything we might all regret.'

'Why don't we mark one of their blokes in retaliation?' Sammy Renton suggested.

Sean fixed his gaze on Sammy. 'That would lead to more retaliation from them. And so on and so forth until it was all-out war. Is that what you want?'

Sammy paled. 'No.'

'Well, neither do I. Because it's a war we'd lose simply because of numbers. We'd be up against something like four to one, maybe more, which are hardly good odds.'

Sean rubbed his forehead. This was a quandary right enough. He must control his instincts and think clearly. That was what leadership was all about. Or part of it anyway. He mustn't react through anger, though God knew he had enough of that.

Big Bill Bremner, he pictured the man again. There would be a reckoning one day, of that he was determined. But in the meantime . . .

Willie removed his tie and draped it over a chair. 'I've been thinking,' he declared.

Georgina glanced over at him from where she too was undressing. 'That sounds ominous.'

He laughed. 'Not really. It's about you actually.'

'And?'

'Dr Duthie is a grand old chap, bags of experience with pregnant women and childbirth and so on. But perhaps you should go and see a specialist in Edinburgh. Just to be on the safe side.'

Georgina regarded him with amusement. 'We're not being a little over-protective, are we?'

'Certainly not!' Willie blustered. 'But I consider it a good idea.'

'Dr Duthie assures me all's as it should be. So why

bother with a specialist? That would only be a waste of good money.'

'To hell with money where you and the child are concerned. It's unimportant.'

Georgina was touched by that. 'It really isn't necessary, Willie.'

He sat on the edge of the bed and began undoing his shirt. 'As I said, just to be on the safe side.'

'You sound like an old woman,' Georgina teased.

'I do not!'

She wagged a finger at him. 'Oh yes you do!'

'I'm only trying to do what's best, love,' he said in a quiet, contrite voice.

He was suddenly like a little boy, she thought, a warmth springing up inside her. But then weren't most men a lot of the time? Even Andrew on occasion.

'Nothing will go wrong, Willie, I promise you,' she said softly.

'I know but . . . Well this is maybe our last chance to have a child. I want to make sure I've done everything I can. I don't want to be negligent in any way.'

She crossed to the bed and sat beside him. 'You really are a sweetheart you know.'

His face lit up. 'Am I?'

'You certainly are. A lovable, adorable man. I was very lucky to find you.'

She had been too, she reflected. With the state of things after the war she could easily have become an old maid like so many women of her generation. In a way she wished she'd never met Andrew Drummond. Life would have been so much easier without him.

She ran a hand over Willie's hair. 'I'll go to Edinburgh if you wish. Of course I will.'

He turned, put his arms round her and laid a cheek on the valley of her breasts. How at peace he felt there, sublimely so. He drew in a deep breath of the scent of her which he so adored. 'Oh Georgina,' he whispered.

She thought again of Andrew. That was gone for ever. She hadn't reconciled herself to the fact yet, but would. She'd have to. And in the meantime count her blessings.

'Do you think it would be all right?' he whispered.

'Would what be all right?'

'You know.'

She smiled. 'I'm only pregnant, Willie. With quite a way to go yet. Of course it'll be all right.'

'I don't want to hurt you in any way.'

'You won't,' she assured him.

'Or endanger things.'

'You must have made love to Mary when she was pregnant?'

Willie closed his eyes. 'To be honest that was such a long time ago I can't quite remember. But I think I must have done.'

'There you are then.'

Willie sighed with contentment. How wonderful it all was. Georgina, a baby of theirs on the way. What else could he ask for?

'I don't care if it's a boy or girl, as long as it's healthy,' he murmured.

'Then we won't be disappointed.'

'No.'

She started to rock to and fro while he continued to embrace her. After a short while she too felt at peace.

'Come in!' Andrew called out when there was a knock on his office door. It was proving a bugger of a day with all manner of things going wrong. And now he'd just found something else to give him a headache.

'Hello, old chap.'

Andrew looked up and smiled. 'Jack! This is a surprise.'

'I was bored and thought I might take a turn up here to find out how you are. Are you busy?'

'Nothing that can't wait. Come and sit down. There's a chair in front of my desk.'

The woman who'd escorted Jack up to Andrew's office closed the door and returned to her duties. Although Jack knew the way to the office it was a difficult route and someone always accompanied him in case there proved to be a problem.

Jack found the chair and sat. 'Any free whisky going today?' he asked hopefully.

Andrew laughed. 'For you there's always some. I'll get it.'

'I hope you're joining me. I hate drinking on my own.'

'You're damned right I'll join you. I could just use a dram.'

Jack sniffed. 'You know this office has always smelt the same as long as I've known it. The same as when your father was here.'

'Really? I can't say I've noticed.'

'Well, you wouldn't when you're here so often. It takes an outsider to recognise these things.'

Andrew poured two large drams and placed one in Jack's hand. 'That'll stiffen your backbone,' he joked, returning to his own chair.

'I wasn't aware it needed stiffening.'

'You know what I mean.'

Jack smiled. 'Your arse in parsley, old boy.'

Andrew smiled also. '*Slainte.*'

'*Slainte.*'

They both drank.

'I confess,' Jack said. 'The real reason for me calling is that I couldn't wait till Friday night to hear what happened at the Seatons. Damned curiosity got the better of me.'

Andrew leant back in his chair. 'What Georgina had to say was something of a shock, Jack. She's pregnant, by me.'

'Aahhh!' Jack breathed.

'She wanted to give me one last chance to change my mind. Which I didn't.'

'And Willie?'

'Is ecstatic, believes the baby's his. He was happy as a dog with two tails when I left.'

'Well, well,' Jack mused.

'Georgina made her announcement that night at dinner after we'd spoken earlier. Carried it off rather well I thought.'

'No regrets then?'

'None, Jack. None at all.'

'That's good, old boy. Now what about Rose?'

'Gave me the cold shoulder all the time I was there. Simply didn't want to know.'

'Give her time. It's hurt pride, that's all.'

'I'm rather coming round to your way of thinking you know. Though Heaven knows how Georgina would react.'

Jack laughed. 'That could be a problem.'

'But that's a bridge we'll cross when we come to it. *If* we come to it.'

Jack drained his glass. 'Dashed fine whisky that.'

Andrew smiled. 'I'll get you another.'

* * *

'I've decided, I'm going to marry you,' Ian stated.

Bridie stared at him in astonishment.

'I'm going to marry you,' he repeated. 'I've thought long and hard and that's what I'm going to do.'

Bridie shook her head. 'You're havering, Ian. I said to you before that's an impossibility. Our stations in life, the fact I work for your father . . .'

His expression became grim. 'Bugger the class system, it's a load of old nonsense anyway. Archaic in the extreme. You're as good as me, the only difference between us is that I come from money while you don't.'

'And that money makes a huge difference, Ian. You're well educated, live in a mansion and own untold acres whereas I hail from the humblest of Glasgow tenements and used to work in a lemonade factory. My accent is as broad as they come while yours is refined, the voice of a born gentleman. And think what people would say. They'd be horrified, accusing you of letting the side down and all that.'

'Gentlemen have married beneath them before,' he argued.

'But not a servant from their own house. One day down on my hunkers cleaning a grate and the next swanning around like Lady Muck, ordering about the self same servants I've been working alongside.'

Ian had to grin at the picture that conjured up. He could just imagine Mrs Coltart's reaction. Not to mention Mrs Kilbride's.

Bridie's tone softened. 'You would shame your father, Ian. And surely you wouldn't do that.'

'Georgina never came from a grand or moneyed family.'

'I know, I've heard. But it is a professional background. And she didn't know anyone in the area when she arrived as your da's bride. She was acceptable, Ian. I would never be.'

He jutted out his chin defiantly. 'I'm still going to speak to my father.'

Her eyes moistened. 'Then you're a fool, but I love you all the more for it.'

'There must be a way, Bridie. There must.'

'No, Ian, I don't believe there is. We're never to be. At least not in this life.'

'I'm still going to speak to Father. And I'll do so tomorrow while he's still in such a good mood over this baby.'

'There'll be a row.'

'Let there. But he'll hear me out.'

'And what if you get me the sack?'

Ian hadn't thought of that. 'I'll ensure you don't. You have my word on that.'

'I still wish you wouldn't. Even though it breaks my heart to say it.'

'I love you, Bridie Flynn, and won't be denied. So there.'

The next evening, he thought. That's when he'd request to see Willie alone.

'Come here,' she said. 'My prince, my hero.'

'You sound very melodramatic when you talk like that.'

'Do I?'

'Very.'

'But you are my prince and hero. Something no one can ever take away from me.'

Chapter 27

Mo Binchy laid Shelagh's letter aside. She might have at least called on him, he thought bitterly, but no, she'd taken the easy way out and written.

It was as he'd known it would be. She didn't want to see him again, she said, because of the violence he was caught up in. But he knew better. Oh, aye, so he did. The real reason was his face and the monster he'd been turned into.

Reaching out for the letter he slowly crumpled it into a ball which he laid on his bedside table.

Tears appeared in his eyes that were soaked up by the swathe of bandages.

'This is a joke I presume?' Willie said, staring in disbelief at an extremely nervous Ian.

Ian shook his head. 'No, Pa. I've never been more serious in my life.'

'Bridie Flynn,' Willie muttered. By all that was Holy.

'I love her, Pa, and she loves me. That's the long and short of it.'

'Is it indeed,' Willie replied sarcastically.

'Yes, Pa.'

He mustn't lose his temper, Willie told himself. That wouldn't do any good at all. 'And how long has this been going on?'

'Long enough for us both to know our own minds.'

'I see.'

Willie rose from the chair in his study and crossed to the whisky decanter from which he poured himself a hefty one. He didn't offer one to Ian. He took a substantial gulp, shuddered slightly, then topped up his glass again after which he returned to his chair. From there he studied Ian thoughtfully.

'The whole idea is preposterous, you must realise that?'

'Unusual perhaps, difficult even, but hardly preposterous.'

'Of course it is!' Willie snapped back. 'She's a servant, for God's sake. A maid.'

'That's right.'

'And you want to marry her?'

'I intend to, Pa.'

Willie took a deep breath, then had another gulp of whisky. 'We'd be a laughing stock, son. Doesn't that bother you?'

'Of course it does.'

'Well then?'

'It'll blow over in time. People will forget.'

Willie barked out a short laugh. 'I doubt that very much. Country folk have long memories as you should well know. And what about the social aspect? You'd never be invited anywhere decent again, and if you were they'd be sniggering at you, and her, behind your backs. Not a very pleasant prospect.'

'No,' Ian agreed in a low voice.

'So let's forget this nonsense and pretend this conversation never took place.'

'I'm sorry, Pa. I can't do that.'

Willie sighed. 'What about the family name, does that mean nothing to you? You'd be dragging it down into the dirt.'

'There's nothing wrong with Bridie,' Ian retorted hotly. 'Except that she's working class.'

'That is precisely what's wrong with her. She probably holds a knife and fork the way a navvy would a pick and shovel.'

'Those niceties can be taught.'

'And her voice? Every time she speaks it's like walking down Sauchiehall Street. Fine for a servant lassie but hardly for the wife of my son.'

Ian couldn't help himself. 'I didn't know you were such a snob, Father.'

Willie's eyes flashed, momentarily betraying his anger. 'But I am, Ian. I most certainly am. Though I would hardly describe it as snobbishness.'

'But it is, you must see that.'

'I don't agree,' Willie said emphatically. 'We have our place and they theirs. That's how things are and always will be.'

'You make me ashamed of you.'

'You ashamed of *me*!' Willie finally exploded. 'Don't be impertinent, boy. It's me who at the moment is ashamed of you. Why, you're beginning to sound like one of those bloody socialists, scum of the earth.'

Willie brought himself back under control.

'And what about the rest of us? Myself and Georgina? Not to mention Rose. Why should we have to live under such a stigma, for it would affect us as well you know. We'd be pariahs.'

'We could get married and go away for a while, Pa. Then return later.'

Willie shook his head. 'That would only be putting off the evil day. No, such a marriage is completely out of the question. I forbid it.'

'And what if I go ahead and marry her anyway?'

Ian was quite capable of doing that, Willie thought. There was a strength in the lad he'd seen growing over recent years. 'Then you'd pay the price.'

'Which is?'

Willie stared his son straight in the eye. 'I'd throw you both off the estate then disinherit you.'

That shocked Ian to the core. 'You wouldn't!'

'But I would, son, and you'd better believe it. At the moment you're my son and heir. Marry that girl and you cease being the latter.'

This was the last thing Ian had expected. Thrown off the estate, leave The Haven. He couldn't even begin to comprehend such a thing. It was unimaginable.

'Isn't that rather drastic, Pa?' he choked.

'Yes, I'd say so. It merely reflects how strongly I feel about all this. Don't forget I've got Georgina and Rose to think about as well. I'm not having our lives ruined because of you and a housemaid.'

Ian swallowed hard. 'Can I have some of that whisky?'

'Help yourself.'

Willie watched Ian's back as he crossed to the decanter. That had certainly put a spoke in the lad's wheel. He knew how much Ian loved The Haven. Well his choice was simple, between two loves. The Haven and Bridie Flynn.

Besides, he wasn't at all convinced Ian did love the lassie. It could well be an infatuation which he didn't realise being young and inexperienced with members of the opposite sex.

Ian noted his hand was shaking as he raised the glass to his lips. To say he was stunned would be a complete understatement. Lose The Haven! It made him feel sick just to think about it.

Willie lit a cigarette and blew smoke in Ian's direction. 'Well?' he demanded harshly.

'I've got to consider this, Pa. It's not a decision I should make on the spot.'

'I'm glad to hear it.'

'And there's no . . . alternative?'

'None.'

The fiery liquid burnt its way down Ian's throat into a knotted stomach.

'You'll get over her in time, I promise you,' Willie said softly.

'I won't, Pa. This is the real thing.'

'I got over losing your mother, though it was hard. Damn hard. Then I met Georgina and look how happy we are. You'll meet someone else, I can guarantee it.'

'It's just not fair,' Ian whispered.

'Life isn't, son. That's a lesson you'll have to learn and which I thought you would have by now. It isn't fair at all.'

Ian replaced his glass, a vision of Bridie swimming before his eyes. He had to talk to her as soon as possible.

'Thanks for your time, Pa,' he said in a cracked, slightly sarcastic, voice.

Willie didn't reply.

Ian turned on his heel and left the study.

Sean and a few others were playing pontoon at 'the place' when Dan Smith burst into the room. Sean was in a good mood as he was winning.

'What's your hurry?' Sean demanded, glancing up. He then took in Dan's expression. 'You look like you've seen a ghost.'

Dan winced while Sean went back to studying the cards.

'It's Mo,' Dan gulped.

'Aye, what about him?'

'He's dead.'

Sean paused for a moment, then laughed. 'Go on, pull the other one. It's no' April Fool's you know.'

'He's dead I tell you.'

Those grouped round the table turned to stare at Dan, disbelief on all their faces.

'Dead,' Sean repeated slowly.

Dan nodded.

'How?'

'I went to see him, take him a few things like. Give him a wee bit of company. But when I got there his bed had someone else in it.'

Dan paused. He couldn't believe this either.

'Go on.'

'I spoke to the Sister to ask where he was. Apparently he died this afternoon.'

'Holy fuck,' Sean swore viciously.

'Of what?' Noddy Gallagher queried.

'Septi . . . septi . . . I can't remember the word she used. But blood poisoning.'

Sean closed his eyes for a brief moment, then opened them again. 'And how did he get that?'

'From being marked of course. The Sister explained they'd done all they could but apparently it wasn't enough. The blood poisoning hit right out of the blue and Mo was gone before they knew it. She was awfully sympathetic.'

Dan slumped into a chair and ran a hand over his face. 'Is there any bevvy in the house?'

Sean reached into a pocket and pulled out a crisp white fiver. 'There's none so go and get some. I think we all need a drink after this.'

Mo dead!

'The fucking Tong. May they all roast in Hell,' Jim Gallagher hissed.

'Aye,' his brother Noddy agreed.

Sean's right hand clasped and then unclasped again. The Tong would pay for this. By God and all His angels they would.

Ian jumped to his feet the moment Bridie appeared in the stables. Going to her he took her into his arms and held her tight.

'What's all this about, Ian? You were in a right old state when you spoke to me earlier.'

'How long have you got?'

'No more than half an hour, then I'll have to be back.'

Ian led her to a bale and sat her down. 'I talked to my father about us.'

She stared into an anguished face. 'I take it he wasn't best pleased.'

'He says if I marry you, or insist on marrying you, he'll throw us both off the estate and disinherit me.'

Bridie was appalled. 'Disinherit you! Oh, Ian.'

'He meant it too, believe me. I expected a row, all manner of reactions, but to disinherit me . . .' He trailed off.

'Well, that's it then.'

'No it isn't!' Ian retorted angrily. 'I'm not going to be beaten so easily. I'm not going to just cave in.'

'The Haven is your whole life, Ian, you told me that once.'

'It was. But now you both are. I can't give up either of you.'

'You're going to have to, Ian. And it's going to be me. I can't have you losing The Haven on my conscience. That would be too great a burden to bear.'

Ian wrung his hands.

'I said it was an impossible situation, Ian, and this just proves me right.'

'There must be a solution. There must be,' Ian croaked in despair.

'You say your father meant it.'

Ian nodded.

'Then there isn't.' But there was, she thought. Though it wasn't the solution Ian was after. There was nothing else for it, she was going to have to hand in her notice and return to Glasgow. What else could she do? If she remained it would just tear them both apart.

Ian put his arms round her. 'I won't give you up, Bridie. Now I've found you I'll never let you go.'

'And The Haven?'

'I won't let that go either.'

'Dear Ian,' she said, and kissed him on the cheek.

He drew the scent of her deep into his lungs. How he wanted Bridie, so much so at times it was a physical ache. But he wouldn't even try and break his promise to her.

She'd only sleep with him if they got married and that's how it would have to be.

They fell silent, each lost in their own thoughts.

Willie stared across the room at Georgina who was reading a magazine. Rose was tinkling on the piano. Despite innumerable lessons when younger she played atrociously.

He'd been thinking about Ian and the conversation he'd had with his son. So far he hadn't mentioned it to Georgina and the question he was mulling over was, should he?

It was rare for him to keep something from his wife, especially something of such importance. And it was the same with her, she told him everything.

He could just imagine what Georgina's reaction would be if he did confide in her. Fury on the one hand, possible hysterics on the other. She would no doubt have it out with Ian which wouldn't help matters one little bit.

No, he decided, it was best he kept this to himself. Best for all concerned.

He smiled, imagining the look of horror on Georgina's face at the idea of being related to a housemaid, especially one who'd been in their service. She'd be mortified to say the least. If he was a snob, which Ian had accused him of being, then Georgina was a far bigger one.

But then, he reflected, that was often the case with the middle classes, from which Georgina had come.

Sean watched stony-faced as the coffin was lowered into the grave. The pallbearers were all relatives of Mo's.

The Samurai were there in force to pay their last respects to a fellow gangmember and friend. They were standing in a group to one side of the official mourners.

The Binchys hadn't been at all pleased when they'd

turned up, but nothing had been said, though Mr Binchy had given them the most contemptuous of looks.

Sean glanced over at Mrs Binchy sobbing loudly and in a state of near collapse. It was only her husband holding her upright that stopped her tumbling to the ground.

'Ashes to ashes, dust to dust . . .' the priest intoned.

Sean fingered his black tie, remembering Mo and the laughs they'd had together, hating the Tong bastards who'd killed him. The heavy marking had been bad enough. But death, that was something else entirely. He hadn't failed to note that the ex-fiancée Shelagh hadn't put in an appearance. Probably too ashamed to do so, he guessed.

He gazed at Mrs Binchy's normally handsome face now ravaged with grief. The woman seemed to have aged ten years overnight if not more.

'I'm glad that's over,' Sammy Renton declared as Sean and his lieutenants sat down in the nearest pub.

'It's the first funeral I've ever been to,' Bill O'Connell confessed.

'Me too,' Noddy added.

'You, Sean?' That from Jim Gallagher.

'Aye, I've been to them before. Though never to one that was a pal and of my own age group.'

'At least the rain held off,' said Don McGuire. 'There were times when I thought it was going to bucket down.'

'Let's have a kitty,' Sean suggested. 'And I don't know about youse lot but I'm going to get pissed as a fart. Deid mockit beyond belief. Mo would have approved of that.'

Several others nodded their heads in agreement.

'So what now, Sean?' Sammy asked.

'How do you mean?'

'About Mo. I know you said we can't take them on because they outnumber us, or mark one of them in return as that would just lead to it all getting out of hand. But surely there's something?'

Sean sighed. If there was he wished he could think of it. He tossed a couple of pound notes on to the table in front of him. 'Bill, you get them in. Whiskies and chasers.'

'Aye right,' Bill replied, rising. He added his contribution to the pile on the table before taking some out and heading for the bar.

An old man shuffled over to their table. He was wearing a dirty shirt without a collar over which was an ancient greasy coat. Grey bristles surrounded a thin, vicious mouth filled with cracked yellow and black stumps. On his head was a cap as greasy as, if not greasier than, his coat. The smell of him was appalling.

'Can I have a word, son,' he said to Sean, doffing his cap.

'Aye, what is it, Tally Jack?'

'I want to say how sorry I was to hear about Mo. I knew him since he used to run the streets as a wee shaver. He was a good lad.'

Sean nodded. 'One of the best.'

Tally glanced about him, then back at Sean. 'There's something I want to tell you.'

He eyed the money on the table. 'No' for cash like. I usually charge, but not this time. This is for Mo.'

'Let's hear it, Tally.'

'I get around a lot, here there and everywhere. All over the city doing a wee bit business now and again. Well, I was in a Tong pub the other night, The Thistle, do you know it?'

Sean shook his head.

'It's their main pub, at one time the landlord was one of them. Anyway, Big Bill Bremner and some of his cronies were there when a newcomer arrived with the news of Mo's death.' Tally Jack paused dramatically. 'Do you know what Big Bill did?'

'What, Tally?'

Tally's eyes opened wide in indignation. 'The swine laughed, so he did. Thought it helluva funny.'

Sean went icy cold inside. 'He laughed?'

'That's right. He even bought a round to celebrate.'

Sean's eyes had become diamond hard. Laughed and bought a round to celebrate!

'Cunt,' Noddy whispered venomously.

'Aye, you're right there, son,' Tally nodded. 'I was disgusted so I was. Fair disgusted. In fact I was so upset I left beer in my glass and just walked out. That's how disgusted I was.'

Disgust wasn't what Sean felt, it was total and utter outrage. Had Bremner no respect whatever!

Sean reached over and extracted a ten-shilling note from the pile on the table. 'Here you are, Tally. Take that.'

Tally shook his head. At that moment, down to his last tanner and with a terrible thirst on him, ten shillings was a fortune. 'I said I wouldn't take cash, son, and I won't. That wasn't why I told you.'

Sean smiled. 'Take it and have a drink on Mo. I insist.'

Tally Jack sniffed, his willpower crumbling. 'Well, if you insist. If you put it like that.'

'I do.'

A filthy claw of a hand accepted the note. 'God bless you, son.'

'And you, Tally Jack.'

The old man shuffled away, heading for a spot further down the bar.

'Cunt,' Noddy repeated.

Sean, a deep frown creasing his forehead, remained silent. When he finally did speak again it had nothing to do with Mo or Big Bill Bremner.

Sean was drifting off to sleep when it came to him. His eyes snapped open and he sat up in bed.

'Of course,' he muttered. 'Of course.'

If Big Bill Bremner would agree.

Wrapped up warm against the bitter cold, Ian was standing outside watching dawn break. Gradually light flooded the landscape, a truly beautiful, magical sight.

A lump came into Ian's throat. How could he give all this up? He couldn't. He belonged here and would die here. He was as much a part and parcel of the estate as any of the trees, fields and all the other living, growing things.

As part and parcel of the estate as he wanted his son to be in time. This was his inheritance and the inheritance he would eventually pass down. An inheritance that had been in the family for hundreds of years.

He sighed, torn inside. There had to be an answer to his dilemma. Some way to make his father accept Bridie as a daughter-in-law.

There just had to be.

'Ah, Bridie,' Willie said, without the customary smile on greeting staff. 'Close the door behind you.'

She did, then crossed to stand in front of his desk. 'Thank you for seeing me, sir.'

He laid down his pen and leant back in his chair. He

stared at Bridie through uncompromising eyes. 'So what can I do for you?'

'Ian spoke about us, I understand.'

Willie nodded. What was she going to do, put forward some sort of argument in favour of the union? He waited.

'Can this be confidential, sir? Just between the pair of us. I don't want Ian finding out.'

'If you wish.'

Bridie clasped her hands in front of her. 'I want to give you notice, sir. If it's all right I'll leave at the end of the month.'

That startled Willie, being so completely unexpected.

'It's best if I simply slip away quietly, sir, without anyone, least of all Ian, knowing. That's why I want it to be just between the pair of us. I appreciate how inconvenient it'll be for you but I'm sure you'll soon find a replacement.'

Willie took out his cigarettes and lit up. 'You must love Ian a great deal,' he said softly.

'I do, sir. With all my heart. That's why I must go.'

He studied her, thinking what a remarkable girl Bridie Flynn was. She'd have made Ian a worthy wife, if only her background had been different.

'This is a big sacrifice you're making, Bridie.'

'I can't stay, sir, that's out of the question feeling as I do about Ian, and he me. Nor will I let him lose The Haven. I told Ian I couldn't bear that on my conscience. Besides, it would be between us for the rest of our lives together. I don't want Ian choosing me and secretly regretting what he's lost.'

Willie nodded. 'You're very wise, Bridie.'

She flushed. 'Not really, Mr Seaton. It's only common sense.'

'There's many wouldn't see it that way, but there you are.'

'So are we agreed, sir?'

'We are indeed, Bridie. We are indeed.'

'And you won't tell anyone. Not even Mrs Coltart. If anyone else knew it would be bound to get out and perhaps back to Ian.'

'Strictly between the pair of us, Bridie. My word of honour.'

'Thank you, sir.'

'End of the month, eh? Pay day.'

'Yes, sir.'

'Then I suggest you leave in the middle of the morning when Ian is out at work.' He made a mental note to instruct Jock Gibson to send Ian to a far part of the estate.

'I'll do that, sir.'

Willie frowned at a sudden thought. 'Does Ian know where you live in Glasgow? He'll try and follow you if he does, I shouldn't wonder.'

'No, sir, I've never mentioned my address. Or even the area I come from. We have chatted about Glasgow on several occasions but I've never been specific.'

That was a relief, Willie thought. Trying to find a single lassie in Glasgow without even knowing her general whereabouts would be like trying to locate the proverbial needle in a haystack.

He then remembered he had Bridie's home address on file. He'd remove that when she'd gone back about her duties and destroy it.

Willie cleared his throat, momentarily embarrassed. 'I must say I admire you for this, Bridie. Very much so.'

She didn't reply to that.

'I shall see, and don't take this the wrong way, that you're amply rewarded for your understanding.'

'Oh no, sir! That's not necessary.'

'You'll need to tide yourself over until you get another position. Making that easier for you is the least I can do. Please accept the gesture as one from a grateful father.'

Bridie bit her lip. It would come in useful after all.

'Well?'

'It seems like a bribe, sir.'

'Nothing of the sort. Don't forget you came to me, I didn't approach you. So how can it possibly be a bribe?'

She was still uncertain. Taking money in the circumstances seemed so cheap somehow.

'Please, Bridie. And even if you say no it'll be in your pay packet anyway.'

She relented. 'Very well, sir.'

'And furthermore, I shall drive you to the station personally and see you safely aboard your train.' And out of our lives, he thought.

'That would be kind of you, sir.'

A great pity, he reflected after she'd gone. He approved of Bridie Flynn. But not her background.

At least not where Ian was concerned.

Chapter 28

A nervous Shelagh was ushered into the room wher Sean was waiting for her. He eyed her coldly. Ther were four others present, including Noddy who'd fetche Shelagh, Jim Gallagher, Bobby O'Toole and Samm Renton. They had no idea why Sean wanted to se Shelagh.

Shelagh's hands were twitching and there was fear in he eyes as she halted before Sean.

'I hope this isn't an inconvenience,' Sean said sar castically.

'No.'

'You weren't at Mo's funeral,' he accused.

She hung her head.

'Felt guilty, did we?'

She gave a small nod.

'I thought as much.'

Sean took a deep breath, and slowly exhaled, enjoyin her discomfiture. For some reason he found himself think ing of her and Mo in the bedroom next door and the cries o passion he'd overheard. That put an edge to his voice when he next spoke.

'I want you to do something for us.'

'Anything,' she croaked.

'Good.'

His lips thinned outwards in an evil smile. 'Ever heard of Big Bill Bremner, leader of the Tong?'

'Mo mentioned him once or twice.'

'Well, I want you to carry a message to him.'

Her head jerked up and her eyes flew open. 'Me!'

'Aye, you.'

'But why me?'

'Because you're a lassie and, as such, presumably safe. It's too risky sending one of us.'

Shelagh gulped.

'There's a pub called The Thistle that he uses a lot. I believe he goes there every Saturday night, sometimes staying till last orders. Other times he and some of his chinas go on elsewhere. Another pub or the dancing probably. The point is that he's there on a Saturday night around seven o'clock.'

She hadn't noticed it before but she did now, a black-handled razor on the arm of Sean's chair. She almost wet herself.

'What's the message?' she choked.

'One to one?' Peter O'Toole said to Sean when Shelagh had gone.

'Aye, just the pair of us, face to face, with assurances there'll be no repercussions from the side that loses. This way numbers don't count, you see. It'll be just Big Bill and me.'

Noddy shook his head. 'You're taking a helluva risk,

Sean. If Big Bill is even half as good as his reputation he'll do for you.'

'Oh I don't think so,' Sean replied confidently.

The others, wary now, stared at him. 'What have you got up your sleeve?' Noddy asked.

'Not up my sleeve, Noddy. But in my hand.'

Noddy frowned. 'What does that mean?'

'It'll be a razor, won't it?' queried Sammy.

'It doesn't have to be, does it?'

'They're traditional. That's what I'd have thought you'd use.'

'As, hopefully, will Big Bill. And you'd both be wrong.'

Sean rose and crossed to the mantelpiece. Reaching up he unhooked the Samurai sword hanging there.

'Holy fuck!' Noddy exclaimed.

'I wonder if Big Bill will laugh when he sees this,' Sean said mildly.

Ian ran a hand over his fevered brow as he prowled the corridors of the house as he'd been doing for the past hour.

He was having terrible trouble sleeping of late. He'd go to bed whacked out, then next thing he knew it was two or three in the morning and he was wide awake again. Tired still, but wide awake. Experience had taught him that once that happened he wouldn't drop off again. If he stayed in bed he just tossed and turned, all the while thinking of Bridie.

Bridie . . . Bridie . . . Bridie . . .

Time after time he found himself creeping past her door imagining her inside. Desperately wishing he was there with her.

Bridie who now haunted him through every waking

moment. Bridie whom he loved. Bridie whom he had to give up The Haven to have.

Ian groaned and again ran a hand over his forehead. Although it was cold he was raging hot inside. If he hadn't known better he'd have thought he was coming down with something. But it was Bridie doing this to him.

There had been occasions recently when he'd thought he was going mad, completely losing his mind. And maybe he was.

Ian Seaton, mad man. He smiled at that. Funny really, if it wasn't so serious.

Despite the earliness of the hour he'd go downstairs and have a drink, he decided. That might calm him down a little. And if one didn't do the job then he'd have two.

Or perhaps even three.

It was shortly before breakfast that Bridie spotted Ian at the far end of the corridor she'd just turned into. She immediately stopped and shrank against the wall.

Had he seen her? How could he when his back was to her?

Dear God in Heaven, she thought. How could she possibly endure this? There wasn't a day passed that they didn't bump into each other somewhere. And now he wanted to meet her in the stables the following night.

Well, she wasn't going to go. She'd say afterwards that she hadn't been able to get away, that Mrs Coltart had set her some extra duties.

Another fortnight before she left, a whole two weeks. Every moment would be torture.

And what would it be like when the time did arrive to leave? Could she just walk away?

She had to, she reminded herself. She simply had to. No matter the pain and anguish it caused her.

Leave and never see Ian Seaton again. For both their sakes.

'How are you today, Georgina?'

Georgina smiled at Rose across the table. 'Fine, thank you. Tip top as Willie might say.'

Willie beamed at his wife. 'You look positively radiant, my dear. Pregnancy certainly suits you.'

'But doesn't help my waistline. I'm fast becoming quite swollen.'

'You mustn't fret about that. Your waist will soon come back after the baby's born. You'll see.'

'It will if I have anything to do with it. That I promise you.'

'But nothing too hasty, darling. Gently does it shall be the order of the day.'

Georgina didn't reply to that. Instead she glanced over at Rose, her expression clearly indicating to Rose that her stepmother wasn't going to pay any heed to that advice.

'Well?' Willie demanded.

'Of course, Willie. Of course. Whatever you say.'

He nodded his pleasure and got stuck back into his plate of bacon and eggs.

'Did you speak to him?' Sean asked the moment Shelagh was brought into the room.

'I did.'

'And?'

'He's agreed. Tomorrow morning, eight o'clock on Glasgow Green. You're to bring two others with you, no more, and he'll do the same.'

'And no repercussions afterwards.'

'He agreed to that as well. Seemed to find it all rather funny if you don't mind me saying.'

'Big Bill seems to find a lot of things funny.' Well the bastard would be laughing on the other side of his face come morning. He was determined about that.

'Can I go now?'

'Aye, beat it.'

There was no word of thanks, nor did Shelagh expect any. She scurried from the room and out of the house. In the street she heaved a huge sigh of relief, thankful beyond belief that was all over.

'So it's on,' Jim Gallagher said softly to Sean when Shelagh was gone.

'Aye.'

'Who do you want to go along with you?'

Sean glanced round the assembled group. 'You and Noddy. That all right?'

'Fine by me,' Noddy replied.

'And me,' said his brother.

Sean picked up the sword that was lying by his chair and placed it on his lap. There the light caught it causing it to gleam and flash.

He took out a clean handkerchief and began polishing it, though it hardly needed that. 'Tomorrow, the morn's morn,' Sean whispered, and smiled.

Andrew threw down his newspaper and stared into the roaring fire. Saturday night and here he was home alone again. Just like the previous Saturday and Saturday before that.

Truth was, he was bored witless and had been for ages. Day in, day out it was the same old routine. Get up, go to work, come home again and that was that with the exception of a Friday night with Jack.

He should get away for a few days, he thought. If only he had a business trip coming up, that would break the monotony, but he didn't have one planned for several months yet.

Call on Charlotte and John? That was a possibility. Then he remembered John wrote his sermon on a Saturday night so that ruled that out.

He tried to think of something to do, and failed to come up with anything.

Jack and Charlotte were right about his getting married. At least then he'd have someone to come home to and share things with. And it was high time he provided himself with an heir. That was another thing.

Which brought him to thinking about Rose. It really was a bit soon to return to The Haven. He'd meant to leave it a while yet.

There again, a weekend away would do him the world of good. And he'd have Willie for company which would be enjoyable.

'Damn it,' he muttered. He would go the following weekend, if Willie agreed that was.

He needed some distraction.

Sean emerged from 'the place' to find Noddy and Jim had arrived while he'd been inside. He was carrying the Samurai sword wrapped in a length of old canvas.

'Christ, it's freezing,' Noddy complained, slapping his hands together.

'Aye, well you won't be when we get there. It's a good walk,' Sean retorted. He was feeling buoyant in the extreme. Almost euphoric.

* * *

'They're already there,' Noddy observed when they got to Glasgow Green, a large expanse of parkland situated on the north bank of the river Clyde.

Three of them as agreed, Sean noted. That was fine then. 'Must be keen,' he muttered sarcastically.

Jim shivered, a tremor that had nothing to do with the cold. He didn't like this one little bit, though he hadn't said so to Sean. His brother Noddy shared his foreboding.

They marched over the grass until they came to the Tong, Big Bill flanked on either side by his companions.

'You're late,' Big Bill said. 'We were beginning to think you'd had second thoughts, Flynn.'

'Not me. And we're not late. You're early.'

'Is that a fact.'

'That's a fact . . . Bremner.'

Big Bill eyed the canvas length Sean was carrying. 'What's that?'

'Something to wipe that stupid smile off your face. Or should I say smirk.'

'Let's get on with it,' Big Bill snarled. 'You talk more than a bloody lassie.'

Big Bill removed his jacket, extracted a razor from an inside pocket, then handed the jacket to the man on his right. He flicked the razor open.

'Let's see if you can fight as well as you can rabbit.'

Sean gave Jim the canvas length to hold while he too took off his jacket which went to Noddy. Accepting the canvas length back again he slowly unrolled it.

'Holy shite!' one of Bill's seconds exclaimed when the sword was revealed.

Big Bill's eyes had narrowed. 'What's your game, Flynn?'

'This is my weapon.'

'But it's a fucking sword.'

Now it was Sean's turn to smile. 'Full marks for bein observant. A sword it is. Or to be more specific, a Samur sword. The sword of an ancient Japanese warrior.'

Sean hefted the blade. 'Ready when you are, Bremner.

'I'm not fighting against that.'

Sean chuckled. 'Scared, are we? Where's the fearless Bi Bill Bremner I've heard so much about? The man who' go up against anyone or anything.'

He hefted the sword again. 'Well run along then . . He paused, then added, 'Poofter. Shirt lifter. Bende Queer.'

Big Bill's face went puce. 'You cunt!'

'Let it go, Bill,' one of the other Tong pleaded. 'No or will blame you or think less of you if you walk away.'

'Maybe not to his face but they sure as hell will behir his back. He'll be a laughing stock,' Sean mocked.

That was too much for Big Bill who launched himse at Sean, his razor whirling in an arc.

Sean danced to one side and the razor whistled harn lessly past. He was enjoying this, his intention being thoroughly humiliate Bill. And hurt him before he w finished.

Big Bill was incredibly fast. A swift change of directi and he was again coming at Sean, razor upraised, rea to strike.

Noddy and Jim watched anxiously, both praying th wasn't going to get out of hand and that Sean knew wh he was doing.

Sean dodged a second blow, then whacked Big B across the seat of his trousers using the flat of his blad 'You should never have laughed over Mo's death, that w a mistake,' he spat.

Big Bill halted to catch his breath and try to think of what to do next. Like a suddenly released spring he galvanised into action.

This time the razor was so close it actually nicked Sean's ear. Sean's reply was a swipe at Big Bill's belly.

The cutting edge made contact, slicing open the front of Big Bill's shirt. Big Bill himself was unharmed.

Big Bill moved forward, then hastily retreated again as the sword carved through the air. Before Sean could reverse his swing Big Bill was on him.

Fear leapt in Sean as, with a roar of triumph, Big Bill went for his throat.

Sean managed to grab Big Bill's wrist, warding off the blow. Using his free hand Big Bill punched Sean again and again.

Sean pushed Big Bill away and thrust with his sword, only instead of cutting Big Bill as he intended, he misjudged the whole thing and the blade of the sword sank deep into Bill's chest.

'Oh my God,' Noddy breathed.

Big Bill looked down at the blade impaling him, his vision already starting to blur. 'You done me,' he croaked.

Sean pulled the sword free, blood gushing and spurting from the wound. Within the space of several seconds Big Bill's front was stained completely red.

It was a miracle Big Bill remained upright as long as he did. He swayed on the spot for several seconds, then tumbled to the ground where he lay still.

The others, including Sean, stood watching in horror. Realising he was still holding the sword Sean dropped it.

One of the Tong hurried to Big Bill and knelt beside him, quickly establishing that he had stopped breathing.

He looked up at Sean with undisguised hatred in hi eyes. 'You've killed him.'

Sean took an involuntary step backwards, his eyes rivete on Big Bill's body. He found he was having troubl breathing. He simply couldn't believe this.

There was the blast of a whistle in the distance. Nodd whipped round to gaze in the direction it had come from What he saw were two policemen racing towards them.

'Come on,' he said urgently, grabbing Sean by the arm 'We've got to get the fuck out of here.'

'What?' A dazed Sean frowned.

'The polis. We've got to get the fuck out of here!'

Noddy, Jim and Sean began running in one directio away from the police, the remaining Tongs in another.

Noddy slammed the front door of 'the place' behind ther and they staggered through to the sitting room where Sea collapsed into a chair.

'Jesus Christ,' said Jim, running a trembling han through his hair. This was disastrous.

'They'll never work out it was me,' Sean declared hop fully.

'Of course they fucking well will. The entire Tong mu know Big Bill was fighting you this morning. With Bi Bill dead one of them's bound to squeal to the police f revenge.'

'There weren't to be any repercussions. It was agreed.'

'That was before you killed him. That alters matters.'

'It would be their word against mine.'

'You left the sword behind, Sean. Your fingerprin will be all over it. That'll be enough to . . .' He traile off and swallowed hard. He'd been about to say 'han you'.

This was a nightmare, Sean thought dully. How had it all gone so terribly wrong?

'I think you should get out of Glasgow, Sean,' Jim Gallagher advised.

'Out of Glasgow?'

'That would be best. If the police do get your name, and I believe they will, they'll be searching for you everywhere. Murder is murder after all. Not to mention you're a gang member and they all loathe the gangs.'

That was true enough, Sean thought.

'Hold on,' said Noddy, and broke away.

'I could use a drink,' Sean muttered.

Jim glanced about, spying an unopened bottle of beer from the night before. He fetched that and handed it to Sean. 'There's nothing stronger in. I finished the last of the whisky myself.'

Sean undid the screwtop and had a long swallow. Closing his eyes he conjured up a picture of Big Bill's body, its front bright red with blood. He shuddered at the memory.

'There's not much left in the kitty,' Noddy announced. 'On account we had the divvy up Friday. But there's enough to keep you for a while.'

Noddy laid the money on the table, then took out his wallet and counted the contents. 'I can add four quid to it. Jim?'

'I've got a fiver on me. Sean can have that as well.'

'Thanks, lads,' Sean mumbled, and had another mouthful of beer.

'So what are you going to do?' Noddy queried.

'As Jim suggests and get out of Glasgow. I don't like it but it makes sense. I'll go home first . . .'

'No no,' Noddy interjected. 'You don't want to involve

your folks in this. And what are you going to say to them anyway? That you're off on a wee holiday. They'd hardly believe that.'

'But I'll need clothes.'

'Buy some more when you get the time. You won't need much. But I'd keep away from your house if I was you. If for no other reason than should the police discover you've taken clothes then they would realise you'd scarpered the city. Leave things as they are and they'll spend more time searching for you here.'

Sean nodded. That too made sense.

'Better still,' Jim said. 'You and I are roughly the same height and weight. I'll go home and get some of my clobber for you. How's that?'

'Good idea,' Noddy enthused.

'I won't be long,' Jim declared, and hurriedly left the room.

Noddy sat facing Sean whose face was white and drawn. 'What a cock up, eh?'

'I never meant to kill him, Noddy.'

'I know that.'

'Mark him, yes. Do him damage, yes. But not kill him.'

'I believe you, but the police won't see it that way. All they'll know, and the jury, is that a man's dead and you did it.'

Sean had another long swallow, thinking his world had just collapsed around him. He knew this was a day that would haunt him for the rest of his life.

Sean stared out the carriage window as Glasgow vanished into the distance. How long before he saw it again? That was anyone's guess. Like the true son of the city that he was he'd miss it terribly.

*   *   *

'Rose, we have to speak.'

Andrew had managed to corner her at last in the library. On entering the room he'd closed the door firmly behind him.

'We have nothing to talk about.'

'Oh yes, we have. This can't go on, Rose. If I've offended you I apologise.'

'Offended me!' she exclaimed. 'Oh, you've certainly done that. You . . . rotter.'

'And why am I a rotter? You have the advantage of me.'

She gazed balefully at him, wanting to slap his face, tear at him with her nails. 'How could you, Andrew Drummond? How could you!'

'How could I what?' he asked patiently. At last it seemed he was about to get to the bottom of Rose's hostility.

Rose turned away from him and crossed to the window. Should she tell him what she knew, or not?

'Rose? I'm waiting.'

'You've been sleeping with my stepmother.' There, it was said.

Andrew went cold all over. 'Why do you say that?'

'Because it's a fact. I heard the pair of you together. It was disgusting.'

'Heard us?'

'I had to go to the bathroom one night and passed Georgina's door. It was the time that Pa was away. There was no mistaking what I heard. The pair of you . . .' She trailed off.

'I take it you haven't spoken about this to Willie.'

She whirled on him, eyes blazing. 'Of course I haven't. Nor will I ever.'

Relief welled through Andrew. Thank God for that.

'The worst thing for me was making such a fool of myself over you. And all the while you were . . . consorting with Georgina.'

'It's over between us, Rose. I swear.'

'Huh!'

'It is, Rose. You have my sacred word on that.' He had a sudden thought. 'Is Georgina aware you know?'

'No. I've kept it strictly to myself until now.'

Andrew nodded, again relieved. 'I'm sorry you found out, Rose. I truly am.'

She glared at him.

'And you didn't make a fool of yourself. I assure you.'

'Why, Andrew? Why?'

He shrugged. 'It was madness of course, sheer folly, on both our parts. I suppose I can only say the flesh was weak. That's not an excuse, merely an explanation.'

'But she's your friend's wife.'

'You're right. I think rotter probably sums me up rather well. I wouldn't hurt Willie for the world . . .'

'And yet you did that to him,' she interjected hotly.

'Yes,' he admitted, shamefaced. 'I did. Though give me some credit for ending the relationship. The guilt just became too much.'

'Have you any idea the effect it would have on Pa if he ever found out?'

'I do,' Andrew replied softly. 'That was why it had to finish.'

'It should never have started in the first place,' she retorted fiercely.

'No, it shouldn't. But life isn't black and white, Rose. It consists of many shades of grey as you'll find out. And we're all only human after all. There are very few saints about in my experience.'

'But to betray a friendship in such a way is despicable.'

'Indeed it is. I totally agree. If I could undo what happened, please believe me, I would. Not only madness but insanity.'

Rose snorted. 'You're pathetic, Andrew.'

'Maybe.'

'Do you love her?'

He smiled. 'That emotion never came into it, Rose. At least not on my part. It was purely physical.'

Rose blushed, marvelling that she was still attracted to him. If only this had never happened.

'I hope in time you'll come to forgive me, Rose.'

She didn't reply.

A heavy-hearted Andrew withdrew, leaving her alone with her thoughts.

Chapter 29

'Bridie, I know you've been avoiding me,' Ian stated, glancing round to make sure they weren't being seen or overheard.

'That's not true,' she lied. 'Honestly, I've been terribly busy.' Only a few more days to go, she thought, and then she'd be gone. Part of her couldn't wait for her departure, another part was dreading it in the extreme.

'How about tomorrow night? We'll meet up in the stables as usual.'

She'd go, she decided. A final rendezvous, a last remembrance.

'Can you manage that?'

'Yes.'

Ian uttered a huge sigh of relief.

'Although it really is silly, Ian. We've no future together.'

'I'll think of something,' he replied desperately. 'There must be a way. There just has to be.'

'Not without you losing The Haven.'

He groaned, wanting to sweep her into his arms, cover her with kisses. Be one with her.

'The usual time,' he said. 'All right?'

'Give or take ten or fifteen minutes. I'm not the free agent you are.'

He smiled. 'I appreciate that.'

Ian couldn't resist it. Reaching up he touched her cheek. 'Till then, Bridie.'

He swiftly snatched his hand away when Andrew Drummond suddenly appeared. Drat the man.

'Right then, you understand,' he said to Bridie, now brisk and businesslike.

'Yes, Mr Seaton.'

'That's fine then.'

Ian turned and walked away in the opposite direction to Andrew.

Bridie gave Andrew a small curtsey before hurrying by.

Sean came up short when The Haven came into view and his mouth dropped open. By all that was Holy! He'd known it was a big house, but not that *big*! It was vast.

He stood for a few moments admiring it, a wry smile dancing on his lips. He couldn't help but compare it with their home in Glasgow. Compare! There wasn't any comparison. Nor with the dirty streets he normally inhabited compared to these lush and rolling surroundings.

He didn't really know why he'd come here, never having been particularly close to Bridie. Yet she was family, and that was what he needed now. Perhaps he could get a job at The Haven. It was at least worth a try. And who would think to look for him there?

He thought of the article in the previous day's paper

saying that the police were wishing to interview Sean Flynn in connection with the death of William Archibald Bremner. He'd laughed at the Archibald bit, but the article itself wasn't funny.

As Jim had predicted someone had given the police his name, and now all they had to do, should they apprehend him, was match his fingerprints with those on the sword.

Well, he was a long way from being apprehended yet. And that's how he intended it would stay.

The future would take care of itself. For the moment only the present mattered.

'Come in!' Willie called out when there was a rap on his study door. He didn't normally work on a Saturday but these accounts were pressing and required dealing with.

Mrs Coltart entered. 'Sorry to disturb you, sir, but there's a young man come to the kitchen door inquiring if there's any work available. He mentioned you by name.'

'Did he indeed,' Willie replied. 'Do I know him?'

'I doubt it, sir. He's from Glasgow. Somewhat rough spoken but pleasant enough.'

Willie frowned. Normally Jock Gibson would have dealt with this but Jock was off ill, bad with arthritis.

'Well, you'd better show him in,' Willie declared, not appreciating this interruption. He was anxious to get finished and join up with Andrew for a couple of drams and whatever.

The young chap Mrs Coltart ushered in minutes later had black hair and black eyes. Willie judged him to be in his early twenties.

'Mr McDougall,' Mrs Coltart announced, and left them.

'Thank you for seeing me, sir. I appreciate it,' Sean said affably. He'd decided to use a false name as he could hardly use his own. He'd chosen a Protestant one thinking that would give him more chance of a job.

There was a spare seat in the study but Willie didn't indicate that Sean should sit. 'So how can I help you, Mr McDougall?'

'I'm after a job, sir, and am hoping you might be able to give me a start.'

Willie grunted. 'You're a Glaswegian, aren't you?'

'That's right, sir.'

'So what are you doing out here so far away from home?'

Sean had his story prepared. 'I got laid off from the iron foundry where I'd been since a lad. I tried and tried but there's just nothing doing in Glasgow at present. It's chronic so it is. I did consider going to Edinburgh or one of the other big cities but from what I hear unemployment's as bad there.

'Then I had the idea of trying my luck in the country where I thought things might be different. And so here I am.'

Willie was curious. 'Why this area?'

'No reason, sir. I got on a train and then got off again when it took my fancy. And that happened to be here.'

Willie laughed softly. What a bizarre way of going about things. 'How did you get my name?'

'I'm staying at a pub called The Clachan, sir, which I'm sure you know. I was speaking to the landlord last night, chaffing like, and he said you're one of the biggest employers around and I should come and see you.'

There was something shifty about McDougall, Willie decided. He couldn't quite put his finger on it, but definitely something shifty. There again, it might simply be because McDougall was a townie.

'Well I'm sorry, Mr McDougall, but I have absolutely nothing going at all. Nor do I foresee anything coming up in the near future.'

'I understand, sir.'

'Besides, agricultural work is hardly what you're used to.'

'I learn quickly, sir. I can graft and labour with the best of them. I'm sure it wouldn't take me long to learn the ropes.'

Willie believed that. Though why he couldn't say. But he'd decided against this McDougall and that was that. 'I'm sorry,' he repeated.

Sean touched his forelock. 'Thank you for your time anyway, sir. I can see you're busy.'

'Goodbye then, Mr McDougall.'

'Goodbye, Mr Seaton.'

Sean found Mrs Coltart waiting for him out in the corridor. She personally escorted him to the kitchen door where he'd entered the house.

When he was a fair distance away from The Haven Sean stopped and stared back at it. Well he hadn't got the job, but no matter. A place like that must be crammed full of valuables, a number of which he intended would soon be his.

He smiled. Bridie hadn't seen him which meant she wouldn't be implicated in the burglary he now intended. No one would make the connection between McDougall and Bridie Flynn. Why should they? Apart from the fact they were both Glaswegian there was nothing whatsoever to link them.

He'd never done a burglary before, but it shouldn't be too difficult. The idea had come to him as he'd been escorted out by Mrs Coltart.

It should be a nice little haul to keep him going for a time. With a bit of luck he might also be able to find some cash, certain that a man in Seaton's position must have some stashed somewhere.

Humming jauntily he continued on his way.

Sean lay on his bed, having bid goodnight to the landlord of the pub and others half an hour previously. Shortly he would open his window and shimmy down the drainpipe situated a little to the right of the window. That was how he'd go and that's how he'd return.

In the morning he'd pay his bill and be off with no one the wiser about what he'd been up to.

Thankfully it was a moonlit night, Sean reflected, as he padded across the terrace at the rear of the house. In his hand he was holding a screwdriver he'd acquired earlier.

The house itself was in total darkness, hardly surprising considering the hour. So far everything was going hunky dory. All he had to do now was get inside.

A pair of french windows presented themselves. These shouldn't be too difficult, he thought, and set to with the screwdriver. Even though this was the first time he'd attempted such a thing he had the doors open in under a minute.

Like taking sweeties from a baby, he smiled to himself.

Ian drifted out of sleep, the memory of his dream about Bridie still clear in his mind. Such a lovely dream it had been too. The pair of them married, happy as could be.

He sighed as he came fully awake, knowing this was going to be another night of tossing and turning unless he did something about it. Something that was becoming all too regular an occurrence.

He wondered what time it was. Two or three in the morning no doubt, that was when he usually woke.

He swore softly as he swung his legs out of bed and reached for his dressing-gown. Standing, he belted it round him. Then he slipped his feet into soft leather slippers.

Sitting on the bed he yawned. God he was tired, but there was no point in trying to drop off again without a few drams inside him.

He'd be seeing Bridie that night in the stables, he thought, which bucked him immeasurably. A short while only, no doubt, but precious, precious time alone together.

He would never have believed a person could be so much in love – aching, agonising love that lifted you to Heaven one moment, then dumped you into Hell the next.

'Bridie,' he whispered. What pleasure saying that name gave him. But not nearly as much pleasure as being in her company.

He came to his feet and headed for the door.

Ian stopped and frowned. Now why were the lights in the drawing room on? How unlike Mrs Coltart who meticulously did her rounds after the family and staff had retired. He'd never known her leave lights on before.

And then he heard a sound, a rustle of movement. Someone was inside. But who? Someone who, like himself, couldn't sleep?

He moved silently forward to investigate what was going on.

Sean couldn't believe it. No money yet, but lots of small knick knacks, all, to his eye anyway, worth a great deal. He picked up a silver and enamel cigarette box which would be easily disposed of and dropped it into the sack he was carrying, making a mental note not to forget the study where he'd been interviewed. If there was cash on the premises that's where it would be. He just hoped it wasn't in a safe.

'What the hell do you think you're doing?'

For a brief moment the two men's eyes locked, Sean frozen to the spot at having been discovered.

'It's the police for you whoever you are,' Ian declared, and strode forward.

Sean remembered the french windows were still open, dropped the sack, and hared towards them.

'Oh no you don't!' Ian exclaimed, and rushed to head Sean off.

Sean cried out as he was taken in a rugby tackle, the pair of them crashing to the floor.

'Bastard,' Ian hissed as he grappled with the smaller man.

Sean, thoroughly frightened now, knowing that if the police got hold of him they'd find out who he was, squirmed and punched at the same time. He managed to land a solid smack on Ian's throat.

But Ian was far stronger than Sean, and far fitter, thanks to his work on the estate. Although dazed and choking he pulled Sean to his feet and hit him hard, Sean flying back across the room to fall in front of the fireplace.

Ian glared as he advanced on him. 'Bloody thief!' he accused in a strangulated voice.

Sean jumped upright, wishing to hell he had his razor on him. He'd soon make short shrift of this bloke if he had. But in the confusion and panic of fleeing Glasgow, it had somehow got left behind.

As Ian closed, Sean threw a lucky punch which connected

full on Ian's chin. Ian staggered backwards, but didn't go down.

Sean tried to dash past but Ian was able to catch him by the jacket and next moment the pair of them were back on the floor again rolling round and round as they fought.

Sean gasped for air, he couldn't take much more of this. His chest was on fire, his breathing agony.

Ian took hold of Sean's arm and tried to force it into a half nelson, a manoeuvre Sean wriggled free from. He aimed a kick at Ian's crotch which missed, though it caught Ian heavily on the thigh.

Again Sean attempted to make a dash for it and again Ian got hold of him and yanked him to the floor.

As they flailed about Sean's hand came into contact with something metal. A sideways flick of his eyes told him it was a poker.

There was a sickening thud as the brass handle of the poker smacked into the back of Ian's head.

Bridie and Jeannie Swanson were chatting between themselves, en route to the kitchen for the customary cup of tea before starting work, when a terrible scream rang out from downstairs.

They both halted in their tracks. 'Holy Mary Mother of God, what was that!' Bridie whispered.

They looked at one another, then, simultaneously, set off at a run.

They reached the drawing room at the same time as Mrs Coltart. An hysterical Meg Somerville, another of the maids, was hanging on to the door post.

'What is it, lass?' Mrs Coltart demanded, grasping Meg by the shoulder.

Meg was wild eyed, her face the colour of putty. 'It's . . . it's . . .' She broke off and gulped.

'It's what, Meg?' Mrs Coltart prompted, in a kinder, more sympathetic tone.

'It's Master Ian. He's been murdered.'

That one word was like a red-hot steel spike plunged into Bridie's brain.

Mrs Coltart left Meg and hurried into the drawing room.

Bridie forced herself to follow. It couldn't be true. There was some sort of mistake.

Mrs Coltart was kneeling beside Ian's body. Around his head was a great deal of congealed blood.

Bridie knew from just looking at Ian that he was dead. Uttering a low, stricken moan she slumped to the floor.

Willie, sitting on a sofa with Georgina alongside, was a man demented. He kept clasping and unclasping his hands, unable to take his gaze away from the bloody stain by the fireplace. Ian's body had been removed a few minutes previously.

Andrew and Rose were also present, they too sitting side by side. Rose was in an obvious state of shock.

Detective Inspector Ralston and Sergeant Murray returned to the room having accompanied the body out to the waiting ambulance. The Sergeant produced a notebook and pencil.

Ralston went over to stand in front of Willie who continued to stare at the blood stain.

'I'm sorry to have to do this, sir, but I must ask some questions,' he said quietly.

Willie didn't reply.

Ralston glanced at Andrew. 'Perhaps a drink?'

Andrew rose. 'I'll get him one.'

'Sir, can you hear me?'

Willie slowly nodded.

'Good. Now as I say, I'm sorry I have to do this. But the questions have to be asked.'

'Can't you just leave us alone,' Georgina snapped. 'Can't you see the state he's in. The state we're all in.'

'That's all right, Georgina,' Willie whispered. 'The chap's only doing his job.'

'Thank you, sir.' Ralston took a deep breath. 'Now, first of all, did your son have any enemies?'

Willie, still staring at the blood stain, frowned. 'Not that I'm aware of. He was well liked by everyone.'

'I see. According to your housekeeper Mrs Coltart a number of items are missing which could mean your son disturbed a burglar and that his death was the outcome.'

'Here you are, Willie, get that down you,' Andrew said, handing Willie a large glass of Scotch.

'Georgina?'

She shook her head.

'Rose?'

'No thank you. I'd be sick if I drank alcohol.'

Andrew returned to the decanter to pour himself a stiff one. He too was in a state of shock, though not nearly as badly affected as the others. Poor Willie, he kept thinking. Poor old chap. What a blow.

'There haven't been any burglaries in the area for quite a while, sir, and we caught that blighter, a gypsy who was passing through. Have there been any strangers around here of late?'

'No,' Willie croaked, and had a gulp of whisky. In his mind he kept envisaging Ian's body and the horror of his first sight of it.

'Are you certain, sir?'

'Quite.' Willie hesitated, frowned, then glanced up at the Detective Inspector. 'That's not true. There was a man here yesterday looking for work. Name of McDougall. There was something about him I didn't like, a sort of shiftiness, so I told him there was nothing available and sent him on his way.'

'McDougall, eh?'

'From Glasgow,' Willie added. He then repeated the story Sean had given him about being laid off and having come to the country to find work.

'Glasgow,' Ralston mused. That was interesting. 'I don't suppose he mentioned where he's staying?' Ralston asked, thinking the man was probably sleeping rough.

'As a matter of fact he did. The Clachan pub. He's staying there.'

'Is he indeed,' Ralston smiled. 'Can I use your telephone again, sir?'

'Help yourself.'

Willie went back to staring at the blood stain.

Sean was about to go down and pay his bill, then leave, when the door to his bedroom opened and two men strode in.

Rozzers, they had it stamped all over them.

His shoulders slumped. The game was up.

'Bridie, can I come in?'

A tear-stained Bridie let Mrs Coltart into her room.

'Are you all right?'

All right? She'd never be all right again. 'I'm sorry, Mrs Coltart, truly I am.'

Fresh tears appeared, to go coursing down her face.

Mrs Coltart was puzzled. They were all upset, dreadfully

so, but why was Bridie taking it so badly? It was clear how distraught the girl was.

'Why don't you take the rest of the day off, Bridie.'

'Thank you, Mrs Coltart.'

Mrs Coltart took Bridie by the arm and guided her to the rumpled bed where they both sat. 'Is there anything you want to tell me?'

'No, Mrs Coltart,' Bridie choked.

'It won't go any further. I promise you. Sometimes it's better to talk.'

And talk Bridie desperately wanted to do. 'Oh, Mrs Coltart,' she whispered, gazing at the housekeeper through eyes filled with pain. 'I loved him you see. And he me.'

That jolted Mrs Coltart who'd never guessed. Not even had an inkling.

Bridie poured out her heart.

Willie lifted the phone which he'd been called to answer. 'Yes, Detective Inspector?' He re-entered the drawing room where the others were still gathered after taking a call from the Inspector. He went straight to the decanter.

'Well, darling?' Georgina queried.

He poured himself a drink then turned to face them. There was a lump in his throat which felt the size of an egg.

'They apprehended McDougall at the pub just as he was about to leave and catch a train. The Detective Inspector said we were fortunate it's a Sunday with a diminished service otherwise he would have already been away.'

Willie paused, then went on, 'They found a number of items in McDougall's luggage, one a silver and enamelled cigarette box which tallies with the description of the one Mary gave me years ago. I've been asked to go to the station and identify McDougall and the items.'

Andrew immediately rose. 'I'll drive you.'

Willie nodded his appreciation, then downed his whisky in a single gulp.

'I can't help it,' he said. 'I simply can't.' And with that he began to cry.

Georgina was swiftly by his side to enfold him in her arms.

'Ian, oh Ian,' Willie sobbed.

Andrew came across Rose halfway down the stairs sitting on a large windowsill gazing out.

'Hello,' he said.

She glanced at him, her expression grim as could be. It was now Monday morning. Nobody except Andrew had appeared for breakfast.

'Have you seen Pa?' she asked.

Andrew shook his head.

'He must still be in his room then.'

'I suppose so.'

She returned to gazing out the window. 'I wish I'd been nicer to Ian,' she said wistfully.

'Nicer?'

'We were always jibing at one another. But there were times when I was downright cruel to him. How I regret that now.'

'You were brother and sister, that sort of thing is common between siblings. We were forever at each other's throats. But it didn't really mean anything. And it certainly didn't reflect how we felt about one another. I admit I really never got on with my brother Peter, but that was a clash of personalities more than anything else. We were so very different you see.'

Rose didn't reply to that.

'Quite normal. Honestly, you've nothing to reproach yourself about.'

'I still wish it had been different. And now he's gone it's left such a big hole in all our lives. I don't think Pa will ever get over what's happened.'

'Maybe not get over, Rose, but he will come to terms with it. Time is a great healer after all.'

She smiled. 'You're very sweet, Andrew. And it's kind of you to offer to stay on for a bit and help.'

'It was the least I could do. Willie needs a friend right now and that's what we are. He'd do the same for me.'

'I'd like to think he would.'

'I know he would.'

Andrew reached out and touched Rose gently on the face. In a strange way Ian's death had brought things totally into perspective. Where there had been doubt before none now remained. It was as though . . . a calmness had descended on him.

'Perhaps this isn't the time or place, but please, and I beg you, forgive me for Georgina. I'm only a mortal man after all, with all the weaknesses men have. Perhaps more weaknesses than many. I desperately want your forgiveness, truly I do. And hope things might go back to how they were between us. I need your trust again, a trust I give you my solemn oath I'll never again betray.'

She gazed up at Andrew, in her heart of hearts wanting to believe him.

He knew he'd said enough for the present. 'I'll leave you to your reflections, Rose.'

Andrew withdrew his hand and strode off down the stairs, Rose staring at his retreating back.

She continued to stare in that direction long after he'd disappeared.

Chapter 30

Willie sat staring vacantly ahead. He was unshaven, his hair rumpled and, despite the fact it was almost noon, still in his pyjamas and dressing-gown. His mind was numb with grief.

Georgina let herself quietly into the bedroom having been about household duties. She gazed in concern at her husband – her heart going out to him.

'Willie?'

He blinked, then focused on her. 'I was just thinking about the war,' he said.

'The war?'

'I remember wondering at the time what it was like for those thousands and thousands of families who received the dreaded telegram. Now I know.'

'Oh Willie,' she whispered. Crossing the room, she knelt beside him.

'The years it takes you to bring up a child. To teach them this and that, go through all the pains they experience while growing up, the emotional expenditure. And then, right at the beginning of manhood, with everything before them, to have them taken from you. I could accept it more easily if it had been due to illness. That, though unfair, you can somehow understand. But to lose them due to an act of sheer wanton violence . . .' He broke off and swallowed hard.

'I know,' she said softly.

'At least in the war when your boy went off you knew it could happen. But we had no warning whatsoever. One day Ian was alive, the next dead. And for what? That's the galling thing, for what? Nothing, when you come down to it.'

'Would you like a cup of tea, Willie?'

He shook his head.

'Anything else?'

'No, Georgina.'

A wave of great tenderness swept over her. She felt bad enough, but how must he feel? The reflection of that was all too obvious in his face.

'Why don't you go back to bed and sleep for a while? You had hardly any last night.'

'I still wouldn't sleep. All I can think of is Ian. In my mind I keep going over conversations we had, times spent together. He was a good lad, Georgina, and I was extremely proud of him.'

He took a deep breath. 'How am I going to face the funeral? It'll be a nightmare. A complete nightmare that doesn't bear thinking about.'

'You'll get through it, Willie, you'll see. And I'll be there to support you. And Andrew. Don't forget we'll be amongst friends. They'll all understand and be with you, my darling.'

There was silence between them for a few seconds, then Willie said, 'We must play "Onward Christian Soldiers". That was Ian's favourite hymn. I remember him mentioning it once.'

'Then we shall.'

'"Onward Christian Soldiers",' Willie repeated, and slowly shook his head.

'How's Rose?' he asked.

'I spoke to her a little while ago and she's bearing up.'

'Good. That's good.'

'Now why don't I take you through to the bathroom and shave you. I haven't done that for years.'

He smiled in memory.

She took his hand and tugged him to his feet. 'Come on. And after the shave you shall have a nice long bath. A proper soak, you'll enjoy that.'

'Yes,' he whispered. Halfway to the bathroom he stopped. 'I keep thinking it's all a bad dream and that any moment I'll wake up and find Ian's still alive. Only it isn't a dream, is it?'

'No,' she said.

The instant Bridie thought of it a sense of tranquillity descended on her, driving out the demons that had been tearing at her since hearing that awful word, murdered, and finding it to be true.

She sighed. Yes, that was what she would do. Had to do.

She slipped out of the house in the dead of night. Underneath her coat she was wearing only a nightdress.

She shivered. It was cold, but not as cold as it had been earlier at the funeral. What a turn out it had been, the church packed, with many people having to stand.

Mrs Coltart had insisted she sit beside her, the only person other than Mr Seaton to know her secret. He hadn't spoken to her since Ian's death. Perhaps he'd temporarily forgotten how it had been between them. *Was* between them, she corrected herself.

She glanced up at the sky which was heavily overcast. It might snow, she thought. The night had that feel about it.

A little way from The Haven she turned and looked back. Her stay there had been a happy one, she reflected. She had no regrets.

She walked to the cemetery and through it to Ian's grave adorned with the many wreaths and flowers that had been placed on it.

She removed some of the flowers to make a space for herself. Then, taking off her coat which she placed aside, she lay down on the freshly dug earth.

'Oh, Ian, my darling, my true love,' she whispered. 'We couldn't be together in this life but we can in the next. It's all been solved, you see. Now we shall be as one for evermore.'

She'd been right about the snow. Large flakes of it suddenly appearing to come spiralling down. Soon the flakes had increased in intensity until there were myriads of them dancing and weaving their way from Heaven.

Bridie closed her eyes and conjured up a picture of Ian in her mind. Sir Ian of Seaton, her knight in shining armour, her prince, her lover for all time.

She began to feel drowsy as the cold seeped into her. Not the unpleasant experience she'd imagined, quite comforting really.

'Ian,' she murmured.

And then he was there beside her, smiling, holding out his hand for her.

'Awful,' Andrew said quietly. 'Just awful.' He'd found Rose on her own. The pair of them were now alone together.

'She loved Ian apparently. None of us knew that.'

Andrew shook his head. 'It makes you think, doesn't it?'

'Yes it does.'

They were silent for a few moments, Andrew thinking how lovely Rose looked. He could just imagine her at Drummond, the lady of the house.

'Do you mind if I sit down?'

She gestured to a chair. 'Please do.'

'Life's a funny thing,' he mused once he was seated. 'As my father Murdo used to say, you never know the minute till the minute after.'

'True enough,' Rose agreed.

'"Father forgive them for they know not what they do."'

Rose blinked at him. 'I beg your pardon?'

'I was quoting scripture. Or as best as I can remember that is. Whatever, the sentiment is right.'

'I don't understand.'

'I was talking about me and how stupid I've been.' He took a deep breath. 'Have I lost you, Rose?'

She glanced away and didn't reply.

'Forgiveness is a great thing, Rose. Do you have that quality in you?'

Again she said nothing.

'I swore to you that I'd never betray you again and I won't. You have my word on that.'

'Do I?' she queried softly.

'Yes.'

She turned and stared into his eyes, looking for the truth. This was far too big a decision to make a mistake. In his eyes she saw the real Andrew, that of a child. But there again, weren't most men precisely that?

'What are you asking?' she demanded.

'Let's give it a bit of time, to get over all this for a start. And then maybe . . . if you'll have me . . .' He broke off in sudden confusion and embarrassment. The latter most unlike him.

'I love you,' he whispered. 'God knows I've fought against it because of our ages. But I do.'

His eyes were pleading, desperate almost as she continued to gaze into them. She melted inside, her feelings rushing to the surface. 'We do need that time you spoke about, most certainly.' Then, huskily, 'I love you too.'

And so it was sealed. There was an understanding between them.

'Dear me,' Jack Riach declared. 'She froze to death.'

'Covered from head to toe in snow when they found her.'

It was the first Friday night since Andrew's return from The Haven and, as usual, he and Jack were in the pub.

Jack knew this was the ending he'd been searching for for his novel. He'd have to re-jig it a bit of course but apart from that it was perfect.

'It only came out afterwards that she and Ian had been in love,' Andrew went on. 'A truly tragic affair.'

'Indeed.'

'A pleasant lass too.'

Jack groped for his pint and had a sip. There was part

of him felt ghoulish, grasping, as Andrew had called it, a tragic affair, but it suited his purposes and he hadn't known either of them. And, after all, hadn't it been worse with his plays about the war? He had been friends, fought and almost died, with many of those people.

'There's something else.'

'Oh?'

'I've decided to marry Rose. We have an understanding. But it'll take time, Jack. It'll take time.'

Jack's scarred face creased with delight. 'That's wonderful.'

'If it does come off I hope you'll be my best man.'

'I'd be honoured, old boy. Honoured.'

'In the meantime keep this strictly to yourself and Hettie.'

Jack tapped his nose. 'Mum's the word. You can count on it.'

Andrew leant back in his chair and sighed, visualising Rose in his mind and wishing she was there. Wanting her company.

Wanting it with every ounce of his being.

Andrew picked up his pen and stared at the sheet of paper in front of him. 'Dear Willie,' he began.

He went on to say he hoped Willie was starting to come to terms with Ian's death and then suggested he might visit again shortly, if that was agreeable.

Andrew smiled to himself. Of course he continued being concerned for his friend but there was quite another reason for the proposed visit.

The letter was the first of many and the start of his courtship of Miss Rose Seaton.

Epilogue

Andrew and Rose emerged from the gloom of the church into brilliant sunshine which made them both blink. Overhead the bells began to peal.

Willie, directly behind the couple, couldn't help but glance across the graveyard to where Ian was buried, and close by Bridie Flynn. He had mixed emotions about Bridie, whose brother it had been who'd murdered Ian. Not only Ian but another chap in Glasgow which made him a double murderer. Murders for which Sean Flynn had now paid the ultimate price. He wouldn't be killing anyone else.

At least the girl hadn't known it was her brother who'd killed Ian, that was something she'd thankfully been spared.

Georgina moved up beside Willie. 'It was a beautiful ceremony,' she said. 'It couldn't have gone better.'

Willie hadn't been too sure about the wedding when Andrew had first brought it up, but Rose had put his worries to rest and so he'd consented to the marriage and given them his blessing. Andrew as a son-in-law, he reflected not for the first time. What a bizarre thought.

'Wasn't James good?' Georgina crooned, and kissed the baby she was holding.

Willie beamed at his new son and heir. As healthy and lusty a boy as you could imagine. He was certain James was the spitting image of Ian. There again, it might only be his imagination.

He thought of how close he and Georgina had become since Ian's death.

As for Georgina, she had no regrets about Andrew. Her feelings for him had vanished. The only man she wanted now was Willie, good in bed or not.

His failings simply didn't matter to her any more.

Jack Riach took Hettie by the hand. 'Don't let me fall down the steps,' he whispered.

'I won't.'

'I'd look awfully silly sprawled on my backside. They'd all think I was drunk.'

'Which you will be later,' she teased.

'Damn right. And you will be too I hope.'

'We'll see.' She smiled.

Jack sighed with pleasure. His novel had been submitted to the publishers some months previously and they were very excited about it. They were certain it was going to be both a critical and financial success. He'd promised himself to start another before the year was out.

Andrew turned to Rose and stared into her eyes. 'Happy?'

'You have to ask?'

'No, Rose. I don't suppose I do. I know I certainly am.'

A cheer and applause went up from the onlookers as the bride and groom kissed.

Passionately.

FLOWER OF SCOTLAND

Emma Blair

'Emma Blair is a dab hand at pulling heart strings'
Today

In the idyllic summer of 1912, all seems rosy for Murdo Drummond and his four children. Charlotte is ecstatically in love with her fiance Geoffrey; Peter, the eldest, prepares for the day when he will inherit the family whisky distillery, while Andrew, gregarious and fun-loving, is already turning heads and hearts. Nell, the youngest, contents herself with daydreams of a handsome highlander. Even Murdo, their proud father, though still mourning the death of his beloved wife, is considering future happiness with Jean Richie, an old family friend.

The Great War, however, has no respect for family life. As those carefree pre-war days of the distillery fade, with death, devastation, revenge, scandal and suicide brought in their wake, the Drummonds are plunged to the horrors of the trenches in France. Yet those who survive discover that love can transcend class, creed and country . . .